Whatsoever Is Just

Augusta Ren

CONTENTS

Content Warning   1

Dedication   3

1. Chapter 1   5

2. Chapter 2   20

3. Chapter 3   30

4. Chapter 4   38

5. Chapter 5   52

6. Chapter 6   54

7. Chapter 7   57

8. Chapter 8   68

9. Chapter 9   73

10. Chapter 10   78

11. Chapter 11   84

12. Chapter 12   87

13. Chapter 13   93

14.	Chapter 14	100
15.	Chapter 15	107
16.	Chapter 16	114
17.	Chapter 17	122
18.	Chapter 18	124
19.	Chapter 19	129
20.	Chapter 20	132
21.	Chapter 21	138
22.	Chapter 22	144
23.	Chapter 23	150
24.	Chapter 24	154
25.	Chapter 25	160
26.	Chapter 26	170
27.	Chapter 27	174
28.	Chapter 28	181
29.	Chapter 29	184
30.	Chapter 30	189
31.	Chapter 31	201
32.	Chapter 32	207
33.	Chapter 33	216
34.	Chapter 34	225
35.	Chapter 35	231
36.	Chapter 36	242
37.	Chapter 37	246

38.	Chapter 38	262
39.	Chapter 39	272
40.	Chapter 40	276
41.	Chapter 41	282
42.	Chapter 42	287
43.	Chapter 43	294
44.	Chapter 44	311
45.	Chapter 45	315
46.	Chapter 46	320
47.	Chapter 47	330
48.	Chapter 48	346
49.	Chapter 49	352
50.	Chapter 50	359
51.	Chapter 51	365
52.	Chapter 52	374
53.	Chapter 53	381
54.	Chapter 54	383
55.	Chapter 55	393
56.	Chapter 56	403
57.	Chapter 57	406
58.	Chapter 58	413
59.	Chapter 59	418
60.	Chapter 60	422
61.	Chapter 61	434

62.	Chapter 62	441
63.	Chapter 63	443
64.	Chapter 64	450
65.	Chapter 65	457
66.	Chapter 66	461
67.	Chapter 67	463
68.	Chapter 68	469
69.	Chapter 69	476
70.	Chapter 70	487
71.	Chapter 71	501
72.	Chapter 72	508
73.	Chapter 73	515
74.	Chapter 74	517
75.	Chapter 75	521
76.	Chapter 76	529
77.	Chapter 77	531
Acknowledgements		533
About the Author		535

CONTENT WARNING

Whatsoever Is Just is a romantic fantasy book with mature themes and thus has some heavy topics including but not limited to: Alcohol, Animal Death, Assault, Blood, Death, Decapitation, Fire, Gore, Kidnapping, Murder, Physical Abuse, Sexual Abuse (off page), Sexually Explicit Scenes, Torture, and Violence.

For Dalton
Unwavering love is hard to come by, I'm glad I have yours.

PROLOGUE

"You could sooner pull lightning from the sky than divert me from my path," He announced as he cornered her, his blade hovering in the air between them.

She smirked, "And so I shall."

In the blink of an eye, she swiped her sword through the air, connecting with his and pushing him backward, freeing herself from the corner. He attempted to take another step away as she prepared to advance, but the back of his knees hit the mattress he slept on. Sensing he was trapped, Wes raised her sword; he attempted to block her, but she was too quick, and his sword clattered to the ground. She stepped forward, keeping her sword between them, and only stopped when she could make out the cluster of freckles across his nose. This close, his breath moved the whisps of her hair. She pushed the sword upwards to poke the bottom of his chin. His eyes narrowed at the touch, a smirk of his own growing.

"I believe you won this round," He whispered.

"I know so," she replied, her smirk turning into a grin as he wrapped his arms around her waist. Her sword dropped as they fell into the bed they had shared many times.

Jaze let his grip on her waist loosen and dipped his head, kissing her exposed shoulder. He lingered and left another kiss higher, closer to her ear.

"And what will your prize be?" He asked, pressing another kiss on her neck.

"Hmmm." While his feather-light kisses left her body scalding, Wes feigned to think, "I think I shall settle for a future prize."

"Go on," Jaze said, his breath tickling her ear.

"That you come back to me in one piece." She paused, considering her words carefully, "And come back to *all* of us in one piece."

His kisses paused, and his hand stilled.

Sensing the weight of her words, Wes turned in his arms to face him. His smile was gone; instead she swore she saw a tinge of pain.

"Promise me you won't tell them. Especially Knox."

Wes searched his eyes. The entire summer they had hidden their *friendship* from Jaze's cousin and Wes's close friend, Knox. And it was just that. A friendship. They both knew they didn't want to settle down and raise kids together, yet they couldn't manage to keep their hands off each other. But in their friend group, no one knew. After the first time, they had promised not to tell the others. Not only would the teasing be nonstop, but their friends wouldn't understand. Jaze and Wes were just friends, that's all they'll ever be.

"Of course, I'm not going to tell them," she said, her voice serious before continuing in a lighter tone, "Plus, I'd be scared the day he finds out."

His eyes widened and a small grin appeared, "You scared? What about *me*?"

"He is your blood."

He reached up to cup her face in his calloused hands, "Maybe so. But his loyalties lie closer than you know."

Wes smiled, pulling herself away from his warm embrace and standing to gather her things, "You're not even in the army and your brain's already rotten."

Jaze just smiled and shook his head, scooting to the edge of his bed to watch as his friend resheathed her sword and set about buttoning the rest of her shirt.

"I am going to miss you Wes Blake."

"They always do."

She finished buttoning her shirt and turned to face him. Standing, he looked the part of a soldier, tall and lean with a womanizing grin. Wes savored the sight of him. It would be months before she saw him again.

He reached for her hand and tugged her inwards so they could embrace. She tucked her head under his chin.

"I'll see you in a few months." He murmured against her hair.

"Maybe by then you'll be able to beat me."

"Oh, I'm betting on it."

They pulled apart and smiled at each other. Wes tilted her head upwards and Jaze responded by bending so that they could kiss. She pressed her lips onto his lightly before leaning away.

"Goodnight," Jaze said, his voice barely a whisper. Wes could've swore he intended to say more, but no words came out. His eyes searched her face before she quietly returned the sentiment with a soft farewell smile.

"Goodnight Jaze."

Smiling softly, Wes came down the stairs of the barn loft and onto the long dirt driveway of the Greene's farm. She headed towards the road and willed herself not to look back. She knew if she looked back, she would see his shadow in the second-story window watching her leave. And if she saw the shadow, she was afraid she would turn around and ask him what he had left unsaid. Or perhaps he hadn't left anything unsaid and was just regretting his career choice. Whatever it was, Wes knew turning and seeing his shadow in that window would make her turn around. And with his early departure time the following day, she knew she couldn't stay. So she kept walking.

When she reached the road, she knew the barn would be no bigger than her thumbnail, but for good measure, she decided to take a few steps in the road before turning to look. Only a few steps.

Two steps into the road, the hair on the back of her neck rose and nausea rolled through her. Something was terribly wrong. The air had shifted and the world seemed to be tilting off its axis. Looking back to the barn, Wes saw the fire spreading over it. As she took off running towards the unnaturally high flames, a small voice screamed inside her and she knew right then.

Jaze is dead.

The gentle *cawing* of a bird is what initially woke Rhyatt from his slumber. Upon seeing the dead, glassy eyes only inches away, he was spurred into motion.

Rhyatt scrambled to his feet to try and back away from the dead man whom he had just been lying beside. As he attempted to stand to his full height, pain ricocheted down his neck, through his back, and spread all throughout his body. He leaned against a barren wisp of a tree as he tried to focus on not emptying his stomach. He failed in his efforts and turned to vomit onto the sandy terrain.

Afterward, his pain faded enough for him to focus on his current situation. He was in a ravine somewhere in his home country of Duran; the barren trees and yellow sand were proof enough. But as he focused, he couldn't remember where he was or how he got there. Looking down at the dead man, he noticed that his arm was tucked unnaturally behind him, and his neck was turned at an odd angle. He was at least two days dead, and the severe sunburn on Rhyatt made him wonder if he had been lying beside him for those two days.

The dead man was clad in black. In Duran City, black was reserved for the rich; it meant you could pay enough to have someone shade you from the desert sun. Both the dead man and him were wearing similar black clothing. Rhyatt was far from wealthy.

Panic began to pulse through him as he took a mental inventory. The only problem was that his memory was failing him. The last thing he could recall was Adriel. Adriel, his little brother, was the only remaining family he had. Panic threatened to take over, and he took action, pushing himself off the tree and running up the steep slope of the ravine. His body worked against him, sluggish and sore. Every hurried step was a battle, and his pain would win if he didn't reach the top soon. Pushing forward, his feet sank into the sliding sand as he clawed upwards.

His body screamed against him as he hauled himself up over the lip and placed both feet on semi-solid ground. His lungs were on fire, his skin taught and sore, and worst of all, his mind was going a mile a minute.

When air wasn't as hard to breathe, he looked up and assessed his surroundings. The sunset determined he was south of Duran City. He took an unsteady step forward and headed towards his home.

When Rhyatt reached his street, his limp was mostly gone. Instead, he clutched at his rib cage. Something had to be broken. The pain pulsed with every breath he took. Limping up the dim street, he stopped to lean against the low brick wall of his neighbor's yard. From where he stood, he could see the window to his home. The curtain was drawn, but he could still make out the shapes as they moved against the brightly lit gas lamp. His mind must've been foggy still because through the window he could make out multiple shapes, two were the size of children. Adriel wasn't fond of children and had never agreed to watch them without Rhyatt present.

Rhyatt shook away his brother's change of heart and headed to the front door. Upon finding it locked, he knocked; he slowed his knocks as he noticed how bloody the back of his knuckles were. Flexing his hand, he decided his skin was not broken; rather, it was someone else's dried blood. The thought sent a panicked jolt of energy through him, and he knocked again, this time louder.

The door jerked open, and a middle-aged man stood in the doorway, shock dancing across his features. Rhyatt's face twisted in confusion. Adriel had never kept older friends.

"Where is Adriel?" Rhyatt asked, surprised at how his voice rasped over the syllables. How long had it been since he had water?

The man in the door shifted so Rhyatt could not see much further. As the man took in his appearance, he wondered how bad he actually looked.

"I'll tell you what I tell everyone else. He can be found at Dalia's bar. Ask for Valvidez." The man paused and squinted at Rhyatt, "And find yourself a doctor." Before Rhyatt could open his mouth to protest, the door was shut in his face and locks were turned.

Anger and fear rose in his throat. He lifted his fist to the door, planning to bang on it until the man returned and told him what had happened to his brother and why he was in their house. His fist hit the door once before he remembered the two small children inside. Rhyatt would just have to go to Dalia's and find Adriel. Turning away from the home he had lived in his entire life, he headed towards The Feed and Seed district. Despite its name, the district was not for livestock nor food. It was a raunchy district where one could buy anything from whiskey to women, and everything in between.

Rhyatt was surprised to find out how easily his battered body blended into the nightlife of Feed & Seed. He was no stranger to the district, but he had never worn the rich man's black clothes. After seeing how the man had reacted to him, he had prepared to be stopped. But no one noticed him. He moved through the streets like a ghost, keeping pace with his fellow pedestrians.

When he arrived at Dalia's, he hesitated before stepping inside. Why was he so nervous?

Inside the bar, it was empty, save for three patrons at the cards table and two at the bar. Rhyatt walked up to the bar and leaned against it for support; his ribcage seemed likely to give in.

"Have you seen Adriel?" He asked the barkeep, his voice still rasped, "Valvidez." He amended, speaking their last name, "Have you seen Valvidez?"

The barkeep looked at him warily. "I don't know anyone by that name. It's best to move along."

"Please. He's my brother. I need to see him." Desperation entered his voice.

The barkeep's look sharpened as he studied Rhyatt, "Valvidez's brother died almost a year ago. So unless you're a ghost, get out of my bar."

The world seemed to shake beneath him. *He was not dead.* The pain in his head and side told him that he was very much alive. His brain struggled to come to a conclusion. It settled on assuming Adriel lied and said he was dead. Why would Adriel tell people he was dead though? And why would he predate it by almost a year? What kind of trouble had Adriel gotten into this time? Is that why he was renting out the house? Was it all a ruse? What about their-

"Rhyatt?" A voice called from the back of the room.

Rhyatt turned at the sound and confirmed with his eyes that it was Adriel. His eyes snagged on his hair. Adriel had cut it short. And his face seemed less round. Had he grown taller?

"Adriel! Thank the heavens above, what mess have you gotten us into?" Rhyatt asked as he crossed the room to where his brother stood frozen, one hand on the stairwell he had just come down. "Why are you here and not at home?" Rhyatt asked when Adriel didn't immediately answer.

Adriel stood still, looking like he had indeed seen a ghost. His eyes were wide, and his brow furrowed. "You're alive?" he asked his older brother.

Rhyatt glanced at the barkeep, "Yes. Why did you lie and say I was dead?"

"Because I thought you were." Adriel responded, his voice now hushed.

Rhyatt reached out to grasp Adriel's shoulder, but his brother leaned away from the touch, fear flashing in his eyes. Rhyatt retracted his hand.

"Adriel? Why would I be dead?" As his confusion rose, his voice stayed steady. He had the type of voice that made people flinch when his voice was raised.

"You've been missing for ten months, I had no choice but to assume you were dead."

Adriel brought Rhyatt up to his rented room above the bar and had him settled on the small stool as Adriel tended to his wounds. Apparently, he had more wounds than he could tell. It had taken every ounce of will for Rhyatt not to lose his shit when Adriel had told him he had been missing ten months. Now he sat thinking everything over. He thought his father's death was a little over a month ago, but judging by the date Adriel told him it was, his father had died almost a year ago. He was unsettled by it.

Truthfully, he was unsettled by everything and only held on by a string.

Adriel blotted at the dried blood, "What happened to you? You look like shit.. and you look huge."

"I... I'm not sure. I woke up in one of the ravines near the canyon pass and walked here." He winced as a sore spot was rubbed clean. "What happened to the house?"

"I sold it a few months ago." He paused, his mouth open to say more, "I sold it when I didn't think you were ever coming home."

A shadow of sorrow passed over Adriel's face and landed like a gut punch on Rhyatt. He began to think about what his younger brother must have had to endure while he was missing. How they only lost their father before he would've gone missing as well. Adriel must've sensed his spiraling and asked another question.

"What's the last thing you remember?"

"That's the problem," Rhyatt winced at the pain in his ribs, "I remember quitting school after Father died. And I remember getting a full-time job. I remember us planning to save up so we could travel to Lita and deliver the news of Father's death in person. After that, the rest is foggy. I can't even remember the last time I saw you..."

"The last time you saw me was when you said goodbye before leaving for work one night." Adriel leaned away, "For three days I didn't see you at home. I thought we were simply missing each other. Bad timing. But on the third night, I noticed you hadn't moved the book you were reading. I got worried and started looking around. You hadn't dirtied any dishes or ate any food. I made a million excuses, but I had this uneasy feeling. I woke early the next morning, walked to your work, and waited for you to get off work. You never came out. I asked one of the workers and he said he hadn't seen you in days." Adriel looked away as his jaw tightened, "It took me three fucking days to realize you were missing. *Three.*"

Adriel continued to look away, refusing to meet Rhyatts' gaze. As tears threatened to fall, Rhyatt reached over and wrapped him in a hug. Adriel fell into it, sighing with relief. To Rhyatt it seemed only yesterday he had hugged his brother, but to Adriel... it must've felt like hugging a dead man.

When Adriel finally leaned away, Rhyat spoke again, "Why sell the house? Why not stay there?"

Adriel's face steeled back into his collected demeanor. "I had to do something. I sold the house and put out a reward if anyone knew anything. I mostly just got drunks looking for money, but there was one that stood out from the rest. He told me details about your tattoo and claimed to have known you before. He said he saw you outside one of the bars where wealthy men liked to hang out. It looked exactly like you but acted the opposite, like an evil twin. He said you and another man held up a merchant and beat him within an inch of his life. He called your name, and you looked back." Adriel's voice grew soft and trailed off.

Rhyatt's chest tightened further, and his heart turned to lead and sank to the bottom of his stomach. His face expressed a similar feeling, and Adriel began to explain himself.

"I know it was foolish of me to believe. But I- I just wanted something to prove you weren't dead too. The next day I tried to track him down to give him reward money, and he was gone."

"Adriel." Fear entered Rhyatt's voice. "Did he say what I was wearing?"

Adriel furrowed his brows. "He said you were dressed like one of them, one of the wealthy."

Rhyatts face paled as he looked down at his dark black clothing. Rearing to his feet, he sent the bucket of bloody water splashing over the boards.

"Get your stuff. We have to go *now*."

Adriel didn't question him and began to pull his stuff out of drawers and pack it.

"Where are we going? Who are we running from?"

Rhyatt bent and helped him shove his belongings into the thick travel bag.

"I don't know. But whoever left me at the bottom of the ravine thought I was dead, and I intend to keep it that way."

When Warden heard of the fire at the Greene's farm he had ridden over immediately, intending to help put it out. But when he got there, all his plans faltered. Wes, his twin sister, was being held down by Knox and Cleo but not by Jaze. At the sight of his friends' tear-soaked faces, he knew why Jaze wasn't helping restrain Wes.

The moments after the realization hit him were a blur, his body working outside of his mind. He put Wes on the horse he had ridden, and Cleo rode with her back to their home. He attempted to get water from the trough, but it was empty. The barn was beyond saving at that point, so he helped the others make sure the fire didn't spread. Luck was on their side; it had rained earlier that day, and the fire was easily contained. The barn burned quickly, and when he left it was no more than a smoking pile waist high.

It was three days before the funeral was held, there were no remains to bury.

Warden walked beside Wes on the way to town, his shoes were a size too small and it made every step rub against his big toe.

"I hate that I have to leave tomorrow." Warden said, his eyes focused on the road in front of them. He was never good with death and its aftershocks.

"It doesn't seem fair." Wes responded, her face blank and eyes focused straight ahead.

"Maybe I should ask Father if I can stay a few more days."

"You know he won't let you."

"I can do what I want."

"You can, but you won't." Her voice was cold, distant even. It was so unlike her that Warden didn't even argue back.

"I know you're right," he began with a sigh, "but it doesn't make leaving any easier... not this time around."

She glanced at him, and Warden saw it in her eyes. The sorrow seeped from them. She looked away quickly as tears threatened to spill. Her eyes once again trained forward as she reached across the space between them and squeezed Warden's hand.

"This is the last time you *have to* leave Warden." She reminded him, her tone gentle.

And it was true; this was both of their last semesters of university and then the world was his oyster. His leaving at the end of every summer had never been easy, but this year couldn't have come at the worst possible time. He couldn't help but feel the guilt in advance. His sister and his friends would stay behind while he moved back down south and saw his friends who never knew Jaze existed and would never ask if he was okay. And maybe this made Warden a terrible person, but he was looking forward to it, to not being reminded of Jaze every single day like he knew the others would. Because of that, silent tears streamed down his face as soon as the funeral began.

Cleo and Knox joined them at the front of the funeral. All summer the five of them had been stuck together like glue. It only seemed right the remaining four of them would mourn and grieve their friend together, away from their families. Wes had taken up a spot between Warden and Knox, Cleo stood on the other side of Warden. As the ceremony went on they all linked hands. Cleo's dainty hands were cool despite the summer heat, however Wes's hands were clammy. It was the only part of her that revealed how she was feeling.

As they had entered town, Wes's face had shifted; long gone was the sorrow and tears threatening to spill. Instead, there was only steel and support. Knox leaned on her heavily, and half way through the ceremony he switched from holding her hand to wrapping his arm behind her back, tucking his shoulder into her side. With not a tear in her eye she comforted him.

Warden held it together semi-well. When the funeral ceremony paused for the allotted grieving time he felt his will waiver. It seemed so unfair that Jaze was gone and not even a bone was left to bury. And so he broke. He turned to his sister and sobbed. She wrapped her arms around both him and Knox, rubbed their backs, and whispered 'let it out' in their ears. They must've stood there half the night, Cleo joining them, but never once did she falter. She rubbed their backs and whispered comfort in their ears.

Warden always knew Wes was the twin who was made of steel, but until that moment, he had never realized how strong she was. Two days ago she was crying and fighting so hard she had to be restrained. Now, she stood supporting the weight of two grown men as they sobbed on her shoulder. Even when tears leaked from her eyes, she still held it together.

When they left the graveyard, they went to town to drink and honor Jaze's memory. And honor it they did. They celebrated his life, no matter how short, and remembered who he was. Throughout the night, Wes kept the celebration going. It was her who made sure to paint Jaze positively and bring everyone warm feelings about him. It was her that listened to the stories and allowed herself to be pulled into corners so people could spill their hearts out about how good of a man he was. Among all the chaos and grief, she became the one that everyone leaned on.

RHYATT

Rhyatt stood outside Saint Saveen's university, craning his neck to see the intricate carvings of Lady Justice at the top of the second level.

He hadn't planned to attend their university, but everything he *had* planned went to shit as soon as his grandmother, Lita, had seen him and Adriel. She had known her son was dead as soon as they darkened her doorstep. Rhyatt beat himself up for not sending word when his father had first passed. It had almost been a year, but with his missing time the pain was still raw.

Any thought of getting a job on one of the lush region's farms had gone out the window rather quickly. When he and his brother awoke on their first morning in Saint Saveen, Lita had already been to town and worked out for both of them to attend the university. She had personally seen the head scholar and ensured they would be placed in an age-appropriate semester. Adriel had been placed in a semester with other 20-year-olds, and somehow, Rhyatt had been placed in the 8th and final semester, set to graduate in 5 months. Rhyatt didn't understand much about the foreign country he had landed in. Still, he knew enough to know Lita had to pull some serious strings to get him into the final semester of school when he hadn't set foot in a university in over a year. So when she had returned beaming ear to ear, proud of her grandsons, he couldn't tell her no. When he questioned her about how they would afford it, she told him university was free here. Baffled, he also asked why they were in the 5th & 8th semesters instead of starting in the 1st. She had mumbled something about 'transferable credits' and said that Rhyatt's time would mostly be spent at an internship. With that, he decided to honor Lita and graduate, only working weekends while taking classes. Afterward, he would find a job and support the three of them in this country. That was all that mattered at the moment. He and his brother were out of harm's reach.

Rhyatt huffed at the humid heat that threatened rain and walked up the stairs towards the set of dark wood double doors. He knew he should be nervous but couldn't find it in himself. If anything, he was excited to get back into a routine, back into some semblance of normalcy. Every quiet moment he had, he'd been questioning the events that led up to his disappearance. It never added up. His mind wandered when he was still, so the distraction was welcome.

Pulling open one of the intricate doors, he strode into the cool darkness of the university. It was opposite from the outside; the outside was all white stone while the inside was dark wood floors. The walls a mixture of white stone and dark wood, and windows on each side were stained glass, letting in colored light. Rhyatt marveled at the beauty. Halfway through the room, a staircase led upwards, a small balcony looking down at the long, empty room. He looked up and discovered the windows went up to the second floor, the enormous size allowing the room to be bathed in multi-colored light.

Stepping further into the room, he noticed the other students lounging around. Their clothes were different earthy tones, and various weapons were strapped to their belts, mostly swords. They sat and stood in groups throughout the room, chatting to each other. A few had stopped to look at him; he was thankful the room's shadows hid the heat that rose to his cheeks. Trying not to stare, he walked to the steps and sat a few feet away from two people deep in conversation. He rested his elbows on his muscular legs. That was another thing Rhyatt couldn't get past, how much more muscular he had gotten. He had never been thin by any means, but now his skin seemed to be stretched tightly across his body. He would be lying if he said he didn't like it. He carried firewood for Lita yesterday, and it seemed almost *easy*. He wasn't even out of breath when he finished an hour later.

Rhyatt pushed away the thoughts before they could turn dark and start assuming what he had done to get them. Instead, he looked around the room at all the other students. They talked to each other casually, with individuals flitting back and forth between groups, the comfort of people who had known each other for years. Most of them had likely grown up together; Lita had mentioned only a handful of students were not from Saint Saveen.

Rhyatt's attention was pulled away as he heard the rain begin. A look at the stained-glass windows told him the sun still shined. He smiled softly. Sunshowers were always his favorite as a kid, proving two waring things could happen simultaneously.

Rhyatt was still thinking about the last time his home city had seen rain when the double doors flung open, banging against the walls and drawing the attention of everyone in the room.

With the sun shining behind them, three slightly wet strangers stepped inside, their faces pulled back in laughter. They seemed oblivious to the stares as they stopped just inside the doorway.

Rhyatt's attention immediately went to the tall, thin woman on the right. Her pale blue silk top made her stand out. She was a timeless beauty and held herself with poise. Her high cheek-bones, full lips, dark waist-length braids, and darker skin added to that beauty. Her gentle demeanor made Rhyatt instantly want to trust her.

On the left was a blonde man who was much shorter and stouter. Everything from his body composition to his face was the opposite of the tall, slender girls. He had broad shoulders and operated his body similar to how a bull in a china shop would. His skin was a peachy pink, and the bridge of his nose was a darker pink. He had likely spent too much time in the sun, just like Rhyatt. With his square jaw and deep-set eyes, he was surely seen as attractive.

Lastly, Rhyatt's vision landed on the woman in the middle. She could've been a prince by the way she swaggered in, but her eyes cut across the room like a hawks. Her features were sharp, and he could already tell if her face was schooled into anger it would be fear-inspiring. She reached up to brush back her dark shoulder-length hair, and even from the stairs, Rhyatt could see the bruises and angry cuts that scattered across her knuckles like stars in a constellation. He pitied the fool who had fought with her.

The trio stepped into the room, and others began to migrate towards them. First was a slim boy who easily looked younger than everyone else. He looked at the middle woman with adoration in his eyes. The others followed. It was like the three of them had a gravitational pull, and other students took turns coming and talking to them. One woman whispered a quick, 'Sorry for your loss.' The blonde man's eyes widened, but Rhyatt could've sworn both women looked away.

A door creaked open from somewhere on the second floor. The students' attention shifted to the stairs, and their voices lowered. Turning, he saw what he presumed was the Scholar. Except she looked young. She couldn't be more than ten years older than them. Despite her youth, the room shifted into silence as she descended the stairs, a pleased smile across her face. By the time she was halfway down the steps, the students had gathered around, and Rhyatt stood and joined the crowd.

"Words cannot express how joyous I am to lead you in your final semester. It has truly been an honor to watch you all grow into the young adults that now stand before me." Her smile was warm, like an older sister.

"But just because I am joyous for our final adventure, do not underestimate how difficult this semester will be. Soon you all will go off on your own, until then I plan to prepare you and push you in all ways possible."

A few students murmured at her words. Rhyatt should've worried more about the challenge she was emulating, but he was too excited to be doing something again. The days of travel and waiting were tiresome and lonely in ways he couldn't express.

"Your struggles will not be for nothing. Because when you take your final exams, I have full faith you will pass with astounding scores." Her eyes softened as she scanned the room, "Now, grab a practice sword and find a partner."

The students began to move toward the far right of the room where a bucket of wooden swords had been pulled out. They formed a line as they picked up one and paired up. Rhyatt was last in line and got one with a small piece of wood missing at the tip, making it jagged.

His stomach flipped as he turned around and saw the students already fighting. Their moves were quick and calculated; for every move, there was a countermove. This type of fighting was new to Rhyatt. He had never picked up on swords in the first place, but this was completely different. He weighed the sword in his right hand; it seemed too short and dense.

Surveying the room, he looked for anyone else still in need of a partner. The only one without a partner was the girl who had stood in the middle of the captivating trio. Maybe it was fear or excitement that grabbed him, but when her eyes caught his, he walked towards her.

He stopped in front of her. She had seemed taller from further away, but up close, she was of average height. She inclined her head in the smallest of bows. Rhyatt mimicked her bow, keeping his eyes on her at all times. At this distance, it was easy to see her dark green eyes and how they danced with excitement, a cat-like grin spreading. She stepped back and pulled up her weapon in one hand. Rhyatt followed suit, praying he wouldn't embarrass himself.

She took the first swing. Rhyatt leaped back just in time to miss the impact that would have landed on his left arm. She paused and her face relaxed. Her lips cracked into the beginning of a smirk. A shiver went down Rhyatt's spine, he was in over his head.

She stepped forward and swung again; this time, Rhyatt was too slow and the sound of the wood hitting his arm smacked in his ears. She pulled away and motioned with her hand for Rhyatt to advance. Rhyatt brought the sword up and tried to copy her first swing. Within a blink of an eye her sword was up and blocked the hit, pushing his sword and him backwards. Rhyatt may have had more height and weight, but she knew how to use her strength and send him stumbling.

She let him get his footing before motioning for him to advance again. Anger and embarrassment had begun to brew inside of him. He tried another similar swing for her legs. Her sword darted out, blocking his hit and driving his arm upwards.

With his arm extended upwards, she shifted her feet and delivered a blow to his right leg.

Then another to his left arm.

And another to his left leg.

When she struck his left leg, he found himself falling backward onto the floor. She loomed over him, silent gloat in her eyes. She gently lifted her sword, pressed the dull tip to his chest and pushed. The message was clear: if this was real, he would be dead.

As Rhyatt sat still, he began to wonder how much torture she would put him through. He looked around to notice everyone else had stopped and was staring at them. Rhyatt leaned forward to get up, but she was still in his path, the dull sword pressing into him. He thought she might mean to hold him there. But after narrowing her eyes, she removed the sword and extended her hand.

Embarrassment and pride pricked at Rhyatt. He scowled at her hand before leaning away to stand on his own.

Her black boots stayed planted in place, so when Rhyatt pushed himself up, they were face to face; she cocked her head like an animal would.

Furrowing her brows, she made a sound similar to a laugh, "You suck."

Rhyatt opened his mouth to deny it, but no words came out. Perhaps the fool who had made her knuckles bloody was as dumbfounded as he was now.

A hand on his shoulder drew Rhyatt's gaze away. The Scholar stood behind him with a scowl on her face.

"Perhaps Rhyatt should begin with me, *and you*," the Scholar looked at her, "should partner with Knox and Cleo."

She nodded, broke her death gaze away from Rhyatt, and walked to the two people she had entered with. Both of them began swinging at her at the same time. With unimaginable grace, she blocked them and delivered earth-shaking blows. The others struggled to block her in time. It dawned on Rhyatt that maybe she had taken it easy on him.

The Scholar led Rhyatt to the corner of the room where she began to show him the basics of fighting with a sword. She was kind and patient but didn't soften her blows compared to the other woman. By the time they finished, his body was throbbing, and his sword had not yet come close to touching her.

After dueling, they met in the classroom upstairs until they broke for a late lunch. When Rhyatt returned, a handful of people chatted idly in the chairs outside the Scholar's office.

"Where is everyone?" He asked.

A girl with tight blonde curly hair turned and smiled at him, "They're all at their internships."

Rhyatt nodded as he sat, still no less confused.

"I'm Olivina." She said with a smile and stretched out her hand. Rhyatt shook it and smiled back at her.

"Rhyatt." He replied.

"Everyone else prearranged an internship. We're the stragglers." She motioned to the others.

"So what do we do instead?" He asked.

"The Scholar places us in internships she thinks we'll do well at."

Rhyatt nodded again. Olivina looked at him, curiosity sparking in her bright eyes. Fear coursed through him as he thought that she might recognize him, but the Scholar calling her name made her look away and the feeling faded.

The next half hour flowed like that, with the Scholar calling each of them into her office until only Rhyatt was left.

"Mr. Valvidez." The Scholar called from her door, her pleated pants extended her tall posture.

They entered her office, and as she walked to sit behind her large, hand-carved wooden desk, Rhyatt marveled at the two floor-to-ceiling bookshelves on each side of a window. He sat across from her as she straightened the paper at the top of her pile. She let out a small sigh before meeting his gaze.

"Rhyatt. I'm not sure where to begin. You've told me you are unsure about your future, which makes placing you in a career-based internship very trying." She tapped her fingers against the paper and glanced at it, "However, there is one placement I have been unable to fill. I believe you could prosper if given the right tools."

Rhyatt sat up straighter as Lita's proud smile replayed in his mind; he would do anything to keep that smile on her face. "I would be grateful for any placement you have."

The Scholar gave him a tight-lipped smile.

"This placement would make you the mentor rather than the mentee. Our younger students are paired up with mentors and are meant to bond with them and learn from them. Unfortunately, we've had one student who has been unable to bond with any of his mentors. I believe that your fresh outlook could help influence him."

"If you don't mind me asking, is there anything I should know about why his previous mentors failed?" Rhyatt asked, but he guessed he already knew; the kid would be a handful. The Scholar's slight turn of head revealed he was right.

"Patience is a virtue many lack. Mentors and mentees spend a large sum of time together. My belief is that the previous mentors lacked the patience to get to know him. I am hoping you will be more patient."

"I can be patient." Rhyatt said and sort of meant it.

"I expect you both can learn a great deal from each other if given time." The Scholar rose and handed Rhyatt a piece of paper with the boy's name and an address.

WES

Wes sat with her closest friends, Cleo and Knox, under the shade of a tree as they enjoyed their lunch. When the trio were together they were never silent, today was no exception. As they sat and ate, the conversation turned to their internships. Cleo was buzzing with excitement at her placement with the town's Historic Councilor, Martin Knoe. Wes knew Cleo would excel, Cleo was smarter than Wes and Knox combined. She wouldn't be surprised if she was offered a job soon after graduation.

On the other hand, Knox had had to fight with his father tooth and nail to intern somewhere besides his family's metal working shop. His father had relented and Knox would be allowed to intern with Doctor Soubi, the town's doctor. Knox had been working under Soubi and assisting for a few years, and his father had still given him grief. Wes had scored one of the most competitive internships in Saint Saveen. She would intern for Commander Pryde, the Chief Commander of Northern Jorjin, and Commander of Saint Saveen. He was one of the three most powerful people in the entire country of Jorjin. Wes had originally applied to be the War Councilor's intern, but the War Councilor wasn't fond of Wes's family, and she wasn't selected. She had switched her sight on the Commander, who favored her family. Wes knew her mother had used her influence to get her the position, but this time she didn't care about her mother's abuse of power. She had worked just as hard to be eligible, and Wes was prepared to work even harder to be ready for her future career.

A gentle breeze blew the pages on Cleo's open book, causing her to look up at a sun bathing Knox.

"Yasmin looked excited to see you today."

"Hmm." Knox hummed without opening his eyes.

"She nearly knocked Wes over trying to get a seat near you."

"I'm just her newest conquest." Knox huffed, "Her newest *toy* to play with until her father takes it away and threatens her inheritance."

"She's a pretty girl." Wes said through a mouthful of apple.

"Then you should date her." Knox opened his eyes enough to glare at Wes.

"I'm far too easy prey. It's you she wants."

"She's very sweet." Cleo added, and Knox's aggravation finally boiled over, which was easy to encourage.

"I would rather jump into a lake of serpents than jump into her bed and risk her father's wrath."

Cleo pursed her lips and sent a disapproving shake of her head Knox's way, "Perhaps your time would be well spent with the serpents, at least you'll have something in common."

Knox bobbed his head and mocked Cleo, "*At Least you'll have something in common Knox. You're a little serpent Knox.*"

He stopped as Cleo chucked a small rock at his leg, and the trio laughed. Wes stood to leave, dusting her palms off on her black pants, the dark soil blending in easily.

"Dinner tonight?" Knox asked, referring to weekly meals served at Wes's house. Wes grimaced.

"I actually might have to postpone any dinners this week. I'm a bit behind on work, and it isn't going to do itself." What she didn't say was she was behind because Jaze's death had thrown her out of her rhythm.

"We understand," Cleo said, "Next week?"

"Next week." Wes agreed and set off towards the governance district.

Wes worked her way through town, the late lunch rush had mostly died down. She picked her path to take her through the garden district. The garden district was full of smaller homes, some of which were rumored to be some of the firsts in Saint Saveen. She admired the gardens the small homes boasted. In addition to the bright gardens, the district had the highest elderly population, and houses were passed down from generation to generation. Wes cleared the district easily before walking into the more lively downtown. She walked through the outer and middle ring without stopping, but as she entered the large open-air circle, she slowed so as to not sweat through her shirt. The late August heat made it easy to do so, and she hoped to make a good impression. Sweat soaking her shirt would not help. She reached the center and slowed underneath the shade of the tree. It was at her slower pace that she watched a young mother come out of a bakery, one hand holding a toddler and the other holding an overflowing basket of goods.

The toddler jerked forward, causing the mother to drop her basket, and wrapped goods spilled forth onto the cobblestones. She sighed and bent to begin picking up the dropped items. Wes altered her path to help but slowed when a tall, broad-shouldered man stooped low and began gathering the items. Wes watched as the man bent, one knee on the ground, and helped pick up the spilled beans. There was something oddly familiar about him. Even with a large build, he moved with grace. His black hair shone in the sunlight, and his dark skin glowed. He stood and reached out a hand to help the young mother stand. She blushed and took it, standing up and dusting her hands on her pants.

Wes slowed to a crawl while watching their interaction. The man hadn't turned around yet, and Wes couldn't shake the feeling of familiarity. The mother thanked him, and he turned towards Wes, giving her a full view of his face.

It was the man from the university this morning.

Rhyatt.

That was his name. And now *Rhyatt* was staring right back at her.

Wes knew she should nod at him and move along, but her actions beat out her rationality. Lowering her chin, she smirked and gave him a wink. If she hadn't been paying attention, she would've missed the small smile and shake of his head as he turned away. She didn't spare him another glance as she went in the opposite direction. The man couldn't fight to save his life, but that didn't diminish how easy he was on the eyes. And he was *oh so very easy* on the eyes.

Wes arrived at the Saint Saveen Governance building and strolled in with her head held high and a polite smile painted across her face. She had been to the governance building many times when her mother and father still worked in the city, but it had been well over a few years since she had been inside. The grandeur of the white marble and glass ceilings still astonished her. The building was one of the largest and most exquisite in the Northern Territory.

She stepped deeper into the building before ascending the six flights of stairs to reach the top level, dedicated entirely to the Commander. Voices echoed upwards to the ceiling as she climbed. She held her head higher with each step and reminded herself how much she deserved this internship. It had been almost 3 years since Commander Pryde had taken an intern; Wes knew this internship was a foot in the door to the future she so badly craved. Commanders of larger towns like Saint Saveen were picky about who interned with them; Their intern was an extension of them and would be seen through the public eye. For someone like Commander Pryde, who was not only the Commander of their town but also the Chief Commander of the Northern Territory, taking an intern was as good as plastering a golden approval stamp across Wes's forehead. All of the town would know about her involvement, and if she did a good job, half of Jorjin would know as well.

Wes didn't want to be a Commander but knew the benefits, skills, and relationships she would gain would help her get the career she did want. Her goal was to lead of the special tasks army, an elite group of 13 that organized and executed tasks for the three chief commanders of Jorjin. When Wes was a little girl, the group was a myth, something children whispered to each other. They were nicknamed 'the legion of ghosts' because no enemy who saw them lived to tell the tale. As Wes grew older, her father let it slip that they were a real group and twice as fearful and elite as she had imagined. Since finding out about their legitimacy, she had set her sights on joining and then climbing the ranks to be their youngest lead ever. Now less than 5 months away from graduating, she had secured the perfect internship to set her on the right path, War Councilor be damned. All that was left to do was excel at her internship and quickly climb the army's ranks.

Wes passed each of the councilors' floors until she arrived at the top. The glass ceilings extended into the Commander's hall, illuminating it with warm white light. Some things had changed since Wes had last been on this floor; notably, the marble and wood walls were now lined with various potted plants. Behind the secretary's desk, the foreign vines were twisted and climbing the wall. Wes noticed the plants were not all local, there were bright pink cactuses from Duran, yellow night flowers from Savia, and black miniature trees from the republic of Widen. It made for a beautiful entrance.

"Hello, Miss Blake." The secretary said with a warm smile. Wes smiled back at her, embarrassment creeping up her spine. She knew the secretary; she had probably met her half a dozen times, but at the moment, she couldn't remember the woman's name. That was the downside of living in her mother and father's shadow; more people knew her name than she'd care to think of.

"It's just Wes." She said, making it a point to find out her name before the next day.

"Well, *just Wes*. Commander Pryde is ready for you." The secretary smiled slyly as she rose from her chair and motioned for Wes to follow her down the hall.

Wes fell in step behind her. She didn't miss the slight swing in the secretary's step as she followed down the hallway. The plant-covered hallway hosted various other offices; some doors were propped open while others were shut tight. The secretary paused at the end of the hall before large double doors with the Commander's crest on them. She rapped her knuckles twice before pushing the door open and stepping aside so Wes could enter.

"Wes Blake has arrived." She announced, her honey voice sending a shiver up Wes's spine.

The Commander sat in a leather chair behind a large dark wood desk. The wall of windows behind him highlighted the growing gray in his hair and neatly trimmed beard. Without looking up from his documents, he waved her in with one hand.

"Thank you, Evalyn." He said dismissing the secretary. Evalyn stepped out, softly closing the door behind her.

"Commander Pryde, thank you again. I'm looking forward to learning from the best." Wes put on what she thought was an ass-kissing voice. On her, it sounded more like a threat rolled in sugar. Commander Pryde bristled at her voice, pausing his work he looked up at Wes, realization rattling through his eyes.

"Wes!" He exclaimed, the pen dropping loudly, "Come, sit."

When Wes had settled herself in a seat across from the Commander, he spoke again.

"Call me Mr. Pryde. Your father would be displeased if you addressed me so formally."

"Thank you Mr. Pryde. I was just telling my father how excited I was to work with you."

That was a lie. Wes hadn't said more than a handful of words to her absentee father in months.

Mr. Pryde didn't notice her lie. He clasped his hands near his face and leaned back in his chair, his eyes roamed over Wes.

In turn, she made sure to sit tall and replicate Evalyn's poised posture. Normally, Wes would have rolled her eyes while under the gaze of an older man, but this felt different. We had known the Pryde family since she was a little girl; she had grown up with his children. His gaze didn't seem sexual. It reminded Wes of a father assessing his child.

"And how is your father? Warden returned to university yet?" He asked after a long pause.

"Good, and yes. He left last week. How is Atticus? The girls?"

The Commander's scrutiny faded at the mention of his children, "Good, very good. Atticus has already started to explore internships for next semester- you know he's only a semester behind you- and the girls are doing great. Winnie is enjoying the Southern territory."

The Commander relaxed with each word he said about his children, and Wes smiled in return. He loved his children and swelled with pride over them—more than some prominent men could say, including Wes's own father.

"That is good to hear about Atticus. Will he not be interning with you?"

"No, I'd like him to do something different for his last semester, and he will shadow me in the summer." Mr. Pryde's smile spread further.

"I'm sure he will be excellent at whatever he chooses." Wes laid the flattery on thick. Mr. Pryde's crutch was his kids. It didn't hurt Wes to dote on them.

"Rightfully so. One day, he may be *your* Commander." Mr. Pryde's smile flashed brightly at the idea, "Shall we discuss your internship?"

RHYATT

R hyatt had stopped to ask for directions three different times. It wasn't until the last time that he showed the elderly woman the paper and he had gotten proper directions. She saw the name and called the house *The BlakeMoore*. Awfully pretentious name for a house if you asked him.

As he followed the woman's directions he came to realize he was traveling the same road he had been down this morning. Not too far from Lita's house, and now his house. As he turned onto the long dirt way he thought maybe the name of the house wasn't pretentious enough. Past the tree-lined driveway sat two barns, one on each side. Men and women walked in between each one, moving animals and equipment to and fro. Past the barns, in the dead center was the house. Its size was intimidating and its white columns were elegant, the pruned greenery all around the front was evidence of the pride that had been bestowed on the home.

Rhyatt's pace slowed as he approached. He was wrong, *The BlakeMoore* fit the looming structure before him.

Before he could get cold feet, he jogged up the stairs onto the porch and rapped his knuckles on the door. Even on this side of the door, he could hear how the sound echoed.

The echo had stopped and Rhyatt was preparing to knock again when the door jerked open.

"How can I help you?" A middle-aged woman with a red face asked while wiping her hands on her apron. A cook.

"Hi, I'm Rhyatt. Scholar Tiunda sent me to see Will Blake. I'm to be his mentor."

"Oh." She pursed her lips and raised her brows, "Are you now?"

"Yes ma'am." He replied with a hopeful smile.

"Well come on in." She pushed the door open further and turned, motioning for him to follow.

Rhyatt stepped out of the sun and into the home's foyer. He had never seen a foyer so big, so much wasted living space. Judging by the way the foyer was separated from the other rooms he presumed the space to be used for parties as well. From the gold-painted staircase and the marble floor, there was no way this wasn't a room for gatherings. Rhyatt began to feel out of place, his clothes too worn, his hair too messy. Perhaps the young lad would eat him alive.

The cook led him through a swinging door next to the staircase, into the kitchen. Heat worse than outside hit him in the face making him sweat like before. The cook paused at the open back door.

"Mister Will is over there." She pointed a round finger at a large tree in the middle of a garden. Sure enough, a small boy sat at a rickety table. His head was bent in concentration.

Rhyatt offered his thanks and stepped back outside, as he walked away the cook whispered *good luck*. His stomach lurched at the thought he might need it, how bad could one child be?

Rhyatt walked through the garden towards the boy. His chestnut hair was all that Rhyatt could see of him. When he reached the shaded area the boy looked up. A misting of freckles was laid beneath piercing brown eyes, eyes that looked right through Rhyatt.

Rhyatt stopped in front of his table and the boy stared at him, his pen frozen on the page. Rhyatt stared back, unmoved by the child's glare.

The boy looked at Rhyatt with bored indifference before speaking.

"What do you want?" His small voice was reminiscent of a child.

"I'm Rhyatt," he extended his hand towards him, "I'm your new mentor."

The boy eyed the hand with suspicion before looking back up to Rhyatt's face. Slowly, he extended his hand and squeezed Rhyatts.

"I'm Will." He said with dismissal and looked back to his paper in front of him.

Most men would have written Will off as an arrogant and disrespectful child, but Rhyatt had a younger brother and had learned patience a long long time ago. He moved away from Will's table and sat down with his back against the tree. Will began to work faster, the pen scratching louder than the chirping birds overhead. His eyes stayed downwards, not even looking up to see the ink he dipped his pen in.

"What are you working on?" Rhyatt asked, straightening to try and see.

"Sentences."

"What kind?"

Will paused, considering his answer before turning to look at Rhyatt, "The kind you do when you get in trouble."

"Hmm." Rhyatt nodded a knowing look. Will returned to his paper, working just as fervently. Rhyatt leaned his head back against the tree and began to put the pieces together. The scholar had given him the troublemaker. That was why no other internship had succeeded.

"How much trouble did you get in on the first day back?" Rhyatt asked and continued the conversation, much to Will's disappointment.

Huffing, Will answered, "Enough that I have to write fifty sentences." He paused again, Rhyatt could almost see the little wheels in his little mind turning, "The scholar said I can't come back until I've done them. And if they're not done by tomorrow my sister will find out."

"What happens if your sister finds out?"

"She'll probably skin me alive." Those brown eyes narrowed and once again found Rhyatts, "And if you want this mentorship to work you won't say a word to her."

Rhyatt couldn't help but smile at the threat from the 9-year-old. He held up his hand in surrender and pushed down a laugh, "My lips are sealed."

Will blinked and returned once again to his paper.

"Maybe when I'm done we could play a game." His voice swung dramatically, morphing back to sounding like a child.

"That would be nice."

There. Will couldn't be *that* much trouble. Rhyatt had already broken this boy and he *offered* to play a game. He couldn't be more trouble than Adriel was when he was younger. Though his brother was only 16 months younger he was more the hellion than Rhyatt ever was. If Rhyatt could survive Adriel then Will would be a piece of cake.

The humid heat had just become bearable when Will stood and announced he was finished.

"What game should we play?" Rhyatt asked, standing as well.

Will paused, only briefly pretending to consider before blurting his game with a smile, "Hide and Seek!"

Rhyatt didn't question the strange smile on the boy's face, instead, he nodded and asked, "Do you want to hide first or should-"

"You hide first!" Will interrupted him, "I'll count to 50." Turning to the tree to shield his eyes he began counting loud and quick.

Rhyatt panicked at the quick counting and took off running, he ran to the side of the house and kept running towards the barns he had seen when arriving. As he got close he realized how big the barn was, it was at least two stories and could probably fit 10 to 15 horses easily. He slowed as he reached the main door, it was already open. Slipping inside he walked to the opposite end and knelt behind bales of hay stacked two high. Not that hard of a hiding place but not easily seen.

Rhyatt began counting at 15, the last number he had heard Will yell. In his head, he counted to 50 and began to wait.

After a minute his legs began to burn from crouching so he sat down.

After a few more minutes of silence, Rhyatt thought that maybe Will had gone to check the house first. He was probably used to playing hiding games in that huge house. He made a mental note to ask the cook about his favorite hiding spots when the roles reversed.

Rhyatt sat and sat and sat.

When he felt his eyelids get heavy he scooted closer to the edge of the bales and stuck his foot out. Anyone who looked inside the barn would see his boot. Maybe that would help Will find him.

Rhyatt sat some more and began to question if his hiding spot was too hard, or maybe the barns were off-limits for someone so young. He hadn't stopped to think about that before.

Rhyatt continued to sit and his head became heavier and heavier until he had nodded off.

He awoke to a loud noise and looked up to see the barn door had been shut. Sighing, he stood and dusted the stray hay off of his backside. He went to the door and attempted to pull it open, but it did not move. He jerked it again. It was locked from the outside.

Rhyatt banged on the door asking for someone to let him out.

It was useless. He hadn't seen anyone the entire time he was hiding and whoever had locked the door was in a hurry to close up. Turning, he looked around for a back door, he walked the perimeter until he found one. It was also locked. Rhyatt was too drained to panic, he kept walking the perimeter.

After doing a full circle of the barn he had come up with two solutions; he could either use the tools to get a few boards loose and slip through, or he could get in the water trough that was half-in-half out of the barn. Rationality said just to break a few boards and be free, but the idea of explaining to the cook, or the owner of the house, what he had done seemed rather unpleasant. Instead, he opted for the horse's water trough.

Stepping into the water he was surprised at the chill of the water, it must be fresh from a well. He settled into the bath-tub-like trough, went under, and used his hands to push him to the outside.

On the other side, the sun had begun to sink lower in the sky, he had learned sunsets here lasted hours. It was one of the beauties he liked about his new home. Gripping the edge of the trough he rose and stepped onto solid ground. Water dripped off him and his clothes.

Rhyatt pushed his soaking hair out of his eyes and headed towards the back of the house. He rounded the corner of the barn and almost collided with a man he presumed to be one of the workers.

"Woah- what the hell happened to you." The man said; he wasn't much older than Rhyatt.

"Got locked in the barn. Had to crawl out through troughs." Rhyatt said, stopping in front of him and ringing his soaking shirt out.

"Oh, man. My apologies. Mister Will told me to lock the barn, I didn't know anyone was still in there."

Rhyatt stopped, his hands still twisted in the white shirt, "Will told you to lock up?"

"Yeah, he usually doesn't say anything to us, but tonight he insisted."

Rhyatt's face twisted into a scowl, he muttered a thank you before continuing to the house. He stopped by the tree to grab his bag, lying on the table were the sentences Will had been writing.

In neat writing 'I *will not lie and attempt to overthrow the scholar house*' was written fifty times. If Rhyatt wasn't soaking wet he would have laughed.

He gripped his bag in his hand and walked towards the still-open back door. The smells of dinner drifted out and made Rhyatts stomach growl.

Climbing the steps Rhyatt paused on the landing so as not to get water inside. The cook had her back turned.

"Excuse me, Miss," Rhyatt said, his words clipped.

She jumped and whirled around. She let out a sigh of relief upon seeing Rhyatt.

"Oh! You startled me!"

"I'm sorry I didn't mean to."

She waved her hand in the air, "No dear, not your fault. William told me you left an hour ago. I just wasn't expecting you!"

Rhyatt gritted his teeth at the new information. Of course, Will had lied and said Rhyatt had left. The pieces were all falling into place.

"Where is Will now?"

The cook turned back to her work, "He went upstairs last I saw him." She leaned forward to look out the window, "But by now he will be at the end of the drive waiting for Miss Blake to get home."

"Thank you." Rhyatt said and turned on his heel, heading back outside. Scowling, he made his way around the side of the house and started down the long driveway.

Rhyatt was a stone's throw from the house when Will and a woman-presumably his sister- turned onto the drive. He paused and stood still. Her arm was draped around his shoulder and he looked up at her chattering away. They were both so caught up in each other that neither noticed the angry and soaking-wet Rhyatt standing in front of the house.

He watched Will and began to feel a sense of regret at his anger towards him. Seeing Will with his sister was like day and night. Around Rhyatt he had been closed off, wary, and almost like a mini adult. Around his sister he threw his head back with laughter and smiled. Even the way he walked seemed more comfortable.

Rhyatt looked to the sister, trying to see what woman had brought about such a change in the boy. He squinted his eyes at the laughing figure, but her dark short hair covered her face as she looked down at him. It wasn't until she threw her head back in a laugh that Rhyatt saw her face.

It was the same woman from the university. The one who had beaten him. She had looked him dead in the eye and told him he sucked.

Rhyatt shook his head, this couldn't be the same woman. The woman at the university was calculated and cocky, her limbs taut and ready to strike. The woman in front of him now walked with ease, laughing and swaying with her little brother. Rhyatt's mind stuttered over the differences until he finally looked down and saw her shoes. They were the same lace-up black boots he had stared at from the floor. Same shoes, same woman.

When Rhyatt looked at her face again her features were no longer easygoing, she had seen him. A moment later, Will saw his sister's reaction and he spotted Rhyatt too.

It must've been the fact that Rhyatt was soaking wet and steaming with anger because Will *smiled* at him. Only briefly. But it was a smile. As quick as it appeared it disappeared and was replaced by tight lips and narrowed eyes, one of the many things Will had obviously perfected.

The dangerous duo stopped in front of him, the sister's hand now resting firmly on Will's shoulder. Will puffed his chest and began readying to talk but his sister cut him off.

"The little bunny who couldn't fight." She said in greeting, amusement coating her words.

"Not everyone can be a killer." Rhyatt replied, a tight-lipped smile on his face.

"Indeed."

She let her words fall and Rhyatt felt her waiting for him to say something. A small voice said he should be intimidated by her, but all he could feel was amusement.

"You must be Will's sister."

She blinked and looked down at Will, who was now looking at her. He began to explain.

"This is Rhyatt," Will began, slightly out of breath, "He was sent to test out a mentorship but I don't think it's going to work." When he finished he put on a small pout as if he hadn't spent the last few hours planning to get rid of Rhyatt.

Rhyatt forced a more natural smile and looked down at the pouting boy, "Of course it's going to work! We just need more time to get to know each other." Will's lips parted to interrupt and Rhyatt continued, "Plus- my lips are already sealed, I'd hate to have to open them."

Will's scowl intensified and he inhaled ready to say more. It was his sister's hand tightening on his shoulder that made him pause. As he looked back up at her his demeanor instantly relaxed again.

"Go inside and wash up so we can eat dinner."

Without missing a beat, Will nodded and began walking towards the house. Rhyatt stared after the boy in astonishment. He turned and looked at the sister in amazement. How on earth had she had such an easy time getting him to do something? Earlier getting Will to talk was like pulling teeth.

When Will was out of sight the sister looked back to Rhyatt, "I'm worried." She said without an ounce of worry in her voice.

"Don't be worried about him. Kids come around when they get older." Rhyatt said, already vowing not to speak of what had happened and why he was soaking wet.

She tilted her head and furrowed her eyebrows, "Not about him, about *you*."

Rhyatt paused to consider her.

"I have other strengths besides sword fighting"

She raised her eyebrows and ever so slowly she looked him up and down. From the top of his head to the tip of his toes.

"I'm sure you do." She said almost playfully, but her tone shifted with the wind as she spoke again, "However Will is a force of nature no one can command. Consider yourself lucky to be leaving here soaking wet and not in pieces. He has driven away other mentors with far more dangerous means."

Rhyatts forced smile faded as a real one replaced it, "I'm not scared away so easily." He stepped forward and began to walk past her, "I'll see you tomorrow Miss Blake."

She cringed lightly, turning to face him as he walked by, "Please. Call me Wes. Just Wes."

"So we're going to be on a first-name basis, Miss Blake?"

"Miss Blake is my mother. Just Wes." She repeated as Rhyatt walked backward.

"Very well Wes," He stopped and bowed at the hips, "Rhyatt Valvidez at your service."

She huffed a laugh and rolled her eyes before turning away.

Rhyatt walked home with the name ringing through his mind, he didn't know why he liked it so much but it was music to his ears.

Wes. Wes. *Wes.*

Rhyatt opened Lita's front door and closed it quietly behind him. The setting sun illuminated the small kitchen in hues of orange and yellow. Adriel and Lita sat at the kitchen table shelling peas.

Rhyatt joined them at the table and began shelling as well. Adriel's face had lit up at the sight of his brother, but Lita now sported a frown. He figured she was still adjusting to having her two grandsons in her house.

"How was your day?" Adriel said, practically buzzing.

"Good." He placed a handful of peas into the bucket, "Yours?"

"Mine was interesting," Adriel said, stretching his words out, hoping for someone to ask him more.

Rhyatt looked at his brother and sent him an encouraging smile, "And why is that?"

Adriel returned the grin, a mischievous glint in his eye, before he began talking a mile a minute, "Welllllll. A few friends and I went to eat lunch in the circle- it's the middle of downtown- and on the way there we almost ran into this woman, only Lila pulled me out of her path. I asked why and she told me that she was the best swordsman this town had ever seen, but her friend- who was rumored to be her secret lover- had died recently so she was likely to cut down anyone in her path."

Adriel ended his spiel and looked up expectantly at Rhyatt. He had to turn his head to stifle his laugh.

"She sounds like an interesting woman."

"They told me she had beaten all the scholars at the university and this summer she started dueling with different people from the army. She beat them all, even the second general. One day she's going to command an army."

"If she's so great why doesn't she already command an army?" Rhyatt asked with a raised eyebrow. Lita stayed silent.

"She's still at university." Adriel said matter-of-fact, "Your grade, I believe. Get this though- when I saw her today she had scratches and bruises all over her knuckles. Lila said whoever she fought probably lost. She always wins."

Rhyatt paused his work to turn fully to his brother, "What did you say her name is?"

"Wes Blake- her family used to be big wigs but rumor has it she beat her twin brother in a duel and he had to move away with their father."

Adriel continued on but Rhyatts chuckle stopped him, even Lita looked up to scrutinize them.

"I met her today." Rhyatt said, still chuckling at all his newfound knowledge of the Blake family.

Adriel's eyes went wide and his hands stilled, "Really? What was she like? How does she talk?"

"She was...something. I'm mentoring her little brother, a wild thing that one is."

Adriel's excitement built, he opened his mouth to say more but Lita cut him off.

"Don't speak ill of the Blake family, boy." Her voice was stern as she looked them both in the eye, "They've been through enough and Wes bears it all." The pea in her hand snapped, "Don't speak ill of them."

Before the silence could settle and become awkward Adriel looked back to Rhyatt, "Well I think she's the best. Maybe you could introduce me?"

Rhyatts stiffened back relaxed and he promised to introduce his brother to Wes. As they finished the peas and began to work on dinner together Lita complained that she wasn't used to cooking for more than just herself. Rhyatt laughed, he had never made a meal for just himself. It was always for himself, his brother, and his dad. Even when his dad passed it had been the two of them to cook for. He began to wonder if Lita was lonely all those years her only son lived in another country. A pang of sorrow shot through him as he thought of how long the news of his death had been delayed. And beneath it all was still the regret and confusion for his lost months.

WES

The clock chimed eleven and Wes finished her rum, slamming the whiskey glass down on her desk. She had been at her desk working since dinner. Will had been disappointed when she had excused herself immediately after she finished. He had stomped up the stairs and made sure to slam his door loud enough for the house to shake. Wes had only left her work once since sitting down to tell Will goodnight. He had rolled over and ignored her.

Now she sat at her desk, her shoulders slumped as she compared documents and wrote in the margins. Business was booming as usual as the summer began to wrap up. Paperwork for both the sales and her employees was always abundant this time of year; it didn't help how many days Jaze's death had put her behind.

Rising from her chair, she walked to the bookshelf where her good rum was hidden. Pouring a finger of it, she began to think of her day. Things with the Commander were going according to plan, and soon enough her friend's schedules would return to normal. But it was thoughts of *Rhyatt* that made her pause.

He was undoubtedly good-looking; seeing him soaking wet in a see-through white shirt made her very aware of that. The fabric had clung to his large frame, showing off every muscle curve on his chiseled shoulders and arms.

Wes sat back down and picked up where she left off. It wasn't long before a sense of grief crawled down her spine. Only weeks ago had she shared her bed with her now deceased friend. It seemed almost rude to think of anyone else with his death still occupying the forefront of her mind. So she pushed the thoughts of Rhyatt in that white top out of her mind.

It was 2 a.m. when she marked the sales of the most recent crop of bananas, blew out the candle, and laid down on the couch to nap.

WES

Class had begun, and Wes was already bored. The Scholar hadn't paired her off with two others, so she sat beneath the stairs and shined her real sword while everyone else practiced. Rhyatt was in a similar predicament across the room. He held his practice sword at his side and slowly looked around.

Wes watched as his eyes stopped on her and widened. Rhyatt returned to the bucket of practice swords, picked an extra up, and strode to where she was sitting. He extended it to her, and she raised her eyebrows in question.

"Looking to get your ass beat again?" She asked.

"Only by you." he replied with a wink before pouting and adding, "No one else wants to spar with me."

"That's because you suck." She replied with an eye roll, still planted in her seat.

"Then you'll lose nothing by sparring with me." Rhyatt shrugged.

She stopped working on her sword and pretended to contemplate it. Before Rhyatt could ask again, she stood and resheathed her real sword at her hip. When it was safely secured, she took the practice sword.

"Have it your way," she said as they stepped away from the wall and took a fighting stance.

"If I learn something—"

"IF"

"—I can say I learned from the best." Rhyatt finished.

Wes revealed her teeth in a mockery of a smile, "Flattery does you no good against a blade."

"Was worth a try." Rhyatt lunged forward in an attempt to gouge Wes's stomach. She was too quick. Her sword caught the inside of his, and she pushed the blade outwards. The left corner of her mouth twitched upward at his failed attempt.

He drew himself back up to his full height, and as Wes side-stepped, he followed, keeping the distance between them. They slowly circled each other, eyes locked as their feet began a dangerous dance.

As Wes stepped, she leaned forward, curving her sword to smack his arm. The loud whack startled Rhyatt, who winced and looked down where the sword had struck. With his head still down, she struck again, hitting the opposite arm.

His head snapped up, fury igniting in his eyes. Her mouth was still set in the half smile she had adopted earlier. He rolled his shoulders and lunged forward, both arms extended. Wes side-stepped his attack with grace.

Rhyatt spun on his heel to face her again. The half smile turned into a full one as she held her arms wide.

"Don't just run at me. Strike me." She taunted.

Rhyatt raised his sword above his head and attempted to bring it down on Wes. Quick as lightning, her free hand reached up, grabbed his wrist, and twisted it the opposite way. She twisted with it until she was on his side. She let go and used her sword to press his downwards. When the tip touched the floor, she put her foot on it, forcing it to clatter to the ground.

In the confusion, they had gotten close—so close that Wes had to tilt her head to stare into his eyes. Rhyatt stared back at her, his chest moving rapidly with each breath. He opened his mouth, but her sword's blunt tip left him speechless.

"Learn anything yet?" She asked, a triumphant smile spreading.

Before Rhyatt could answer, The Scholar's voice rang across the room, stilling other pairs.

"Why is my best student sparring with my worst student??" She neared them and stopped to assess them. "You," she looked at Rhyatt, "Will get beat to a pulp. And you," she turned to Wes, "will get lazy. Do *not* spar together again."

Wes dipped her head in acknowledgment as The Scholar strode away from them, anger rolling off her. She looked at Rhyatt once more,

"Not too bad, *little bunny*."

He smiled, showing straight white teeth, "Eh, you could've done worse, *killer*."

RHYATT

R hyatt walked to the BlakeMoore home with his head held high. He was determined to make today better than Monday. The Scholar told him that internships would often begin with a focus on schoolwork and develop deeper as time went on. At this point, Rhyatt just hoped to live through it. He had had a lot of time to think about it and think about how cruel Will could potentially be. The possibilities were endless. The only thing bringing him here today was the drive to not be broken by a child. This was his new home, and he refused to let one rotten child break him before he had even settled.

It also helped that Will's sister was so intriguing.

Rhyatt knocked on the door and listened as the sound echoed through the foyer. The cook opened the door quicker than before.

"Oh!" Her brows raised in surprise, "You came back!"

Rhyat flashed her a handsome smile, "Of course. Is Will home?"

She pushed the door open, beckoning him inside. As she shut the door, she stood still and smiled at him, "I just knew a strong boy like you would last longer than a day."

She turned and headed towards the kitchen, motioning him to follow. She called over her shoulder, "Come. Have some lunch."

Rhyatt frowned, "No thank you, I don't want to impose."

They rounded the corner of the kitchen, and the cook went back to the counter.

"Nonsense. Soup will be done in a moment."

"No thank you, I'm fine, really." Rhyatt stepped closer to the open back door and peered out, "Is Will outside?"

"Not home yet." She responded, turning her back to him.

"Oh." Rhyatt pushed his shoulders back.

"A wild one that boy is."

"Does he give you much trouble?"

"Oh, sometimes," she said with a faint smile, "But not nearly as much trouble as Miss Wes used to give me. Now look at her-running the house and business better than before, I couldn't be more proud."

Rhyatt looked away from the back garden, "Wes runs all this?"

"Mhm." She hummed a yes. Of course she does.

"Where are Mr. and Mrs. Blake?" Rhyatt asked and winced as the cook stopped her motion. Slowly, she turned her head to look at him. He couldn't decide if the question made her look cautious or just plain tired. Either way, the mere mention of the parents was enough to still the cook.

After a long pause, she spoke carefully, "They both took jobs in different cities. Miss Wes took on the responsibilities when they left." She lifted her chin: "And she's done a *fine job*. She keeps us all going and keeps Will tame—well, as tame as can be expected."

"I see." Rhyatt paused, "And how long has she been the head of household?"

The cook scrunched her eyebrows and seemed to do a mental tally before answering, "This will be her fifth year."

Rhyatt nodded, and the cook went back to her work. As her back turned, Rhyatt's mind began to race. He had thought it odd how easily Wes had controlled Will, but now it made sense. It came easy to Wes because she was more than just his sister. She was his caregiver. His guardian. That was why Will had listened to her so quickly before.

"What does Will like to do?" Rhyatt asked, interrupting the silence.

Without looking up, she responded, "He likes to do whatever he's not supposed to do."

An easy smile spread across his face, "I've gathered that."

The cook looked over her shoulder at him and smiled back, "When he's not getting into trouble, he likes to be a kid. Running foot races, swimming in the creek, playing games." She turned away before continuing, this time quieter, "So many people forget he's just a kid."

"Do you think he'd do any of that with me?"

"Possibly. He might take a minute to warm up to you, but if you stick it out, he'll come around."

"It's the sticking it out part I'm worried about. Wes told me his actions can be... *less than ideal* when trying to rid himself of a new mentor."

"No one is going to tell you this, but you seem like a good enough young man that I'll tell you. Will isn't fond of men. Don't take it personally." She paused again, picking her words carefully. "He has a particular dislike of the male workers here. Been known to play a few nasty tricks on them, that's why they all avoid him like a demon."

"The workers don't retaliate against him?" Rhyatt asked, and the cook turned her face towards him again.

"Heavens no. He may be a menace to them, but they all respect Wes too much. And if you ask me, the ones who don't respect her fear her."

"I see," Rhyatt said as a chill ran down his back. He remembered the cuts across her knuckles and wondered if they were somehow related to Will.

"He may not be fond of you now, but give it time. I'm sure he'll grow to love you once he gets to know you." She picked up another onion, "He's a very likable child when not causing trouble. Very intelligent. Creative. And dare I say, kind-hearted."

"*Kind-hearted*?" Rhyatt asked, and the cook laughed at the question in his voice.

"Trust me, dear boy, he can be kind when he wants to be."

Rhyatt huffed a laugh, "I'll believe it when I see it. I don't think the boy has it in him."

Before the cook could scold him, a gentle *thump* came from upstairs. The cook looked up expectantly, and Rhyatt followed her gaze. After a moment, no further noises were heard.

"He's home. He'll be down in a few minutes."

Rhyatt nodded and looked out the open back door and into the woods beyond the creek. He had to admit, The BlakeMoore was beautiful in a classic way. In Duran, the gardens were full of desert plants, brown and muted greens were the only colors visible. Here it was different, lush and vibrant green was everywhere, from the trees to the grass. The plants in the gardens themselves were shocks to Rhyatt as well, pale yellow flowers, bright green moss, and rich green vines climbing the house. If the humidity wasn't so bad here, Rhyatt may come to enjoy Jorjin.

At the sound of the door swinging open, Rhyatt turned to see Will walk into the kitchen. As he sat at the island, his face was void of any emotion. In a polite voice, he asked the cook for lunch and she set about serving him. She sat down two bowls on the counter and looked at Rhyatt.

"Come, you must at least try it."

Rhyatt nodded, stepping towards the table. "Of course," he said, not wanting to be rude. He took his place carefully, leaving a chair between him and Will. Will ignored him, content to eat his soup and pretend Rhyatt didn't exist. They ate in silence, the only sound being the continuous chopping coming from the cook. When Will was over halfway done, Rhyatt looked at him.

"How was your day at school?" He asked innocently enough.

Will paused, his spoon held in the air, as he turned his head to look at Rhyatt. "Good." He took a bite, swallowed, and put the spoon back in the bowl. "How was your day at university?"

"Good." Rhyatt paused before adding, "I got beat real bad while sparring."

Will scrunched his eyebrows and assessed Rhyatt, "You look like you'd be good at fighting."

A small smile formed in the corner of Rhyatts mouth, "Looks can be deceiving. I'm not good in any way that counts."

Will blinked and returned to his soup. Rhyatt shook his head. This wasn't exactly progress, but it was a step in the right direction. Will continued to eat his soup in silence. The cook had switched from chopping vegetables to cracking eggs. When Will's bowl was almost empty, Rhyatt leaned back and asked him a question.

"How fast do you think you can run?"

Will took a bite, considering the question. He swallowed slowly and took his time placing the spoon back in the bowl before narrowing his eyes and responding.

"Why?"

"I was just thinking about how I could outrun you," Rhyatt replied, shrugging his shoulders in an attempt to look bored.

"No you can't. You're too heavy."

Rhyatt feigned shock, pressing a hand to his broad chest.

"Oh- that's not nice Will." The cook chided with her back turned.

"It's true. It's why Wes never wins. She says she's too heavy to go long distances fast."

"Maybe so, but it's still rude to say." She replied.

"It's okay," Rhyatt said to the cook before turning to Will, "There's only one way to find out."

A few minutes later, Rhyatt and Will stood underneath the large shade tree as Will explained the route they would take. They would start in the garden and end by the flat banks of the creek. The first person to set foot in the sand wins.

Will had taken on a serious demeanor, laying out the route like a professional would. Rhyatt nodded along. He found himself excited for something as trivial as a race. His body itched with anticipation. Will placed a hand flat against the tree; Rhyatt copied him.

"Are you ready?" Will asked, his small voice taking a competitive edge. Rhyatt nodded in response.

"3-2-1-go!" Will shouted, and they both took off running.

They kept stride with each other as they exited the garden, both of their arms swinging wildly. Once on the open grass, Rhyatt pushed ahead, gaining on Will. The sun shone down on both of them, making beads of sweat roll down their faces, necks, and back. At the halfway mark, Rhyatt had the lead by a handful of feet. He kept that lead until his feet hit the coarse sands of the creek.

Rhyatt had won.

Both boys paused in the sand, resting their hands on their knees to catch their breath.

"What's my prize for winning?" Rhyatt asked.

"It's no fair." Will said between breaths, "You're much bigger than me."

Rhyatt laughed, the deep sound echoing, "In the kitchen, you said I'd lose because of my size."

"I forgot how tall you are. It gave you an advantage." Will whined, and the sound sent a jolt through Rhyatt. Perhaps he was just a child who wanted to win a game. Rhyatt sighed.

"And what do you think would make it fair?"

Will paused his labored breathing to send a menacing smile at Rhyatt.

10 minutes later, Rhyatts' wrists were bound in front of him, and Will was grinning ear to ear. He had to give it to the boy, he knew how to tie knots. Rhyatts' wrists were bound so tightly he couldn't wiggle free, and they would most likely need to be cut to release him.

Will put a hand flat against the tree, and Rhyatt mimicked him, half his body pressed to the tree as well. Will counted down, and they were off. Will took the lead as they headed out of the garden, his arms swung wildly while Rhyatts' shoulders moved awkwardly. As they exited the garden, Rhyatt caught up and kept stride with Will, their feet beating a pattern against the soft grass. At the halfway point, Will began to slow down, only by a hair, but enough that Rhyatt noticed. He adjusted accordingly so they were neck in neck again. They ran like that until the sands were only yards away. And ever so slightly, Rhyatt's rhythm faltered, putting Will a couple of steps ahead. Their feet hit the sands as they came to a stop.

Will had won.

Rhyatt bent at the waist, his tied hands hanging limply between his knees, Will copied him, catching his breath as well.

"I won." Will laughed between breaths.

Rhyatt echoed his laugh, straightening against his restraints, "You did."

"See- I told you I could beat you."

"All you needed was a fair playing field," Rhyatt responded and Will nodded, his chest swelling with pride.

"What will my winner's prize be?"

"I planned to make you play tag."

"Let's play tag," Will agreed, stopping to wipe the sweat from his brow, "but you have to keep your hands tied."

Rhyatt tensed, to run a race with your hands tied was one thing, but playing tag seemed a bit too difficult. He had only agreed to the idea to appease Will.

"I don't know if that's a smart idea," he said, concern lacing his brow.

"What? Afraid you'll lose?" Will taunted.

Rhyatt knew he was a grown man and shouldn't give in to teases from a child, but the way he said it had lit a fire in Rhyatt.

He may have backed off during the race, but there was no way he would back off during tag.

"Fine." Rhyatt lunged forward, tagging Will, "You're it!" he yelled as he took off in the opposite direction.

Will ran after him, and for the next few hours, an intense game of tag took place on the BlakeMoore property. Between Rhyatts' awkward running and Will's ability to scale trees, there was never a dull moment. Both boys got tagged at least a handful of times, and by the time they heard the clock strike 5, they agreed to a truce so they could sit at the creek and get water.

Rhyatt sat hunched over near the water's edge while Will had reclined onto his back, staring at the sky. Rhyatt was amazed at the past few hours. The boy he had just played tag with was nothing like the boy he had met earlier in the week. Okay- maybe that was a bit of a lie, Rhyatt's hands were still bound. But the attitude was different, almost like a completely different person.

"I think you picked a good prize," Rhyatt said, bringing his cupped hands to his face and washing away some of the sweat.

Will said nothing, he continued to stare up at the clear blue sky.

"Why don't you cut my ropes, and we can play one last game before I leave."

Will said nothing. Instead, he sat up and looked at Rhyatt, his little face hardening into stone. His brown hair was pushed back from his face, and Rhyatt could see a faint white scar that ran down from his hairline. As his face hardened into the boy Rhyatt had met previously, the scar added to what Rhyatt already thought. He was as mischievous as they come, likely having got the scar while doing something he wasn't supposed to.

"I don't know if I'm *kind enough* to cut the ropes," Will said, venom lacing his words as his lip snarled. He had been waiting to say something.

"Kind enough?" Rhyatt trailed off as he realized.

"I overheard you and the cook in the kitchen. You don't think I can do anything good." Wills ground his teeth together as he clenched his hands in the sand.

Rhyatts face dropped as shame washed over him. How could he have said something so stupid?

"Will, I didn't mean it like that,"

"People mean what they say and say what they mean." He recited from memory, huffing at the words.

"Will, I'm sorry." Rhyatt tried again.

"You're only sorry because I heard." Will rolled his eyes and turned away, his shoulders slumping.

"No, that's not true. I'm sorry because I was wrong." Will kept his face hidden, and real shame and sorrow washed over Rhyatt. Oh gods, what an ass he had been. "I'm sorry because I'm wrong. I made a judgment about you before ever getting to know you, and I was wrong. It was rude of me to say it in the first place. I am sorry, Will."

Will kept his face turned, but his shoulders relaxed.

"If it makes you feel better, I'll stay tied up the rest of the day. I'll walk home tied up. Eat dinner tied up. *Sleep* tied up." Rhyatt's voice rose as the exaggerations got sillier.

Will finally turned back to him, a childlike grin on his face. The breath was almost knocked from Rhyatt. That was the same smile he had seen Will wear when he thought he and Wes were alone. This childlike smile made all the others seem fake, like part of his ruse at pretending to be a kid. It sent an ache through Rhyatts chest. What had happened to make this young boy hide so much away?

"It would be your punishment?" Will asked.

"Of course. Seems a fitting punishment."

Will nodded his agreement.

"In that case," Rhyatt said, pushing to his feet, "tag your it."

Rhyatts' hand brushed Will's hair, and he turned towards the creek, his long legs jumping to a flat rock parting the water. Rhyatt looked back, and the boy scrambled to his feet, ready to lunge after him. Will took a step into the water and paused, assessing the situation. He walked toward the left of the rock, where the water was more shallow. Rhyatt tensed, ready to jump when Will came closer.

Will stepped another foot into the water, and Rhyatt grinned, shifting to the edge of the slippery rock. He bent his knees, ready to jump. Will stepped forward.

"William Blake!"

Rhyatt and Will snapped their heads to the source of the woman's call. None other than Wes Blake was striding out of the gardens, her hair blown back and scorn in her eyes. Rhyatt shifted at the sight, but he turned too much. His boot was wet, and the rock was slick and worn down by the water. He went tumbling face-first into the creek.

He put his bound hands out to catch him, but something sharp hit his forehead, and his world went dark.

RHYATT

When Rhyatt opened his eyes, he noticed a great deal of things. Three of them took the forefront of his mind. First, he was upside down and watching the world move beneath him. Second, he was sopping wet, and the heat and humidity made him feel sticky. Third, his head felt like it had been split open.

Rhyatt lifted his head and stifled a groan. He was being carried by Wes. She had somehow thrown him across her back, and they were in the gardens, headed towards the house.

"You can put me down now." He grumbled.

"Gladly," she said and released him without warning. He hit the ground and lay in an ungraceful slump.

"Ow." He said, rubbing his head. He felt like he was still under-water.

"When you can stand, come inside," she said before disappearing up the stairs.

Rhyatt slowly sat up and noticed Will squatting down beside him, something similar to worry in his eyes.

"I fell?" Rhyatt asked him.

Will nodded, "You hit your head and passed out. Wes fished you out before the current could carry you off."

Rhyatt groaned. Just what he needed. Wes having another thing over him. Was there anything she wasn't good at? She beat him at swordplay, was far more advanced at taming Will, and now she was good at saving lives.

"That's all?"

"She did give you a good tongue lashing, but I suspect she'll give it to you again inside." Will leaned closer and whispered, "Don't worry, I'll stay nearby."

Rhyatt attempted to smile his approval but the pain in the side of his head resulted in him grimacing instead. He pushed off the ground, and together they went into the house. Rhyatt left wet footprints in his wake.

Inside the kitchen the cook sent them a look of pity, "Wes is in the library, she got the bandages."

Rhyatt followed Will out of the kitchen, through the main foyer, and towards a set of dark wood double doors. Will pushed on the one that was partially open and walked in, Rhyatt went to follow but stopped in the doorway. The library was larger than the kitchen, and the ceiling rose above the second floor. From floor to ceiling, there were thousands and thousands of books. The only break in the walls of books was for two large windows facing the front drive and a mammoth fireplace. There were more books in this single room than Rhyatt had seen in his entire life. He took another step into the room and noticed its furnishings. On the right, a desk sat pulled from the wall, an oversized black leather chair behind it and smaller, lighter-colored leather chairs in front. In front of the fireplace sat a large ornate rug, a coffee table, a comfortable couch, and three armchairs surrounding it.

It was on the edge of the sofa Wes was perched, her face pulled tight as she uncorked a bottle of clear liquid.

Will had already entered and was settling into one of the armchairs when Wes called to him, her eyes still fixed on the bottle and bandages in front of her.

"Come. Sit."

And like an obedient dog Rhyatt listened. He sat on the couch beside Wes, leaving more than enough space between them. She didn't seem to notice. He glanced at the coffee table, off to the side was an open ledger and an empty whiskey glass.

She followed his gaze and snapped the ledger shut, pushing it further away. The scowl on her face deepened. Rhyatt was right about his earlier assumptions, when her face was contorted into anger it was *very* fear-inspiring.

She had a cloth draped around her hand and used it to turn his face, ensuring their skin never touched. She studied the cut on his forehead, narrowing her eyes as if it was an opponent. She decidedly dipped another rag into a clear liquid before pressing it to the wound. This close he could clearly make out the small cuts and bruises along her knuckles, noticing they were layered. Old scars were thin and white with newer pink scars above them.

"You fool, you could've died." she hissed.

Rhyatt lifted his brows, considering. He knew he could've died. He knew he should apologize and thank her, but in this moment he could only focus on how angry she looked. So naturally a smart remark tumbled out of his mouth.

"Will would've saved me."

The boy covered his mouth with his hand to keep his laugh from sounding. In turn Rhyatt smirked. This did nothing to sway Wes.

"No, he wouldn't have." She snapped as she dabbed the wound harder than necessary .

"Then I trust he would have led someone to my bones."

Wes's scowl deepened as she looked at Will who was now outright laughing. Her scowl softened ever so slightly and she paused, considering something.

"Perhaps. But it seems he prefers you alive."

Will stopped laughing and put a hand to his chin, stroking a nonexistent beard. "I'm undecided." he said in a croaky voice.

"You're undecided if you prefer me alive?" Rhyatt asked with a snort.

"Hold still." Wes grumbled.

Will shrugged, "I haven't seen you dead, so I can't decide which I prefer."

Perhaps it was the childlike voice or the glint in Will's eye, but something was enough to make Wes crack. Her scowl melted away as the corner of her mouth twitched upwards.

"Ah." Rhyatt replied, raising his eyebrows as he noted the small change in the sister.

Wes pulled her hands away and looked back to Will, "Quit being morbid and go get the clean bandages from Rhina." Her voice was softer than the one she had used on him.

Once Will had left the room and was out of earshot she turned back to him, "What happened to those "other strengths" you have?"

Rhyatt raised his eyebrows, Wes was sharp as a tack and he was beginning to see the similarities between her and Will.

"I consider winning tag while tied up to be a strength." Perhaps it was the gash on his forehead or the high he was riding from successfully making Will not hate him, but he was getting cocky.

71

"You agreed to play tag. While tied up. And got in the creek." An exasperated sigh escaped her, "It's a good thing you're pretty."

"You think I'm pretty?" Rhyatt asked and felt heat begin to creep into his face.

Wes was saved from replying as Will entered the room carrying a bowl of freshly boiled bandages.

"HotHotHot." He hurried to place them on the table. Wes thanked him and began to bandage Rhyatt's wound. She made quick work of it, her hands slightly rough but quick nonetheless. When she was done she stood and gathered the supplies and headed towards the door, she paused in the frame and looked back at him.

"Take care and make sure it doesn't get infected." Rhyatt nodded and she disappeared again.

Feeling rather tired after a long day, Will gathered Rhyatt's belongings and then walked him to the front door. He paused with his hand on the handle. Sheepishly he looked up at Rhyatt.

"I wasn't going to make you go home tied up."

Rhyatt grinned, "It would have been okay if you did."

WES

"I don't see why they haven't sent his last will yet," Knox grumbled as he shoved the last bite of his lunch in his mouth.

"It will come soon," Cleo assured him.

"It better. Otherwise, the entire war council will have all the hells to pay."

"It will," Wes said, reassuring him as much as herself. She felt a bit guilty for hoping Jaze's last will had a goodbye to her. She knew he would have included Knox and Knox's parents. He may have thrown in a general goodbye to their friend group, but a selfish part of her hoped he had written individual ones. At least that way she could get her own form of closure. She pushed the thoughts away and assured herself that his last will would arrive in Knox's hands by the end of the month.

"Give it until the end of next week. If it hasn't arrived, Wes can ask the Commander." Cleo said.

Knox hummed his agreement, his temper cooled for the moment.

Not long after, Wes excused herself and headed back to the university. The scholar had asked her to meet before her internship. If she was being honest, a bolt of fear had struck her at the request. Her first thought was that she had already messed up, and Commander Pryde wanted her gone. The scholar had quickly assured her that wasn't the case and insisted on seeing her fifteen minutes before two.

Wes opened the large wooden door to the classrooms and strode inside. She turned to close the door, but upon hearing voices float down from the second floor, she paused.

"A Jorjinian education can open a lot of doors for you. If you let it." Scholar Tiunda was saying.

"Thank you again for letting me in." A man's voice floated down from the scholar's second-floor office. Not just any man, it was Rhyatt. Wes put her hand to the door, shutting it with precision. Not a creak.

"Since your swordsmanship skills are lacking, I am forced to give you an ultimatum. If you have not improved greatly by mid-semester, then I will be forced to move you to a lower level. From there, you will be able to fully immerse yourself in learning the art of the sword."

A strangled noise came from Rhyatt. "But Scholar Tiunda—I can't be in school that long. My grandmother." He paused, and Wes could imagine the pain on his pretty little face. "My grandmother is getting older, and I—" He paused again, struggling with the words. Wes crept closer to the staircase.

"It may sound foolish, but I cannot be in school for more than this semester."

Scholar Tiunda was silent. Wes had been in her office many times when the eerie silence had settled around her. Her silence took on a presence, weighing on you, sinking its claws into your shoulders.

"I understand your urgency," she spoke at last, "but if you are not improving, I would be doing you a disservice by allowing you to continue. Our university may be free, but that does not mean we do not have standards."

It was Rhyatt's turn to be quiet. Scholar Tiunda spoke again, filling the silence.

"It has been a week, and you are a quick learner. However, you are not my only student. I can only spend so much one-on-one time with you. I wish it were different, Mr. Valvidez. I really do. But as it stands, I will give you until the midterms to show your improvement."

There was the sound of a chair scraping as someone rose; a breath later, another chair followed.

"Please note, I believe you can accomplish this. Hard work and determination make all things possible. Your advancements with young Mr. Blake are proof of that."

Rhyatt's reply was so soft that Wes almost didn't hear him thank her. Then the office door creaked open, and she heard his heavy footsteps exit and head for the stairs. Wes moved from her hiding spot and began walking up towards him.

She wasn't expecting what she saw. Rhyatt's head was downwards, and his limbs were loose. The opposite of how she had seen him last time. She hated that it stirred something in her. He was about to pass her on the steps when she paused and faced him.

"Do you plan to continue mentoring Will?" she asked, no greeting, as she slanted her chin upwards.

At her words, he looked up and a tired smile appeared, "Hello Wes, good to see you too."

She blinked, impatient. "Do you?"

Rhyatt sighed, his smile falling away. "Yes. I'm assuming you have an objection?"

"Quite the contrary."

Rhyatt leaned back against the wall and crossed his arms, looking weary to the world.

"You see," Wes began, stepping up, making her gaze even with his. "If you plan to continue mentoring Will, I will owe you. And as it happens, I hate being in debt to anyone." She shook her head, the idea annoying.

"I see."

"But I have the perfect way to repay you."

"Go on."

"Tutoring. In swordplay. I can get you up to par."

Rhyatt raised his eyebrows in irritation, "You were listening."

Wes shrugged and looked away, "I overheard."

"You were eavesdropping."

She rolled her eyes, "Same difference."

Rhyatt paused, seeming to mull it over, "It would take a lot of time."

"Consider it a repayment plus interest."

He shook his head and pushed off the wall, his arms still crossed, "You would do that just so you wouldn't *owe* me?"

Wes nodded. Rhyatts' eyes flickered, and she swore she could see all the sorrows of the seven seas in them.

"It's a good thing you don't owe me anything. I like mentoring Will. It is not something that requires repayment." He looked towards the bottom of the steps and unfolded his arms. Wes panicked at his leaving. Why did she want him to say yes so badly?

"I know you are new here and don't know how things work, but if I do not repay you now, I fear you will ask for repayment when I am unable to give it. Please help us both and take my offer. You will become a better swordsman—trained by the best if I remember right—and I will once again be debt-free."

Rhyatt tilted his head and held her eye contact. He was contemplating something. Wes held still, forcing herself not to turn her chin up or look away. Whatever he was thinking through was more important. He finally spoke.

"I accept."

"Good."

"I guess I should say thank you."

"You're welcome." Wes paused and looked him from his head to his toes. Perhaps it appeared she was assessing what material she had to work with, but in truth, she was considering what mess she was getting herself into. "Stay after your internship with Will and we can begin today."

She turned her back and took another step upwards, looming over him.

"It's like this Rhyatt, you scratch my back and I'll scratch yours." Wes spun on her heel and began walking up the stairs before he could answer. She heard a soft chuckle before he called out to her.

"Next time, just tell me where the itch is and I'll scratch it for free."

RHYATT

It had been a particularly long evening with Will. He had asked for help with a mathematics problem, which had been easy enough to figure out. But then it spiraled. Will was indeed a very smart and curious lad. He had moved from the equation he was having problems with and was now trying to work through a problem he had found in Wes's old stuff. It was far less easy than his actual work, and Will had become frustrated *many* times.

"You can't just erase the one." Rhyatt said with a sigh, hovering over Will, who was sitting at the desk under the tree.

"Why not?" Will asked, rewriting the one as he complained.

"Because it doesn't work that way."

"It worked that way in the last problem."

"No, it didn't."

"Yes, it did."

"No, it didn't. We just moved it."

Will narrowed his eyes at the problem. "Fine," he said and left the number alone.

It had been like this for the past hour. Will would try to do something, and Rhyatt would tell him he couldn't. He would then argue and eventually give in. Rhyatt had been trying to convince Will to call it quits for the evening, but Will refused until he found the answer to the problem. Stubborn had become an understatement.

When Wes came down the stairs from the kitchen, Will started to rewrite the problem on fresh paper. She looked much more tired than she had just a few hours earlier. Rhyatt thought she looked how he had felt in the Scholar's office.

She approached them, two practice swords in her hands and an unpleasant look on her face. Without a word, she leaned over the desk and examined the problem. Her dark green eyes darted around the upside-down paper. She leaned away.

"The answer is 21."

Will looked up and scowled at her, "I was trying to solve it on my own."

"I know you were, but you haven't yet taken the classes that will give you the skills to solve this problem."

Her tone was matter-of-fact, but Will still scowled at her.

"I'm going inside." He said, picking up his supplies a little too hastily.

As Will slipped in the back door, Wes eyed Rhyatt. He had been somewhat excited when Wes had offered him the help he sorely needed to graduate, but now, standing before her, he tried to mentally prepare himself for all the pain she was sure to cause. He could tell she was in a foul mood, and he was sure it would soon be taken out on him.

She handed him a sword, and he felt his shoulders tighten in anticipation. She must've sensed it because she gave a tight-lipped smile.

"I'm going to go easy on you. Only the basics today." her voice lowered, like talking to a frightened animal.

Rhyatt nodded, "Sounds good." His voice had more confidence than he felt.

"Copy me." She said and raised her sword. Rhyatt followed the move, mimicking what Scholar Tiunda had shown him. She nodded in appraisal, then shifted and stepped to the side. Rhyatt followed, keeping her in front of him. She took another step, and Rhyatt followed, his feet moving carefully so as not to trip.

"Have you fought before?" she asked. The softness had left her voice, and it had returned to normal.

"When I was younger, I used to box."

"Why did you stop?" She asked, her eyes locked on his.

"My father asked me to stop."

"And you do everything your father asks you to?"

"When he was alive, I did."

Wes faltered in her steps, realizing her mistake. She lowered her eyes.

"My condolences."

Rhyatt felt a bubble of panic rising. He didn't want to think about his father—not now, at least.

"He asked me to stop because my brother was starting to follow in my footsteps. Fighting isn't the safest in Duran. Most fighters only fight to win, but some fight to kill."

He changed the subject quickly, and Wes kept up.

"What a barbaric waste of life."

"I agree."

Wes stopped their circle and stood still. She explained she was going to show him a move and asked him to copy it. She raised her arm and cut in a downward arc. He raised his and attempted to copy her, but it didn't quite go the same. He felt odd, out of touch with his body as he moved. Wes had made it look easy.

"Try again, but watch the way your arm bends." She stood back in front of him as a target.

Rhyatt tried again, but much to his dismay, he felt just as awkward as before. Wes demonstrated again, and Rhyatt once more failed to follow correctly. She pursed her lips and seemed to think.

She stepped forward, her hand outstretched towards his, but paused, "Do you mind?"

"Not at all."

Her hand reached forward and Rhyatt noticed the cuts on her knuckles had mostly healed, only red scratches remained.

She closed her hand over his, and a current passed between them. Stronger than a shock.

They jerked apart and stared at each other, bewildered. Wes let out a small laugh, breaking the tension.

"You shocked me!" Rhyatt said with a lighthearted smile.

She raised her eyebrows and held up her hands in innocence, "How do you know it wasn't *you* that shocked *me*?"

Rhyatts lips twitched before his smile spread, "That's a fair point."

Wes shook her head, and placed her hand on top of his again. The quick shock happened again, but not as strong. Both chose to ignore it. Wes stepped behind Rhyatt, her forearm pressing against the top of his as she led him through the motion. He was tense as she did it the first time, but by the second and third, he had loosened up and was following.

She stepped away, releasing him, and instructed him to do it again. He executed the move thrice before Wes approved and stood in front of him again.

"Now try it on me."

Rhyatt nodded, lifted his sword, and executed the move, his sword clanking against hers. She nodded approval and signaled for him to continue. He did the move again and again.

"Good. Now do it quicker and put some muscle behind it."

Rhyatt nodded, and they reset. This time, he brought his sword down in a quick arc. With the added speed, Wes deflected the sword to the side.

"Again, with some muscle." She said simply.

He reset, raised his sword and hit again, feeling a bit more confident he sped up. Wes did not move her feet, instead she stood still and easily deflected him again.

She shot him an accusing look, "I know that's not all you've got."

Rhyatt shrugged and looked away from her accusing stare. She wouldn't understand.

Wes paused, and instead of resetting, she began to circle him. Rhyatt knew turning and following would have been best, but a voice whispered for him to stay still. To stay still was to leave his back unguarded, to put his trust in Wes.

"You know," she began, her voice gaining a dangerous edge, "It's insulting."

"What is?" Rhyatt focused on her footsteps behind him, slow and deliberate.

"Many things. First and foremost, not listening to your instructor. Secondly, not using your strength against me." She paused directly behind him. He stood still, refusing to turn. He didn't want to see her piercing gaze. He wasn't quite ready to spill all his secrets.

"I don't mean to insult you." He paused, willing his words to not sound insulting. I just don't want to hurt you."

She scoffed and finished the circle, standing in front of him again.

"You're doing a piss poor job of not insulting me. If you are able to *hurt me*," she spat the words, "then I will be very surprised."

"I don't mean to insult." He began again, but Wes cut him off.

"Prove it." The ice in her eyes was so cold it threatened to give him frostbite.

Rhyatt understood, he either used his strength and potentially hurt her, or he didn't and insult her more. Looking into her eyes, he sensed that her scorn would hurt more. He reset, and she followed. He raised his sword and brought it down, this time using his strength. Wes blocked his blow, and to his surprise she also made another move, pushing his weapon away and whacking his ribs in the same motion. He lurched forward, and in his confusion, she moved behind him. He didn't know how it happened, but one moment he was standing, the next he was on his knees, and she had her sword pulled taught across his throat.

"Point taken." Rhyatt's voice rasped.

She released him and sauntered to her spot before him, "You train with everything you've got, or not at all. Consider this your first lesson." She dropped her sword back to her side and stepped away, making to leave.

Rhyatt stood and shook off any lingering embarrassment, "Let's go again."

He was ready to learn

RHYATT

R hyatt hadn't meant to fall asleep shortly after getting home, but he was out as soon as his head hit the pillow. The only problem was that it gave him more time to dream. Since moving to Saint Saveen, his dreams had been less than favorable. Every night, it was something new. Sometimes, they were so vivid he was convinced it was a long-lost memory.

Rhyatt tossed in his bed. His face screwed up into a grimace.

Duran City will always be a dangerous place. Rhyatt was one of the reasons it was so dangerous. Everyone knew he was a watchdog for hire. Pay him the right price, and he would handle any problem you had.

Tonight was no different. He was waiting in the back alley behind a bar. Her bar. She would likely take the trash out at any second. Then he would strike.

He blinked, and his friend was beside him, waiting. Both of them were an intimidating sight. Both tall and broad. Dressed in all black. A signal of the wealthy.

The door creaked open, and music from the piano drifted out to them. As light spilled into the alley, her arms poked out of the entrance, each carrying a bag of trash.

She stepped fully into the alley and took a handful of steps to deposit the refuse. When her back was turned, he struck.

Rhyatt knocked her down to the ground, and his partner came up alongside him.

"Tell us what we need to know, and no one has to get hurt." His partner said.

"I know nothing." She said through gritted teeth as she kept her head down and face hidden.

"Then this will be very painful," Rhyatt replied and kicked her in the side.

She fell back to the ground, and the partner kicked her other side. She yelped in pain as both men took turns kicking her. She was soon coughing up blood.

The partner reached for her arm and jerked it backward; she yelled in pain.

"Tell us."

"Go burn in the seventh hell." she spat.

The partner jerked, and her arm dislocated. She turned so her body followed her arm.

Wes was staring back at him.

Rhyatt tried to stop, he tried to scream, to do anything. But his voice didn't work. Instead, he kept kicking her, and the blood kept flowing.

The worst part was that he felt himself smile.

Jerking awake, Rhyatt sat up in bed. His hand instantly went to his sweat-soaked chest.

It was all a dream, he told himself. He hadn't hurt anyone. Wes was safe at home.

He hadn't hurt anyone.

He repeated it to himself many times before lying down again. He was thankful that sleep did not find him again.

WES

If Rhyatt had thought the first training with Wes had been brutal, there was no way he would think this one was anything but a death sentence. Wes had spent half a night buying her grade school teacher drinks and convincing her to spill the secrets on the best ways to train someone. The effort had been fruitful. Not only had she spilled training secrets, but she had also revealed that Wes was her favorite student, even above the ever-smart Cleo. Her ego had been stroked, but she would never venture to hurt Cleo's feelings so that little fact stayed in the back of her mind for now.

Wes now stood, sweat dripping down her back and dirt smeared across her forehead from where she had wiped it. Rhyatt looked ten times worse, he was nowhere near out of shape, but his movements were stiff and unsure. He stood hunched, his practice sword hanging loosely at his side as he caught his breath. They had been working on footwork with the move she had shown him last time. Wes knew footwork was just as important, but Rhyatt was already so balanced and moved like an agile cat, she didn't think it should take up too much of their time. Her old teacher had told her differently.

"Again," Rhyatt said, releasing a huff of air and raising his sword once more.

Wes replied by raising her sword again and sidestepped, making him move with her. He took another step towards her, his attack clear. Wes knew he was new to all of this, so his moves would be easy and predictable, but every time he used that power that shook her arms, she felt a thrill. It would possibly take years, but once he was trained, he would be a force to be reckoned with. The seed had been planted, and Wes was excited to see the result.

Rhyatt struck, and her arms shook as she shoved aside his sword; he regained his composure quickly before they began the same sequence again.

It felt like they had done this exact thing 100 times today...

101

102

103

"One more, and let's break." She finally said. Will had opted to watch today, which meant she controlled her tongue, only silence and learning. It had been a long, sweaty afternoon.

Rhyatt made his final move, and they set their stuff down beside Will and walked down to the shaded area of the creek.

The garden offered little spots of shade, but at the back, where it met the creek, the trees took over and faded into forest. They cast deep shadows, a harsh difference from the golden early sunset that filtered through the garden. The creek itself wasn't more than ten feet wide, and a few feet deep at the center, it bubbled as the water ushered by.

Crouching down, Wes leaned over and cupped her hands in the clear water. She lifted it to her lips, enjoying the cooling sensation of it running down her throat. She preferred the creek over the well water. After two handfuls, she lifted more above her head and let it soak her hair, run down her face, and drip off her chin.

Rhyatt followed her lead and dipped his head into the cool water. Wes watched as his loose curls flattened and swayed in the water. He leaned back up and pushed his hair back out of his face, causing water to drip down his face and his rolled-up sleeves to get wet. Wes had gone from watching to straight-up staring. The way the water ran down his muscular arms made her breathing increase. It was barely a passing thought before a memory of Jaze's arms clutching her surfaced in her mind. Then, the sharp flare of guilt rose in the back of her throat. She blinked and opened her mouth.

"So why Saint Saveen?" She asked, her voice softer than she had meant for it to be.

Rhyatt looked at her with his brows furrowed, his hands still in the water, scrubbing dirt from them.

"Why did you move to Saint Saveen?" Wes repeated, her voice returning to normal, nothing but curiosity driving her now.

Rhyatt paused, his body stilling. Wes thought he was thinking about his answer.

"My father passed away, and after a while, I realized there was nothing left in Duran for us." He looked back down and continued to move his hands, "Plus, I realized I'm barely fit to take care of myself, much less my brother." His tone was light and airy.

"I'm sorry about your father." Wes said, looking down at the water, "How old is your brother?"

"Adriel just turned 20. He's rather rambunctious, but our grandmother has a way of calming him." A small smile formed at the edge of his lips, and he seemed to speak mostly to himself more than her. "I think Lita needed us just as much as we needed her."

Wes paused and stared at him, "Lita is your grandmother?"

Rhyatt tilted his head and narrowed his eyes tentatively, "Yes... Do you know her?"

"Know her?" Wes barked a short laugh, "She's my neighbor. You're my neighbor!"

"Neighbor? But the road-"

"It curves!" Wes interrupted, joy trickling out of her, "It curves left, and the back of your property is pushed up against mine." She stood and pointed to the far right side of the BlakeMoore, "See that tree line? If you walk straight for about 5 minutes, you'll be home."

Rhyatt smiled as he stood to look. He must've deemed it possible because he looked back at Wes and nodded. She started walking forward, back to the tree that Will and their stuff were under.

"Now I know where to find you." She said over her shoulder with a wink.

Rhyatt's face almost instantly flushed, which only made her grin even more as they returned. Once under the shade of the tree and Will's ever-watchful eye, Rhyatt asked her a question.

"How long have you known Lita?" he said, stooping to pick up the sword.

"It would be easier to ask how long she's known me. She was always around growing up; it's only in the past few years that she's started to stay home more." Wes smiled fondly. "She used to yell at me and Warden to stay out of her barn, then hours later we would return with cookies, and all was forgiven."

"Warden?" Rhyatt asked.

"My twin brother." She said in a way of explanation and left it at that. She did not owe Rhyatt the whole sob story of her family.

"It's funny," she continued, changing the subject, "I bet we've met before."

Rhyatt smiled, a soft, secretive smile, "No, I would remember meeting someone like you."

Wes returned the grin and drew up her sword, motioning for him to strike. He did, and they continued their conversation in between movements, their breath uneven.

"How is Lita doing these days?"

"Good-" he inhaled deeply, "She planted too big of a garden this year, so Adriel and I have been working on it every chance we get."

Wes nodded, trying to even out her breathing as they went again.

"Do you miss Duran City?"

"Only in the way people miss things that are familiar to them."

"I see."

Will lifted his head, his interest piqued.

"What is Duran City like?" he asked, his eyes wide in childlike curiosity. Wes cherished the look; it was so rare that he looked like the young boy he was.

"Well," Rhyatt began but paused, presumably considering how much to disclose, "Duran is mostly a desert," his voice had shifted. When he talked to Will, he became protective, the playful side still there but tampered down. "The city is an oasis where trees and plants grow. It's the biggest city in the country. Not only do a lot of people live there, but many people visit." he paused again, weary. "Sometimes it can be dangerous."

Will uncrossed his legs and squinted up at Rhyatt, "What *kind* of dangerous?"

"The criminal kind," Rhyatt responded, looking over his shoulder to the curious boy staring him down.

"Like what?" Will egged on.

Rhyatt looked at Wes with a questioning look. She lowered her sword an inch and nodded at him, giving him permission to be truthful.

"Thieves, burglars, killers, the likes. It's not safe after dark. They call it *sin city*." Rhyatt responded, his tone ominous.

"I want to go." Will said, excitement seeping into his voice.

"If you're bad again, I'll take you and drop you off after dark," Wes threatened, her smile giving away her lie.

"Do it." Will encouraged, his smile mirroring hers.

Rhyatt let out a sliver of a laugh as he looked back at Will, a small smile spreading. It was the purest thing Wes had ever seen, and it took all her might not to ask Rhyatt what he was thinking. For the first time in a long time, she couldn't read someone. And that someone was Rhyatt. She would've paid top dollar to know just a single thought in that pretty little head of his.

WES

"Who do you think would win in a fight, me or the immigrant?" Knox pondered while lazily tossing a berry into his mouth.

"You, obviously," Wes responded, plucking another berry and putting it into the basket, "He's strong, but it'll be a while before he's coordinated enough to do anything worth a damn."

"How have the lessons been going with him?" Cleo asked, eating every other berry she picked.

"*Rhyatt*," Wes said, emphasizing his name while shooting a look at Knox, "is doing well. He learns quickly and understands a lot of the footwork. I'm willing to bet he would be decent in a fistfight."

Knox leaned against the garden statue and squinted his eyes in the bright sun. "I bet I could take him," he said.

Wes rolled her eyes.

"I doubt it," Cleo said.

"He's taller and got more weight." Wes agreed.

Knox looked back and forth between the two women, "The bigger they are, the harder they fall." He smirked, "It sounds like you want him to win."

Wes and Cleo looked at each other. It was no secret that they had both discussed how attractive he was. They shared a secret smile before Wes looked back at Knox and chucked a berry towards his face.

"I'm the only one who can beat you. Let's keep it that way."

Knox dodged the berry and laughed. They continued to pick berries, only half making it into the basket and the other half straight into their mouths. The baskets were only half-full when Will came out with new ones and announced that a letter had come for Wes.

"Who was it from?" Wes asked as Will turned and began to run back inside.

"It didn't say who," he yelled over his shoulder, "Just a red seal with a 'J' on it."

Jaze.

Wes's mind raced as she glanced at Cleo and then Knox. His face was twisted in confusion as he met her gaze. The basket was dropped, and berries bounced and rolled in the grass. The three of them took off sprinting towards the house.

They bound up the steps and hauled through the kitchen, narrowly avoiding Rhina. Wes thought she heard Cleo yell an apology as they slid through the door and into the foyer. On the table, there was a single envelope facing down, showing off a bright red seal.

Time stopped as Knox picked up the envelope and stared at the seal. Wes and Cleo stood on each side of him, all slightly out of breath. If this was Jaze's last will, the three of them were severely underprepared to read it. But was anybody really ready to read the last words of their loved ones?

Knox held the envelope in both hands and slowly turned it over to reveal Wes's name. His mouth parted as he read the name.

"It's for you." He muttered and reluctantly passed the letter to Wes.

She slowly opened it, prying the wax seal up instead of tearing it in two. Inside lay a single sheet of paper and a key. Holding her breath, she pulled the key out and placed it on the table. Next, she pulled the letter out, pausing before opening it.

Cleo shifted her weight. "Maybe we should give you some privacy." Her voice was small, and despite her words, she made no motion to leave. Knox stood still, a tree rooted to the spot.

"No," Her breath was shaky, "Stay, please."

Cleo moved to stand on the other side of Wes as she unfolded the letter and held it away from her body so everyone could read it. They stood with no space between their bodies, bent their heads, and began to read the words from their dead friend.

Wes,

If you are receiving this letter, I have passed. I send my sincerest apologies and hope the funeral will be something to marvel at. Please do not grieve for me too long. Keep an eye on Knox and stand by his side as he will need it the most. Remind him to stand tall and strong, the best is yet to come.

As far as last wills go, this is a shitty one. My last request of you is to retrieve some of my belongings. Before you curse me, remember I am dead. In Duran City there is a bank on the corner of 3rd and Pritchard. In box #143 the remainder of my things are hidden. Please go quickly and go alone. Don't tell anyone where you are going. You will understand more when you get there.

I wish I had more time in this life, but I'll be seeing you where I'm going.

Whatsoever is Just,

Jaze Greene

Silence settled around the three of them like a thick fog. It took on a living presence, hugging their shoulders and sticking to their hair. No one moved, no one breathed. If someone broke the stillness, the reality would set in.

Knox was the one who broke the silence, his rage not willing to hold the disbelief anymore.

"Why is his stuff in Duran City?"

Wes looked up at him. He was still staring at the letter, but his jaw had tightened, and his hands were balled into fists.

"I'm not sure Knox," Wes muttered and began to reach for his shoulder to comfort him.

"No-" he backed away, avoiding her touch like it would burn him.

"Why did he send his last will to you, Wes?" he spat her name like it was a curse.

She looked from Cleo to him, "Knox," she began gently, "I didn't find it important at the time."

He moved quickly, closing the distance between them and wrapping his hand around her neck. She slammed against the marble wall. Her head made a *thunking* sound as it connected. Almost instantly, he let go of her throat and instead put his hands on both sides of her head, pinning her in.

"Don't fucking lie to me." he seethed.

Cleo stepped closer, her hand reached out to grab Knox. A flicker of Wes's fingers told her not to intervene. Wes tilted her chin upwards. It was time her friends knew the truth.

"At the time, we didn't think it was important," Wes began again, and this time she told the entirety of the story.

She reminded them how summers always meant Jaze and Warden were home from school and that the trio became a group of 5. When all 5 of them were together, not much else mattered. They all felt like kids again. The sorrows of their everyday lives didn't drag them down. This past summer had been no different. The only significant difference was that Jaze would be leaving soon, this was their last summer together. For some reason, Wes and Jaze had grown closer because of it; what started as just a friendship quickly turned into something physical. But they were both level-headed people, and they understood the difference between physically desiring someone and wanting them romantically. So they had hidden it from the others. There was no reason to make a big deal out of nothing.

By the time Wes was done talking, they had moved to the stairs and sat down. Knox seemed to be lost in painful thought, his hands clasped under his chin. Cleo had wound her arm through Wes's and rested her head on her shoulder.

After a deafening silence, Knox spoke, "Did you love him?"

"Fiercely." She said without missing a beat, "The same love that runs true for you both."

Cleo squeezed her arm in support, and Knox seemed to relax his shoulders a little. He scooted closer to Wes so their legs touched.

"Do you remember the night he died?"

Wes shook her head. She hadn't remembered almost anything. She knew the fire had happened and that when it was over, Cleo had bandaged her fingers and told her everything was going to be okay. Of course, nothing had been okay at all.

With a deep sigh, Knox began to speak.

"When Father and I saw the flames, we knew it was too late to save the barn, but nevertheless we ran down to help Jaze get the animals cleared of the fire. When we arrived, I knew by your face alone that he hadn't made it out. You were still pouring buckets of water onto the barn." The tiniest twitch of a smile made it out, "Your knuckles were so bloody from scraping the bottom of the trough, your face was red and hot from the heat.... You moved so quickly that I was partly convinced you were a ghost. When you ran out of water, I was scared you would run after him. When you started to walk towards the barn, I feared you might actually do it. That's when I grabbed you. You fought like hell. It took Cleo helping to hold you back..." he paused and looked away, "If you hadn't already been trying to fight the fire, I fear you would've gotten away and made it inside."

He paused, his voice wavering as he continued, "I couldn't have handled losing both of you."

Jaze's words resurfaced. *His loyalties lie closer than you know.*

"I'm sorry we both lied," Wes said, looking from Knox to Cleo. "We didn't want anyone to think it was something it wasn't. And then after the fire," she shrugged, "It seemed useless, like an attention grab."

"To outsiders, it may have looked like that, but that is what we are here for," Cleo said, extending her open hand to Knox, "We're here to help carry the load, whether it is sorrow or joy."

Knox nodded his agreement before Cleo began again, "I can't imagine what hells you've been in, holding in that secret while missing him."

Wes nodded, but no tears fell from her eyes. She contemplated what Cleo had said. It had been burdensome, no one knowing what had transpired in the last few moments of his life. How happy he had been, how excited.

"Now everyone knows, no more secrets," Wes said with finality. And she meant it.

"So... anyone ever been to Duran City?" Cleo asked, ever the planner.

"It's not far from the border, but the city is huge and apparently dangerous." Wes offered, her voice already lighter now that her friends knew.

"How are we supposed to find a bank in a city ten times the size of Saint Saveen that we have never been to?" Knox questioned.

And then the idea occurred to Wes. The best way around a new city was a personal tour guide, and she knew the perfect one.

"I know somebody," she glanced at Knox before adding, "but you may not like it."

RHYATT

R hyatt had been reluctant to agree to go. He had sworn he would never return to Duran City, but when Wes asked him to draw a map instead, he had changed his mind. There was no way she was getting around Duran by herself. She most likely didn't even know the full dangers of the canyon. So he had agreed, and two days later, she had four of her finest horses saddled and ready to go at dawn. Rhyatt was less than enthused that Knox was going. The angry blonde didn't particularly like him. Cleo, however, was a different story. He had learned she was the kindest of the three. She always greeted him and never had any snarky comments. Even so, Rhyatt had to admit he had only agreed to come because of Wes; he felt drawn to her. In class, he found himself wanting to sit near her. It seemed almost silly, someone like her would never give him the time of day.

They rode through Saint Saveen in silence, the early morning dusk casting the town in a haze. When they reached the town's northern border, the number of homes decreased and Inns began taking over. Rhyatt thought it was wise of the business owners to make the Inns one of the first things travelers would encounter after crossing. They continued towards the mountain tunnel, the peak stretched high into the sky. Although it did not grow lush green trees, it still managed to be covered in bright green moss and clumps of vines and bushes clinging to any spot they could take root.

The entrance to the tunnel was empty of other travelers. When the young guard saw them, she perked up and held her entry book to her chest. Wes dismounted and made quick work, passing the guard a few coins and giving false names. The guard pocketed the money and didn't bother to check their saddlebags. When they entered nobody was coming or going.

The tunnel was so long that the other side seemed to be a speck of light in the distance. Rhyatt fought to even his breath as they rode through the dark tunnel. The hanging gas lamps didn't do much to illuminate the space. His thoughts continued to go back to the last time he had been here and how he and Adriel had looked over their shoulders every step of the way. But it had been almost a month, and no one had come for them.

The tunnel ended, and the desert began.

Below them stretched the canyon, a tremendous yawning thing. To the right was the mountain pass. It arched downwards in switchbacks before curving away from the canyon and eventually leading to the east side of Duran City. The city wasn't yet a glimmering speck this early; instead, it was a blob about five miles out.

Rhyatt had told Wes the honest truth, that you can take the traveler's road, but it would take you two full days to get there. Or you could take the canyon and risk a flood and the canyon dwellers. The canyon was a trip that took a few hours, so she wisely chose it, pending the weather. If it rained, they would be trapped. But now, there were no clouds in the sky and no hint of rain on the horizon, so they headed down into the belly of the canyon.

They rode for an hour in the orange rocky canyon before the stream widened, and they dismounted to get water. They went in pairs, leaving the horses to rest. Knox and Cleo went first, then Rhyatt and Wes.

She was bent down refilling her canteen when she asked, "So how dangerous is Duran City *really*?" she glanced over her shoulder towards where Knox and Cleo waited out of earshot.

"In the daytime it's not bad. As long as you stay out of the wrong neighborhoods." He replied, glancing back at her friends. He didn't know much besides that she had received a letter to go alone and that she couldn't do so because both Knox and Cleo had been there to read it. He got the sense she was worried about them.

"And after dark?"

"We'll be long gone."

"If we're not?"

"Then I guess you'll get to show off your moves, *killer.*"

She grinned at him, "Sounds like someone is a little scared." she reached her hand out and rested it on his shoulder, "Don't worry, I'll protect you."

He huffed a laugh, "I have no doubt you would Wes."

Her grin expanded at her name, and the sun caught her green eyes, making them sparkle like emeralds. She gave him a shove, and he stumbled to the side laughing.

They continued through the canyon, the sun scorching them the entire time. Cleo was the only one wise enough to bring a hat and stayed at the front of the group, picking the path they would follow through the rocky terrain. It was slow and careful going. Rhyatt hadn't mentioned the canyon dwellers to Wes. He didn't want to strike unnecessary fear. There was no need to fear as long as they left the canyon before dark.

When the canyon finally opened up, the four of them walked together, conversation flowing more easily than when they had to yell back and forth.

"Did you hear The Historic Councilor's speech the other night?" Cleo asked Wes.

"No, Commander Pryde said it was optional, and I didn't think anything of importance would be said."

Cleo hummed. "Importance? No. However, Atticus was lingering, which made doing my job very hard."

"Ick. Atticus." Wes rolled her eyes, but Cleo laughed.

"I'm surprised he hasn't started in on you yet," Cleo said, the smile still on her lips.

"It's because I've been hiding. He can't ask me to dinner if he can't find me." Wes replied.

"Oh, he's going to find you. I'd give it a week, two max, before he corners you in daddy's office." Knox had a wicked gleam in his eye.

"I say he'll find her before the weeks over," Cleo added.

"For my own sake," Wes interrupted, " I hope it's another month."

Laughter broke out between the three friends, and for the first time in a while, Rhyatt felt something akin to jealousy. He enjoyed being in their company, but watching them talk made it clear he was an outsider. They were friends who had known each other for half a lifetime, and he was just their tour guide. But maybe he could change that...

"Who is Atticus?" Rhyatt asked, and all three heads turned towards him.

"Atticus is Commander Pryde's son-" Wes began but was cut off by Knox.

"And he has it *out* for Wes."

Wes's back stiffened as she shrugged, "He only wants me because it would make his father happy."

"Maybe that's the only reason you don't want him." Cleo raised her eyebrows, "and because it would make your mother happy."

She shrugged and looked forward, Rhyatt's interest piqued. Then he did something stupid: He opened his mouth.

"Why would them *being together* make their parents happy?" he asked Cleo.

Cleo and Knox shared a knowing glance before she turned back to him.

"Because Commander Pryde wants his son to marry a 'peoples person'. He thinks it'll help how people view him if someone like Wes marries into the family."

Someone like Wes.

"It would help. She's well-known and liked. If the Blake family backed him, he would win an election by a landslide." Knox spoke like Wes wasn't there, but out of the corner of his eye, Rhyatt swore he saw Wes tip her chin upwards slightly when her family name was mentioned.

After a pause, Wes added in a haughty voice, "And Atticus would do almost anything to please his father."

"He loves his daddy," Knox added, a malicious grin forming.

On all accounts, he sounded like a man someone like Wes would be interested in—powerful, connected, and obsessed with her. With this assumption, Rhyatt did the second stupid thing of the day: he opened his mouth again.

"But you won't give him the time of day because your mother wants you to?"

His words were meant to be innocent enough, but as they echoed, they twisted, and all went silent. Knox and Cleo suddenly found the road straight ahead *very* interesting. Wes slowly turned her head to face him completely. With rage burning in her eyes and her mouth in a tight line, Rhyatt felt a prickle of embarrassment—or maybe fear—tinge his face.

"I don't dislike Atticus at all." Her words were sharp and clipped. "However, my love interests are not controlled by others' suggestions. Especially not my *mother's*." She spat the name like it was poison, and Rhyatt could've sworn he saw Cleo flinch.

He broke eye contact and stared at the road ahead, pretending to find the rocks and sand just as interesting as Cleo and Knox had. They slipped into silence again, the clopping of hooves on rock the only sound. It had been just long enough to begin to be really awkward when Cleo let out a little laugh.

"I'd like to change my bet." She stated, a giggle escaping, "4 days."

"5 days," Knox said, changing his wager as well.

Wes's face relaxed ever so slightly as she said to her friends, "3 days before he finds me, 2 more for him to come up with a good enough excuse to ask me somewhere."

An easy smirk rose to her lips, and the tension was gone as if it had never existed. Just like that, she diffused the situation and changed the mood. Rhyatt couldn't help but admire it. There were leaders all over the world, but it seemed rare you saw one who hadn't been officially handed the title of 'leader'. They just naturally respected her and followed from there. Rhyatt felt another bout of jealousy rise. Not only was he jealous of their friendships, but the way she made everyone feel. Even as an outsider, he felt *safe* with her, and going into the city he had nightmares about, it was a comfort he allowed himself to feel.

WES

Wes had been trying not to gawk at the canyon's vastness the entire trip, but whenever they saw the city, she couldn't help it. With her eyes wide and mouth slightly parted, she took in the view of the oasis city as they approached.

From a distance, you could see the green trees. *Palm trees*, Rhyatt had called them. They stood tall and vibrant green at the tops. They were small and scarce in the outskirts, but towards the center, they thickened and towered over homes. The blur of red and tan homes grew larger until the streets became packed with merchants and people. The houses were all earthy tones with flat roofs. None had a hard edge; even the window sills were curved. It made Saint Saveen's carved marble buildings seem sharp and intimidating.

The city quickly earned its nickname 'Sin City.' It seemed that every other building advertised gambling, liquor, or sex. The signs for the businesses were either painted with bright colors and imagery or made of stained glass. A few businesses' glass signs were set up so the sun would shine through them and display an image on the sandy stones. There were tame ones that displayed cards and others that showed lewd acts.

The streets became too packed for them to ride, so they dismounted and led their horses onward. Rhyatt reminded them to hide their weapons out of sight; they had all left their swords at home since it was frowned upon to walk around armed. Wes, however, had two daggers in the band of her pants and a small knife in her boot. She wished she could pinch herself for not coming here sooner. Duran City was less than a 2 hours ride away, yet it felt like a different world. But when would she have had time? She couldn't bring Will, and a few days ago, she hadn't even heard about the canyon pass.

As the throngs of people grew, she noticed how many were dressed in similar shades of color. The style of the clothing varied, but the pale colors remained. Wes, Cleo, and Knox stood out slightly as their garb was similar on top, but they all had dark pants. Rhyatt, however, looked the same as everyone on the street: off-white top, light brown pants, and dark hair. It was his expression that made Wes pause. His eyes would land on a street vendor, and he would smile, happiness flickering through him. Seconds later, he would shift his gaze and become uneasy. His shoulders would tighten, his head drawn back, a grave look on his face. Wes noticed his expressions flickered back and forth, never staying on one thing for too long. Maybe he was as nervous as her.

They continued through town until the buildings became taller, casting shade on them. It was surprisingly easy for Rhyatt to find one of the streets the bank was on. Duran City's streets were straight, and much thought went into their planning. They continued on the street for another ten minutes before the bank came into view.

It wasn't quite as ominous as Jaze had led her to believe. It was a sandy white two-story building with only two windows in the front and one door. It was small and quaint compared to the neighboring buildings. It was not at all what she expected.

It had been decided that Rhyatt and Wes would enter the building, posing as siblings. They shared no common features and were built very differently, but their dark complexions and darker hair were enough for them to say they came from the same household.

We took one last glance at Cleo and Knox, who stood across the street before she looped her arm through Rhyatts and pushed open the bank's door.

As they stepped inside, their eyes struggled to focus. The dark hall was lit only by candlelight, a severe adjustment from the white-hot sun outside. The darkness was not the only adjustment; the inside was eerily silent. They entered the main room and saw the patrons whispering to the clerks in hushed voices. Posted throughout the room were large guards, all stony-faced and armed to the teeth.

Together, they got in the back of the short line, only a handful of people were in front of them. Wes's eyes were focused on the back of the man in front of them when Rhyatt's low voice sounded a little too close to her ear.

"Nervous?"

She cocked an eyebrow and looked up at him. He glanced at her slightly shaking hands.

Shit, why now?

She knew why but that didn't stop her from cursing the reasoning. Her reply was soft, matching the tone of the bank.

"No. It's just something my hands do." She glanced down at her hands. The cuts and bruises had mostly faded away; only the worst remained.

"That seems concerning." His brow furrowed and concern leaked into his voice.

"My father used to say the gods gave me too much power when creating me."

Rhyatt huffed a laugh and rolled his eyes. He was quiet for a moment before speaking again.

"They didn't shake the other day."

"Nope."

"You can control it." he guessed. When she said nothing, he continued, "How do you get it to stop?"

"The three F's," she smirked.

Rhyatt opened his mouth to ask yet another question, but the clerk on the furthest corner motioned them over. They walked forward in unison and stopped in front of her chest-high desk. She smiled coolly, her dark eyes appearing black in the low light. She glanced at Wes before focusing her attention on Rhyatt.

"How can I help you?" She asked him.

"Hi," Wes drawled, "We are here to collect the contents of our deceased cousin's account." She held the key up, "Number 143."

She smiled curtly at Wes before turning her attention to a large ledger. Its pages turned with ease. The clerk stopped, tapping the page and returning her attention to Rhyatt.

"What was the name?" She asked him.

"Jaze Greene," Wes responded before Rhyatt could open his mouth. She hadn't planned for the clerk to be so interested in Rhyatt otherwise she would have divulged more details.

The clerk blinked, annoyance spread across her features, tightening her eyes. Closing the ledger with a thud, she reached behind her for keys and gestured for the pair to follow her.

They approached a guarded metal door, and the clerk waved her hand, motioning the guard aside. She put a wide circular key into the door and leaned into it as she turned it. Rhyatt glanced at Wes, something akin to nervousness. She smiled back at him. She had no idea what to expect. Rhyatt had guessed something illegal, she hoped he was wrong.

The door opened without a peep, its hinges frequently oiled. The clerk grabbed a lantern hanging from the wall and motioned for them to follow.

"Follow me." She said with a smile to Rhyatt and stepped forward into the dark. Wes stepped forward, and Rhyatt followed behind her. They descended a set of stairs, the temperature growing cooler until they hit the bottom landing. They were in a long, narrow underground room. The lantern flickered and lit up the wall, revealing lock boxes ranging in size. The clerk led them away from the smaller ones and kept walking towards the back, where the boxes became bigger until they were as long as an arm. She stopped towards the end and motioned to the box second from the bottom. The numbers 143 were carved on the metal door.

"Here we are." The clerk placed her lantern on the shallow shelf along the back wall and motioned to the door. We crouched, taking a deep breath as she slid the key into the lock.

"I'm sorry to hear about your cousin. He was very kind." The clerk said to Rhyatt.

Wes was too focused on opening the box to respond.

"It was very unfortunate. A life taken too soon," he said, and Wes glanced back at them.

"Mhm. A tragedy indeed." The clerk said as she shifted, touching Rhyatts' arm in an attempt of comfort.

Wes rolled her eyes and returned to the box as it snapped open. She blinked in confusion. Inside was a black leather saddle bag. Both bags were stuffed full. It took every bit of self-control to keep from opening the bags right then and there. Instead, she focused on the intricate stitching that went over the leather. This was an expensive bag, far too expensive for Jaze. Worry creased her brow and settled in the bottom of her stomach. What was Jaze doing to afford such an expensive bag and lock box, all of which were in a different country?

She ran her fingers down the stitching before picking it up and throwing it over her shoulder. Relocking the box, she stood and extended the key, attempting to hand it to the clerk.

"The box still has a little under five years left." The clerk began and once again turned to Rhyatt, "Since Mr. Greene has passed, shall we change the name to yours?"

Wes's blood began to boil. Sure, Rhyatt was attractive, but the clerk was doing everything in her power to ignore Wes. It was Wes's friend who had passed. It was Wes's lover who had burnt to nothing. It was Wes who grieved his loss every day. Rhyatt was merely an accessory. Her shoulders tensed, and she was on the verge of lashing out when Rhyatt spoke.

"Not me, my sister." He looked at her, and she could feel him willing her to remain calm, "Put it in her name, Wes Blake."

The clerk's face dropped. A second later she recovered and a smile was in place.

"I can make it a dual account for you both, Mr. Blake."

Now it was Rhyatts turn to be aggravated. He clenched his jaw and gave her a tight smile.

"That's perfect." Wes cooed and, without another word, turned towards the stairs. Her eyes didn't need to adjust; she saw red, and the room was clear as day. She just wanted out of this damn room with this dumb clerk.

"I'll change it immediately. What was your first name, Mr. Blake?"

"Rhyatt, Rhyatt Blake."

That was the last thing Wes heard before she pushed open the heavy door, astonishing the guard that she was alone. He began to ask her questions but she kept walking. He could walk his ass down the stairs and figure it out on his own. She wasn't in the mood to answer to anyone.

WES

"A saddlebag?" Knox said once the four of them were seated alone in a private room at a restaurant nearby.

No one answered him, nerves were high. Wes had paid for the room to be left empty for half an hour, buying them some privacy. Without speaking, Wes pulled the bag onto the table. She began opening one side while Knox took the other. On the other side of the table, Cleo and Rhyatt watched.

Knox was the first to unlatch the clasp. He pulled out a mass of black clothing that was wrinkled and hastily shoved into the bag. While he rifled through the pockets, looking for anything of importance, Wes opened her side. Unease crawled up her bones. The first thing she saw was a white shirt with blood stains. Gently, she pulled it out of the bag and noticed something was wrapped inside. She unraveled it to reveal a leather-bound journal wrapped tightly with a cord. A letter was shoved under the cord—a letter with Wes's name on it.

Guilt came for her quickly as she saw her name and not Knox's. He had been so hurt that Jaze's last will had been given to Wes, another item with her name on it would surely upset him. But as she glanced at him, she didn't see hurt or even jealousy. Instead, it was just sorrow.

Wes took a deep breath and removed the letter, and opened it.

Wes,

If you are reading this something has gone terribly wrong and I need you to finish what I've started. I'm so sorry to ask this of you but it must be seen through. Please keep this to yourself and don't let anyone know you have my belongings. The less you know the better. I need you to get this journal into the hands of someone in power in Jorjin, preferably someone in Saint Saveen since we will be the most affected. It has to be someone you trust wholeheartedly. At the time of writing this there is a rat in power. Please just make sure it is someone you trust, not everyone is as innocent as they seem.

It is not safe for you to read the journal, but I know you too well and know your curiosity will be the death of you, so I will sum it up.

In late spring I was approached by a woman offering me coin to do some digging on an independent military agency in Duran. The agency was posing as an advanced medical treatment center, but they had hundreds of soldiers living on site. I found out they did do some medical treatments but more often than not the 'medical treatments' were more of medical experiments. Some people came willingly, others were dragged in the middle of the night. They have someone in both Duran and Saint Saveen covering for them. Supplies have been coming in from Jorjin that passed without inspections.

The worst is the soldiers. I have never seen men so willing to do another's bidding. They seem not to care for their own life. They are like dogs who jump on command. Avoid them at all costs.

Be careful my little tiger, avoid people you don't trust. I hope I have satisfied your curiosity and I hope you can help me finish outing the rat.

-JG

PS Don't let Knox know. Keep Cleo and Warden away too. Sorry to bring you into this, but if anyone can do it you can.

Wes sighed and handed the letter over to a waiting Knox and Cleo. If she had felt guilt at her name being on the letter, she felt even more guilty now. She should've listened and left her friends out of it. They wouldn't have let her willingly go alone, but she could've left earlier than their expected departure date. Cleo would figure it out, but by the time she did, Wes would already be on her way back. How could she be so selfish about including her friends?

Knox finished reading and folded his hands into his lap. Cleo took the letter from him and passed it to an oblivious Rhyatt.

"He doesn't get to read it." Knox objected, anger lacing his voice.

Rhyatt paused, taken aback by the harsh voice. He began to outstretch his arm to return the letter to Cleo.

"He's lived here his entire life. He might know something we don't." Cleo closed her hand around his and pushed the letter back towards him.

"He should be on a need-to-know basis." Knox leaned forward, ready to defend his point.

"This is need to know. He deserves to know why we're here." Wes responded, her voice stern. To tell the truth, she was getting nervous about what mess they were getting into.

Knox turned his gaze to Wes, a challenge on his lips. "*Okay.*"

Rhyatt waited, the letter still held away from his body. When Knox didn't say anything else, he quietly began to read.

Knox became impatient, tapping the fork against the table until its rhythm became hurried and frantic.

"This doesn't change who he was." Knox spoke mostly to himself.

"No. It doesn't." Wes put a hand over Knox's, stilling the fork.

"No one action can condemn anything that is whole, and no redeeming action can piece together anything that is broken." Cleo said, quoting one of the many life mantras she had learned.

"And Jaze was whole." Wes added, clarifying Cleo's quote. Knox still looked down, so she spoke again, "This won't change who he is."

Cleo nodded, adding her hand over his other free hand, "We can keep it between us. No one has to know it was Jaze who wrote this journal."

Rhyatt finished reading and looked up, catching Wes's eye. He nodded once, agreeing to keep the secret.

"No one has to know," Knox said again.

For so long they had covered their grief, but the letter exposed the cracks in their facade. And the group that never quieted was left silent. They didn't trust their voices enough to speak, so they sat there and let their own thoughts run rampant. Jaze was dead. There was nothing they could do about that. But he had unfinished business, he had one last task they could see to. And that was good enough for Wes, it was a goal to work towards. A goal to blindly distract her from how she was feeling.

No one was prepared for the late afternoon heat. Jorjin's humid heat made you sluggish, Duran's heat made you want to drink water continuously. The only one who was faring fine was Rhyatt. Wes didn't think he was even breaking a sweat on their walk out of town. There was no breeze in the city's busy center, just hot bodies. Wes was disappointed to find out the outskirts were just the same but slightly less crowded. The morning had bamboozled them into thinking the heat wasn't that bad. The afternoon heat had shown them otherwise.

It was so hot they didn't even waste the energy complaining about the heat; it was no use drying your mouth out. Or perhaps it was the contents of the letter that left them still distracted. Cleo stepped to the side to look at a street vendor, causing the entire group to stop. She rejoined them, a faux smile plastered on her face, and leaned in closer to Wes.

"Back left, short man with long dark hair. He's following us."

Wes didn't allow herself to tense as her heart jumped into her throat. Of-fucking-course they were being followed. They had left a bank that housed fortunes with a saddlebag, presumably full of money. How unfortunate someone was about to find out it was worth nothing, but they still would not be giving it up.

Looking back, she nodded a quick confirmation to Cleo. This sucked. The day was long, and the heat was relentless. A wanna-be-robber was the last thing she wanted to deal with right now. But it had to be done. She mentally flipped the gods the bird and handed her horse's reigns to Cleo, dropping back to walk between Knox and Rhyatt. They both glanced at her with curious expressions.

"Smile at me and laugh like I just told you the funniest joke in the world." Her voice was flat despite her grin.

Knox caught on instantly, smiling and leaning his head back in laughter. Rhyatt followed suit with a tight-lipped smile and a shake of his head.

"Good boys." She purred, her voice low, "Don't look now, but there's a man following us- *Knox I said don't look now*- We need to get rid of him before the canyon."

Rhyatt's eyes widened, and he swallowed hard.

"Any side streets we can use to get rid of him?"

Rhyatt paused, looking at the street names and getting his bearings.

"In three streets, take a right, Helman Street."

Wes patted him on the shoulder, a flirtatious smile taking over, "Thanks boys." she said before rejoining Cleo at the front and passing along the plan. Even with the potential robber on their tail Wes found herself thinking about Jaze. There were so many things she wanted to ask him, first and foremost, why he accepted a mysterious job like this. How good did the pay have to be? What about the blood-soaked shirt? How many times had he gotten hurt doing this? Had he planned to continue when on breaks from the army? She had so many questions and none of them would ever be answered.

Cleo led them towards Helman Street. The street was narrow but still navigable for two horses side by side. It was empty, more of a back alley than a road. It was perfect.

Like a unit, Knox and Wes handed over their reins and slipped behind opposite walls, putting them out of view of the main road.

"Don't look back." She whispered, her head held high, focused on the road in front of them.

Wes tucked herself in tight and signaled for Knox to do the same. They waited, arms loose at their sides and legs bent.

The soft sounds of footsteps echoed at the entrance of the street. Knox looked to Wes for direction. Without their weapons they would not deliver killing blows. Killing blows were not necessary for a common thief anyways. Wes held her hands up to her throat.

Knock him out.

Knox nodded. The message was understood.

The footsteps got closer, too careful to be someone casually wondering. Then, the man came into sight. Wes instantly sprung to his back, wrapping her arm tightly around his throat. Knox stepped out to restrain his flailing arms.

Wes's head was yanked backward by her hair. Surprised, she loosened her grip and went to the ground, scraping her elbows.

There was a second man, who now hovered over Wes, a gleam in his eye.

Knox had been caught unaware by the second man, so when the first man head-butted him, he released him and stumbled backward. He shook his head, but the first man had gained the advantage. He swept his foot out, knocking Knox to his knees. He kicked him twice in the side before Knox was down completely.

Wes pushed herself up, ignoring the red her elbows had left on the cobblestone and the gritty sand in her open wound.

The second man was much taller than the first, and his hair was cropped close to the scalp. They looked at each other, assessing the other's skill. The second man decided Wes was easy prey and aimed a blow at her face.

But Wes was quick. She dodged him and hit him hard in the ribs.

He didn't move. He didn't react. It was as if she hadn't hit him at all. Instead, the gleam in his eye sharpened.

She paused, she could sword fight all damn day, but this was different. She had only ever been in fistfights with friends or acquaintances. This was going to be a straight-out brawl. She had little clue how to handle it. When he took another swing at her, she chose to avoid first and attack later.

The only problem was that as she avoided the second man's punch, the first one rounded to focus on her. In her haste, she stepped too close to him.

He reached out his arms to grab her, but she skitted back and right within the second man's reach.

Without warning, he wrapped his large arms around her waist, picking her several feet into the air before slamming her back into the hard cobblestone.

The air was pushed out of her chest, and her vision blurred as both men stood over her.

RHYATT

Rhyatt and Cleo had kept their cool and stayed focused on the path in front of them. It was when they heard commotion they finally turned to see Knox kneeling and Wes avoiding punches from a second thief.

Despite his fears of this city, his first thought was to run and help them, but footsteps coming from in front of their horses made him pause. He looked back to see another man running towards them, his eyes focused on the saddlebag that sat on Wes's horse.

Cleo caught his eye, unsure what to do.

"Go help them. I can handle myself," he informed her.

With his words, she took off running towards her friends, leaving Rhyatt alone with the approaching man. He stepped forward, putting himself in between the thief and the saddlebag.

The man slowed his running when he was a handful of feet away. Unease ran through Rhyatt. There was something familiar about the third thief in front of him, something scarily familiar. The thief seemed to see it too, because he cocked his head to the side.

Rhyatt shook away the recognition on his face and focused, it had been years since he had boxed. He knew how to take a punch and how to throw one, hopefully his strength would cover what muscle memory did not.

The thief closed the space between them, the sharp glint of metal appearing as he did so.

WES

Wes blinked rapidly, fighting the dizziness surrounding her. The second man bent down and grabbed the collar of her shirt. He started to pull her up towards him, but Cleo came out of nowhere and jumped on his back. He released his grip and began trying to get Cleo off.

She wrapped her arms and legs around his body, locking them together. In seconds, she was tightening her arm around his throat. He stumbled backward, still grabbing at her arms as he struggled to breathe.

Wes used the distraction to push herself to her feet, her mind swirled as she rose. Out of the corner of her eye she caught sight of the first man grabbing for her hair. What was with these men and her hair?

Before his fingers could find purchase in her hair, she turned and grabbed his wrist and twisted so his arm was at an unnatural angle. If he moved forward he would break his wrist.

And then the dumbest thing happened. He looked down, seemed to acknowledge what would happen, and then *did it*. A nasty crack sounded, and he jerked forward, headbutting Wes in the nose.

Her blood instantly flowed, splattering on the ground.

Anger flared through her, hot and strong.

She used his broken wrist to push him away, and with the added space she landed two punches to his face. Breaking his nose and cracking her knuckles open.

His broken nose proved to be more distracting than the wrist. Knox took advantage of this and wrapped his hands around the man's ankles, yanking to make him fall.

Wes stepped forward, put one foot over his shin, and applied pressure. For a change he seemed to care about breaking his leg. Perhaps it was more valuable.

She looked over to where Cleo now stood, pushing the unconscious body of the second man out of view. She looked back to the man below her foot, and a guttural laugh escaped her.

"I hope it pains you to know you attempted to steal a saddlebag with old clothes and a *journal* inside it," she said to him.

Knox rose and stood beside her. The man looked back and forth between the pair, hatred in his eyes. Then he looked at Wes and spat on the ground.

"Very well. I'd be upset too." Wes said, a deadly calm entering her voice as Cleo stepped up to her other side, "My only remaining question is, which one of those idiots at the bank tipped you off?"

The man shook his head and smiled, red blood running across his teeth.

"I said," she applied more pressure, and he grimaced, "*Which one talked?*"

He laughed and once again spat blood, this time at Wes. It landed on her boot. Knox stepped forward to reprimand the man, but Wes clicked her tongue.

She knew he wouldn't talk. She knew she should just knock him out and be done with the situation.

"He won't talk," she said, lifting her boot from his shin. Relief shown in his eyes. "I guess we'll have to make him squeal."

She brought her foot down in the middle of his shin, and a resounding crack split through the air.

Screams of unbearable pain rang out and echoed in the alley.

Cleo glanced at Wes, and Wes cocked her head to the side, a feral grin forming. But Cleo had the sense to run.

Grabbing Wes's hand, she said, "Let's go before someone shows up."

All three of them took off running towards where the horses stomped impatiently. As they got closer, they could make out the outline of two men, one on top of the other. The man on the bottom was trying to fight back, but the man on top was relentless with his punches, landing blow after blow.

They got closer and through her hazy vision Wes could tell the man on top was Rhyatt, relief flooded through her.

Rhyatt landed a knockout punch to the man's jaw, and the man stilled, his arms slack at his side. But Rhyatt didn't seem to notice. He reared back again, punching the man three more times.

"Rhyatt lets go." Cleo yelled from atop her horse. Both her and Knox were atop their horses, that's when Wes realized she may have gotten hit harder than she thought because they were on horses and she was still standing there.

Rhyatt didn't seem to hear them and reared back again.

"Go!" she yelled at Cleo and Knox. She would get Rhyatt. There was never a man left behind, Jaze had taught her as much.

Wes ran to him and bent at the waist, grabbing his fist before he could swing again.

Rhyatt looked at her with a wildness in his eyes. No, he wasn't looking at her, but rather looking *through* her. For the briefest moments she thought he would turn his fist towards her and strike, but slowly recognition spread across his features.

"He's good. He's down." urgency filled her voice. The first man was still wailing at the other end, and someone had begun to walk down the street to see what was going on.

Rhyatt blinked, his eyes darting back to the body underneath him.

"Rhyatt." she said his name, and he looked back at her, "It's okay. He's down."

He looked at her face, searching. Slowly, she released his wrist. He brought it down to his side, still balled in a fist. He looked back at the body again, and his face shifted. The wildness was gone, and it was replaced by fear.

Wes went to her knees beside him and gripped his face, forcing him to look away from the man beneath him.

"Rhyatt. Rhyatt." she ushered him, "We have to go. We have to leave now. Alright?"

He nodded back.

"Right now, we have to go. I need you to stand up and get on this horse with me, alright?"

He nodded again. She let go of his face, grabbed under his arm, and pulled him up.

Seconds later, they were on their horses riding towards Cleo and Knox, who were waiting at the mouth of the alley. By the time they exited the alley, Rhyatt was sitting tall in his saddle again, and any trace of the wildness or the fear was gone completely. Instead, he just remained the solid man she had come to know. He led them into the canyon with speed, trying to avoid the consequences of their actions.

RHYATT

The sun had set when they returned home. Cleo and Knox had split off to their own homes, leaving Rhyatt and Wes walking alone. Rhyatt had a thousand questions spinning in his head. For starters, how did she so effortlessly break that man's leg? Once they had gotten far enough in the canyon, Knox mentioned it, admiration lacing into his voice. No one had mentioned how he had blacked out on top of that man, and for that, he was thankful.

They were walking on their road when she turned to him, a sparkle in her eyes.

"It seems you are less of a bunny than I thought."

"Yeah?" he asked, his cheeks heating at the same time a laugh escaped him. Leave it up to her to make him laugh about something he was ashamed of.

"Maybe you have more *killer* in you." She continued.

He broke eye contact and looked forward, focusing on the dark road ahead. That was not something he wanted.

"That's not a bad thing Rhyatt." her voice was soft and a shiver ran down his spine at the sound of his name. He looked back to see her light smile, it touched everywhere but her eyes. "You've earned some respect. I cannot thank you enough for coming with us." She continued.

"It was nothing."

"But it was." she glanced back at the saddlebags, "It means a lot. Thank you." Her voice hardened and now it was her turn to look forward.

Rhyatt thought of giving her space, but something in the back of his mind told him to ask anyway. At least when she didn't answer he wouldn't feel bad for not asking.

"What's on your mind?" he asked, turning to face forward so they wouldn't have to look each other in the eye. Some conversations were easier that way.

"He had five years left on the box... five years." Rhyatt kept quiet until she spoke again, "He expected to live at least five more years. He didn't make it but a few months."

"I'm sorry Wes-"

"I don't want to talk about it." she cut him off, "I just. I couldn't tell Knox and Cleo. I didn't want them to know and to come to the same realization. They deserve some peace of mind. They deserve not to be reminded of his short-lived life."

Rhyatt decided to hells with facing forward and turned to look at her. She was already staring at him, her face set into a hard line, determination written on the firmness of her mouth.

"You deserve the same peace of mind." Her brows wrinkled like she'd never heard those words before. And that was when Rhyatt thought maybe she hadn't. Maybe her friends hadn't ever protected her peace of mind. Was that the cost of being Wes Blake?

She nodded but said nothing.

"What are the three F's?" he asked after a moment.

Her brows unknitted, and she smirked.

"Knox came up with the name, not me." She began.

"Ooh, now I'm *very* curious."

"Very well," she said with a playful sigh, "Fighting, fucking, and getting fucked up. Anything that drains energy."

A light blush crossed his cheeks, "Ah, I see."

"Cleo's theory is that they stop shaking when I'm tired."

"And what's your theory?"

She shrugged, "I don't think I care much why it happens, only that I make sure it doesn't happen often."

Rhyatt nodded. He could understand that. Caring less about the why and more about the solution. It seemed he had been living that way lately. They approached the BlakeMoore's drive, and Rhyatt found himself reluctant to say goodnight.

"It's nothing to be ashamed of. You're still a *killer* with or without it."

"Thanks *bunny*."

He smiled at the nickname and walked home in the dark. This late at night, the birds were silent, and only the insects sang. It was almost nice. He had returned to his home country and no one had known him or attacked *him*. Sure, they had been attacked in general, but the saddlebag and bank had been to blame. He sighed, his shoulders relaxing. He had been told to wait and give it time for his memories to return, but maybe he didn't want them to. Maybe he was okay with his fresh start.

WES

W es went the rest of the weekend without seeing anyone outside her household. Even the friendly faces of Will and Rhina were sparse. She was up to her eyes in paperwork, fall was always busy, and classes at university never paused. She worked all day Sunday without stopping, falling asleep in her office and being woken by Rhina telling her to go to bed. The excitement of the Duran trip and a late Sunday night made for a groggy Monday morning. Or maybe it was the rum she had drank. Either way, it had taken a heavy dose of strength to wake up, hide the journal in her bag, and begin the walk to the university with Will in tow.

Exiting the Blakemoore's drive, she noticed Rhyatt and his brother walking a hundred feet in front of them.

Will tugged on Wes's sleeve, "Let's catch up with them."

"Go on." She said, pushing him forward.

Will took no time running, his feet quick but silent.

She watched as he ran behind Rhyatt before wrapping his small arms around the man's waist. Rhyatt acted surprised even though Wes had seen him glance back and notice them earlier.

She followed them from a distance, ensuring Will went inside the schoolhouse and didn't attempt to return home. Last year, he had gotten away with sneaking home and climbing the lattice inside one too many times.

When Will's shaggy hair disappeared inside the building, Rhyatt turned, his eyes instantly finding hers. A wrinkle creased his brow as he looked at her. It must be the dark circles under her eyes. He almost had a matching pair, *his* were less noticeable.

"Rough weekend?" he asked with a knowing smile. She had begun to like that about him. He spoke as if their conversation had never stopped, only paused. He didn't do awkward greetings, and for that, she was thankful.

"Oh, just a little." she said as they fell into step, heading towards the university, "My back is the worst. It looks like someone crushed blueberries on it."

He frowned at her, his brow creasing, "Can I see?"

Wes nodded and stepped in front of him. She loosened the collar of her shirt so he could look down the back.

She went unnaturally still as his fingertips brushed the back of her neck. And her breathing stalled when his breath dusted across her ear.

"Maybe you should see a doctor?" He said, letting go of her shirt and stepping away.

She shrugged and resumed walking, "Possibly, they'd just tell me to rest."

"Then perhaps you should consider rest?"

"There isn't any rest for the wretched."

"That's a bit worrisome," he paused, and before he could continue, Wes began.

"Thanks again for everything, we really do appreciate it."

133

Rhyatt dipped his head, the crease in his brow disappearing, "Anytime. But please don't ask me to return to the city anytime soon."

"No promises." she said and tried to forget the strange stirrings of feelings as they walked into class.

Wes walked towards the governance district. Over lunch, she had told Knox and Cleo her plans of handing the journal over to Commander Pryde. Sure, he was occasionally full of himself, but he was dedicated to Saint Saveen. With the journal handed over, Jaze's last wish would be completed. He could rest in peace, and so could they.

Wes entered the cool building and walked up the tall stairs to the Commander's floor, a ball of nerves growing in her stomach with each step. When she reached the top, the secretary nodded her forward. Down the long hallway she could see one of the Commander's office doors was open. She assumed the midday heat had gotten to him. The cool marble could only stop so much heat on the top floor.

She neared closer to her office when the whisper of voices caught her attention, but instead of coming from the open office, they were coming from the meeting room right next to *her* office. Wes continued to the Commander's office. Sure enough, it was empty. A tendril of relief curled around her. She almost felt guilty at that relief. But it was another few moments she got to hold onto the last piece of him.

She entered her office, leaving the door open and plopping into her chair. Pulling the journal out from her bag, she placed it on the edge of her otherwise empty desk. Her fingers hovered, and with a sigh, she placed her hand flat on it and began tapping a gentle rhythm, as if touching it would bring her closer to him.

Wes didn't know why she was so worked up. It was just a journal. She didn't even know the contents. Although she had been tempted to read it. Commander Pryde may ask questions, but she had thought of just about every excuse in the book to deflect the blame from Jaze. The journal's contents may very well implicate him as the author, but she had promised Knox that she wouldn't willingly tell anyone.

Her fingers stopped when a raised voice made it through the meeting room wall. The voices were muffled, but it was evident someone was not happy. She leaned closer to the wall and listened. At first, she could only hear vague voices, but after a few minutes, she could make out four distinct voices: one female and three males. As their voices continued to grow louder, Wes could make out more of their conversation.

"No. You know what will happen if they don't get their shipment."

"For god's sake, it's *flood season*," another voice said just as loud.

Their voices quieted again, pushing Wes out of their conversation. Curiosity got the best of her. Standing, she pressed her ear against the wall.

"Outpost... canyon floods can be... land.... North of the city.." A woman's soft voice was barely audible, even with her ear pressed against the wood.

"-giving them power we can't take back." A man spoke this time.

Either the other side was silent, or Wes could no longer hear their conversation. A few heartbeats later, a man's voice came through crystal clear, as if he was leaning against the wall she was listening to.

"Do what you must. But don't involve me in it."

Wes backed away from the wall. *That* voice belonged to the Commander. She would know the cadence of his aggravation anywhere.

The only thing North of Jorjin was Duran City. The only thing between the neighboring cities was a canyon that Rhyatt had informed her did flood often. It was uncanny how the meeting's whispered words sounded like an echo of Jaze's written ones.

Trust.

He told her to trust the person she handed his journal off to.

A gut feeling now told her the Commander could not be trusted. Not fully.

The sound of the meeting door being thrown open and banging the wall startled Wes into action. She scrambled for a blank sheet of paper and rapidly began writing. Half the words she was writing were nonsense.

Heat came to her face as the quick steps of people leaving echoed in the marble hallway. Out of the corner of her eye, she saw Commander Pryde walk by and enter his office. She refused to look up and notice him. Refused to unnecessarily draw his attention.

She continued writing.

And then the dog ran and ran, but no, it didn't

She focused on the words, making no sense but still scribbling away. When the Commander stopped in front of her doorway, she forced her to continue, pretending to be deep in concentration.

He gently knocked, and Wes jerked her head up quickly, feigning surprise.

"Commander Pryde!" she said a little too loud.

He smiled at her, his posture rigid with his hands in his pockets.

"I hope we didn't disturb you."

"Disturb?" She asked innocently enough.

His shoulders relaxed, and in turn, Wes's chest tightened.

"Our meeting ran over." he motioned to the room next door.

"Oh, I saw your empty office and thought you had stepped out for lunch." An airy laugh bubbled from her lips.

Commander Pryde smiled briefly at her and turned to leave.

Wes glanced at the journal, willing it to melt into the desk.

She looked up, and The Commander's eyes were on the journal.

"For me?" He asked, motioning to the journal as he stepped into the room.

"Oh, no." She looked at him with feigned sorrow, "Borrowed from a friend." She placed a palm down on the journal, covering any markings.

"My mistake." he placed his hands back in his pockets and stepped backward. Pryde had seen her grow up, known her family. How much did he know about her? Did he know how terrible of a liar she was?

His brow rose marginally, but he blinked and was back to normal.

"I have some files I need you to deliver." He said and returned to his office.

Wes stood, shoving the journal deep in her bag, and followed him.

WES

"**I** didn't give Pryde the journal," Wes said as soon as Will was out of earshot.

Rhyatt and Will were sitting under the tree when Cleo and Wes arrived. Knox arrived moments later, and Will promptly excused himself and headed inside. Rhyatt got the feeling Will didn't like Wes's friends that much. The boy wasn't exactly rude to them, but he didn't interact with them the same way he did with Rhyatt. The same could be said of Cleo and Knox. They were polite to him, but when his razor-sharp wit came out, they leaned away.

"Why not?" Cleo was the first one to ask.

And like little animals, they huddled close with their heads bent and listened to what Wes had overheard today.

It made sense that she was weary of their commander. The only canyon close to Saint Saveen was the one leading to Duran. The canyon was too steep and uneven that you couldn't bring any sort of cart or carriage into it. Most people instead traveled the Traders Road. It took a day and a half to travel between the two cities that way, but it guaranteed safety. The canyon was not only susceptible to flooding but also only accessible during daylight when the cave dwellers slept. Most who traveled the canyon were either in a rush like they had been or wishing to go unseen. Not much else made the risks worth it. Wes and the others seemed to understand the gravity of it.

"Maybe it was a trade deal," Wes paused, her hand absentmindedly going to the small bag the journal was in, "But trustworthy people don't take the canyon."

Rhyatt nodded his approval. The motion caught Knox's eye, and he was reminded of his place. He stilled and tried to stay as silent as possible, hoping he wouldn't be noticed.

"Then who do we trust?" Cleo asked, turning the conversation and planning. She was a planner that way, always looking for what was next.

"What about your parents?" Knox asked, his gaze firmly away from Rhyatt.

"If this is something we can't trust *the commander* with I don't think we should put it in my parents hands." Cleo paused before adding, "I trust them, but their power is fleeting."

Rhyatt raised an eyebrow. He had only gathered a bit about the Saint Saveen government; he hadn't known Cleo's parents were employed by them. As if sensing his confusion, Wes turned to him and explained.

"Cleo's parents are ambassadors from Genvi. They may have the council's ear about foreign matters but much less domestically."

"Who has more power than your commander?" Rhyatt asked and earned Knox's attention again. This time, a nasty look accompanied it.

"No one. But maybe we don't need someone with more power," Wes mused, "just an equally loud voice."

"One of the council of five?" Cleo asked, and Wes nodded before turning to Rhyatt and explaining again.

"The council of five are the elected officials directly under The Commander. There is Trade, Law, History, War, and Treasury. They each have a crew they manage. The Commander works closely with them."

"Wes, you have the most contact with them. Who are you closest with?" Knox asked, crossing his arms. He was not shy showing his displeasure about Rhyatt being included in the conversation.

"When my Father was on the Council, he was close to the Trade Councilor, but I haven't spoken to him in years. I doubt they keep in touch." Her lips pressed together into a tight line.

"Anyone else?" Cleo prompted.

Wes shook her head, "I know all of them, but I trust each of them about as far as I can throw them. If you think the elections are brutal, the inner workings are worse. I thought Commander Pryde was our best option."

"Maybe we should thumb through the journal and get an idea of what it says." Cleo suggested with a shrug.

"Jaze said not to read it." Knox snapped, his voice low and threatening. Rhyatt stepped closer to Cleo.

"I'm with Knox on this one," Wes said, her tone even and soothing, "Jaze requested we didn't read it, and we should respect that. We should approach this cautiously. He didn't expect his last will to be read so soon. We have time to get this into the right hands."

Rhyatt was dumbfounded as he watched Wes diffuse the tension that had appeared. Knox relaxed, and Cleo's shoulders drew back. He wondered if she knew how easily her friends had calmed down at her words. How quickly she had stopped an argument before it even began.

"What do we do in the meantime then?" Knox asked, any evidence of his rising anger had vanished.

"We keep it to ourselves and gather information. At my internship, I'll learn more about the council members and see what they're up to these days. Cleo, talk to your parents more and see if anything weird has come across their desks or any of the other ambassadors' desks. Knox, keep an eye and ear open at the bars and with the jewelry clients." She paused and turned to Rhyatt, "I'm not asking you to do anything, but if you happen to hear something odd, even if it seems trivial, we would appreciate it if you let us know."

Rhyatt realized two things simultaneously. The first was that he wished she would have asked him to do something, he liked being useful. The second was that there were more differences between Duran and Saint Saveen than he had realized. When he had first arrived, he thought it odd that swordsmanship had been taught in class, that previous battles and wars were broken down and analyzed. But now, standing in front of someone who had just made a strategy within seconds, he understood. Every person in this town had a basic education on being a warrior. In theory, every person could fight if a war called for it. Duran was the opposite, the City was too large to teach everyone about fighting and war. They relied on soldiers who had a minimum of a year's experience. The group before him had been raised on war tactics and politics; he couldn't remember who his former city's current mayor was. They had taken the journal and seen the need to get it into trusting hands; when their first option was deflated, they reorganized and planned. *That* was the difference. He had no idea how to think like them. So he nodded and agreed to keep his ears open.

"We appreciate it," Cleo said with a soft smile. Even she, the sweetest of them all, thought like that. Maybe his joke of calling Wes *killer* wasn't too much of a joke.

They circled back and began to talk about the council members. Rhyatt remained lost throughout the conversation, but he learned a few things. Wes's parents used to be *very* close to the Commander and the Trade Councilor. During her father's time on the council, they were his closest confidants. Her father's involvement and ties to Saint Saveen had ended almost five years ago; he presumed that was the same time her father and brother had both left home. Wes knew the Treasury Councilor in passing, as she had only been elected in the past two years. The only person she truly didn't trust and didn't care to get closer to was the War Councilor, Anouk. She blamed it on an old family feud, but her hollow laugh left Rhyatt unconvinced.

"Dinner!" Will's voice called from the back door. Knox and Cleo began walking, but Wes stayed still. She looked at Rhyatt, giving him a tired smile.

"Will said he invited you for dinner."

"Yes," he hooked his hand around the back of his neck, "but I don't want to impose."

"Would you like me to tell him that you chickened out?" Her smile turned sly. He stared at her, open-mouthed.

"No, I–"

"Then come on in." She began walking away before he could protest further. He was left with no choice but to follow. To be fair, he wanted to have dinner with them, he just didn't know Knox and Cleo would also be there.

He followed her inside and into the formal dining room. The room was meant for large dining parties, but the leafs had been removed from the table and leaned up against the wall, making the table small enough that six spots could be set and not feel like they were a world apart.

Rhyatt paused at the entry, unsure of what spot to take, before he could think too long. Will beckoned him, "Sit by me Rhyatt." he gestured to the spot beside him. He took his seat, and Rhina joined them. It should've surprised him, but it didn't. In Duran, if you were wealthy enough to have any household help, they would not talk to you, much less sit and break bread with you. His first day in the house had thrown his expectations to the wind. Rhina seemed less of household help and more of family.

When everyone sat at the table, they began eating, conversation flowing easily. Never once was the journal mentioned. Will was more likely to turn and talk to Rhyatt than anyone else. As the meal went on, he started whispering little rules to Rhyatt. *No arguing at the dinner table. If challenging someone, you wait until after dessert is served. No one should have to eat dinner worrying about an upcoming fight.* And lastly, but certainly not least to him, *The person to finish the water pitcher is required to get the next one.* Rhyatt watched as Will purposely only drank water when the pitcher had been freshly filled. Most times it was Wes who would finish it and retrieve more. On the third time, he noticed she finished the pitcher with her cup still half full.

Rhyatt smiled as she retrieved more water. Perhaps Saint Saveen didn't raise their children as differently as he thought.

WES

According to Knox, Wes had laid low all week. She couldn't disagree. Retrieving the journal on the weekend and then distrust being planted in the Commander had tired her. After lessons with Rhyatt, she found it entirely too easy to crawl into bed and sleep like the dead. And so she had been. She would come home from class, teach Rhyatt, eat dinner with Will and Rhina, and then crawl up the stairs to her bed, where she would attempt to complete some paperwork for the farm. Half the time, her eyes would shut before she read more than a sentence.

She would spend tonight training Rhyatt. It was not her first choice of how to spend her night, but he could be enjoyable at times. She had arrived home, and Will had gone inside to get a snack while she dropped her stuff off at the tree. Rhyatt was rising and stretching.

"Let's make this quick and easy. I've got places to be," she said, tossing him a practice sword.

"We can reschedule?"

"No, we're both already here." She lifted her sword, "Show me what you remember."

He lifted his arm and demonstrated the first move she had ever shown him. When she blocked him easily, he reset and demonstrated another move. She blocked again. When they reset again, she instructed him to block her. When she struck, she did so hard and fast; luckily, he responded just as quickly.

"Good *little bunny*, it looks like you've been practicing." She wanted to sneer at him, but it sounded like a compliment instead.

"I've done as you told me," he said while resetting himself.

"Do you always do as you're told?"

"Only for you," he said with a wink.

"Oh, a little flirty today, hm?"

Rhyatt laughed a throaty laugh, still holding his sword up, anticipating her next move.

"Would it be too much to say 'only for you' again?"

Wes smirked at him, "It's your life, Rhyatt. You gamble it anyway you see fit."

She raised her sword and struck him in a new way. He was quick and got his sword in front of his body, but he didn't block the correct way, leaving her to strike his chest.

"When I strike like that, block like this." She lifted her sword and showed him how to block correctly, her movements fluid.

He reset himself, and they began again, this time slower. She repeated the move twice before picking up the pace. He was a quick learner and blocked her correctly. She nodded her approval.

"Tell me more about yourself. I feel like Will knows you better than I do," Wes said to him as they continued with the new moves.

"What do you want to know?" He asked.

"What are you willing to share?"

"I'm an open book." he moved his arms wide.

"What's your guilty pleasure?"

"Ooh, straight for the deep stuff, huh?"

"You're an open book, remember?"

Rhyatt smiled, "I like to eat my dessert before dinner."

Wes tossed her head back in an exaggerated laugh, so *that* was his guilty pleasure. She was hoping it would be picking his nose and eating it or kicking puppies, something to make him not as charming.

"And what about you, Wes Blake? What is your deepest, darkest, guiltiest pleasure?"

She rolled her eyes at him and struck.

"Oh, come on, tell me the tiniest of secrets about you. I swear to keep it to myself." Rhyatt crossed his heart with his finger.

"I never said I was an open book." she mused, a catlike grin on her face.

He put on a fake pout and struck out at her, "Humor me then."

"Fine." she tilted her chin, "When no one's looking, I like to eat strawberries," she paused and looked away, "with butter and sugar."

Rhyatt's hearty laugh echoed as he bent over, "That's it? That's all you've got?"

"Like yours was much better!" she exclaimed.

"Touchè. Now it's my turn to ask a question."

"Fire at will."

"What is your favorite childhood memory?" he asked, his laugh dying as he moved his feet to block her blow.

Without pausing, she launched into it, "When Warden and I were twelve, we became really competitive with each other. The sibling rivalry is heightened when you're a twin," she added, "Whatever he thought he could do, I aimed to do it better, same for him. We had been in this unspoken competition all summer to see who the better twin was. Who could fight better- me. Who could run faster- him, damn those long legs. Who was braver- still undecided. The end of the summer was coming, and Knox saw a snake on the riverbank. The challenge went: if you're brave, you'll pick it up. Of course, Warden and I had something to prove, so he picked it up with two fingers, grimacing the entire time, and put it down as quickly as possible. When my turn came, I picked it up and held it for way longer than he had. I stepped towards him and saw the fear in his eyes, so I did what every child does to their siblings. I threw the snake at him. The sound of him screaming is still imprinted in my brain to this day. I've also never seen him run quicker." She ended with a smile.

"That is-"

Wes cut him off with a wave of her hand, "I know it's awful, but it wasn't poisonous, and he was the one who wanted to be brave."

"I was going to say it was hilarious." Rhyatt shook his head.

"I'm glad you find more humor in it than Warden does. It's still a sore spot for him."

"Reasonably so."

"Go on then, let's hear yours."

Rhyatt smiled softly, "It's not much, but when I was younger, we had this game we would play, it was similar to hide and seek. We would put out all the candles, and all but one of us would hide. Then, the remaining person would quietly seek out the others until everyone was found. The only rule was that you couldn't make any noise. Sometimes, the game would go on for hours, everyone quietly shuffling around the house trying to find one another. The thing I remember the most is the muffled giggles from when someone found you, how you wanted to laugh but didn't want to alert everyone that you'd been found." he looked away from her for a second, the memory making him smile fondly. Wes was mesmerized by the smile on his face, so innocent and pure.

"What's your next question?" he asked, pushing her backward.

"Best joke you've ever heard?"

"This one's a little lewd, that alright?"

She raised her eyebrows at him, "Go on."

"So," he huffed as Wes swung at him, "A man walks into a bar and sees his friend sitting next to a 12-inch pianist. He says that's amazing, where did you find him? His friend says it is a funny story and pulls out a-"

"Wes!" Will called from the steps, "Wes! There's a delivery here for the farm!"

"Coming," she called to him before turning back to Rhyatt, "I guess I'll have to finish this joke another time."

She tossed the practice sword onto the ground, wiping her hands on her pants.

"And Rhyatt?" She said, taking a step towards the house.

"Yeah." His head snapped up, and his eyes immediately focused on hers.

"Don't doubt yourself so much. You're going to learn quicker when you make mistakes."

"I don't-"

"Yes, you do. You didn't get to think about your doubts when we were talking, and you performed better. You even gained a few steps on me."

Rhyatt stared at her momentarily before responding, "Perhaps you should talk me through it more often?"

Wes felt her lips involuntarily tug into a smile.

"Perhaps."

CLEO

C leo lifted her hand to Wes's face and used the makeup brush to gently place the dark powder near the outer corner of her friend's eye. Wes scrunched her nose at the contact.

"Can you please sit still?" Cleo asked, an inch of frustration entering her voice. Nothing irritated her more than when she was trying to do an extremely detail-oriented task, like painting makeup on her friend, and her canvas kept moving. Cleo's mother was no different. Every time Cleo applied lip color, Mother Nafin would twitch. It was a level of irritation she did not like. She enjoyed when things were within her control. Both Wes and her Mother's faces were not controllable.

"I'm trying, but your sleeve keeps touching my face," Wes replied, huffing a blast of air towards the sleeve in question.

Cleo put the brush down long enough to push her billowy sleeves past her elbows and resume her work.

"Better?"

"Much."

Cleo continued, moving slow and gentle over her friend's eyes. She was surprised that Wes had agreed to go out to the Lucky

Duck Bar tonight. It had been easy to get Knox, but Wes needed convincing. She had to arrange for Rhina to stay with Will, and even then, Wes had wanted to say no. However, Cleo was not taking no for an answer. Her friend was slipping, and she could tell that a night out, away from all their worries, would help. They had promised to pretend to be normal university students with no care in the world. No dead friends with a troubling journal left behind. Just friends spending a Friday night together, like all their peers did.

"How long do you want your lashes to be?" Cleo asked, placing one brush down and trading it for another.

"I want them to tickle everyone I kiss," Wes replied with a raise of her brows.

Cleo didn't say a word, instead, she began brushing the black lash creme through Wes's already dark lashes. Wes cooperated.

"Is there a reason you've decided we need a night out?" Wes asked after a few strokes on the opposite eye.

"We haven't been out together in a while." Cleo lied with a shrug. They hadn't visited any public bars or drinking establishments as a group since before Jaze died. It had been the night before he died when they all had last piled into a bar together. Their hair was still wet from their last midnight swim together. It seemed like another life.

"I don't like how many eyes we have on us when we go out," Wes replied. And that was a fair assessment.

"It can be annoying," Cleo agreed, reaching for the lip color she knew Wes loved, "but drinking at home is no fun." Which she also knew Wes had been doing.

"What if I see someone I don't like?"

"You're Wes Fucking Blake. Turn your back on them?"

Wes had no response to that. Likely because she knew it was true. As much as Wes complained and drug her feet, Cleo knew Wes would go and have a good time.

Cleo continued applying the dark lip color onto Wes, which was more purple than red. It suited her well.

"I agree with you about the journal," Wes said when Cleo paused to wipe away the excess lip color. "About reading it." She added.

"You didn't agree with me when Knox was present," Cleo stated.

"You know how he is." She started before breathing a deep sigh, "He will honor Jaze's wish, even if it means waiting until it's too late."

"How long do you plan to wait?" Cleo pulled away, placing her hands behind her and leaning back.

"What do you think? A month?" Wes's freshly painted lips thinned.

"A month seems adequate." Cleo agreed. "Will you tell Knox?"

"Fuck no. He won't say it, but he's still upset that Jaze sent his last will to me instead of him."

Cleo said nothing. Wes was more gentle with Knox than Cleo ever had been. They had had many arguments over it, and it ended the same. Wes would say that Knox had a hard life and was prone to lashing out. What Wes never said was that both she and Cleo had equally hard lives. Wes ran the family's farm and took care of their business, while Cleo was the daughter of foreign ambassadors. Their lives not being normal is what made them such good companions. Cleo continued her silence, letting Wes talk if she felt up to it.

"I'm hoping we can talk to the councilors in the meantime and get a good idea of who to give it to. That way, no one has to read the journal, and his secrets can stay safe."

"Yes." Cleo mused, "But are you willing to read the journal when, we are still unsure of whom to trust in a month?"

"I said I was willing." Wes repeated.

"Saying and doing are two different things." Cleo countered, pushing herself off her floor and to her feet. She bent at the waist and offered Wes a hand.

Wes narrowed her eyes before a coy smile appeared. She grasped Cleo's waiting hand and allowed herself to be pulled upwards. Wes smoothed the emerald silky top she wore. Its buttons were mother of pearl and glimmered in the low lamp light. Despite Wes's protests she had put effort into her clothing.

"You look good," Cleo said.

"And *you* always look good," Wes replied.

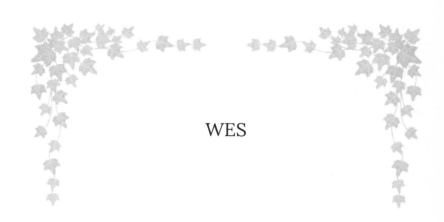

WES

Wes stopped outside the door to the Lucky Duck and tucked her dagger into her boot.

Knox tapped the sign that said No Weapons Allowed in big, bold letters. "I wonder how many people got hurt before Higgins put up this sign."

"One too many," Cleo replied, pushing the door open and motioning for her friends to follow.

Wes straightened her spine, tilted her chin upwards, and let all the air leave her lungs before following.

Immediately, the cheers of her peers erupted at the sight of the three of them. Approximately half of her class was here, and half of the University was scattered around the bar.

"Wes! Where have you been?"

"Let me buy you all a round."

"It's been so long since we've seen you all."

Three people talked to them all at once. Wes fought the urge to tell them that she hadn't been in lately because her friend had died and then left her a seemingly impossible task.

Wes, Cleo, and Knox stood around the bar with the others from their class. Olivina stood closest to them, and within a minute of being there, she handed Wes a glass of dark rum.

"Thank you," Wes said, taking the glass and swallowing it in one quick motion. She placed the glass back on the bar. "How's your internship going?"

Olivina smiled that gorgeously sweet smile, and Wes felt her stomach tighten. Olivina had an irresistible beauty around her. With her light brown curls and round face, she was sweet and lovely—the opposite of a man—just what she wanted right now.

"Good. Working with lace is much harder than you might think!" She ended her sentence with a soft laugh, and Wes found herself thankful Cleo had made her lashes especially long.

"Really? My hands were never steady enough to-"

Wes was cut off by a drink being put into her hand. Dutifully, she gulped it down and turned to thank the gifter. It was a girl a year or two below her. Her shorter friend stood tight against her. Wes had seen both girls in between classes. They had a competitive spirit about them and could often be seen sparring on the lawns during lunch.

The friend held out another glass. Wes took it but paused before drinking it.

"We want to know how you beat three soldiers at once." the taller one asked.

Wes nodded and tossed the drink down. Ew, it was whiskey. She should have sniffed it first.

"Well, the first thing you have to know is that they were all idiots," Wes was handed another drink by a younger boy. He looked to be the same age as the girls, maybe 19.

"But what led to you being able to beat them? How do you train? What sword do you use? The weather?" The boy asked. He ended his sentence by tapping his drink against Wes's and tossing it back.

Out of habit, Wes brought the cup to her lips and tilted it back. This time, it was rum. The band in the corner chose this moment to begin. The drum beats instantly filled the air and increased the noise tenfold.

Wes wrinkled her nose, motioned the three younger students closer, and began to tell them all her secrets. Which was honestly not much. She told them how she had begun doubling up her lessons at 13 and how she practiced daily and twice on certain days. She left out that Rhyatt now occupied the second practice. When the stringed instruments joined in and raised the noise, she left the students with one last piece of advice: to practice with a wide variety of people.

She slipped away from the trio and began to look for her own trio. The band ended their current song, and the crowd cheered. Closest to them, the tables and chairs had been cleared, leaving room for a makeshift dance floor. Next to the dancefloor, Cleo and Knox stood, half watching those who danced. Knox held a pint of ale, drinking it quicker than he should. Cleo's slender fingers were wrapped around a glass of clear liquor. Even drinking, she was poised.

Wes joined her friends and slumped against the bar, her face was already warm.

"How many rounds have you been bought? I had four in under ten minutes." Wes said.

"Four," Knox said.

"Two," Cleo added.

"It's because you have the gall to deny them." Knox huffed, "You should be passing them to me instead."

Wes was tapped on the shoulder.

She turned, and the barkeep's son placed three glasses of rum on the bar behind them. The boy motioned back towards where her peers were standing. Michal waved at her, a sheepish grin on his face. Michal was in their class and somewhere in the middle when it came to swordsman skills. Wes smiled and waved back, collecting the three drinks before turning around and distributing them to Cleo and Knox.

Wes drank hers immediately. Knox followed suit, but Cleo put hers down on the bar.

"We need to start going to the Brothers bar. It's nothing but old folks in there." Wes said, picturing the three of them standing among the older folks. It would be quiet, and none of their peers or friends would be there. But there wouldn't be dancing, and Wes loved to watch those brave enough to dance. The later the night went, the worse the dancers got. They lost rhythm but gained liquid confidence.

Wes watched the few dancers in front of them. A man not much older than her twirled a woman around, switching direction with the changing rhythm. Her eyes flickered to another couple, two friends with their arms linked who were performing a dance with little kicks. It didn't go with the music, but it was likely what they knew. She watched them for a moment before moving her eyes again. This time, she landed on Atticus Pryde, the Commander's son.

Her brain clicked on and told her she had to move before the song ended. She searched the crowded bar, her vision landing on Olivina. That would be a conversation he wouldn't interrupt. But

Olivina was talking to someone, he was tall with broad shoulders and dark short curly hair. She would recognize that frame anywhere, Rhyatt.

Wes paused, watching them interact. Olivina put her hand gently on Rhyatt's elbow and laughed.

Her mind took an immediate left turn and pictured them both naked, bodies tumbling in between the sheets. And Wes wanted to be in those sheets, between them both.

She reached around Cleo and grabbed the spare drink, tossing it back.

Cleo eyed her with suspicion.

Wes nodded her head toward the duo.

"Oh." Cleo grinned wide. "Here." She motioned Wes forward before using one hand to quickly open two buttons on her blouse. The top of her bra peeked out, the light fabric stark against the dark green top.

Wes turned away, and Cleo smacked her ass. Wes blew her a kiss before weaving through the crowd. The later it got, the more packed the bodies became.

She was halfway there when Olivina caught her coming and smiled, the light instantly reaching her eyes. Rhyatt paused and followed her line of vision to see Wes.

He raised his brows at her before nodding in acknowledgment.

Wes could envision exactly how it would go. Olivina and Rhyatt were on the shyer side. It would have to be Wes to make the first move on both of them. Her best bet would be to encourage them to kiss while Wes used her hands to–

The movement of a woman walking caught her eye, causing Wes to stop in her tracks.

It was her Mother.

Her Mother was here.

Her long black hair swished against her back as she rounded the corner to the back hallway.

Wes felt her chest tighten as she turned to follow.

Why was her mother here?

She turned towards the back hallway, pushing people aside to get there quicker. Sweat trickled down her back, and she could feel her heartbeat in her fingertips.

She rounded the corner just in time to see her Mother getting pulled into a private room by a man half her age.

RHYATT

R hyatt watched her slip out the side door that led to the ally. He thought about leaving it alone, leaving her to whatever thing she was dealing with. But every time he refocused on Olivina his eyes would drift back to the door. His mind began to whir and he thought of her admission. That her dead friend had left five years on a bank box, he thought of how she had kept it to herself and not told her friends.

He smiled at Olivina and bid her goodbye before heading towards the door. The spine rattling thumps of the drums were enough to hasten his walk across the dance area.

He pushed the door open and stepped into the slightly cooler, but still very warm, night air.

It took a moment for his eyes to adjust to the darkness, but when they did, he could make out her form perched on a crate, her legs dangling and her back pressed up against the opposite wall.

He glanced down the alley. They were alone.

"It's too loud in there," Wes said, her words slightly slurred.

"It is." Rhyatt agreed. Then, he promptly cursed himself for being so lame. He committed himself to silence, and Wes closed her eyes, extending her silence to him.

He decided to take a seat on a questionable wooden crate that only went up to his knees. It held his weight as he sat down.

"Are you okay? Really?" He asked before his bravado faded.

She sighed and shook her head, "I'm okay."

The door burst open, banging against the wall as two figures poured out it, drinks in hand.

It was Knox and Cleo.

Knox went to Wes, handed her a drink, and leaned beside her. Cleo, however, looked both ways down the alley like she was crossing a street and took a seat next to Rhyatt. His unstable crate groaned slightly at her added weight.

She extended a drink. Rhyatt shook his head, he had had enough for the night. Cleo only shrugged and began to take small sips.

Across from them, Wes had placed her empty drink down and returned her attention to Knox.

"Are we not good enough for you, Wes?" Knox asked.

Wes smiled and shook her head. But that smile... That was it. That was the smile she wore all the time. With a shock, Rhyatt realized it wasn't real. It was for show. A way to ward off any unwanted questions. A way to appear to be the happy woman she wanted to be seen as. An unsettling feeling climbed through Rhyatt and up his bones.

When she didn't respond aloud, Knox moved from her side to stand between her legs. She looked him in the eye before reaching for his drink and finishing it off.

She set it down beside her, then Knox was leaning in, pressing his lips to hers. Rhyatt stared. Knox reached his hand up and wrapped it around her neck, attempting to pull her closer.

Wes pulled away, using her hand to gently press on his chest and separate them.

"What are you doing Knox?" She asked quietly, confusion in her brow.

With Knox's back to him, Rhyatt saw the man tense, and then anger entered his voice.

"I figured if Jaze could get it, so could I."

For the briefest of seconds, no one reacted, no one breathed.

Like a flash of lightning, Wes drew back her fist and it connected with Knox's jaw.

A switch had been flipped inside her. No longer was the faux smile or even the tinge of sadness. There was only rage. Her eyes hardened as she stood to her feet, Knox stumbling to the side, clutching his jaw.

"Don't be disrespectful." She sneered.

Both Cleo and Rhyatt stood up. Knox narrowed his eyes at her before straightening up and striding towards her.

Rhyatt stepped forward instinctively.

"Don't," Cleo said, wrapping a hand around his wrist.

Rhyatt shot her a confused look.

"It's best if you just let them settle it."

"Let them fight?" he asked, still pulling towards Wes.

Cleo nodded, but Rhyatt didn't relax. He feared her with a sword in her hand but had never seen her in a close fight. The most he had seen was in Duran, but even then he was too focused on himself.

Knox reached Wes and grabbed for her shoulder when she swung again. Only he had been expecting it. He dodged her punch and wrapped his arms around her middle, pulling her and sending them both to the ground in a scramble.

Rhyatt cringed as they rolled on the filthy ground. Wes was sluggish and a bit slower than Knox. She had had more to drink than he had. Rhyatt wasn't surprised with the way drinks were given to her. Cleo's hand remained loosely wrapped around his wrist, holding him to the spot.

They were a blur of blond and brunette hair as they struggled for power. Knox won the struggle and took the upper hand, straddling over her waist. He reared back and landed a punch on her cheek. Rhyatt jerked forward, but Cleo held him tighter.

Wes's head had turned to the side, facing them. Even beneath a man, she had *that* look about her. He wondered if she had made a deal with a demon. Knox pulled his fist back again, but she had time to get her hands in front of her and blocked the punch. Wes bucked her hips, bringing Knox closer to her face, but that freed her legs. She brought her knee up until it connected with his back.

Knox arched his back and yelped out in pain.

She saw this and used it to her advantage, twisting her body and throwing his weight to the side. She followed his roll until the roles were reversed, and she straddled him. Her dark hair made a curtain and closed off her face. She wrapped her fingers in Knox's collar and then pushed down, using his own shirt to choke him.

"Conceed," she said between clenched teeth.

"No." he snarled back.

He reached up and grabbed a fist of her hair, yanking it towards the ground. Her head bobbed, and he used the temporary distraction to free himself and stand.

Rhyatt felt Cleo stiffen as Wes ran her fingers through her hair and stood. Rhyatt leaned forward, wanting to stop this madness. Cleo only tugged on his arm.

"It's going to get worse before it gets better." She muttered, resigned to the fighting.

Wes swayed on her feet, using the back of her hand she wiped the sweat off her cheek, effectively smearing the dirt. Knox pushed up his sleeves, in response Wes spat blood onto the ground.

They lunged at each other again.

Wes landed a solid punch on his nose, her surprise costing her a brief disorientation. Knox must have been expecting it because he shook his head before grabbing her and slamming her to the hard ground, his weight landing on top of her.

She gasped loudly, the air knocked out of her.

Knox got on top of her again, put his forearm across her throat, and began to push.

"*Conceed,*" he said, mocking her earlier attempt.

She gasped, struggling for air and her free hand clawing at his neck.

"No... thanks.." she said between gasps.

Knox pushed down harder, and her face began to go red, her free hand still barely leaving a mark on him.

Rhyatt pushed forward, meaning to break Cleo's grip and help Wes. He was surprised when she not only held tight but also jerked his arm, forcing him to turn and look at her.

"She'll concede when she's done," Cleo said with undoubted confidence in her friend.

"But she's choking–" Rhyatt sputtered.

"She's not done yet," Cleo stated, a fierceness he had never seen before entering her voice.

Wes gasped again, then calmed herself, her hand stopping. She jerked her shoulders to the side, then her waist. Her knee was now bent underneath her. She jerked again, shaking Knox around. When he was jilted, she pushed her knee forward, kneeing him in the groin.

Knox instantly released her and doubled over in pain. She shoved him off of her. He rolled on the ground, clutching himself in pain and groaning.

She remained on the ground, gasping for air. She didn't move. It was clear the fight was over between them.

Cleo released his wrist and he instantly went to Wes's side as she sat up. He knelt and offered her his hand. She barely glanced at his outstretched hand before swatting it away and using the crate to pull herself up. She sent him a look that could've frozen a man in his tracks. He understood though. She didn't want or need his help. So he backed away and went back to Cleo's side. Cleo reached out a comforting hand on his shoulder.

Wes stood and put her hands on her hips, slightly bent as she still struggled to catch her breath.

Looking at Knox, she said, "You pulled my hair." her voice was raspy.

Knox narrowed his eyes at her, "That's different." he let out a wet cough and sat up. Any anger clearing from his face.

Wes wiped the blood off of her cheek. Rhyatt was still studying her and noticed that her almost healed knuckles were once again split and bruised. He had yet to see the woman with clean hands.

"Fair." She stumbled to where Knox was leaning on his knees and reached out a hand, an offering. Knox looked up at her before taking her hand and pulling himself up. He swayed on his feet, Rhyatt wondered how much the both of them had drank and what a fight without alcohol would look like between the two of them. Knox found his balance, and then the two of them linked arms behind each other's backs, leaning on each other. Without another word, they walked back into the bar.

Rhyatt stared at the closed door in confusion. Cleo squeezed his shoulder before sitting back down in her spot.

"It's been far too long since they've fought." She paused to think on it, "Since before Jaze," she trailed off again.

Rhyatt said nothing.

"I'm surprised they went so easy on each other." She continued.

"Easy?" Rhyatt asked in disbelief as he remembered the sound of knuckles hitting a jaw.

"Very."

"Why do they fight like that?"

Cleo turned away from the fire to look him in the eye, "They're like siblings."

Rhyatt furrowed his brow, "I don't know a set of siblings that kiss each other."

"Not like that." Cleo rolled her eyes, "Sometimes they do things to piss each other off. They know exactly how to push the others' buttons. He knew what to do and say to get her to take the first swing."

Rhyatt could understand that. He and Adriel had come to blows multiple times in his youth. They always knew exactly what to do to stir the pot. He also knew exactly what to say to hurt Adriel enough that he would leave him alone for the day. He wondered if he still knew Adriel that well. The large gap in his memory made him curious about how much had changed about his little brother.

"They have set rules?" Rhyatt asked, a vision of Wes's disbelief when her hair was pulled.

Cleo nodded.

"Then why did Knox break them knowing he could get worse treatment?"

Cleo only smiled and looked forward. "I used to think he did it to let her win, but I've realized he's encouraging her to cheat."

Rhyatt tilted his head to ask why, but Cleo was speaking again, as if reading his thoughts.

"Wes always plays fair, always by the rules. Sometimes it's her own rules, but rules nevertheless. Whatever is *right*."

"Whatsoever is just," Rhyatt whispered the phrase he had heard her say a handful of times.

Cleo smiled fondly at the words, "Her and Warden both took those words to heart."

Rhyatt frowned slightly at the mention of her brother, he had never met the man, but it was clear there was animosity around his name.

"Why does he go to school elsewhere and leave her here to deal with everything?" He hadn't meant for the anger to slip into his voice, but judging by Cleo's wariness, he had failed.

"That is not my story to tell."

He understood. Cleo was happy to talk about her friends and their fighting, something they felt comfortable enough to do in front of him, but when it came to the sore spots she was tight lipped. Rhyatts' interest piqued at the knowledge, but he made no move to pry, instead he shifted the conversation.

"What about you then, what is your story?" he asked and when she made no notion to talk about herself he instead asked her more directly, "Tell me about your family. Do they like being ambassadors?"

"They do. They find Jorjin to be a very... *interesting* place."

"The violence?" Rhyatt asked.

"The lack of it. The constant preparation for it. I have lived here for over half of my life, so perhaps I am biased, but there is comfort in knowing that everyone is semi-trained to handle an act of violence. It makes going out in public feel safe. Even if there was a madman roaming the street, there's confidence in knowing over half the population has been trained to stop them."

"Huh. I guess I never thought about it like that." Rhyatt said, and for some reason, he felt like being uncomfortably honest with her, "I think that's why I'm so uneasy here. Because everyone could take me out without another thought. I hate feeling like a child amongst the gods."

"You are not as helpless as you think Rhyatt. I saw you in Duran. Most people here would beat you with a sword, but without that, you'd stand a good chance."

Rhyatt blushed, partly because of the compliment and partly because he didn't want to remember what happened in Duran.

"Do you ever miss Genvi?" he asked.

It was Cleo's turn to blush and look away, "I have lived in Saint Saveen too long. I would never tell my parents, but I do not remember Genvi all that much. I know she had a rocky sea and warm climate."

"I've heard it's a beautiful country."

"I'm sure it is. When I return, I'll have to let you know."

"When will you return?" Rhyatt asked, sad at the thought of losing his newfound friend.

"I want to visit my brothers and their families soon. Hopefully, post-graduation. My parents have a job lined up for me if I choose to stay there." She looked down, looking unusually sheepish. "I'm afraid my heart belongs to Jorjin. Even with all her flaws, she is home."

Rhyatt nodded. He understood where you grew up had a massive effect on what you liked. He still missed the dry heat of the city, instead he was constantly glistening with a sheen of sweat here. And even though green was his favorite color it seemed to be the only color here. He missed the orange sands.

"I'm sure you'll make the best decision for yourself," Rhyatt told her with a comforting smile.

"And what about you? You must be missing Duran. Will you return?"

Rhyatt shook his head, "Duran was my first home, and I miss the city terribly. Oh-what I wouldn't give for a smoked cactus pheasant- but I think I needed a change of pace." he glanced towards the door, "I think I ended up where I needed to be."

"We all end up where we need to be," Cleo said with a knowing smile, glancing back to the door as well. "I hope wherever you end up, you'll stay in touch. You're good people, Rhyatt."

KNOX

It didn't matter what time he arrived home, Knox was always bitched at. It was no different when he showed up an hour past midnight. Even though he was quiet, his father still leaped from his chair to yell at him.

"Where the hell have you been?" the older man yelled.

Knox curled his lip before calming himself enough to respond with a lie, "It was the Blake's fall dinner tonight, I told you days ago."

"You didn't tell me shit." his father crossed his scarred arms over his chest.

Knox stared blankly ahead, too tired to engage with the waste of space.

"You don't have nothing to say to me, boy? Why is your face busted up like that?" When Knox didn't respond instantly he continued, "If you got into a fight at the Blake's I'm going to tear you a new one."

"It happened on the way home." Knox lied between his teeth.

"Good." his father said, satisfied for the moment. "You need to bring the young one over here soon. I know that farm goes through metal workings like crazy. You obviously can't woo her to invest her business in us, so maybe I can."

"She doesn't want to do business with you," Knox said, turning to head towards his room, not in the mood for his father's shit.

His father smiled like a cat who had caught a mouse in a trap, "And why would that be?" He advanced on his son, blocking his path to the hallway.

Knox wanted to rage back at his father, but he was too tired. His fight with Wes had left him weak. He opened his mouth to apologize so that his father would move and let him into the hallway, but he paused as his parent's bedroom door squeaked open, and his dainty mother stepped into the hallway. Her thin nightgown did nothing to hide the dark splotches across her arms.

Knox refocused his eyes on his father, a shit-eating grin appearing, "Because you're a piece of shit businessman who drinks too much and forgets to open the shop on time. Because I refuse to encourage her to invest in someone as terrible as you."

His mother's eyes widened. Knox knew what came next, so he simply closed his eyes.

When Knox regained consciousness, he was on the kitchen floor, his head resting in his mother's lap. One of her hands brushed his blonde curls out of his face as the other dabbed a damp cloth over his face. She whispered words to him he could not understand. He wasn't entirely sure it was in his language.

Forcing his eyes open was a chore in itself. When he finally pried them open, she gasped. His mother had begun to show signs of aging, and it always pained him when he looked at her from this angle. Looking up at her like this reminded him of when he was a boy, only now her face was different, much different, showing all her age and then some. It pained him to look at her like this, her eyes glassing over as he awoke.

"Mijn Zoon," she whispered to him, relief flooding her face.

Knox blinked up at her, "How bad was it?"

She looked to the hallway. The rest of the house remained silent and dark.

"You were only out a few seconds before he stopped."

Knox moved his arms, and his body tensed. Wes hadn't done much damage to him, only his face. Now, he felt the pain ripple through his chest, down his arms, and in his torso. He blinked and relaxed once more. His mother clutched him tightly.

"It's not that bad." Knox lied, staying still in his mother's arms for a moment longer.

She looked at him with horror in her eyes, "He used the belt."

Knox sighed. His belt had a metal tip that bit into his skin and always left purple triangular bruises. He always looked -and felt- the worse when he used it. He glanced down at his arms; bruises had begun to form all the way down to his wrists. Great. Now, he would have to wear long sleeves in the early fall heat for the next few weeks. He didn't want to think how bad the side of his head was. His Father always made sure his head was the final blow.

With a deep sigh, he bit down his wince as he sat up and out of his mother's embrace.

"I'm okay," he said, keeping his head turned away lest she would pick up on how bad his pain truly was.

He stood slowly, then hobbled to the door frame.

"Knox," His mother whispered, still frozen on the floor.

"Goodnight, Ma." He turned back and mustered a smile for her.

RHYATT

"When the Queen's war began, Saint Saveen wasn't even a blimp on the continent. It would be hundreds of years before Jorjin became a country. We sometimes find artifacts from the war as this was the last stopping place before they crossed what is now the Duran desert. At that time, it was the grassy plains that provided very little coverage or food. Hundreds of years ago, current day Duran City was the last standpoint for the Queens." The Scholar paused her lecture to look over her pupils.

Rhyatt stared intently back at her. Today, they had been doing a deep dive into the Queen's war. In Duran, he had glazed over the basics sometime in late grade school and since forgotten anything but the name of the war.

"At this point, each Queen had amassed massive armies and many allies. The final battle would allow bloodshed the world had never seen before. Both Queens knew this and agreed to meet. It is still unclear who proposed the meeting. At their meeting, Queen Cecilia proposed single combat, where each Queen would choose a victor for combat, and the champion's side would claim the battle as a victory. Traditionally, the fight happened until first blood. Queen Cecilia proposed two new rules. Their single combat could only be between the highest-ranked leaders at the battle, and the champion was only crowned after the other's death. Queen Cecilia and Queen Beryl were the highest ranked in their entire armies. Thus, they would fight each other."

"At this point, I would like to remind you of some important things that make Queen Cecilia's offer much more interesting. Beryl and Cecilia had grown up together. Until their mid-twenties, they were seen together constantly. They were *very* close." The Scholar glanced around the room, her students more lively than before.

"And, remind me. What happened to Queen Beryl only a few days prior?" The Scholar asked.

"She had injured her fighting arm," Rhyatt replied.

"Thank you, Mister Valvidez." The Scholar replied before launching back into her lecture. "She had injured her fighting arm, and it was still being held aloft by a sling. Queen Cecilia knew this. Her offer was not only rude but a death sentence if Beryl took it. Wisely, Beryl refused. The two behemoth armies finally clashed, and the resulting battle would last for ten days. In the end, Queen Beryl stood victorious, but with Queen Cecilia still alive, she did not rest. At the beginning of the 11th day, the Queens met again. Queen Beryl had not forgotten Cecilia's offering. Beryl broke Cecilia's arm and proceeded to offer her *Eligere*, a choice. Queen Beryl offered a choice only out of respect for the twenty years they spent together in their youth. The choice was that Queen Cecilia could submit and be Queen Beryl's willing prisoner, or the two would battle in single combat until the death. Queen Beryl made her soldiers promise that if Cecilia was the winner, they would allow her to be free. But Beryl also made it very clear that if she was the winner, she would not only kill Cecilia but also slay all of her remaining soldiers, completely eradicating her country and ally's fighting forces."

"Queen Cecilia chose to fight. Not much is known about their combat, but the outcome is agreed upon. Both women were mortally wounded. They lay beside each other and died breaths apart. It is unknown who died first, and the outcome of their *Eligere* fight is still a mystery to this day."

"Let's review." Wes said, stretching her hands upwards, causing her shirt to come untucked and reveal the skin of her lower abdomen. It was odd practicing at this time of the day, Scholar Tiunda had dismissed them extremely early. Will was still in school and only an occasional worker was seen about the property, it felt like they were weirdly alone for the first time. Not to mention the midday sun shone down on them making it feel twice as hot.

Wes stepped forward and struck, quick and fast as per usual. Rhyatt blocked her and counter-attacked. To his surprise he moved with ease, Wes deflected him and launched a counter attack, not giving him much time to gloat. Her counter attack was a move he'd seen her use but she had never instructed him how to block it. When her sword smacked him he grimaced.

"You're a quick learner." She stated, pulling her weapon away, "Ready to learn something new?"

Rhyatt nodded, "Always."

"When I go low, you go low as well." She positioned her sword to gently touch the outside of his thigh. "But be careful; if you go too low, I will have the upper hand." She motioned for him to position his sword under hers, and he followed her instructions. "The key is finding balance, so that way you can block and prepare a counterattack."

Rhyatt nodded and tried to push her sword up and away, but she held steady. He glanced up and she was making eye contact with him, a smirk on her face.

"What're you playing at Wes?" he asked, his sword still underneath hers, as he cocked an eyebrow.

"Just waiting on you to push me off." She pressed her sword down harder.

Rhyatt rotated his wrist and pushed upwards, to his surprise she released easily and backed up. She gave him no break as she launched back at him, the wooden sword coming at him hard and quick. He blocked and attempted a counter attack, she blocked easily and went back to being relentless.

Blow after blow, she continued. To his credit, he kept up, only stumbling once. She went on like this until sweat began to coat the both of them. Rhyatt hated this humidity, it always made him sweat like a pig, like he was in constant need of a shower. Wes must have been feeling the same about the sweat dripping down her face, she paused her assault to grab the front of her shirt and fan herself with it.

She pulled the fabric to and fro twice before muttering *fuck this* and began unbuttoning it before pulling the damp clothing off.

Rhyatt looked away as she took it off. But then it was off, and there was nowhere else to look. She wore her pants at her navel, and her brassiere covered most of her chest. Even so, there was more skin on display than he had ever seen of her. His eyes were drawn to the dark tattoos. Around her waist was a snake. It wrapped around her body, and above her navel, the snake bit its own tail. She turned and threw her shirt at the tree, revealing her back. In the center of her shoulder blades was a tattoo of a scorpion, its tail poised and ready to strike. Two deadly animals tattooed on a deadly woman.

"See something you like?" She asked, her eyebrows raised.

He blushed and looked away quickly, "Admiring your tattoos."

"As you should. They took hours."

Turning back to face her, he rolled his eyes at her confidence and began pulling his own shirt off. Her eyes were anywhere *but* his face.

"See something you like?" He asked, mimicking her confidence as he tossed his shirt aside.

"Matter of fact, I do." She replied, her eyes still southbound. Rhyatt resisted the urge to look away, instead waiting for her to finish.

"Do you like snakes?" She met his eyes. She was referring to the twin snakes tattooed on each of his shoulders.

"No."

She cocked an eyebrow and picked her sword back up. He could almost hear her next question.

"I don't like them, but I do think they are something to marvel at." He said as he picked his sword up.

She didn't speak again, instead she launched into an attack, this time she did the new move. Rhyatt didn't react quick enough, the sting of the wood slapping his bare skin made him hiss in response.

"Come on Rhy, you marvel at snakes, you must be prepared to strike like one."

His heart fluttered at the nickname, *Rhy*. He didn't know why, but it slowed him down. No one had ever shortened his name into a nickname, and coming from her, it sounded all the more sweet.

Distraction was Wes's friend. While he was still thinking of the nickname, she struck him again. He winced.

"Are you even paying attention?"

"Yes, I-" he paused, unsure how to explain that he had been so poorly distracted by a *nickname*.

"Here, let me show you." She lowered her sword and came to stand behind him, placing her hand over the top of his like she had the first day.

The shock happened again, only this time it was less on the first touch and more of a continued feeling. She wrapped her hand around his and her entire forearm laid flat against his.

She guided his hand down and then up. Her body pressed against his side as she showed him. Rhyatt knew he should be focused on the movement, but the only thing he could process was how her warm skin was pressed against him. He could only focus on how she was still slightly out of breath and how her chest moved up and down, touching him with every breath.

"I think I've got it." His voice came out gruff, but she didn't release him. He turned his head to look at her, and she was so close. Too close. He swallowed slowly, his thoughts lost.

She pulled away, biting her bottom lip before going to stand in front of him again.

"Let's see it then." her voice was low, almost threatening, but her face was calm, something else entirely.

Rhyatt lifted his sword and waited for her.

Will came home, and Cleo and Knox followed not too long after. Wes and Rhyatt excused themselves to wash up. Rhyatt finished before her and took his seat at the table, to his surprise only a pie sat on the table.

"Did I miss dinner?" he joked as he sat down next to Will.

"No." Will turned his bright eyes to him, "Wes insisted we have dessert first tonight. Rhina argued, but I kept quiet."

"You? You kept quiet?" Rhyatt teased and ruffled the boys' hair.

"Hey! I can be quiet when needed. I'm actually a great spy."

"I'm sure. What do you spy on? The barn animals?"

"Actually, I've overheard some interesting things." Will countered.

"Yeah? Did the cow whisper what a lousy neighbor the horse is?" Rhyatt joked. Will looked up to him, chin jutting out.

"No." He narrowed his eyes before motioning for Rhyatt to move closer. Rhyatt obliged, and Will whispered in his ear, "I've seen Peni and Leroy kiss."

Rhyatt leaned away and laughed. He didn't know the couple but still said, "Good for them."

"Zonny also sings to the horses as he feeds them," Will said loud enough for the table to hear.

"Are you spilling everyone's secrets, Will?" Wes asked as she entered the room, gliding to her spot.

"Nothing important," Will responded, sinking into his seat.

Wes eyed him briefly and then picked up the pie in the middle, cutting and serving it.

"Why pie first?" Knox asked, accepting his slice.

Wes grinned and looked up to Rhyatt, "Because sometimes we all need a little change."

She winked at him and continued serving the dessert.

WILL

Will had been working on a flower crown for his sister for the better part of the hour. Rhyatt had shown him how to make one, twisting the stems around each other and knotting them. He had done the last four knots without Rhyatts' help. He had left early, saying to let Wes know he would be back soon.

Wes and Cleo joined him as he was working. Wes plopping down on the ground closest to him, Cleo on the other hand took her time sitting gracefully. Will disliked that about Cleo. She acted like a princess, too afraid to get dirty.

"You seem to have taken a liking to Rhyatt," Cleo said softly. Will also disliked that. So soft-spoken.

He shrugged, "He's okay."

What Will didn't say was that Rhyatt was quickly climbing the list of his favorite people. He passed Knox and Cleo quickly, but now he was above even Rhina. Wes's 'dessert before dinner' had allowed her to keep the number one spot, but Rhyatt was certainly competing for it.

"He's more than okay if you ask me," Cleo replied, folding her arms in front of her.

"Good thing no one asked you," Will replied, a childlike grin growing.

"Will," Wes warned.

He put his hands up in defense, "I'm just joking."

Cleo raised her eyebrows, a peaceful look on her face, obviously unbothered by Will's remarks. She was hard to bother like that. "You've got too much of your sister in you."

Will dipped his head and refocused on the flower crown, a proud grin prowling his features. Some people compared him to his sister as a compliment, others used it as an insult. But the older he got, the prouder he became to be compared to her. Someone had once made the mistake of comparing him to his father. He had been kicked out of school for a week. He took the comparisons to Wes and wore them like a badge of honor.

He twisted and tied another two flowers together, remembering how Rhyatt had shown him. He looked up at his sister's big head. Two more flowers and it would be done.

His little fingers worked diligently around the flowers. Twisting and tying them carefully.

Wes checked her watch again, "Where did Rhyatt go again?"

"He said Lita and Adriel would be out of town, so he has to feed the chickens."

"And how long ago did he leave?"

Will sighed and looked down at the crown, "About four flowers ago."

It was Wes's turn to sigh.

"I'm going to walk over and see if he's still training today." She pushed to her feet and looked at both Will and Cleo. "Do you all want to come?"

"Yes," Cleo said, rising.

"No. Wait!" Will said, his fingers working faster, "I'm almost done with the flower crown!"

Wes paused, and he tied the final knot, making the crown a complete circle.

"Here," he said, pushing to his feet. Wes bent at the waist so her head was level with him. He gently put the flower crown on her head. Pushing the white circular flowers down against her dark hair. His sister smiled at him, a soft smile, the one he liked to see. He couldn't stand how soft Cleo was, but when Wes was soft, he became softer too.

"Thank you Will." She said, straightening up and gently touching the flowers, admiring them.

Will beamed back at her, "Don't lose it!" he called as she and Cleo began to walk towards the road.

WES

They had just cleared the drive when Cleo looked over at Wes and smiled.

"Do you think he knows they are weeds and not flowers?"

"Oh, don't ruin the boys' fun. You're just jealous that I got a crown and you didn't." Wes teased back, the crown of weeds situated across her brow.

"Very much so." Cleo responded, and they continued walking for a few steps before she added, "Any updates about the journal?"

Wes knew she meant who to trust with the journal. And no. There were no updates because Wes had not done any digging this week. She found that every time she tried, it just reminded her of Jaze, and at that moment, she couldn't think of him for too long without all of her thoughts turning to him. It was just too much, but Cleo would never understand.

"No updates. I'm going to talk to Scholar Tiunda soon."

"Are you going to tell her?"

"Of course not. But she is the most knowledgeable and trustworthy Scholar I know."

"I know." Cleo said, shaking her head, "Just be careful what you say to her. She may get suspicious."

Their boots crunched against the dead leaves lining the road, and the bugs picked up their afternoon song.

"So what? Even if she does, we can trust her."

"I know you like her a lot, Wes, but that doesn't mean she can be trusted."

Wes rolled her eyes. "You don't know her like I do Cleo."

"Yes, Wes. My family isn't as privileged to have connections to the entire town like yours does."

"That's not what I meant. You've had just as many opportunities to get to know her as I have. It's not my fault you didn't-"

Wes cut herself off and stopped cold in her tracks.

"Stop." She whispered to Cleo.

"What now?" Cleo asked, stopping to turn and look at Wes. The look on her face must've been enough to let Cleo know it was serious because she froze, holding eye contact with Wes.

The entire forest had gone quiet. Not even a bird chirped in the distance. The insects, who had been singing at the top of their lungs only moments ago, were now quiet. The forest had gone still and nothing good came out of the quiet.

"Something's wrong," Wes whispered.

"What is it?" Cleo whispered back, her brow furrowing in worry.

"Listen." Wes instructed. And they both paused, their eyes moving but bodies still. There was no sound, the entire forest had decided to quiet down. But then there was noise. A whimpering of sorts. It came from just beyond the tree line. Both women turned towards it.

"It's probably a jungle cat. We should go." Cleo stated but didn't move.

Wes shook her head. It was something else. Something was terribly wrong, and it was making her stomach turn. Wes looked back to the trees, straining to see anything. The trees were too dense, and the world too quiet. She looked back at Cleo. Cleo shook her head and mouthed, 'No'. But Wes had already made up her mind. Pushing her breath out, she drew her sword and stepped toward the tree line. Cleo, a true friend, rolled her eyes and followed.

Ten steps away from the road, the whimpering came again, and this time, it was closer. They paused, the hair on the back of Wes's neck standing up. The women looked at each other once more, speaking without words, before altering their path to head towards the whimpering.

Cleo did not wear her sword frequently and instead pulled the small dagger at her hip. They slowed, the only sound was their breathing.

Then they saw it.

Half hidden behind a tree was an animal. A skinny brown hind leg poking out.

They split up, both swinging wide to avoid being seen by the animal.

Wes was the first one to see the animal. It lay in a pool of its own blood, a red trail leading in the opposite direction.

"It's Rhyatt's dog," Wes called out, coming closer to the poor animal.

"Rhyatt has a dog?"

Wes shook her head and inched closer, "It's not actually his. He just feeds it."

"Something mistook it for dinner," Cleo said, joining Wes in front of the dog.

The scraggly dog had seen better days to begin with, but it looked raggedy today. Its short brown fur was damp and splotchy, covered in blood. Its eyes darted to the women, and it let out another whimper.

Wes told herself not to look away, but when the animal's eyes met hers, she moved her head involuntarily. She was still focused on a tree in the distance when Cleo sighed and asked, "Should we put it out of its misery?"

Wes's eyes darted to her friend's face. Wes knew the circle of life better than anyone. Countless farm animals have passed over the years. But she couldn't help being worried about Rhyatt. It wasn't exactly Rhyatt's dog, but he had made sure to feed the thing twice a day since arriving. The damn dog barely left Rhyatt's side whenever he was outside.

"If we don't do it now, it will only suffer," Cleo added, sensing her discomfort. "You see how much blood it's lost, whatever did this will come looking for it soon. Better a quick death now."

Wes thought for a moment. She wished she could go and get Rhyatt, let him say goodbye. A selfish part of her wished he would come and do it. But she knew wishing only got you so far, no one ever came to save you from doing the hard things. You had to do them yourself.

"Knife." She reached a flat palm towards Cleo.

"I can do it." Cleo turned her chin up, a facade of bravery.

Wes shook her head. The offer was nice but she knew if it was carried through Cleo would have nightmares for weeks. This was something Wes could bear.

The warm metal of the knife soothed her hand. She inched forward, talking to the dog in a low voice.

"Shh. It's okay." She kneeled down, using her free hand to caress its dirty fur, "It's all going to be okay." She ran her hand down again, noticing the lack of wounds.

A moment later, it was done, and the dog stilled.

Wes removed the knife and cleaned it in the nearby grass. Standing and still looking down, she returned the knife to Cleo.

"Turn it over so we can see what happened."

Wes turned her head to glare.

"Rhyatt is owed an explanation," Cleo added, and Wes knew she was right, but to her, it felt that *Cleo's curiosity* wanted an explanation.

Wes bent down before she could argue back or make excuses. Her hands shook as she reached for the animal, gently turning it.

She paused, there were no teeth marks, no scratches. She pulled the animal over further and then saw it. A black hilted knife was wedged in its ribcage.

Her mind jumped to and fro on different conclusions.

She turned to tell Cleo what she had found when it caught her eye.

The trail of blood.

It came from the direction of Rhyatts' house.

"Rhyatt." She whispered as her feet led her towards him.

RHYATT

"Tell us their names and what was in the journal, then we'll leave. You can continue your safe little life in Jorjin. No one has to know we were ever here." The shorter of the men sneered.

Rhyatt stared back at them stony-faced. His attackers were not the smartest. The only reason they had gotten the better of him was because he was playing with the dog and hadn't heard them sneak up.

He strained against the restraints on his wrists, firmly putting his hands out of use behind his back. He was just thankful that they had brought him outside to beat him. At least Lita wouldn't have to clean up the mess. He rocked from one knee to the other, annoyed at the rock that dug into his right knee.

"Hit him again." The shorter one told the big, burly one.

And sure enough, the big one hit him. It was more of a back-handed slap, sending his head to the side and the blood from his nose slinging across the grass.

Gross.

"Just tell us. We don't have all day." Shorty said

"I told you." Rhyatt spat at Shorty's feet. "They paid me when we got back, and the only thing that was in the bag was clothes and jewelry."

Rhyatt was getting very irritated. Stupid and Stupider had been 'interrogating' him for the past ten minutes. It was more of just getting bitch slapped by Biggy.

"Don't lie." Shorty almost screamed. Apparently, he was irritated too. "We saw you with her. You knew her."

"Protecting your new toy is only going to make it worse Rhyatt," Biggy added calmly, folding his arms across his chest. "Tell us names, and we promise to take them alive."

"I don't know," Rhyatt said through clenched teeth. That was one thing for certain. He wasn't telling them any names. Not even fake ones. He didn't want the satisfaction to cross their face.

Biggy looked back to Shorty. Shorty nodded in confirmation, and Biggy raised his hand again.

"Are you boys looking for me?" A sweetly sultry voice came from the trees.

Wes stepped out of the trees, her hands held out, showing off herself. A crown of white flowers sat in her dark hair.

"Wes," Rhyatt whispered, fear and adrenaline pumping through him.

Both men turned towards her, a hungry look in their eyes.

"This must be the pretty little bitch who broke Finso's leg," Shorty said, casting an evil look at Biggy.

Rhyatt struggled against his restraints, rage coursing through him as they called her names.

"She fits the description. Rhyatt picks well, doesn't he?" Biggy added with a slow laugh.

"Let's keep her alive and take her back for our own *personal testing*."

Wes took another step forward, her smile shifting as she tilted her head down.

"Come and take me boys."

Her sword was pulled from her sheath in the blink of an eye, and she ran forward, all the hell's rage in her eyes.

Rhyatt had seen some of her fight in Duran, her fight in class, and her brawl with Knox. But this was different. It felt *personal*. She advanced with no fear in her eyes, just rage. If Rhyatt hadn't been seething with anger, he might've felt sorry for the men. Now, all he felt was a pang of excitement at the goddess of a woman running in his direction.

Biggy was closer and had his knife in front of him, ready to attack Wes. She gained on him, and when she was in range, he swung his knife at her. She ducked. Her sword scraped his knees, red blood spilling onto the green grass.

Shorty's eyes widened at the bloodshed, and he began to walk towards them.

It was when Shorty began to walk Rhyatt noticed movement from the left side of the tree line. As Shorty walked further away the movement increased. Then he saw Cleo, running towards him on the blind side of Shorty.

"What the hell is going on?" She asked as she stopped in front of him, a dagger in her hand as she began to cut through his bindings.

Rhyatt meant to help; he meant to talk, but the only thing he could focus on was Wes.

Wes stood to the side of Biggy, he was too big to move quickly and Wes used that to her advantage, darting around him. Her eyes flashed to Shorty approaching her, he had pulled two blades out, and a feral grin crossed her face.

Quick as lightning, she darted to Biggy's side, the hilt of her sword connecting with the side of his head. Like a sack of potatoes, he crumpled to the ground.

Shorty was in range now. Stepping away from the unconscious body, the two began to circle each other. Two jungle cats circling, deciding who would be dinner.

Shorty attacked first, he lurched forward and Wes moved out of the way, striking back. What he lacked in height, he made up for in skill. He blocked her and attacked again. Her feet moved quickly, switching from offensive to defensive. She blocked his blow but didn't push him away. She let him get closer, then her lips moved. Whatever she whispered, it only made the man angrier.

Rhyatts restraints were cut free, and with the use of his hands, he pushed himself to his feet, ready to help. Cleo must've sensed his intentions because she reached out, the dagger in her hand, hilt facing him.

He grabbed it and rushed towards the pair, who were once again circling each other. His eyes briefly connected with Wes, that rage still burning.

Shorty swung at her side, but instead of blocking, she stepped away. Only she was too slow.

The tip of his sword scraped her arm, her dark shirt turning wet. She didn't glance at it.

While he was still off balance, she rotated, getting close enough to knock one of his swords from his hands.

It had been a sacrifice.

With only one sword, the man seemed off balance. He attacked again, and Wes sidestepped, a laugh bursting out of her.

"This is it?" She asked him.

Rhyatt was close to them now, but the man still hadn't noticed.

Rhyatt reached his hand up, ready to slit the man's throat.

The man darted forward, reckless with abandon. But Wes was waiting; as his sword was extended near her hip, she stepped closer, her sword slicing the inside of his wrist.

His weapon dropped to the ground, and Rhyatt wrapped his arm around him, pulling him close.

He drew his dagger across the man's throat, his lifeblood spilling into the grass and onto Wes's boots.

He crumpled.

It was just Wes left. Her chest rose and fell rapidly, the feral grin on her face fading as she looked at him.

They stood there, saying nothing but understanding everything.

Behind them, Cleo let out a loud gasp.

The pair turned quickly to see the same man from the alley now had his arm wrapped around Cleo's shoulder, a knife pressed to her throat.

"Stay where you're at, and I won't hurt her." He called, his voice unsteady.

"What do you want?" Wes replied. Her voice, on the other hand, was neutral.

"Just some information. That's all I need. Information."

Wes nodded her head, "What would you like to know?" She stepped forward, standing on Rhyatts' right side. He felt her elbow brush against his arm.

"I said *stay back*." The man called again. He was nervous.

Wes stuck her sword into the ground and held up her empty palms. "What would you like to know?" She repeated.

Rhyatt began to sweat at the deadly calm that had taken her over. Only a moment ago, she had an entire inferno raging behind her eyes; now he looked at her, and she breathed steadily. Her back was straight, her face calm.

"What was in the bag?" The man shook Cleo, "What was in the traitorous scum's bag?"

Rhyatt was close enough to see a muscle in her neck flinch. Despite that she responded in the same calm tone.

"A journal."

"Have you read it?"

"I've read enough."

"Then you know what I must do." He pulled his hand away and lowered it to Cleo's stomach.

A gentle clopping of hooves sounded from the direction of the road.

Panic flooded Cleo's features, and the man holding her looked to the road, looking for the sound.

The slight distraction was enough to set Cleo into action. She stomped her foot down on top of his and slammed her head back into his nose. His hand wielding the knife jerked across her abdomen, a gash in her clothing and skin appearing. She bent at the waist in pain.

Cleo gasped, and Rhyatt felt Wes take the knife from his hand. A second later, the knife was being hurtled through the air.

There are many ways to describe the sound of a knife entering a man's skull. But the sound of a knife entering the eye socket has no words. Rhyatt flinched.

The man seemed to fall in slow motion, his face stuck in a horrified 'O' as he fell to the ground.

When his body hit the ground time seemed to speed up, but instead of returning to normal it seemed faster.

Before he knew it, he and Wes were over Cleo, helping her. The horse from the road had been Knox coming to check on them. He joined them, his skilled hands assessing her wound.

"It's fine." Cleo gaped, "Not that deep, just painful." She clamped her teeth together as Knox shook his head.

"It needs stitches," Knox replied, his mouth set in a firm line as he wrapped an arm around her, preparing to help her up.

"Take her to the house. Rhina will get you supplies."

Knox nodded, a frown setting into his mouth.

The three of them helped hoist Cleo into the saddle; she winced as Knox joined her. Clutching her stomach, they rode off towards the house, leaving Wes and Rhyatt alone in the bloody aftermath.

Wes stood still, staring at the spot they had last seen Cleo.

"She's going to be okay," Rhyatt said, following her line of vision.

"I know," Wes said.

Rhyatt turned away from her, sensing she didn't want his attention on her. Instead, he surveyed the lawn, which looked like a battlefield. The man from the alley had a pool of blood growing around his head; he was face down. Shorty was also lying in a pool of his own blood. The only difference was the splatters in front of him. Biggy, however, had no blood around him, and his chest still rose and fell.

"That one is still alive." Rhyatt motioned to Biggy.

Wes turned and looked at him, her face hardening. Tilting her chin up, she responded, "We'll have to do something about that."

She walked towards the man with the knife in his eye. Using the toe of her boot, she flipped him over. Rhyatt saw the beginning of the grimace before she turned her body away from him. Her face out of sight, she pulled the knife from his eye socket. A sickening suction sound came from the dead man. As much as he wanted to look away, he didn't. He focused on her back as she pulled the knife and then wiped it in the grass. When she turned around, her face was once again made of stone. She walked towards the still-breathing man, and Rhyatt met her there.

"It feels wrong to kill a helpless man," Rhyatt muttered, his stomach turning at what was about to happen.

"It does." She said, no hint or remorse in her voice. "But if we let him live, he will only lead someone else back to you. Back to your home. Where your family lives." She paused before adding, "No strings left uncut." Her tone was one of finality.

Rhyatt nodded. It had been a stroke of luck that they had found him in the first place. If none of them survived, then his family would be safe. He would be safe. Maybe this man didn't deserve to die, but his family deserved to live.

"Help me flip him." She said, interrupting his thoughts.

Together they flipped the large man onto his back, his head lulled to the side but he did not stir.

Rhyatt held out his hand for the knife, "I can do it."

Wes waved his hand away, "I got you into this mess. I plan on getting you out."

She bent down quickly, eager to be done with it. She pressed the knife to his throat. But she paused. It was a fraction of hesitation. He had never seen her hesitate. She was always so sure of everything she did.

"Can I say a prayer?" Rhyatt asked. He wasn't particularly religious.

Wes moved the knife away from his throat but stayed crouching. He saw the slightest sag in her shoulders as she nodded.

"For though you are of flesh and bone, your soul will find its peace in death. May the gods lead you to the heavens and forsake you the journey of the hells."

Rhyatt recited the prayer of the dying he had heard at executions in the City. Wes blinked, her jaw clenching. She jerked the knife across his throat, and red began to flow from his neck.

Rhyatt felt stuck again. He wanted to look away. So badly he wanted to look away. But as long as she was looking, he felt like he had to look as well. She confirmed he was dead, and he allowed himself to look away.

His heart pounded. It seemed only seconds ago he had been on his knees awaiting his untimely death. The woman before him seemed unflinching. She hadn't batted an eye throwing a knife into a man's eye.

"Let's take him to the woods. We'll bury them there." She bent again and wiped her blade in the grass.

Rhyatt nodded, his body going on its own accord. He thought of nothing as they lifted the still-bleeding man and carried him into the woods. He felt nothing as he saw his dog lying dead. He recalled the skirmish with the dog. But even now, seeing its dead body, he could feel nothing.

They walked back to the bloody field, he heard the crunch of twigs under his feet, but he felt none of it. He knew that sweat trickled down his back but it seemed distant, as if it was someone else's body. He heard Wes give him directions, but it was a dull sound in the back of his mind. He felt like a stranger watching someone else operate his body.

He was standing in front of Shorty. He was standing in front of the man whose life he had ended. When it had happened the only thing on his mind was vengeance. Vengeance for holding him captive. Vengeance for talking to Wes that way. But now his mind slowed, all the gritty details coming back to him.

He remembered how the hilt of Cleo's knife had felt foreign in his hand. It was too smooth and polished. Only ever been used as a default. Wes had held out from killing the man for him. Their eyes had connected, and she had known. The man had lost his sword when Rhyatt wrapped his arm around the man and pressed the knife to his neck. But Rhyatt hadn't hesitated like Wes. The knife had moved smooth, like butter. It wasn't until he had seen the blood on the ground and her boots that he felt his body relax.

The smoothness of the knife cutting flesh replayed in his mind. The weight of the knife. How easily it moved. Flesh wasn't supposed to cut like that. It had been so easy. It had been too *easy* to end a life.

Rhyatt had taken a life.

He had ended someone's life.

And he had done it like it was nothing.

He hadn't hesitated.

Rhyatt didn't realize he had closed his eyes until he reopened them. He was on his knees, the man he had murdered a few paces away. How had he gotten here? He looked up to see Wes, her eyebrows furrowed in question and concern.

He looked down and saw the body again.

His breath became ragged and irregular. No matter how hard he tried, he couldn't get enough air.

"Rhyatt," Wes said, her voice was distant, like she was underwater.

He knew he should get up, but his legs turned to lead, anchoring him to the spot. He closed his eyes, trying to get the image of the body in front of him out of his mind.

It didn't help. With his eyes closed, he could *feel* the knife in his hand again. He opened his eyes and gasped. But all he could smell was blood. Since when was the smell of blood so bad? Rhyatt stopped breathing. Maybe it was the fact that it was human blood. He began to take shallow, shaky breaths through his mouth.

He closed his eyes again, trying to focus on anything but the body in front of him.

Breath. Damn you breath. He commanded himself, but it didn't work.

After a moment he felt a hand on his shoulder and another on the back of his head. He opened his eyes to Wes kneeling in front of him. She pulled him into her chest. He went willingly. His head rested on her chest, her chin perched on top of his head. Gently, her arms wove behind him, holding him tightly to her. After a moment he wrapped his arms around her, pulling her closer. He grabbed a fistful of her shirt and held tightly.

"You're okay." She whispered to him, her voice softer than he had ever heard it be. It was enough to make him pause, his breath suspended.

She whispered it again, "You're okay."

Then, her voice was all he could focus on. It was the only thing that mattered at this moment.

"You're okay, Rhyatt." She moved her hand so it was tangled in his hair. "You're okay."

Softly, she began stroking his hair. His focus switched to a tree in the distance. His cheek was pressed against the bare skin of her chest, and he could hear her calm and steady heartbeat. He breathed in as she repeated the phrase to him again. This time, he didn't smell blood. He smelt the salt from her skin and the light tones of honeysuckle from her perfume. His breathing became less labored as she stroked his hair and whispered to him.

He released the fist he had made in her shirt, and they sat in silence. The warmth and weight of her arms grounded him. He inhaled again, taking in her scent. And they continued to sit like that, no words being passed, just the soothing touch of one another.

When a sense of guilt crept into him, he removed his arms and removed his cheek from her now sticky chest. He leaned away and opened his mouth to apologize, but she spoke first.

"Go get a drink and return with two shovels." Although her voice was still soft, it allowed no room for arguing.

Without any protest, Rhyatt did as he was told. Returning with the shovels, he saw the second body had been moved. All that remained was the man with the missing eye.

He nodded a thank you to her.

WES

Two shovels and three bodies later, Wes and Rhyatt arrived under the large tree where she had killed the dog. It was dusk and in the forest it seemed darker. Her eyes struggled to adjust. The birds had already quieted and the only sound was the crickets and the toads singing their night song.

"I'm sorry about your dog." She said as her shovel dug into the damp ground.

Rhyatt said nothing, still visibly shaken. He dug his shovel into the ground and they began a rhythm, working together on one mass grave. Their boots clinked against the metal of the shovels as they worked. In no time, the sun had completely set, leaving the pair in darkness. Their eyes adjusted as the moon rose and peeked through the canopy of the trees. She had purposely not brought a lantern for fear of people seeing them from the road.

They worked in silence, sweat dripping off of them as they pulled shovel after shovel of dirt out of the hole. The grave was halfway done when Wes stopped for a moment, using the bottom of her shirt to wipe the sweat dripping off of her face.

She looked at Rhyatt, he continued to work, absorbed by the task in front of him. She thought he didn't notice but a second later he spoke.

"I've never killed anyone." He admitted without turning his head or breaking his rhythm.

Wes nodded, even though he couldn't see it. "I'm sorry I got you into this mess, Rhyatt. But I swear it, I'll get you out of it. No matter what."

He said nothing for a moment, continuing digging.

"Have you killed someone before?" he asked, his shovel going down harder than normal.

Wes's features shifted.

"Yes." She said simply before returning to digging.

Rhyatt paused and turned to face her, but she had already picked up her shovel. He waited for an explanation, but he could keep waiting. Wes wasn't ready to dig those skeletons out of her closet yet. Besides, he wouldn't understand.

They worked in silence once more, pausing once when someone passed by on the road. They likely couldn't hear them over the clopping of their horse's hooves, but they aired on the side of caution.

"This is deep enough." Wes said, the sweat poured off the both of them in droves. Although the sun had set, the night hadn't cooled yet. Rain was on the horizon and it made the air feel sticky.

Rhyatt stabbed his shovel into the ground and turned, walking towards the dog.

"No." Wes said and he stopped, turning to look at her. "Men first, then dirt, then the dog."

"You think so lowly of them you would put them beneath the dog?"

A grim smile formed in the corner of her mouth. She wanted to laugh, but instead, she smiled. Rhyatt's shoulders relaxed as he watched her and waited for an answer.

"Yes, but that's not the reasoning." She said, moving to the larger man's body and grabbing his wrists.

"Oh?" Rhyatt asked, his voice light and free of all the worries it had carried all night. He bent and grabbed the man's ankles.

"It's a safety net." She said as they worked together to lift the body. They tossed it into the grave.

"If anyone comes around and decides to do some digging- literally- all they will find is a dog."

They lifted the shorter man a lot easier and tossed him into the grave rather violently.

"Do I even want to know how you know to do this?" Rhyatt asked, a grim sort of amusement entering his voice.

"If I tell you, I'll have to kill you," she replied with a wink.

Something about her wink broke free any remaining worries between the pair. Rhyatt moved and stood at the top of the grave, holding his arms out wide.

"I'll save you the trouble of digging another grave if you promise to do it quickly."

Her white teeth shone in the moonlight as a laugh escaped her. It had been so long since someone had joked with her like this. It seemed lately everything was so serious. But it was different around him. He smiled and made light of situations that otherwise would have been difficult.

"Unfortunate for you," she said as they picked up the last body, "I think we're even as far as favors go. I would have no qualms killing you however my heart desires."

Together, they tossed the body into the grave.

"Oh, you've been keeping score of our favors?" He asked, his tone playful.

"And you haven't?"

"No. Remind me of the scores, then?"

She raised her eyebrows at him as they began shoveling dirt into the grave.

"You're serious?" she asked.

"I'm always serious with you."

She rolled her eyes but told him anyway, "You are Will's mentor, in exchange, I am tutoring you."

"Mhm."

"You agreed to take me to Duran City, and I do believe me saving your ass back there is payment enough."

Rhyatt laughed, and it was the sweetest sound she had heard him make.

"Saving *my* ass?"

"Yes. That is what we call it when one person gets another out of a bad situation." Wes tilted her chin up in mockery.

"Alright smartass." he shook his head with a smile as he threw another shovel of dirt in the grave. "What if we weren't even anymore?"

Wes looked up at him, "We haven't been squared away for an hour, and you're ready to climb back into bed with me?"

Rhyatt looked away, and even in the dark, she swore she saw a blush creep into his cheeks.

"I was hoping to teach you how to fight."

"I know how to fight," she said with a smirk.

"I was hoping to teach you how to fight *without* the sword."

She raised her eyebrows, but he cut her off.

"And without a knife."

"So with what? My fists?" She asked.

"Yes, you are already skilled in many ways. I thought you might want to add another."

"How old fashioned."

"In Duran, there is a lot of money to be made in the fighting rings."

"Oh, is that your plan? Train me and stick me in a fighting ring to make you money? It sounds like I will be in debt to you."

Rhyatt paused his shoveling to look at her, "This can be your favor to me so that I will owe you."

She only raised her eyebrows and made a humming noise.

Rhyatt shrugged sheepishly, "I need a sparring partner."

Wes considered, she was decent in a fight but she had always had a knife handy. It would be a good advantage to have another skillset in her arsenal.

"And you would actually spar with me?" She questioned.

He nodded, "After some training, you would be an equal opponent."

"Equal? Ha. More like superior."

He laughed, the type of laugh that comes from your belly, and Wes almost asked him to do it again. She didn't know why, but that little laugh of his was so sweet. It was even sweeter when it was she who had made him laugh.

They paused their shoveling of dirt to move the dog into the grave. They placed him much more gently than the bodies. Once he was in the grave, they began to shovel dirt again. After a short silence, Rhyatt spoke, focusing on his task in front of him.

"I'm sorry I ever questioned you Wes. When we first started I knew you were talented, but even so, I didn't follow your instructions. I just didn't want to use my strength against you and hurt you." His body kept working as his words paused. "I don't want to hurt anyone."

A light sprinkling of rain began to fall, making its way through the canopy and onto them.

"We all make mistakes. It's how we atone for them that matters."

Rhyatt nodded, "So, will you be my sparring partner? Let me show you the error of my ways by teaching you better ways to kick my ass?"

"I would *love* to discover more ways to beat your ass." She replied.

Rhyatt smiled back at her as they put the last shovels of dirt on the grave. Perhaps it was more on her plate than she could handle, but it felt right. Anything with him felt easy.

RHYATT

Wes had led them down the path in the forest that had once connected her and Lita's house. Rhyatt wondered how long it had been since it was used. For the majority of the walk, they were in the knee-high foliage. When they crossed the creek onto the Blake's property, it lessened. She guided them around the thorn bushes, and in a few minutes, they were approaching the BlakeMoore from the right side.

Wes led them to the back door, all of the lights were off, except the kitchen. She opened the door soundlessly, Rhyatt followed after her.

Knox was standing in front of the sink with his shirt in his hands, exposing the pale skin of his back. There was a strange triangular pattern of bruises across his arms and back. If you focused, you could make out the white scars in the same shape. He didn't notice them entering and continued to scrub at the blood stain on his shirt.

"How is she?" Wes asked, pausing in front of the counter, her hands balled into fists at her sides.

Knox snapped his head to her, his eyes becoming slits as he looked her over. Both she and Rhyatt looked worse for wear. The speckling of blood had mixed with the dirt from digging the grave. Then, the sweat and rain had made them look like they'd crawled here.

"Rhina and I got her stitched up. It wasn't too deep, but it'll take her a while to heal. She was asleep before I even left the room." His lips were in a tight line, and his words were clipped.

"Thank you," Wes said and slumped against the island. Rhyatt stepped forward, placing his palms down on the island beside her.

"You should be happy that's all that happened," Knox replied under his breath.

But both Rhyatt and Wes heard.

"She told me everything that happened." Knox continued, the anger inching out. "She tried to cover you, but I could tell how *impulsive* you were. How *stupid* you were."

Out of the corner of his eye, he saw Wes turn ever so slightly away.

"Tell me Wes, what if there was more than one person out of sight? What if he hadn't wasted time asking questions? What if he would've slit her throat first? Why did you go in so unprepared? You didn't even tell her what you were doing. You are so much smarter than this, so why be so fucking dumb?"

"I was about to have my throat slit." Rhyatt interrupted. He sounded more aggressive than he meant to, but he had a real issue with Knox's tone.

"I don't care if it was *my throat* about to be slit," Knox said to Rhyatt before turning his attention back to Wes. "She got hurt because you ran in without a plan. You went in half-assed and didn't even say anything to her. Didn't tell her to run, to fight, *nothing*. She got hurt because of you. *That* is on your hands." He pointed to the bloody rags strewn on the counter.

Knox huffed, pulled his hand away, and went back to scrubbing his shirt in the sink. Rhyatt looked at Wes, waiting for her response. Instead, he found her face void of emotion. She stared absentmindedly at Knox's back. Rhyatt felt a twinge of sadness. The woman had buried three bodies with a grim smile on her face. Now, before her friend, she stood empty, quiet.

"It was my fault. She acted quickly and saved my life-"

"Don't care." Knox cut him off.

Rhyatt bristled, ready to say more than a few words to the hot-headed asshole in front of him. But Wes placed her hand over his, a gentle cease-fire.

She began unbuttoning her shirt and walking to the other side of the island where Knox was. Rhyatt felt himself tense up far more than he should. What was he preparing for?

"Can you stitch me up before you leave?" She asked, pulling off her dirty and drenched shirt. It slapped against the tiles when she dropped it.

Knox turned again; this time, his expression was different. Worry creased his eyes as he searched her exposed midriff. "You need stitches?"

"I think so." She placed her palms on the counter and jumped so she could sit on it facing him.

He dropped his shirt in the sink and stepped forward, his hand reaching gently towards a cut at her shoulder. He gently touched the skin around it.

"It's fine. Just bandage it." He said with dismissal and began to turn back to the sink.

"Will you look at this one too? I don't think it's too bad, but…" She trailed off.

Knox turned around again, annoyance radiating from him. Rhyatt, on the other hand, tensed, he had known about the cut on her shoulder but he hadn't seen her get a second one.

She leaned back and unlaced her pants, rolling the right side down to reveal a large open wound on her hip.

"You didn't think it was that bad? Are your godsdamned eyes broken?" Knox shouted at her.

Wes winced and shushed him. Rhyatt walked to the other side to get a better view. The cut was as long as his finger and looked deep.

"How have you not bled out?" Rhyatt asked.

She only shrugged in response.

"We just dug three graves, and the entire time you were missing a chunk of your hip." he continued, ridiculing her.

"It's a miracle you didn't pass out and fall into one of those graves," Knox added, and for the first time, Rhyatt agreed with him.

Wes rolled her eyes, "There were more important things to be done."

"You can't do anything if you're passed out from blood loss." Knox fired back.

"It really doesn't even hurt." Wes continued ignoring him.

"I don't see how." Rhyatt crossed his arms.

"Oh, it's going to hurt when I'm stitching it up," Knox replied with a wicked grin.

"Try not to sound so happy about it."

"No use in hiding my feelings," Knox said, pressing his fingers to the dark and angry flesh around the wound. Wes stared down at him.

"Get comfortable, this is going to take a minute." Knox instructed and she laid back onto the island counter.

"What can I do to help?" Rhyatt asked.

"Get me a bottle of rum," Wes replied, her eyes closing.

Rhyatt looked to Knox for approval; when he nodded, Rhyatt walked to the liquor cabinet. Opening the door, he pulled the first white rum he saw. He walked back to them, and Wes held out her hand for the bottle. Leaning forward, she uncorked it and took a long sip.

When she had taken a second sip, she grinned at Rhyatt, "For the pain." She extended the bottle to him.

To his own surprise, he took it and sipped.

"For the nightmares that are sure to follow," he replied as she took the bottle back.

She laid down once more, and Knox began to work, pushing the needle through her skin. To Rhyatts' surprise, she didn't wince or call out in pain. Even when Knox jerked the needle, she didn't make a noise; she only lifted her eyebrows briefly. She looked relaxed to all the world. Knox's large hands were nimble and worked quickly. The stitches were done in a matter of minutes. He was quicker than some of the professionals Rhyatt had seen. Wes lay there even as he cleaned the wound and dressed it.

"Keep it clean," Knox said, tossing his wet shirt over his shoulder and walking towards the door.

"And Wes?"

"Hmm." she hummed without opening her eyes.

"Use your brain next time."

He walked out the door, not giving her enough time to respond. She only laid still, her eyes still closed.

"Go to bed, I'll clean up," Rhyatt said, giving her knee a small nudge.

She nodded, and he set about cleaning up the kitchen. He piled up all the bloody rags, dumped the bloody water down the drain, and threw the extra thread away. He ran warm water and began washing the needles and basins that had been used. They would have to be sterilized later. After setting them out to dry, he gathered all the rags he had put into a pile earlier. He took them to the washroom and put them in a separate pile, not wanting to stain anything else.

When Rhyatt returned to the kitchen, Wes had sat up but still hadn't gotten down. He stood in front of her and crossed his arms, waiting for her to go to bed like a disobedient child.

She looked at him and with a roll of her eyes, jumped off the counter. Only her knees temporarily failed her and she began to buckle. Rhyatt reached out, grabbing her forearms to steady her. He noticed the shock wasn't as noticeable this time. Dulled even. It worried him.

"I may have lost more blood than I thought," she said, wincing.

Rhyatt furrowed his brows at her. The entire time she was getting stitches, she hadn't shown any sign of pain, but now, just standing, she winced.

"I'll walk you upstairs." Rhyatt said repositioning himself so one arm was wrapped around her, holding her up and close to him.

"I'm okay." She lied but leaned into him nonetheless.

They walked through the kitchen at a snail's pace. When they finally made it to the dark foyer, she paused in front of the steps and leaned onto the railing, resting her head on her arm. She was out of breath and trying to hide it.

"Godsfuck." She mumbled, looking at the staircase in front of her like it was a mountain. "I'll just sleep in the library."

"Let me help you," Rhyatt said, looking at her in the dark, but she didn't look back.

"Wes, can I help?" He asked again.

"What? Are you going to pack me up the stairs?" She looked back at him with an eye roll.

"If that's okay with you."

She looked left to right as if checking for someone. And then, reluctantly, she nodded.

He bent and scooped her into his arms. He didn't know what he expected would happen, but this wasn't it. She didn't cradle into his arms instantly like he'd imagined. She was tense and resembled dead weight. Less like someone being carried to bed and more like an unwilling farm animal. But she was warm, far too warm. And the spark between them turned into a current everywhere their skin touched, like something invisible being passed between them. He chalked it up to the adrenaline of the night and the fact that he had a growing attraction to the woman in his arms. Halfway up the stairs, he felt her relax and slump her head against his chest.

"Speak of this to no one." She tilted her head up and whispered.

A shiver went down his spine, "It's our secret."

He crested the top of the stairs and looked down the hallway at all the various doors.

"Which room?" he whispered in her ear.

"Third on the right." She whispered back, her eyes closed.

Rhyatt resumed walking towards her door, his large feet making soft thuds against the carpet. He stopped in front of the door, shifting her in his arms to reach the knob.

Walking into the room, he tried to hide his surprise. Her room wasn't at all what he'd expected. He'd pictured a neatly organized room with dead animals and weapons on display. Maybe dark, hard-edged furniture. Instead, it was a bit messy, with drawers half open and garments hanging out of them. Books and notes were scattered across the vanity that doubled as a desk. Elegant paintings hung on the walls, gilded in gold. Not a weapon nor a dead animal in sight. The furniture was soft, comfortable even. Well-loved chairs and a loveseat made a semi-circle around a fireplace. Rhyatt started to think it wasn't a reflection of her, but he stopped. Wes had many sides, and this was just another one, the most private one.

He walked to her unkempt bed and gently put her down. She sat up slowly and began to unlace one of her boots.

"Let me." Rhyatt bent on one knee and worked on the laces, until they were loose enough for her to pull her feet out. Half way through she laid back down, her heavy eyelids closing. He took the boots and placed them by her door.

"Pants." She muttered.

"Pants?" Rhyatt asked, heat coming to his cheeks instantly.

"Pull the ankles."

Rhyatt suddenly felt very nervous. With shaking hands, he gripped the ankles of her pants and gently pulled. She lifted her hips, and they slid off easily. He looked away quickly, not wanting to see her in her undergarments without her knowledge.

He folded them and placed them in the chair by the vanity turned desk. When he turned around her eyes were closed and she was still, her breathing evening out.

With careful steps, he walked to her bedside and pulled a blanket up to her shoulders. She hummed in response, snuggling deeper into the bed. Rhyatt couldn't help but feel like he had seen straight through to her core tonight. He had watched her react in pure rage. She had helped put him back together when he began to break. She had made jokes, making him feel better. And when she was getting yelled at by her closest friend, she simply took it in silence. And she hadn't winced or even shown an inkling of pain around others. It was only when she was alone with him that she had shown it. The facade she put on for everyone around her had faded completely when she allowed him to help her up the stairs. Rhyatt looked down, her face peaceful in the beginning of sleep. And a horrible thought rambled through him. How much of who she was was a facade? How much of it was put on, even around her friends?

Overcome with an emotion he could not name, he bent closer to her, pushing her hair out of her face.

"You're always safe to be yourself with me Wes. I don't know you that well, but I hope to know *you* more. I hope to know who you are when no one is looking."

He knew she was likely too far asleep to remember his words, but he hoped she understood. Hopefully, somewhere deep down, she understood. Because he had meant it, he had meant every word.

WES

Wes crossed the room and circled her arms around Jaze. She stared into his eyes, knowing this was the last time she would hold him. He was going to die. And in some strange way, he knew it as well.

She closed her eyes and pulled him closer, resting her head against his chest. She smiled. He was warm and felt like home. She listened to the steady beat of his heart. This was the last time she would hold him, but that was okay.

When she opened her eyes again he was gone and she was standing on the back side of the barn she had just been in. Her body moved of its own accord, she looked down and understood this was not her body, it was a man's body. In her hands she held a large metal pitcher, the contents inside were clear and had a sweet smell.

She watched as the body she occupied poured the liquid over the back side of the barn, spreading it out on the old boards. When the pitcher was empty, she pulled out a box of matches, lit one, and threw it at the barn.

The liquid lit on fire so quick and hot that she had to jump back. As soon as the flame touched where the liquid was, green flames erupted. In seconds, the entire barn was engulfed.

The body she occupied began to run away, then she heard it. A yell. A man yelling something over and over.

The man was Jaze, and he was yelling for Wes.

Wes awoke panting. The dream had felt too real. It hadn't felt like a dream at all. It felt like a memory. She pushed the covers off of her and rested her elbows on her knees, cradling her head.

It was just a dream. She told herself over and over.

After the fourth time, she stretched out, pushing aside the dream and opening her eyes fully.

Annoyance ebbed at her as she saw the state of her sheets. She had gone to bed muddy, bloody, and wet last night. It would take her half a day to clean the giant smeared stain. Her body was no better. There was dirt permanently lodged underneath her nails and blood smeared around the wounds. She looked like dammit, and felt even worse.

She rolled out of bed, staggering to the curtains. She opened them slowly, grimacing at the bright light and the shooting pain behind her eyes.

Staring out into the garden she watched Will's small frame move from bush to bush. She squinted her eyes and realized he was eating berries. Likely picking the biggest, ripest ones.

He was up early.

Wes checked the watch on her bedside table. Nevermind. She was up late.

She heaved a sigh and padded into her bathroom. On the bright side, the water would be warm from the sun. She stripped away the torn and dirty shirt, faint memories of being carried to bed resurfacing.

Gods. That was embarrassing. Her body had been so weak she couldn't make it up a single flight of stairs. What would others think if they knew?

Wes slipped her undergarments off before stepping into the off-white limestone tiled shower. She turned the faucet and waited for the water to begin spilling out of the overhead pipes. Stepping under the warm water, she sighed. She could stay under the steady stream half the day. And with the upgrade to the rooftop water tank, she actually could stay half the day. Last summer, she had traded the small tank for one the same size as the bunkhouses. The only true downside was that the water stayed hot constantly. In the dead heat of summer, she would have to pump cold water from the well and mix it with the hot water for baths. Both she and Will had opted to take partial baths in the creek instead. Until the heat became unmanageable, and algae grew, making the creek stink. But with the worst of summer behind them, they only used the water from the tank.

She closed her eyes and stood still, letting the water run in rivulets down her hair and face. The dream reappeared, and she snapped her eyes open, willing the images of Jaze to go away.

Scrubbing her nails, Wes tried to think of anything but his screams. They were fictional. She had been there, and he hadn't been screaming. Why was she so disturbed by something that wasn't real? Something that was a trick of the mind?

She took the rag and began to gently wash the wound on her hip. A dark thought crept in.

What if it wasn't a dream?

What if it was something different? Her body trying to make her remember something she forgot during her grief.

Wes walked slowly towards the garden district, the wet tips of her short hair creating dark splotches on the shoulders of her top. She didn't have a limp, but she feared if she walked too fast, she might develop one.

This time of year, the bright, colorful blooms had faded, and the various gardens were being thinned. They would remain green through the winter but not regain their fullness until spring.

Wes loved the smaller one story homes of the garden district, she could see herself and Will living in one of them one day. Their neighbors would all likely be old, but at least she wouldn't have to worry about the noise level like the block of apartments that housed the out of town university students.

Wes smiled at a woman she thought might be ten times her age before pushing the small gate open to the house with a light green wash. Tiunda's home was well polished in most aspects, the stone pavers were clean, the porch never dirty, but there was a row of wildflowers on each side of her house that grew unruly. Tiunda claimed the wilder they were the more it helped the bees.

Wes stepped onto the immaculate porch and raised her fist, knocking on the wooden door. Her knuckles were cut up again. They would be itchy until they healed.

Tiunda opened the door, her skin pale next to the warm wood. She smiled at Wes, not like the usual smile she gave all of her students, but something warmer. Wes's shoulders relaxed and she exhaled a breath. Cleo was wrong, Tiunda could be trusted.

"Looking to catch up on the last lesson you slept through?" Tiunda asked.

Wes opened her mouth to argue that she had not slept through the last lesson, and if she had, she had done the responsible thing and copied Cleo's notes. But she was working to be less *impulsive*, so she closed her mouth and redirected. Never mind the fact that coming to Tiunda in the first place might be impulsive.

"I need your advice."

Five minutes later Wes was seated on a pastel settee in the small but well lit living room. Tiunda bent to hand her a cup of steaming tea, loaded to the brim with honey and sugar, just the way Wes liked it. The scholar took the seat across from Wes in a pale green settee with an intricate brocade pattern. Despite the small home it was filled with light and potted plants, making it cozy.

"Is this to do with Mr. Greene?" Tiunda paused before quickly continuing, "If it is, I think you know my feelings."

"It's not the Greene you're thinking of," Wes replied, setting the hot tea on the table between the settees.

"Oh." Tiunda's neutral face faltered.

"There's more to his death," Wes found her voice caught in her throat. She swallowed, "When I got his last will, it contained a request."

Wes proceeded to tell Tiunda everything, well, everything she needed to know, which wasn't much in comparison. She clued her in on the journey to Duran and the attack but left out who was with her. She included that there were multiple objects in the safe but didn't say which one had further instructions. She included that Jaze was weary of those in power but left out that Wes herself was weary of the Commander. She left out the details of last night's attack and simply said that she feared others would be coming after her in the near future.

"Why are you telling me all this?" Tiunda asked, never one to beat around the bush.

"You believe dreams have meaning?" Wes asked.

"The universe has a way of relaying information when we are ready to know it."

"Last night, I had a dream about his death. One moment, I was in his arms, and the next, I was behind the barn, lighting it on fire. I poured a liquid on the boards, and when ignited, it went up in green flames." Wes paused, her head turning slightly so she wouldn't look Tiunda in the eye, "It felt *real*. It didn't feel like a dream, but rather a memory."

Wes leaned back into the cushions, her rigid back relaxing a fraction. Tiunda was the first person outside of her close friends to know the truth, and now she was the first person to know about the damning dream she had had.

Tiunda raised her teacup to her lips, slowly sipping the hot liquid. It was clear she was waiting for Wes to continue.

"What does it mean?"

"Ask me a question you don't already know the answer to," Tiunda said without missing a beat.

Wes proceeded to miss several beats and went slack jawed. She had forgotten that Tiunda was never one to give answers away, even in lectures she made them work for it.

"You believe the dream could be real." Wes landed on a statement.

"Perhaps."

"Was the person from the dream real?"

"I did not dream with you; therefore, I do not know."

Wes resisted the urge to roll her eyes and instead let out a loud sigh. Wes was here for a reason. She knew Tiunda believed in the things we cannot see and would understand her dream. She knew Tiunda wasn't questioning the legitimacy of her dream. Gods damn. Why was Wes here then? Just to tell someone about her issues? What question did Wes not have the answer to? She bit her inner lip, forcing herself to remember the dream and its details. Her eyes flicked upwards to Scholar Tiunda's patiently waiting blue gaze.

"What flame burns green?"

Tiunda smiled, "Finally, a question I can answer. At festivals, they burn copper to make green flames, but since your dream had a liquid, it was likely a newer product called Liquid Fire."

Liquid Fire. Wes had never heard of the substance.

"So it's a fire accelerant." Wes mused, "Where can it be bought?"

"To my understanding, It isn't being sold."

How was Wes supposed to track down a product that isn't sold locally? Unless...

"Who is making it then?"

"No one with half a brain," Tiunda moved her teacup in its saucer dish, "It can be extremely explosive."

"Then..." Wes trailed off, her mind whirling like the gears of a clock. Was her dream false? It couldn't be a lie. Wes hadn't known about the liquid before and had seen it as clear as day in her dream. Someone was making it and selling it privately. That was the only other option.

"What is it made out of?" Wes asked.

"Green Mountain Corn," Tiunda responded, her eyes twinkling.

Wes thought of the green corn that grew only in high elevations. It was mainly used for feeding animals. You always had to cover it and keep it cool; otherwise, the sun would heat it up, and it would begin to smoke and eventually light itself on fire.

"What else do I need to know?" Wes asked, sensing Tiunda wasn't telling her something.

"Only you know what you need," Tiunda responded.

"I *need* to know everything." Wes pleaded, then softened her voice, "Please Tiunda, tell me everything you know about Liquid Fire."

Tiunda raised a brow, consideration crossing her features.

"Knowledge is power, but it can also be dangerous, Wes. There is a reason Liquid Fire isn't being sold at the market, and there is a reason why you didn't know of its existence. The council works hard to cover up things that could put us in danger."

Wes stilled, her body going taught. The Council. They would know who had successfully created Liquid Fire. And if Wes could track who created it, then she could find who they sold it to and find out who lit the barn on fire.

Wes sprang to her feet, her body moving towards the door. A jolt of pain at her hip slowed her.

"Wes." Tiunda called and waited to speak until Wes turned, "Make Rhyatt do more offense with you; he is learning to defend just by training with you."

Wes winced. She figured Tiunda would eventually learn about their deal.

"How did you know?"

"Did you think I would not recognize your stylistic flairs?"

Wes nodded her head and walked out of the quaint home back to the lively streets and headed towards her home.

Alone with her thoughts, she began to think of the night the fire happened and the dream, how they were similar yet different. She began to think of his death and how the barn was lit on fire, how it wasn't an accident. It had been someone's plan to murder Jaze.

The horrifying reality crashed on her. The animals had all been let out, and the fire didn't start until he was alone. It didn't start until she was clear of the barn. It had also rained earlier in the day, which meant an accelerant would have to have been used. She breathed in deeply. The attack last night, they had known about the journal.

She kept her breathing even as the rage built. Someone who knew about Jaze's side job had killed him. They had burned him alive and used Liquid Fire to do it.

She gritted her teeth and began to plan. But first, she would have to tell Knox.

KNOX

Knox had been working in the field half the damn day when he heard the sound of hooves approaching. It had been a long morning. He had gotten back late last night, and luckily his father had passed out drunk. Unluckily, this morning, it meant he had to tend to the small field by his lonesome. He was pissed he had to do it, but at least he was doing it alone. His mother opened the shop today while his father slept off a nasty hangover.

He looked up to see Wes and Cleo riding Sugar, Wes's horse, towards him. They dismounted and started towards him on foot. When they were in range, he whistled at them.

"What did I do to get two pretty women calling on me while I'm workin'?"

"You almost done for the day?" Wes asked as they stopped in front of him.

He frowned slightly, "Yeah. Why? You two just couldn't stay away?"

"We just wanted to check on you," Cleo said, her eyes darting away from his gaze.

"Me?" he asked, looking back down. "It should be me checking up on you all. That's the most stitches I've done in one night in a while. How are they holding up?"

"Fine. Thank you again." Cleo said softly, her gaze still averted.

"Anything for you. Wes?" his voice edged as he turned to her.

Wes winced as Cleo turned on her. Her gaze swept her entire body.

"You needed stitches?" Cleo stepped towards Wes, her face contorted.

Wes's lip twitched before she grimaced and nodded.

Knox chuckled at Cleo's realization. The little rat Wes hadn't told her. "Serves her right too."

Wes rolled her eyes at him, "The alternative was worse. I'll take my injuries."

"It really just pains you to admit you're wrong, doesn't it?" Knox shot back before he could check his rage.

"Show me," Cleo said, stepping closer, cutting off his line of sight to Wes.

Wes huffed and began untucking her shirt from her pants. Once it was free, she unbuttoned the pants and rolled down the right side until the bandage on her hip was revealed. Cleo leaned in closer, and Knox stepped up to appreciate his handiwork.

She slowly pulled off the bandage, revealing the red and puckered skin. Surprisingly, it looked decent for only happening last night. The purple and blue bruises on her skin had looked worse yesterday.

"Why is it so bruised?" Cleo turned and asked Knox, but Wes responded first.

"It was a hard hit." She straightened and began putting the bandage into place.

Cleo backed away as Wes buttoned her pants again.

"You should've told me." She said to Wes, her face tight.

"Wouldn't have made a difference." She shrugged and began to look away but Cleo wasn't done yet.

"I wanted to know."

"I'll tell you next time."

"I hope there is no next time."

Knox slapped his hand against the tool in his hand, "I hope there is, and I hope it's more painful than the last."

"Thanks Knox. I can always count on you to wish me the best." Wes sneered.

"Always." he replied with a smile of his own, and picked up the tools around him, gathering them to head back towards the shed.

Wes stepped forward quickly, and her expression shifted, turning soft. His heart stalled. She was never soft.

"Actually," she stepped closer to him, "I did come here to talk to the both of you. And I'd prefer it to be in private."

Knox felt his face hardened into something serious, he glanced at Cleo and found a similar expression across her features.

Wordlessly the three friends stepped closer, forming a triangle, all within arms reach.

Wes exhaled a shaky breath and began, "I've been thinking about the night Jaze died. And the one thing I haven't been able to figure out is how fast the barn went up in flames. Even if it had started as I was leaving, it wouldn't have been as bad as it was when I ran back." She looked down and licked her lips before continuing. "All of the animals got out. And I. I was gone. I was gone before it started. We originally thought he was the one who let them out. But it doesn't add up. There were no casualties besides him. Why would he have gone back in with no one there?"

Wes broke and looked him in the eyes, "I think Jaze was murdered because of his side job with the journal. I think someone set the fire with an accelerant, Liquid Fire, and killed not only him but put to rest any secrets he had collected." Her words began to rush out of her, "I think whoever did it knew about the bank box but couldn't buy the bank teller off, so they just waited and watched until we finally showed up. When they couldn't get it in Duran, they used whoever recognized Rhyatt to bring them here. And that's why he was attacked last night. They knew about the journal. Whatever Jaze was doing is more serious than we thought."

Her hands were shaking at her sides as she paused and looked between the two of them, "I know the time for grieving is over. And I know saying this aloud makes it hard not to.. But you both deserved to know. And I'm sorry. I am so sorry." Her voice cracked on her last apology.

Cleo's eyes had gone wide while Knox's had set into slits. He took a step back, needing space to think. It made a clear barrier between him and his friends.

"You're telling me a sympathetic murderer waited until you were gone, then let the animals out before they killed a man?" His voice was louder than intended and echoed across the field.

"Yes. I think-" he cut her off before she could go into detail.

"Who would do that Wes? Do you hear yourself? It doesn't make any sense." Knox took another step back, his rage building as his hands balled into fists.

Cleo took a small step towards him, the balance of the triangle being thrown again. "Someone who would lose money if you lost money. Or even a fellow farmer. Just because they *had* to kill him doesn't mean they were heartless about it."

Knox crossed his arms at his chest, Cleo was right, he hated it but it all made sense. The immediate battle was lost, but many more raged inside him.

"Why the hell did you tell us this?" he asked.

"You deserve to know," she said with pity, and he sparked again.

"And what the hell are we supposed to do in the meantime? Guard Rhyatt because he helped us once?" He huffed at his own thoughts.

"What happened last night was pure luck mixed with bad timing. They won't be looking for him again. In the meantime, we carry on as normal. But we have to get this journal into the right hands for Jaze... That's why I'm going to start reading it."

"You really have lost your godsdamn mind." Knox unfolded his arms, his balled fists at his sides. He would not strike her first. He was not his father.

"It will give us insight on who to trust. If we've learned anything, it's that everyone is guilty until proven innocent."

Knox knew his rage was burning out of control. He opened his mouth and went for a low blow, even for him. "You really think you're hot shit because you were sleeping with him, and he chose to give you the journal, huh?"

He watched as Wes drew back, his words clearly hitting its mark. She seethed a deadly calm. "He asked me to do it because he didn't want either of you involved. He didn't want you in danger."

"And yet, look where we are," Knox said, stepping forward so that he and Wes were closer, only a hands width away.

"I should have never taken you with me." she snapped, shaking her head and attempting to step away. But Knox's arm darted out and gripped her at the elbow.

"And then where would you be, Wes? Dead. You'd be just as dead as him. You would've gotten attacked all the same, but *we*," he motioned to himself and Cleo, "Wouldn't have been there to save your ass."

Wes jerked her arm from his grip but didn't back away. "Is that what you want?" She yelled in his face, "For me to admit I need you both? Because I do. Is that what you want to hear?"

"What do I want?" Knox tilted his head back, and a dark chuckle escaped. "What I want doesn't matter. He's dead. And now you come here with that bullshit about reading the journal. You're going to end up just like him, burned to nothing but ashes."

He pushed past her, knocking her shoulder as he went.

"Knox," she called.

"Fuck off Wes," he replied without turning to face her.

WES

D<del>ear Diary,</del>
I was approached tonight by a man from out of town and offered a deal I couldn't resist. Not only would I be helping my country I would also be given 100 silver now and 50 silver every time I report. They wish for me to report weekly, and if my findings are good their pockets will be good to me. The job is simple, I am to go to Duran City and investigate a medical facility. They are located on the outskirts of the town, closest to Saint Saveen. My new employer gave me a map of how to get there using the canyons. Turns out they aren't as dangerous as I thought.

Yours truly,

Jaze G.

Monday morning, Wes was able to walk normally. The cut at her hip had been healing rather nicely. Her pants rubbing at it was the only bothersome thing about it now. Though she was starting to feel better physically, mentally she was tired. Telling Knox and Cleo had taken so much out of her. It had been a horrid enough realization for her, but his retaliation had drawn from her.

Furthering her exhaustion. It was because she was tired that she purposely walked fast, attempting to hide the worn look on her face. Her hustle had placed her at the university far earlier than normal. So early, in fact, that she didn't see Cleo nor Rhyatt. Only a few other people were inside. Without making a sound, she slipped inside the open door and silently plopped into a sole chair tucked into the shadows beneath the stairs. The three women talking nearby didn't glance her way. Good. She wasn't in the mood to make light conversation anyways.

From this angle, she had a great view of the door, and she was able to watch others enter without them seeing her. After a moment, more of her peers filed in. They didn't even glance at her. A small part of her was relieved that no one noticed her. She looked like shit. When Graham, a boy who wasn't very fond of her, came in the door and looked over her like she didn't exist, she got suspicious. Looking down, she realized she was wearing Warden's old shirt. It was brown and blended in with the wall. She smiled softly at her own accidental camouflage. Although it was an accident, it was convenient.

Because of her spot on the wall and unobstructed view, she had the pleasure of witnessing Rhyatt's arrival. Every time he had watched her walk through the door, he had been awestruck. Now, she began to understand why. As his body filled the sunlit doorway, the light dimmed, creating a glow around his back. He had the vague appearance of a sun god. His large frame filled the single door, and the golden light bounced off his dark curls, shining through in spots and giving him a halo effect. His light-colored clothing gave him an ethereal look.

Wes gawked.

He stepped into the room and the light seemed to intensify on his clothing, making the cream shirt semi transparent, showing off the curve of his shoulders, the structure of his chiseled arms.

Wes stared, unashamed. No wonder so many of the women whispered about him. She had never witnessed his arrival, but now she understood.

She watched as he crossed the room, running a hand through his hair before leaning against the far wall, not too far from her own hidden spot.

Only there was something off about him. He ran his hand through his hair a second time before briefly closing his eyes and breathing in. When he reopened them, he looked... tired. Perhaps he was just as tired as Wes was.

She stood, readying to approach him when Graham stepped up to him, Michal and Beth at his sides. Graham began speaking but she was too far away to hear what he said. She did notice as Rhyatt crossed his arms, his face hardening at whatever was being said.

Wes inched closer, wanting to hear the conversation without being seen.

"And *who* did you get into a scuffle with this weekend?" Graham was asking, addressing the cut across Rhyatt's nose and the bruise on the side of his face. She hadn't noticed how deep they were.

"So you'll fight others, but you won't fight me?" Graham continued, snickering.

Rhyatt stared blankly ahead. Unfazed. Unbothered.

"There's no use fighting when you know you'll lose," Michal added, egging Graham's nastiness on.

Graham placed a hand on his sword hilt, "I heard your brother isn't afraid. He steps up to his fights. Maybe I'll find him and see what he's made of."

Rhyatt's eyes sharpened, and his mouth set into a taut line. It was the first recognition he showed. But there was none of the raging fire she had seen a few days prior. Only an aggravation. Like a horse upset that there was a fly buzzing in its ear.

"Leave us alone." He said, pushing off the wall and turning to walk away from where Wes was waiting in the shadows. But Graham was quick. He threw out an arm, slamming his palm into the wall. Michal stepped to the far side, effectively trapping Rhyatt in.

Rhyatt cocked his head and looked to Graham, who was now entirely too close.

"When I beat him like a bitch maybe then you'll step up," Graham whispered.

But Wes had heard. Before she understood what her body was doing, she was in front of Graham, her fist connecting with his nose.

He hit the floor with a soft thud. Looking up at her, he clutched his nose, now spurting blood.

"He may be too nice to beat your ass, but I am not." Wes spat at the boy on the ground.

In a hurry, he pulled himself from the floor and stormed towards the door. Michal and Beth followed him from a safe distance.

When they were all out the door, she turned to Rhyatt. His face was drawn. He shook his head, "You didn't have to do that."

"How long has he been talking to you like that?" She asked.

"It doesn't matter." He crossed his arms again, leaning back against the wall. "Some people are just looking for a rise out of others. And now you've given it to him."

Wes stopped and thought about it. It was true. But if only Rhyatt knew how easy it would have been to get Graham off his back. A few punches would've lowered his ego and gave Rhyatt peace.

"You could've taken him in a fistfight." Wes responded after a pause, "He leads with his left and is slow to defend his right."

Rhyatt shrugged, looking above her head, his eyes unfocused. "I don't want to fight."

I don't want to hurt anyone. He told her that he didn't want to hurt anyone. Even when they were attacking him, he hadn't *wanted* to hurt anyone. The unspoken truth rang out in her ears. Rhyatt didn't want to fight. He had been forced to fight for his life days ago. He had killed someone. His first kill. *That* was the reason his eyes were glassed over, shoulders slumped, and the usual easygoing grin was missing. Her heart sank. She had done this. This newest version of him was her doing.

She tilted her chin up to him, mouth open to say something. But his eyes were still focused somewhere beyond her. When he did focus on her, she almost withdrew. An emptiness had settled on him, taking away the sunshine.

She instinctively reached out, grabbing his large hand and entwining their fingers. His grip was limp. She sent him a small smile and squeezed. His fingers twitched before tightening around hers.

"Let's get out of here." She whispered. Rhyatt nodded at her, and the duo walked out of the hall, hand in hand.

Wes felt every set of eyes on them as they walked through the university courtyard.

She wanted to cringe and release his hand, but she didn't dare. Instead, she tilted her chin higher, keeping her face blank. She had never been in a public relationship, her mother forbidding it, banishing all of her children's relations to the dark. Before she left, she had actually helped cover up one of Warden's mistakes. He had been caught kissing a girl in the middle of Saveen's Festival. She had hidden them with her dress and whisked them away somewhere private. Warden had, of course, not wanted to continue after his mother intervened. It had always been a rule in the Blake household to keep your relationships private. Even those that are not romantic. It was one of the many reasons her home was her friend's main gathering spot. No one knew how close they truly were.

Wes tightened her grip on his hand as she walked. She had been so private in all her sexual relationships that holding hands in broad daylight felt like having sex in the circle. Even if she and Rhyatt were nothing more than friends, this felt oddly intimate. Judging by the stares she was getting from just about everyone, they thought just as much. The word would spread quicker than wildfire. She hated that. Being a Blake meant nothing she did went unseen. There was no doubt this would eventually reach her mother. On the bright side, Rhyatt would fall under her umbrella of protection.

They exited the university courtyard and headed towards the square. Rhyatt followed at her side, matching her steps and never looking anywhere but straight ahead. He either didn't notice the attention they had just received or didn't care.

When they cut through an alley, she dropped his hand and linked their elbows instead. The silence between them stretched on, at first quiet and knowing, now it seemed ominous... almost dangerous.

They exited the alley and entered the outermost loop of the square. Early in the morning, it was slow, with very few citizens milling about. Rhyatt's shoulders relaxed in the less crowded area.

"Are you okay, Rhyatt?" She asked when they were out of earshot.

"Yes." He said, facing away from her.

"Something is eating at you."

"It's nothing." He said, his voice flat.

"You're not acting like it's nothing," she responded, slowing their pace.

"I'm fine." His whispered reply was strained.

She rolled her eyes. So that's how it would be. With a small grin, she nodded.

"Fine. You're okay."

He slowed his pace and narrowed his eyes in her general direction without fully looking at her, "Why did you say that to me the other night?"

Finally, a foothold.

"Because, even if you weren't okay in the moment, it was a promise that one day you will be okay." She toed a rock, "Sometimes I tell myself I'm okay, even if I'm not. It helps knowing that it can't always be insufferable. One day I'll tell myself, 'You're okay,' and mean it."

He broke, looking at her, his eyes glassy with his mouth in a tight line.

"I can't stop thinking about it," he said, barely audible.

"We did what needed to be done." She replied, gripping his arm tighter.

"That's not it." He said with a shake of his head, "I-" he broke off again. "I go back and forth from feeling so awful about their deaths to wishing they would've lived longer so worse things could've happened. It's so fucked up-I'm sorry. That's awful of me to say."

"Don't apologize. You don't have to explain yourself to me."

Rhyatt pulled away a fraction of an inch and she knew she had said it in the wrong way. The wrong tone. She wanted to be there for him, her misunderstood words were not working in her favor.

"Not that I don't want to hear about it, I do." She quickly amended. "I mean that you don't have to justify your actions to me. If you want to talk, then I'm all ears. But do not apologize for hoping bad things would happen to bad people."

He huffed, shoving his hands into his pockets, "Bad things rarely happen to bad people."

Wes could've sworn his eyes flicked toward her. Did he think she was a bad person?

"There are exceptions, and this was one of them." She assured him, pushing her own welling emotions down.

"I know all too well about the exceptions." he replied with a slight eye roll, "Some people deserve what they have coming. It doesn't stop me from feeling guilty that I was the one who dealt it."

They had made a circle around the outer loop of the square and began retracing their steps in a second pass. Wes silently thought while Rhyatt stared forward. Although his expression was blank, he hadn't pushed her away. As they walked, she debated with herself. Wes was a woman of many secrets, but this one was detrimental. She had sworn she would take it to the grave. Not even Knox or Cleo knew. But as they continued, Rhyatt flexed his arm, forcing her closer to him. And the thought of sharing it grew on her. He could be trusted. Even if he thought less of her, he would take it to his grave as well if she asked. Unsure of why, she began in a low voice.

"We have to do what is just. And sometimes, that means getting our hands dirty. The killing was *just*, Rhyatt. We both know what would've happened if they had lived." She paused her speech, her feet carrying her forward. She looked and caught Rhyatt's eye, holding it for the first time that day. "You asked me if I'd ever killed someone. What you didn't ask is why I feel no remorse about it." She paused once more, gathering a kernel of strength to continue, "Because I had the ability and strength to do it. If I had not acted, more people would have suffered. *It was justified.*"

Rhyatt looked at her, curiosity sparking in his eyes. To her relief, he showed no signs of fear. No judgment.

"I shouldn't have asked." He dipped his head lower, getting closer to her to speak.

"No. I want you to know." She nodded her head slowly. "I trust you."

His eyes widened slightly at her last statement and she nodded to a sole bench under a shade tree, together they sat down, disentangling their arms. Instead of arms locked, their knees pressed against each other. The gravity of what she was about to say made Wes look out, avoiding his gaze.

"A few years ago, a mother caught a man with her young daughter. I'll spare you the details- but even with the mother's account, the law council failed her. Because the young girl could not speak, they would not convict the man. At the time I had a friend on the law council who told me of the results. That night, I brought a meal to the home. When I arrived, the kitchen was full of women, of mothers, who had the same thing happen to their daughters. Time after time, the law council failed them." Her voice cracked, the only show of emotion she had allowed. "The rest of the evening, I sat in that kitchen and listened to mother after mother describe the horrors of what had happened to their daughters. Their *young* daughters."

Wes took a shaky breath and flicked her eyes to the sky. With time, she got better at talking about the hard things, but she had never spoken of this to anyone. And with each word, she was transported back to that kitchen. To the hard wooden chair, to the tears, to the rage. At the time, she had been taking care of Will for a couple of years. She had started to understand a mother's love. She came back down when Rhyatt placed a hand over hers. She breathed deeply before continuing in the same calm voice.

"As long as I live, I will never repeat the horrors I heard in that room. At the end of the night, I knew what needed to be done. And I knew who needed to do it." She paused, considering her words. "There are women like me, and then there are the women like the mothers who gathered in that room. They didn't have the ability to do it. They were important and needed. So I promised it would be taken care of. And it was. I have no regrets about what I did. I sometimes wish *things* about it. I wish I could've put his head on a spike in the center of town. I wish I could've kept him in a cage until the girls were old enough to take their own revenge. And lastly, I wish I wouldn't have given him a quick death. He deserved to suffer for his horrendous crimes."

She looked down from the sky, her sorrow had dried up and been replaced by the rage that always came with thinking about that man. She turned her body towards Rhyatt and he was staring at her. Fear still did not taint his face, but something different. She couldn't place it. She willed her voice to even out before continuing.

"Whatsoever is Just is more than just a saying to me, Rhyatt. Sometimes, it means doing things because they are right and fair. They are *just*. Sometimes, it means doing things to your own version of just. And on a rare occasion, it means doing things because no one else has the ability and strength to. If we wouldn't have done what we did, who else would have? How many of our friends and family would be suffering because of our inaction?"

Rhyatt nodded slowly, and Wes took his silence as a cue to continue.

"We are not awful people because of what we did to protect others. We are not awful for hoping bad people suffer. We are just *human*."

His hand tightened around hers, "Thank you. I appreciate you, Wes." He nodded his sincerity.

Before the emotion could become too overbearing, Rhyatt cocked his head, and a playful smile appeared, "Anything you can do to help with the dreams?"

She flipped her hand and tightened it in his grip.

"I have something to fix that. Hope you're not fond of your beauty sleep."

RHYATT

W es and Rhyatt hadn't returned to class that morning, instead opting to walk through town and talk until it was time for their internships. Now, they circled each other under the BlakeMoore tree, wooden swords gripped tight and sweat dripping off their faces. Underneath the tree, Cleo flipped through a newspaper, and Will ate fresh berries he and Rhyatt had picked earlier that day.

"Wes!" an angry voice bellowed. Rhyatt paused and looked up just in time to see Knox round the corner, his pace quick and irritated. As he neared them, he threw his bag to the ground and looked at Rhyatt.

Rhyatt fought the urge to roll his eyes. Knox couldn't still be mad about the other night.

"Can I see that?" Knox asked, motioning to the practice sword in Rhyatts hand.

"Yeah," before Rhyatt could say anything else, Knox swiped the sword from him and pointed it at Wes.

"I'm irritated with you," he said simply, rolling his shoulders back.

242

"So take it out on me," Wes said, her tone playful as a smirk appeared. Rhyatt stepped backward as Cleo and Will scooted forward, paying more attention.

"Yasmin won't talk to me." Knox lurched forward, swiping at Wes. She sidestepped and avoided him without raising her sword.

"I thought you weren't interested in her." Cleo pondered loudly behind them.

Knox grunted and moved to block the attack coming from Wes.

"I remember you choosing a lake of serpents over her," Wes added with a nod.

"Well, it doesn't matter now because she won't speak to me."

"What did you do?" Wes asked, blocking his strike above her head.

"No, no, no," Knox clicked his tongue, "Not what I did, but what *you did.*"

Wes furrowed her brow and stepped away from him, a question on her lips. But Knox continued.

"Your little stunt with Graham. Now she's 'afraid of your wrath.'" He continued.

Rhyatt scoffed and smirked at the other man's back, "I'm afraid of it too."

Cleo let out a small laugh, and Rhyatt swore he heard Will whisper a defiant 'not me' under his breath.

"What can I say?" Wes said with mischief, "Poor Rhyatt was in distress."

Rhyatt's smirk disappeared, and he stepped forward to defend himself, but once again, Knox began to speak. He had a talent for interrupting others.

"Rhyatt is built like a godsdamn brick wall. I think he would've been fine."

Cleo was tight-lipped from keeping in a laugh. Rhyatt furrowed his brows and turned back to the dueling duo. Wes had cocked her head and was examining him. Her eyes roved from the top of his head down to his toes. He felt the heat creep into the back of his neck. This always happened when she stared at him for too long.

"Yes, but he's still shit at fighting." She moved and tossed the sword to him. Out of instinct, he reacted and caught it. "Your lesson isn't done for the day. And Knox is irritated with you."

"With me?" His voice got higher as she prowled closer and stood behind him, nudging him forward.

"Yes. He's irritated you didn't tell Graham to shove it where the sun doesn't shine."

"No." Rhyatt shook his head, "He's irritated with you."

"No." Knox said, ending their spat and rolling his neck, "I'm just irritated."

Before Rhyatt could respond, Knox struck hard and fast. Luckily, it was something he knew how to deflect. With ease, he pushed the sword aside. Unfortunately, he had not yet been taught the counterattack. When Knox struck again, he deflected and moved away.

"You need the practice anyway!" Wes said with enthusiasm, following at his back.

"And I need to work out some anger," Knox added, lunging again. This time Rhyatt was a hair too slow. Knox's sword nicked Rhyatts arm just enough to sting.

"I don't see how this is going to help. He's much better than me!"

"Yes, but he's not as good as me. And his style is different." The two began circling each other, Wes following at Rhyatts back.

"Think of it as facing a really good opponent." Her feet moved quietly over the ground. He felt her breath on his neck when she leaned forward and whispered, "I'll have your back the entire time."

"That's comforting," Rhyatt replied with an eye roll. But what he didn't say was that it was comforting, knowing she was there, that he appreciated it. That he appreciated her. Even if she did put him up against an angry Knox.

RHYATT

*I*t took me three visits to find out enough information about the medical facility to make my first report. Which was three nights away from the farm and my friends. I have to leave before sundown and wait until sunrise to return, lest I be caught in the canyons after dark. I'm beginning to wonder if 50 silver per report is enough. This week I reported that the facility specializes in experimental medicine. Which I have learned is the polite way to say they have no idea if what they are doing is working. They take in patients with a variety of sicknesses, even the ones that their sickness has no cure to. I've learned very few are cured but many continue to try because for some it is their only hope. Sometimes the cures come with additional problems like blindness, tremors, and weakness. For a medical facility the building is massive and hundreds of soldiers live on site. I suspect the soldiers are the reason I was hired.

Whatever is Just,

Jaze

Rhyatt lay awake in bed and stared at the ceiling. He hoped Wes would come by with a tea or something herbal to help him sleep, but as the clock neared midnight, he decided to close his eyes and attempt to sleep. But there lay another problem: every time he closed his eyes, he saw her face. And it was a lovely vision. It truly was. But with Adriel awake and sitting only ten feet away, he didn't want to think of her. Adriel sat at the desk, the gas lamp illuminating him as he wrote letters to his friends back home. Rhyatt was proud of his brother; he had been adjusting well, making new friends, and so on. He had only continued writing to two or three of his friends from Duran. He was doing a good job of moving on, unlike Rhyatt. He had thought of his former friends and the ache in his chest was always too painful, so he had stopped thinking of them. Instead, pretending they didn't exist. It was easier that way.

Rhyatt closed his eyes and tried again. This time, he tried to count lizards. He reached one hundred and forty-three when a gentle tap came against the window. Lifting his head he saw Adriel was already up and pulling the window open. Apparently, he was *very* well-adjusted. Rhyatt propped his head up, waiting to see which of Adriel's new friends appeared.

"You're Wes Blake," Adriel whispered, excitement in his voice.

Rhyatt perked up.

"The one and only." Came her amused reply. Rhyatt moved towards the window.

"Is Rhyatt home?" She asked at the same time he shoved his brother to the side, poking his head out the narrow window.

"Hey." he said with a soft smile. And gods was she beautiful in the moonlight. Her dark hair shone and her eyes were hidden in the shadows. It made all of her sharp features that much sharper, it made her that much more *her*.

"You ready?" she said, a mischievous smile growing as she looked down at his bare chest.

"For?"

She only raised her eyebrows, playing coy. He wouldn't deny her.

"Let me get dressed." Rhyatt pushed himself back into the room and began to scramble for clothes as quietly as he could. As he got dressed, he could hear Adriel talking to her again.

"Is what they say about your fighting true?" He asked, unashamed.

"And what do they say?" Wes drawled.

"That you are the best Saint Saveen has seen in years. That you take on three at once."

She laughed, and Rhyatt poked his head out the window, turning and reprimanding his brother.

"Adriel." he hissed a warning as he began to climb out of the window, only one boot on, the other in hand.

Wes turned her attention to him, "Ever heard the phrase 'too tired to dream'?" she leaned forward as he put his boot on, "Tonight I'm giving meaning to it."

He smiled at her wicked glance. With no idea what was in store for him he was anxious, excited even. Once his boot was on she began to walk away, motioning for him to follow.

"Wait!" Adriel whispered loudly. The pair of them stopped and turned back to him, his hands still on the windowsill, torso hanging outside. "You didn't answer my question!"

Wes snickered to herself, and Rhyatt rolled his eyes at his insolent little brother.

"Stop by practice some time, and you'll find out."

When the house was out of view Rhyatt shook his head and chided her, "You shouldn't have told him that. Now he'll pester me everyday until I tell him when and where practice is."

"Oh, let him come. Maybe he'll learn something."

"Or maybe he'll drive the both of us insane," Rhyatt said, walking beside her as the trees lessened. "He thinks you are the coolest thing since sliced bread."

"I am," she said, turning to look at him and wink.

He only laughed at her, "Are you going to tell me where we're going, or is it a surprise?"

"Telling you would take all the fun away."

"So it's a surprise?"

She said nothing, biting her lip and stepping further in front of him.

"Nothing's ever easy with you, is it?" he grumbled to her back.

"Never," she said airily, not bothering to look back at him.

They continued through the forest. The sounds of crickets and night birds cawing surrounded them from every angle. The dense trees ended abruptly as they entered a field of cane sugar. He guessed it was her family's; otherwise, she wouldn't be traipsing through it. She confirmed as much before leading them on in silence. When the field ended, a barn and a few large cabins came into view. They were plain looking, but sounds of vibrant life, music, and voices came from inside. They snuck between them to re-enter the forest, only this time it was denser, wilder. The brush around their feet had grown up, making it harder to walk. Wes must've sensed his aggravation because soon they wandered to a creek and began following it upstream. Not long after, the trees broke, and a lovely lake came into view.

Closest to them the lake funneled into the creek, small but steady. On the far side, large rocks loomed high overhead, they jutted out towards the top, giving the appearance of half of a cave; water trickled down from them, pattering against the lake. On top the forest continued, roots and vines hung down framing the lake. It was a beautifully secluded place. In the daylight the rocks would keep the sun off the lake, keeping it cool.

He looked to Wes to comment on the beauty, but when he looked over, she had her shirt over her head in a state of undress.

"Wes?" he asked tentatively, heat rising to his cheeks.

"I have yet another surprise for you. But we have to swim to it." She smiled at him, her eyes glinting as she reached down and began loosening the laces of her boots.

"I...um." Rhyatt stuttered and winced. "I can't swim." He admitted, looking down to avoid her gaze.

"See!" a voice shouted from the forest, making him jump, "I knew he couldn't be *that* perfect."

Rhyatt snapped his head to the voice as Knox and Cleo emerged from the tree line, the former saying the statement and shaking his head with a broad, shit-eating grin. Of course, Knox would prey on his inability to swim.

"Lay off Knox. He's from a *desert city*. Why would he need to know how to swim? You probably wouldn't know how to ride a camel." Cleo chided.

Knox held his hands up, "Only joking."

And for the first time, Rhyatt believed him. Something had shifted today. Even when they were fighting, Knox hadn't been as nasty as he could have been. Perhaps it was the news Wes had told him about his cousin. She had only told Rhyatt that he was possibly murdered and not to take it personally if Knox lashed out.

"She's right." Rhyatt offered with a smile. An olive branch. "This much water would have kept the entire city alive for a day or two. Swimming would have contaminated it."

"Yet another imperfection attributed to your birthplace." Knox pulled off his shirt and tossed it into a pile, "Do you have any imperfections of your own person?" He looked at Rhyatt.

"I didn't know you knew so many big words, Knox." Wes chimed, drawing his attention as she shimmied out of her pants.

"I know more than you'd think," he replied with a wink.

"The bar isn't very high," Cleo added, tossing her own clothing onto a small rock instead of the ground.

The three of them continued undressing until they were all in their undergarments. Rhyatt was careful not to look at anyone for too long, not wanting to be disrespectful. Knox and Cleo started walking towards the water, hands swinging and bickering. Wes stayed behind.

"I can teach you."

"Teach me?" he asked, confused and still keeping eye contact.

"How to swim." She prompted, stepping closer.

His face warmed at his own idiocracy, "Maybe I'll just stick to the shallows." he offered with a sheepish smile.

"Suit yourself." She turned and jogged towards where her friends now waded waist-deep in the water. Alone, he began taking off his clothes and folding them into a neat pile beside Wes's. He hustled to the water as their laughter rose up and echoed off the semi-rock ceiling.

Rhyatt hadn't been 'swimming' since he was a boy visiting Lita. That didn't stop him from hustling into the lake. The temperature was surprisingly refreshing. The water was at his elbows before Cleo turned and noticed him.

"What are your tattoos?" She asked, her observant eyes tracking his movement. Wes and Knox turned to look at him. Under their examination his body felt too large. His chest too broad, neck too thick. The water wasn't covering nearly enough of him, he inched deeper, until it was at his chest.

"They are a rare cobra found outside the city." He said as he reached for the ink, his fingers hiding them. When he reached the depth Knox and Cleo were at Wes, who had been further out towards the middle, swam back and rejoined them.

"You like snakes too?" Cleo asked, her eyes flickered over his shoulders.

"No." he glanced at Wes. Her dark hair was wet and slicked down against her head and neck. "I'm actually terrified of them."

"Not everyone is dumb enough to mess with them." Knox cast a glance at Wes.

"Not dumb," she shrugged, "Just patient. You should try it sometime." She grinned at him, and in return, he sent a splash of water at her face. She stared at him, open-mouthed with surprise. Knox only smirked and held his arms wide in a 'come get me' motion. In a blink, Wes's mouth closed, and she dipped under the water.

Knox's smirk disappeared entirely. He began backing up, heading in the opposite direction of her. He had only made it a few steps when her head rose from the water behind him, silent. Eerie. She had moved far too quick. Perhaps this is how good swimmers move.

She touched his shoulder, and he let out a startled yelp in surprise.

"Tag. You're it." she crooned loudly before dipping back below the surface of the water. This time, she didn't go as deep into the water; instead, the outline of her body could be seen just below the surface.

Soon enough, Knox regained his footing and came for them all. The three of them split into different directions and began an hours-long game of tag. They laughed and splashed like children, making an ungodly amount of noise. They were all 'it' at one point or another. Like an unspoken rule, when Rhyatt was 'it' no one veered too deep where he could not swim. He was thankful for their kindness. He did, however, notice that Wes *was* quicker than the others. She was borderline uncatchable. At times, she seemed to slow and let them catch her. If Cleo and Knox noticed they did not say anything. They went on playing until their limbs were tired and their pace had slowed. Knox was the first one to exit the lake, journeying to find a stash of firewood they kept nearby. Cleo soon joined him. She sent a knowing look over her shoulder at Rhyatt.

"Are you ready for your second surprise?" Wes asked, appearing behind him. He jumped.

"Another surprise?"

She nodded, "But you'll have to trust me."

"I always trust you, Wes," he replied sarcastically. She had already turned her back on him and was heading towards the edge of the faux cavern ceiling. The rocks cropped out into the water there, and he wasn't able to go far before they dropped off. He followed her, wary.

When they reached the rocks, she looked back at him, that mischievous smile forming on her face. The moonlight reflected off the water and into her eyes, giving her an empyrean glow.

"The second surprise is on the other side of the rock." she said with a nod, her chin bobbing, "The only problem is the entrance is currently underwater. If you are willing, I will take you to the other side and bring you back."

Rhyatt paused, he had no earthly idea how to swim. His flailing about for the last hour had proved that. If he were dropped in the middle of the lake he would sink to the bottom like a rock. Although his earlier statement had been made with the roll of his eye, it was true he trusted her. If there was anyone he trusted to bring him underwater it was her.

"Promise you won't let me drown?"

Her smile faded away, and her face tightened into seriousness, "I will not let you drown."

He nodded once, nervousness sinking into him.

She inched closer and offered her hand. As he took it, the moonlight flashed across her eyes, temporarily turning them silver. He sucked in a breath and tried not to notice the current between them, that feeling cycling between them.

Hands clasped, she led them into deeper water. When the water was to her neck she looked back at him, the smallest of smiles on her lips.

"Hold your breath and keep your eyes closed until I tell you." With that, she pulled him forward and down beneath the water.

Rhyatt held to her hand tightly, afraid the water would loosen their grip. His eyes were shut tight, and his mouth even tighter. He thought they were going deeper, but he had no idea. She could have led him in a circle and he wouldn't have known. He only knew she was pulling him forward because he could feel his hair moving behind him. He thought they were moving upwards, and when his feet touched the stone, he surged forward towards it. Wes jerked his hand upwards twice, and he began to resurface.

She released his hand as he took a deep breath, his hands going to his eyes to wipe the water out of them.

"Don't look yet!" her voice echoed, and as he listened, Rhyatt heard the sound of multiple streams of water dripping and echoing.

He continued wiping his eyes but did not open them. He heard the swishing of the water echo as she moved around. She moved away from him, and it sounded like she doubled back around him before stopping in front of him once more. He could hear her breath, the excitement in her voice.

"Okay, you can look now."

Rhyatt opened his eyes. Wes stood directly in front of him, her own eyes full of wonder as she watched him. She was lit by a blue glow. Rhyatt blinked and looked away from her. They were in a cavern of sorts, all illuminated by a deep blue glow. He looked down and noticed the source. In the water, there were thousands upon thousands of glowing blue specks. They swirled in the water, moving counterclockwise around the cave. There were so many of them that he could see through the water clear as day, all the way down to the slats of rock he was standing on. Even above the water, it illuminated the cave in a soft glow. He stared in wide-eyed wonder at the glowing water.

"It's an algae." Wes whispered, "During a cloudy new moon, you can see them all across the lake. But they always light up here, in the dark."

He put his hand back in the water and scooped some up. The tiny blue flecks illuminated his hand. He poured the water back into the pool and watched as a few of the flecks stuck to his skin and stayed illuminated. He lifted his hand in front of his face in wonder. All his life, he had never seen something so magical. He had thought the dry heat and sands of the desert were enough. He had thought he enjoyed his life in a large, bustling city, shifting sands and cool nights. But now he wasn't so sure.

He looked back up to Wes, her eyes still filled with wonder. She hadn't stopped watching him like she had been enjoying his reaction. His fascination. It was odd seeing a look of wonder on her. She shed the skin that made her seem older and wiser and instantly became younger. He couldn't help but feel a pang of jealousy as he wondered who had shown her this place, at whoever had gotten to witness her joy for the first time.

"How did you find this place?" He asked, his voice barely above a whisper.

"My parents found it." her expression shifted, the wonder gone. Rhyatt regretted asking the question, but she continued. "They found it when they were younger. When the water was low, you could see the entrance. It wasn't until years later when the lake's water had returned, they swam in and discovered the algae always glowed in the dark of the cave."

Rhyatt frowned; the mere mention of her parents had changed her whole demeanor. He wanted to ask, but it wasn't the time, certainly not the place.

Wes looked away from him, staring at the walls of the cave. She looked around for a minute before leaning back, submerging herself in the water again and then floating. Her eyes gently closed. Her dark hair fanned out and she looked peaceful like this.

"Float with me," she whispered.

"I'm not sure how." Rhyatt returned her whisper, keeping the noise level to a minimum.

Her eyes flew open as she regained her footing to look at him, the specks of blue were stuck in her hair, her arms, her chest.

"I can teach you." she nodded, assuring herself.

"Will I owe you another debt?"

A raucous laugh burst from her, "Do you *want* to owe me another debt?"

Yes. "No."

"Then no. Consider it a gift." she smiled, but it wasn't cat-like, it was simple. Patient.

He nodded, and she stepped forward, the water going higher up to her waist.

"On your knees."

He raised his eyebrows at her, but she only smirked. "I'm going to cradle you like a baby."

Rhyatts ears grew hot, but before he could protest she closed the distance between them. One hand on his shoulder guiding him down, the other pulling his arm so his side was pressed to her body. He went willingly and instantly felt the warmth of her body against him. He was so distracted by the warmth of her skin he almost missed the shock that ran down the entire length of him that was pressed against her. He assumed she had felt it as well because she shivered.

Quickly, she bent in the water and scooped his legs so that he was cradled against her, he wrapped an arm around her back to steady himself. She had done as promised, held him like a baby. Rhyatt pouted.

"I feel like a child," he complained, his voice returning to a normal level.

"You look cute like this." She cooed at him. He used the hand wrapped around her to gently pinch her arm. She shook her head before focusing.

"Stretch out and relax. I'm going to support your neck and back. Your ears will be underwater. Just focus on my voice."

Rhyatt did as instructed. She loosened her grip on his legs, and he stretched his legs flat, his abdomen taught. Wes moved her hands to where she had promised, his lower back and neck. Panic began to rise as his legs sank downwards. He jerked his head out of the water to look at his sinking legs. Wes poked his hard abdomen.

"You have to relax. All the way. Nothing tense. Like lying in your bed about to fall asleep."

Rhyatt huffed but gently put his head back in the water and closed his eyes. He began to sink again. He felt her hands drift away, and he tensed once more. His entire body dipped below the water. He struggled and regained his footing, pushing himself upright.

"Why did you move?!" she questioned.

"I was sinking!" he said, pushing his hair out of his face.

"You're going to sink before you float, Rhy. You have to trust that I am there to catch you."

There was that nickname again. Gods, he loved it.

Nodding, he reclined back into the water, her hands finding their spots once more. This time, he shivered at her touch. He laid back until his ears were underwater again. Closing his eyes, he prepared to sink.

But he didn't.

His legs had gone down, but his arms and chest stayed above water.

"That's it." he heard her muffled voice and began to relax more, focusing on her reassuring touch.

"Doing good." She praised him. Slowly, her hands began to move away. To his surprise, he didn't dip lower in the water. He stayed buoyed on top.

"You're doing it," she said, quieter this time.

"I'm floating," he replied, excitement entering his voice.

His excitement grew until he was giddy. He never thought he would know how to swim, and he still couldn't. But he could float, and that was a step in the right direction. The desert boy could float in water. He stood back on his own feet and faced Wes.

"I did it!"

"You did it!" she exclaimed back, matching his giddy energy. She placed her hands on his shoulders and shook lightly, repeating herself.

He wasn't sure what came over him, but he bent and wrapped his arms around her thighs, lifting her into the air and spinning.

Wes let out a sharp laugh, echoing around them. She looked up at the cavern ceiling as if tracing the laugh. He laughed loudly in turn, echoing hers.

Then, she looked down at him. And time slowed.

Blue algae was still dripping off of her hair, and the light from the water below illuminated her face. She looked down at him, smiling. Only this smile was different than any other he had ever seen. It made the rest seem shallow in comparison. This was her *real* smile. Every other time had been a forced smile. This open mouth, teeth showing grin was the real one. The rarest one. He cherished it.

She seemed to understand the shift in him and flung her arms out wide as they spun. Closing her eyes, she tilted her head back, that smile still plastered on her face. At that moment, she appeared to be every bit the goddess he suspected her to be. He wouldn't have been surprised if she sprouted wings and took flight. He wanted to tell her exactly that, but he didn't know how to say it. So he spun, holding her close and watching that beautiful smile stay on her face.

He would've spun forever to see that smile, but as her arms came down to his shoulders, he stopped and released her. She slowly slid down the front of his body. Back on her own feet, she stared up at him, smiling. He smiled down at her, his hands loosely at her sides.

He had never wanted anything more than to keep this smile on her face. He would have made a thousand debts if that meant her smile. He wished he could stop time in the moment so that way they would forever be in the cave together, in this moment of pure bliss.

A rock clinked somewhere in the cave, and Wes's head snapped in the general direction. When she didn't see anything, she looked back at him and stepped away. The smile was gone, and he felt his stomach sink. He felt himself returning to his body and felt the guilt wash over him.

"I'm so sorry. I should've asked before touching you." He looked down, "I didn't mean to. I'm sorry-"

"You have nothing to apologize for." She said sternly, pulling herself up straight, pushing her shoulders back, and tilting her chin up. A faux smile appeared, and in seconds, the Wes that was readily available to the public appeared. He tried to hide the hurt of the demeanor change, but she had seen it anyway. He schooled his face into neutrality.

"They should have the fire going by now." She walked closer to the ledge and offered her hand. He took it, and when the current didn't pass between them, he felt his hurt grow and take root in his chest.

RHYATT

The next day, Knox did not show up for class. Rhyatt wished he would've done the same. Wes acted the same as always, smiles and jokes. But now that he knew the difference in her smiles, he didn't think he'd ever view her the same. Her words had rang true though. He was too tired to dream. And he was thankful for it. If he had to see her smile in the cave in his dreams, he probably would've gone out of his mind by now. 'Ignorance is bliss' never had so much appeal to him as it did now.

When Scholar Tiunda released them for lunch, Wes caught his eye and nodded towards the door. His heart skipped a beat, but he soon realized she was inviting him to eat lunch with her and Cleo.

The three of them walked through the courtyard together, Wes in the middle. As they walked, he noticed both women's eyes were focused forward. They paid no one else any mind. Rhyatt, however, was not as good at ignoring the eyes that followed them. Everyone in their classes and everyone below looked up when they walked by. And shockingly, they were looking at Rhyatt.

A cloud of self-consciousness covered him and he curved his shoulders in. Were they looking at him because of what happened yesterday? Did they think he was the one who punched Graham? Surely they didn't. Maybe they knew about the man he had killed. But wouldn't they look at Wes, too? She had killed someone as well. Or just maybe- they were looking at him because he was in Knox's spot. This is where Knox usually stood with them. Now, he was in that spot.

"Don't look them in the eyes," Wes whispered to him, a smile on her face. It was the same thing she had done in Duran.

"Why?" He asked, not able to match her smile.

"They're like vultures. They circle if you give them a reason." She didn't break stride as she looked at him and spoke.

"Why are they staring?" Rhyatt asked, his voice sounded small, even to him.

"For many reasons," Cleo said, loud enough for not only him to hear but anyone close to hear as well. "Possibly because you were the first person to be seen doing anything slightly romantic with Wes Blake. Possibly because she punched Graham for you yesterday. Or, even better, that your brother told his friend he was invited to spar with you and Wes, which then spread the word further that you two are in cahoots."

Rhyatt's steps faltered. They were clear of the courtyard, but he was just as confused. What had he done romantically with Wes? No one could possibly know about the cave, could they? No. Wes wouldn't tell anyone... but what- oh.

"Us holding hands is romantic?" He asked both women.

Cleo nodded, looking at him.

Heat crept to his cheeks, but then another question rose in his throat.

"That's the *first* romantic thing you've ever done?" He asked Wes.

She smiled like a cat and rolled her eyes, "In public."

Rhyatt scrunched his eyebrows together, another question on his tongue, but Cleo spoke first.

"Everyone thinks you're either engaged or soon to be engaged."

Wes's laugh ricocheted off the cobblestone streets. "They'd think I'd been married and divorced half a dozen times if they had seen everything the library has."

Cleo's laugh joined hers, a little sharp and twisted. Rhyatt's blush had to have deepened because now his cheeks felt like they were on fire. Wes looked at him, her smile dimming into concern.

"Don't worry Rhy, they'll forget soon enough."

He nodded. Not sure if she was telling the truth. Wes was many things, but optimistic was one of them. She hoped they would forget soon enough. But he saw the way people watched her, how they gravitated towards her in a crowd. He was starting to understand that Wes Blake, the idea, and Wes Blake, the person, were two different people. Wes Blake the person was funny, courageous, smart, and determined. But Wes Blake the idea was different. Colder, yet somehow more readily available to the public. She was calm, confident, and ambitious. It wasn't real. He felt like he knew something everyone else didn't. But they still gravitated towards that version of her. It was because of that he knew he would still be getting stared at until something else became better news.

They had entered the square when a short, stout man began walking towards them, his eyes focused. Wes and Cleo both slowed their pace drastically. They looked at each other and nodded. Both of their mouths drew into tight lines.

The man stopped in front of them, looking directly at Wes.

"He's been there since last night."

"How much do I owe you?" Wes asked, her hand going to the small pouch around her waist.

"Nothing." The man replied, shaking his head. "His tabs paid. Just get him out. A sleeping man is bad for business."

Wes nodded, her face hardened. Cleo's expression mirrored hers. The man turned, and they followed.

He led them to one of the nicer bars in the circle, the kind whose name was long, signifying its importance. The Oak's Refinery. Pushing open the heavy door they followed him in. The room was dark, the windows were made of stained glass taking the edge off the light. A few patrons sat at the bar, the rest of the room housed empty circular tables. Empty all except one.

In the middle of the room, a mop of blonde curls was slumped across a table, presumably asleep. Knox didn't move as they entered and walked towards him. When Cleo poked him, he let out a soft snore.

It was then that Wes looked up and looked at Rhyatt. She raised her eyebrows, almost in surprise, as if she had forgotten he was there. She straightened her spine and tilted her chin up slightly.

"When you return to class, will you tell The Scholar that Cleo and I had an emergency to attend to?"

He nodded.

"Whatever she asks, just don't say anything about Knox."

Rhyatt nodded again, "What are you going to do?"

She looked down at the sleeping man before looking back at Rhyatt, "Going to put him to bed."

Rhyatt opened his mouth to ask if she needed help, but he thought better of it. She had lifted him like he was nothing more than a sack of potatoes. Between them, Knox would be nothing but a bag of onions. So, he set out to eat lunch and return to the university alone.

The following morning, Knox appeared normal in class, almost chipper. The opposite of the groggy man who was carried out of a bar at noon the day before. Rhyatt wouldn't have thought it was odd, except it was Knox. Chipper was not in his vocabulary. In addition, he did not eat lunch with them. He disappeared only to be back to class early. At the end of the evening, he had been one of the first to leave. Scholar Tiunda had barely closed her books when he rose and walked out of the room. Rhyatt did not miss the worrisome look Wes and Cleo shot each other. Cleo had told Rhyatt that Knox often acted like this when he was down. Rhyatt had asked what she meant, and she looked away, repeating that it was not her business to tell.

Rhyatt could respect that. However, he couldn't respect Knox's actions, which seemed to punish his friends as much as he did himself. He suspected this was a reoccurring thing. The barkeep had been awfully familiar with them. He had even known to go to Cleo and Wes instead of Knox's family. Rhyatt began walking home, his anger growing as he walked up the drive.

It didn't seem right. Cleo and Wes had their own families to worry about. They shouldn't have to babysit a drunk Knox. He lacked many things. Accountability was one of them. Another was brain cells. Rhyatt pushed open the door and paused, standing in the frame.

It wasn't his business. But it bothered him. It bothered him deeply. He and Knox weren't even *friends*. Knox was actually quite the asshole to him on more than one occasion. He had only started to be friendly towards him a few days ago.

Knox was an asshole.

But he was also a man who was hurting.

Rhyatt sighed, calling out a clumsy excuse to Lita and Adriel before turning and heading toward the bars.

Rhyatt walked up the long dirt drive that led to Knox's home. After checking all five of Saint Saveen's bars he had given up and asked for directions to Knox's home.

He had no idea what he was doing. He didn't know what he would say to Knox if he found him. Would he lecture him about how his selfish actions affected others? Or perhaps he would just stare at the man until it made him angry enough to swing. As long as the fight was without weapons, Rhyatt knew he could win. Rhyatt heaved a sigh. He didn't know why he was doing anything, only that it seemed important.

Rhyatt continued up the dirt drive, the setting sun casting long shadows across the land. The tree's shadows stretched out and joined others, putting the majority of the path in the shade. But ahead, there was a break, a large one, where golden sunlight streaked through.

As he approached the patch of sunlight, he noticed that the trees bordering it were dead and blackened. Burnt.

His steps slowed. Not too far from the drive sat a scorched piece of earth. The deepest burns laid in a square on the ground, the grass immediately surrounding it was gone. Beyond it the landscape was dried out like it had gotten too close to the sun.

Rhyatt stepped off the path and crept closer. This piece of land was a stark contrast. A blackened streak across a lush green landscape. It was a place of death. A place of sorrow. A place of-

"Come to get a live look at the shitshow?"

Rhyatt jumped and turned to the voice. Knox was propped against a fallen tree, a bottle in his hand. His shirt was holding on by two buttons and his face had black streaks, upon further inspection so did his hands. Soot. Rhyatt shook his head, looking from the ashen land to the collapsed man.

"No," he replied gently. "Just checking up on you."

Knox paused, the bottle halfway to his mouth. "Why?" His voice fell flat, any intended venom not reaching him.

"It's what friends do. Or so I've been told."

Knox gulped another mouthful and narrowed his eyes, "Did Wes or Cleo send you?"

"No," Rhyatt replied truthfully. Knox studied him, looking for a lie. After a moment of concentrated staring, he glanced down at the bottle in his hand and lifted it.

"You thirsty?"

"Thought you'd never ask." Rhyatt joined Knox, sitting less than an arm's reach away, and took the bottle. Surprising himself, Rhyatt took a generous sip. Whiskey. He grimaced and handed it back without a second sip.

He stared forward, not looking at Knox, and began to understand why Knox had picked this spot. He wasn't visible from the road, but he had a perfect view of the scorched earth. The place where his cousin had perished. A nasty thought rambled through him before he could stop it. Every day, Knox had to pass the spot where his cousin had died. Every time he left his home he was reminded. When he came home, it was the first thing he saw. Sorrow nestled into his chest.

"What was Jaze like?" He asked, his voice quiet.

Knox inhaled deeply. It was the only sign Knox had heard him. But he did not reply. He took another sip, and Rhyatt wondered how much whiskey he had started out with. The bottle was half empty now.

"He was my cousin, but I often thought of him as a brother." He took another sip. Rhyatt reached out his hand, sensing the only way to stop Knox from drinking the entire bottle was to drink it himself. Knox obliged and handed it over. "He was a good man. A better man than I'll ever be." Knox said slowly, as if gathering his thoughts, before twisting his mouth and adding, "A much better man than my father."

"You all speak very highly of him. He was a good man and is mourned greatly."

"Not mourning." Knox shook his head violently, and his eyelids began to droop. "We have already mourned him, and he has moved on. We are simply remembering his life. It is what keeps his spirit happy."

"Ah," Rhyatt said carefully, unsure of Jorjin's death customs. Knox reached his hand out for the bottle. Rhyatt lifted it to his lips and began taking long pulls. Knox put his hands back in his lap for the moment.

"We used to joke that if Wes was the father figure of our group, then he was the mother hen." Rhyatt turned his head, and out of the corner of his eye, he could see the smallest smile forming on

Knox's face. "Don't get me wrong," he continued fondly, "He was rowdy and adventurous, but he was also the one to bring you soup when you were sick. The responsible one. The mature one. He cared about everyone he ever met, even if he acted like he didn't. He went to great lengths for all of us." Knox looked down to his lap, losing himself to his own memories.

"Share a memory with me." Rhyatt encouraged gently, not wanting to push too far.

Knox reached for the bottle again. This time, Rhyatt handed it to him. After another swig- this one thankfully smaller- he laughed a brittle sound.

"This is a good one. When we were still juveniles, we decided to play a fun little joke on a friend. We broke into their home and *rearranged* some things. On the way out, something fell and we all took off running. Warden had just grown another few inches and was clumsy as hell. He fell and got scraped up pretty badly. It was Jaze who turned back and helped when the rest of us were too spooked and waited in safety." He laughed again, this one not as brittle. "He was always so protective of us. Even as a kid, he would always fight my battles for me, getting me out of the messes I should've had to deal with. When we got older, all I had to do was ask for help, and he would step in. That's just who he is." Knox paused, realizing his mistake, "Was. Who he was."

"He sounds like a good friend," Rhyatt said quickly, hoping to distract Knox from his own thoughts.

"You two would have been fast friends." Knox's words began to slur.

"I'm honored you think so." Rhyatt reached for the bottle that now sat limply in his grip.

"Maybe that's why I didn't like you. You remind me of him."

"You admit you don't like me?"

Knox swung his head to look at Rhyatt. The liquor was clearly running its course and running it fast.

"I said I *didn't*."

"Ah." Rhyatt hummed and stared back out across the land, the sun had disappeared completely, leaving the afterglow of dusk. Knox copied his movement and they stared out, not looking at the scorched earth before them, but looking beyond. They sat in silence as the crickets began to chirp and night settled over them, bringing a cool breeze.

Rhyatt wondered if that was the sole reason Knox had been unpleasant to him. He doubted it. Although he did not seem it, Knox was complex. Multi-layered in his burning rage. A fire like Knox's took more than one stimulant to keep it going. Rhyatt remembered the strange triangle-shaped bruises he had seen on Knox's back the night he was attacked. He would bet that those bruises were another stimulant in the fires. Would Rhyatt have the same rage as Knox if he had the same circumstances? That was a dangerous question and a dangerous game to play. One can say you'd react reasonably in certain situations, but until those situations happened, one was merely guessing.

It was dark when Knox rose to his feet. Or rather, he tried to but stumbled. Rhyatt stood and steadied him. He took a step towards the house but stumbled, Rhyatt wrapped an arm around him and they took a tentative step forward together. Then another one.

"Iss the least youcando." Knox slurred, his steps uneven as Rhyatt guided him towards the house.

"It is." Rhyatt agreed with a chuckle.

WES

The facility is in constant need of supplies. They do not make much money, if any, off of their medical treatments, and yet the deliveries are nonstop. The majority of the deliveries are food and they come from Jorjin, which is to be expected since they are our number one export. The deliveries range from fresh fruits, vegetables, and livestock. However, there are religious deliveries in a grain bin, they always have stamps of approval from the mountain pass, but never once have they come with papers detailing what is inside. I wonder who they are paying to get things across the border without papers. I was cautious when giving details in my report.

~~Whatever~~ Whatsoever is Just,

JGreene

Many things were inevitable. Birth was inevitable. Death was inevitable. And most of all, Atticus was inevitable. Wes had spent the entirety of the semester avoiding him. It was like a game of hide and seek, and only she knew they were playing. He would round a corner, and she would turn the other way. He would enter the bar she was at, and she would dissolve into the background. But he was indeed inevitable. No matter how long she turned away, he would eventually capture her. Wes had decided that the capture needed to happen sooner rather than later. With the devastating realization around Jaze it made getting rid of the journal that much more dire. It made getting the journal into the right hands that much more important. And Atticus was smart. He listened in on his father's meetings. He knew more than she would from her internship. So he was necessary.

It wasn't that Wes disliked Atticus. He could actually be pretty funny. But he was also very entitled. They had grown up in similar circles, and he only had to bat his eyes to get his every wish. Wes wasn't that far removed to know she had grown up entitled as well. Only her parents had made her earn everything. Her first horse had cost her three months of work on the farm. It was because of that she didn't venture towards Atticus like everyone else. But today was different. She had soaked in her newest trouble long enough. It was time for a solution.

She waited until everyone had left the university before leaving, ensuring Atticus would be in his normal spot eating lunch. Walking out the double doors into the courtyard crowded with students eating and lounging in the sunshine, she tilted her chin up and pushed her shoulders back. Just because it was her plan to 'accidentally' run into Atticus didn't mean she had to act sweet and innocent. Everyone knew who she was, and she wasn't going to sacrifice it now.

She saw him almost immediately. In the middle of the courtyard was a set of steps leading to a square platform. He sat at the top of the platform, three other boys around him, all a step below. His shiny black hair reflected the sun and protected his large, deep-set eyes. Atticus had favored his mother; Commander Pryde had married her for her beauty and she had passed it on to all three of her children before dying in childbirth. Wes had to admit Commander Pryde was an average-looking man, but his son had succeeded him in looks.

She walked on the cobblestone path, her back straight but her stride slow. It took only seconds for him to take the bait.

"Wes!" she heard him call from behind her but continued.

Footsteps slapped the brick pavers in the distance.

"Wes!" he called when he was only a few steps behind her. This time, she acknowledged him.

"Atticus," she raised her brows in surprise as he reached her. He smiled with his teeth, and she slowed her stride even more, allowing him to walk with her.

"What have you been up to?" Wes asked first, wanting to take the upper hand. He shoved his hands in his pockets.

"The usual." He said with a shrug before continuing, "I feel like I haven't seen you in forever. It's been so long you've got a boyfriend now."

Wes laughed. He was feeling bold. Or curious.

"So that's what everyones been saying?" She sighed through her smile, "Much to everyone's disappointment, I am not seeing anyone. Although- I think Mr. Higgins may be happy to hear that."

It was Atticus's turn to laugh, "I think more people than Higgins will be glad to hear the news." He bumped her shoulder, "Which reminds me, Father is having a dinner party Sunday. Winnie is coming home, and he's invited a few officials from Duran. Just a small soiree. I'd love it if you'd be my date."

Hook, Line, and Sinker.

"Are you saying the idea of me being your date is lovely, or are you asking me?" Wes teased.

Atticus raised an eyebrow before smoothing his features into seriousness.

"Lovely Wes, would you be my date and save me from listening to the country's problems being rattled off by our elders? Oh- and save me from Winnie's watchful eye."

Wes lowered her chin to share a conspiratorial smile with him, "I'm not sure I can do much about Winnie, but I will save you from listening to the country's gossip."

Atticus smiled back at her, "Great, I'll see you Sunday then!"

He turned and jogged back to his friends, once Wes was out of his line of vision her smile turned sinister. Some boys were too easy to manipulate.

RHYATT

Rhyatt and Will had spent the majority of the afternoon lying underneath the shade tree in the garden playing hangman. A last little burst of heat had made the evening almost unbearable. Rhyatt thought he had adjusted to the sticky Jorjin humidity. He thought wrong.

"Any L's?" Rhyatt asked.

"No." Will replied quickly and returned to the story he had been telling, "After our teacher told him to quit pulling her hair, he stopped. But at lunch, he waited until she was alone before doing it again. I just knew he was going to wait until the teacher was gone."

"Mhm." Rhyatt marked the L out on the paper, "And where were you?"

"I was under the tree eating with Kat and Xavier."

"Why didn't you help her? Any E's?"

"No E's." Will marked the letter down before continuing. "I didn't help because I don't think I could've done it peacefully, and I can only get in trouble three times this year. I didn't want to use one of them up too soon."

Rhyatt frowned down at him. Will stared back at him, refusing to be shamed.

"So you didn't help her because you want to cause chaos at a later date?"

Will, in turn, frowned at Rhyatt. He had struck a nerve.

"It sounds bad when you say it like that."

Rhyatt raised an eyebrow, "If saying the truth makes it sound wrong, then perhaps there may have been a wrong done." Will twisted his mouth to the side, but Rhyatt continued, "People come first."

"What if I get in trouble more than three times?" Will asked, his voice contemplative.

Rhyatt looked up to see Wes coming out of the back door, two practice swords in hand.

"You're smart. Figure out a way for the blame to go elsewhere." He pushed off the ground, rising to his feet. "That girl doesn't deserve to have her hair pulled, and *you* can stop it."

Will noticed his sister getting closer and stood, gathering his paper and supplies. He had been watching their lessons less and less lately. Wes had told him that she thought it was because he didn't want to share Rhyatt. Will turned towards the house but paused.

"You're not wrong." He nodded his small head before walking towards the house.

Rhyatt smiled after the headstrong boy. Something that had begun as a challenge had become one of his favorite parts of his day. To be honest, any time he spent with the Blakes was a high-light of his day. He usually left drenched in sweat or aggravated, but they strangely felt like a second family. He almost felt guilty about it. He had Adriel and Lita, but the fact remained that his father was dead, and the family he grew up with would never be the same. But with the Blakes, it was different.

Wes approached him, extending one practice sword toward him. A faint smile played on her lips, but her eyes didn't fully focus on him. She was distracted, he concluded.

She had just begun to position herself when he struck out, fast and hard. In a heartbeat, her eyes focused, and her body reacted. Her sword flew up to protect her, but she didn't counterattack. Her eyes narrowed on him, and she tilted her head.

"Surprise attacks require more surprise than that."

"Was worth a shot." Rhyatt shrugged, drawing himself back up and striking again.

This time she let him get closer before pushing him back and counter attacking. She attacked hard and fast. Rhyatt kept up. Barley. But he kept up. He blocked her and attacked. But she gave him no mercy, stopping his attack in its tracks and countering. He was forced backwards as he regained his wits. She seized his loss and went again. This time he was able to hold his ground.

"Someone's been practicing." She crooned.

He resisted the urge to smile at her compliment.

"Did you expect anything less?"

"No." She stepped sideways, attacking again.

They trained in silence, the heat beating down on them, making their strikes angrier than normal. After Wes took a break to teach him something new, he ventured to ask her a question he had been wondering since the previous night.

"What are the customary death rituals?" he asked as he committed the new move to muscle memory.

"Why? Do you plan on dying soon?" She asked, her brows knitting together.

"No." Amusement tugged at the corner of his mouth as he spoke. "Just trying to understand."

She cocked an eyebrow before nodding, "When someone passes, we wait a few days before burying them. The days between are the days of mourning. On the day of the funeral family and friends gather to mourn and say their goodbyes. When it's over, we return to town and celebrate their life," her voice dropped low, and she added, "No matter how short."

Rhyatt paused to process it, "The days of mourning-are they the only days you are supposed to mourn?"

Wes looked at him like he had two heads, her sword pausing its slow path, "Yes, in theory. But grieving is never a linear process."

It was Rhyatt's turn to be perplexed as he lowered his sword. "Explain."

"You can listen and learn. Sword up." She said, refocusing on him. He had noticed that she could carry on a conversation easier when she was in motion. The fluidity of her body made the words come out with the same grace and speed. He raised his sword, and they continued practicing the new move.

"Being in mourning for too long is hard on the body. That is why you are to mourn them until *their* body is gone." She slowed before continuing, "Some believe when we speak about our dead we allow them to see us from the afterworld. When we talk fondly, they experience our happiness."

"And what if you talk ill of them?" Rhyatt asked.

Wes chuckled darkly, "Only you would think of that." she shook her head, "If you believe they can see us and experience our happiness, then the opposite is true."

"That's why my father told me to never speak ill of the dead," Rhyatt muttered.

"Indeed." She pursed her lips, seeming to contemplate something. "When I was younger, I threatened Warden that I would kill him just to speak ill of him. I told him if he died before I was ready, I would speak so ill of him that he would come back as a ghost. My logic was that if he was haunting me, we could still be together."

Rhyatt laughed, a rough laugh from the back of his throat. "Seems very on par for you."

"It is." She struck again. "Tell me, your father grew up here. Did he never tell you of our beliefs?"

"Yes and no. He always kind of followed my mother's lead on how to raise us. And when she left, he continued as she always had. He always said little things like not speaking ill of the dead. My mother often said being good would get us into the heavens, and being bad got us into the hells."

"The heavens, as in the skies? The hells as in below the ground?" Wes asked, her curiosity piquing and spilling into her eyes.

"Yes."

"I didn't know they were places your soul could go." She hadn't asked a question, but he could tell she was waiting for more.

"Maybe they aren't." Rhyatt shrugged.

Her eyes narrowed again, "And what do *you* believe, Rhyatt?"

He paused his motion, lowering the weapon to reset, "I'm not sure if I believe anything happens to us after we die. Maybe we just cease to exist... If I was to *choose* something to believe, it would be that when we die, our souls go to new bodies and are reborn." He watched Wes's smile widen before he continued. "Something about the idea of souls who are meant to be together continuously finding each other- well, it seems nice. Maybe it's just the romantic in me."

Her smile expanded, showing her teeth and meeting her eyes. The real smile. Rhyatt found himself hopelessly lost as he stared at her.

"You are definitely a romantic," she concluded, shaking her head.

He nodded in agreement. He would agree to almost anything when she smiled like that. But he was too wrapped in memorizing her face to notice her body had shifted.

Quicker than a dart, she struck, her sword slapping his arm, sending a sting down it. Her eyebrows rose as shock crossed her features.

"Where's your mind at?"

He shook his head, trying to clear it, "You've smiled like that twice."

The shock and grin faded and were replaced by her cat-like grin and the raising of a brow, "Like what?" she asked, her weapon still pointed at the ground.

"Not like that," Rhyatt said, laughter lacing his voice as he raised his sword again. He thought she would ask again, but instead, she wrinkled her nose and drew herself up.

WES

Wes had ended up pushing Rhyatt harder than she ever had before. When they finished both of them were coated in sweat and out of breath. Opting to wash up, they walked to where the creek met the forest, in hopes it would be cooler than that of the banks nearest by that soaked in the sun.

They both knelt down together to drink the cooler water. Afterward, Rhyatt stood, allowing Wes more space to splash the water across her face and arms.

"You never took me up on my offer to train you." Rhyatt attempted to tease, but Wes could tell he was hurt. She knew she had unintentionally hurt him in the cavern. She still hadn't found the right words to tell him what had changed. Turning back to look at him, she focused her calculating eyes on his face.

"I didn't know you were serious."

"Why wouldn't I be?" His shoulders straightened.

Wes shrugged, returning to dip her hands in the water one last time. "Most people say things they don't mean after something like that."

She stood and backed away, allowing him space. He knelt beside the water, rinsing his hands.

"I meant what I said."

"Of course you did." Wes rolled her eyes and crossed her arms, "When do we start, *bunny*?"

Rhyatt stood and faced her, a mischievous smile growing, a flash of white against his dark skin. "I was thinking right now, *killer*."

A smirk grew on her face. She enjoyed him like this, playful and light. "Looking to get your ass handed to you one more time today?"

To her surprise, he stepped forward, leaving only a hand's width of space between them, "Only if it's by you." His voice was a whisper, and it sent a shiver down her spine.

"The rules?" She asked, pretending not to be affected by how he was looking down at her. How unfair it was that the gods had gifted him thick, long eyelashes. Don't even get her started on the lips.

"No biting-"

"-That's my favorite-"

"No pinching, no scratching. Hits and kicks are fair."

"And I don't need to pull my punches?"

"No." He stood taller.

"I'm not like you, Rhy. If you say don't pull them, I won't."

His hand covered his heart in faux hurt, "My pride would be wounded if you went easy on me."

Wes broke eye contact, looking down, "Have it your way."

Without warning, she stepped closer and hooked her ankle behind his legs, sending him falling. His free arm went wide, but the one that had been on his heart reached out to steady himself.

To both of their surprise, his hand grabbed her belt and sent the both of them scrambling to the ground.

He landed on his back with Wes on top of him.

His hand was loosely held at her hip. She moved to get up, but one of her legs was tucked under his. She wiggled her hips, trying to free her legs. Once they were free, she tucked her arms under herself to push up. But her elbows had hit a sensitive spot on Rhyatts' ribs, and he grunted, the hand on her hip jerking her upwards, forcing her to straddle him. The shift had also put them eye to eye, their chests heaving in union as they caught their breath.

Wes pulled her head back, and this close, she could see the golden streak in his right eye. She could see the faint scars on his cheekbones from punches, she realized. Despite the barely visible scars, he still had a very straight nose. It had never been broken.

"You've never broken your nose." She whispered, their faces still close.

"I wasn't ready," Rhyatt grumbled at the same time.

Wes sat up but didn't get off of him. She ran her tongue across her exposed teeth and repeated back his words, "The rules were no biting, no pinching, and no scratching. I did none of those. Not my fault you weren't ready." Triumph coursed through her. She was so proud she almost didn't notice the current that was *everywhere*, not just where they touched. It seemed like this much of them touching made the current faster and wilder. She wanted to ask him if he felt it, too, but he let out a low laugh.

"I haven't broken my nose."

"You either didn't fight much, or you were a *very* good fighter."

She reached her hand up, gently tracing her pointer finger along the light scars on his cheekbones. Leaning forward she touched the bridge of his nose, admiring the smoothness of it. Her finger paused at his lips, looking for any trace of scars.

"Which do you believe?" he asked, his voice gruff.

Her eyes flickered to his, and she noticed the shift. As she had been studying him, he had been doing the same to her. And now his attention was focused on her lips. Her heartbeat increased as she remembered the position they were in.

His hand left her hip and followed the length of her arm up until his fingers ran across her cheek. Then his thumb gently went across her lips.

"I know you fight a lot, so you must be a good fighter." His words were slow, methodic. She blinked back at him, heat spreading through her body. When he looked at her like that, she wanted nothing more than to rip his clothes off. She instead opted for something more subtle. She parted her lips and pushed his finger into her mouth. Slowly she closed her mouth and sucked, pulling her head away until she reached the tip and pulling back completely to bite her own lip.

His face of shock was worth it, but the face of arousal afterward made it that much sweeter. His hand snaked to the back of her neck, but before he could pull her down, she heard the clopping of hooves.

Her head snapped towards the house, a few heart beats later a boy riding a horse rounded the corner and looked for them.

By then Rhyatt had seen too, she pushed up off of him and brushed herself off, stepping out of the forest so the boy could see her. Rhyatt stood beside her as she waved him down.

The rider approached until he was close enough for Wes to recognize him. Dylin. He was still a boy, the hair on his upper lip just beginning to grow.

"Dylin." She said, nodding her head in greeting, her lips tight. This couldn't be good.

"Wes." he dipped his head, returning her greeting before continuing, "Knox showed up to the Lucky Duck half an hour ago. My father sent me to let you know."

"Was he alone?" She asked.

"Yes." he nodded and glanced at Rhyatt.

"Thank you. Give your father my thanks and let him know I'll be there soon."

"Of course," Dylin said. He turned his horse towards the house and took off again.

As soon as he rounded the corner of the house Wes heaved out a breath. She looked down to the ground, a small patch of moss grew beside her left foot. She stared at it for a moment, contemplating the simplicity of it. All moss had to do was grow. What a simple life it must be to focus on nothing but your own survival. But it also must be a lonely life.

Taking a deep breath, she looked up and squared her shoulders to Rhyatt, "Accompany me?"

RHYATT

R hyatt had kept his mouth closed as he helped her prepare the horses. She had insisted on them, and Rhyatt had a suspicion that she didn't anticipate Knox being able to walk home. So they rode into town in silence, only the clopping of their horses' hooves across the dirt path. Not long after they left the stables, the sun had set completely, leaving them to ride in the dark.

He wanted to ask if she was worried about Knox, but he knew she was. There was no point in stating the obvious.

"I spoke to him yesterday," Rhyatt said. When she didn't respond, he continued, "He told me about Jaze."

"Jaze," She whispered softly, the name a prayer on her lips.

"Yes," Rhyatt said more confidently. "I think he's.." he paused, searching for the right word, "*upset* about what you told him."

"Upset?" She turned towards him, "Does he not think the rest of us are upset? You don't see Cleo and I drinking ourselves into oblivion every night."

"I'm not defending him." Rhyatt forced himself to sit higher in the saddle, pushing his shoulders back before continuing. "I just think he's hurting more than you think. And maybe cutting him some slack would help."

Wes scoffed and turned away.

They rode the rest of the way in utter silence. Perhaps he had spoken out of turn. After a very awkward few minutes, they arrived at the Lucky Duck Tavern.

The room had a yellow glow from the gas lamps hanging from the high ceilings. It was still early, and many people had dishes of food in front of them. In one corner, a group of loud elders played a card game. The oldest-looking woman he'd ever seen rose as she flipped them all the bird and raked in her earnings. The others sighed and returned the gesture. The bar was lined with lone travelers who had large bags with all their belongings. And in the very middle, closest to the bar, sat Knox.

He sat at a round table with another man, both laughing open-mouthed laughs. Judging by the neat dark green uniform, the other man was military. Knox looked up and saw them, but he did not react as Rhyatt had expected. Instead, he smiled, waving them over.

Wes walked towards them, Rhyatt on her heels. She bent down and whispered something in the soldier's ear. When he stood, his ears were turning pink and he slithered away like a thief in the night.

"Oh, come on Wes. Join the fun, don't ruin it!" Knox chided, his cheeks red in color and his curls pushed back from his face with sweat.

"I'm sorry, friend," Wes said, sorrow lacing her voice before she held her hand over his mouth and nose. It took three heartbeats before Knox stopped trying to pull away, his body going limp.

With her free hand, she grabbed his head and gently guided it down onto the table.

When she pulled away, Rhyatt noticed the small vial that she had held over his nose. She corked it and returned it to her pocket. Rhyatt had not seen her remove it upon entering, nor had he seen her pack it. She patted Knox's arm gently before turning and striding to the bar. Rhyatt followed.

"How much do I owe you?" She asked the barkeep who stood pouring drinks.

"Forty-two silver." He replied, a disappointing frown on his face.

"I have only twenty on me," Wes said, pulling two silver ten pieces from her pocket and placing them in the barkeep's hand. "Send Dylin to the BlakeMoore tomorrow, and I will supply the rest," she leaned closer and whispered, "*plus interest.*"

The barkeep put the silver pieces in his pocket with one hand while the other passed drinks to a bartender. He shook his head the entire time, disappointment radiating from him.

"What is it?" Wes asked and glanced back to where Knox still lay.

"Soon, your money will be no good here." His voice was gruff but not harsh.

"You know I'm good for the money." Wes inched forward, furrowing her brows.

"I know you are," he said dismissively. "You need to stop interfering on your friend's behalf. Falling hard on your ass is what makes you fearful of the fall."

"And you fear me altering his fall makes him ignorant of his wrongdoings?"

"Somewhat." he shrugged before continuing, "What I fear more is the day he truly falls, it will be a *hard fall*. And because the boy has never fallen, he will have no clue how to handle it. You, of all people, know how much there is to learn from climbing back up."

"I do." She pushed her shoulders back, and her tone shifted, "Let us hope I am able to interfere before it happens."

The barkeep saw the shift and followed suit, growing distant from her. "For your sake, I hope you are not."

Wes returned to Knox, her mouth set in a tight line as she and Rhyatt wrapped an arm underneath his shoulders and stood him up. He wasn't as heavy as he looked. Together, they drug him outside, and as one they lifted him onto the saddle of the horse. Wes climbed up behind him, leaving Rhyatt to ride alone.

When they arrived at Knox's home, Wes led them to the back side, light spilling out of the house windows illuminating their path. They tied their horses up before hauling Knox down, sitting him against the small brick wall that made up a raised garden bed. She pulled something from her pocket and wafted it in front of his nose before he stirred.

Bursting to his feet, Knox immediately found Wes and his eyes bored into her, "You had no right to do that."

"Knox," Wes said quietly, her voice steady.

"It's embarrassing. To be drugged and then taken from the bar. Do you know how bad we both must look?" He continued, ignoring her.

"This has got to stop. I know you miss him, we all do, but this." she raised her hands, motioning towards him, "This can't go on. He's gone. And there's nothing we can do to change the past."

Knox blinked, drawing himself up straighter. And the nastiest look Rhyatt had ever seen began to spread across Knox's face. He was looking to hurt something. But instead of raising his hand, he opened his mouth.

"Maybe if you weren't sneaking around with him, he wouldn't have died. If you had just *loved him-* and it had been out in the open, he would still be here."

Wes recoiled, her nostrils flaring. She spoke low, "You have no right declaring I didn't love him."

Knox only smiled and stepped closer, the action anything but warming. "Not in the way that mattered." he spat. "But you don't deny that if you weren't sneaking around, he'd still be here."

It wasn't a question but rather a statement. Either way, it got the response he was looking for.

"You don't think that exact thought doesn't run through my mind every. Damn. Day." her voice rose louder, meaner. "If we hadn't seen each other in secret, perhaps we would have been at the BlakeMoore that night or perhaps in town. But at the end of the day, the fact remains. That barn would've been lit on fire with him in it."

"You don't know that." Knox snarled. "The sway your family has- You loving him could've changed everything."

"If you want something to be angry about, be angry I left the barn, be angry that I didn't notice it on fire sooner, be angry I didn't get inside to drag him out, be angry I didn't die trying." Her voice wavered as she stepped closer, her pointer finger pressing into his chest. "But don't you dare try and tarnish my memories of him. Don't you dare tarnish what I have left of him by trying to make me wish it was something else. Don't you fucking dare."

Knox didn't have an immediate response, Rhyatt stepped forward, meaning to diffuse the situation. But instead Knox's hate filled eyes only turned to him, deciding on the next target. He stepped away from Wes to face Rhyatt.

"I understand now," a guttural laugh escaped him. "You are just a sorry replacement for him. I bet she hides you all the same. Be careful. You may find yourself burnt to ashes after she leaves."

Rhyatt knew the jab was meant to hurt Wes, but after their night of talking he felt the sting all the same.

"Enough," Wes commanded, her voice was again low.

And it was very much a command. It left no room for question, no room for interpretation. With all the fire of a newborn star in her eyes, she had commanded Knox to stop, and he did. A sinking feeling started in Rhyatt's stomach and rose its way up as he looked between the two and started to understand. Wes would take all the verbal beatings from her friend, but the moment he brought others in, she shut it down. Likewise, Knox understood this. He understood the way to hurt her was by hurting others. They understood each other in a way only people who had known each other their whole life did.

Wes turned and remounted her horse. From her high horse, she looked down upon Knox.

"If the ideology you're sticking to is that us hiding is what got him killed, perhaps you should think about why we hid it. It certainly wasn't my mother's rules."

It was how Knox would have reacted to their relationship, Rhyatt realized. Knox must've realized this too because as soon as she was out of eyesight, his shoulders slumped.

Rhyatt mounted his horse and took one last look at Knox.

"I'm sorry, Rhyatt." He mumbled, staring after where Wes had disappeared. He walked into the house without another word.

Rhyatt rode to the end of the long driveway and found Wes waiting for him. Silently they resumed riding back to the Blake-Moore. The night was partly cloudy, making them ride by the moonlight that faded in and out of clouds.

"I shouldn't have said that." Her voice was distant.

WES

Wes hated taking the carriage anywhere. It was pretentious and slow. But at least Zonny, her field hand, had offered to drive her. He was good company on the drive to the Pryde's home. And if she was honest, he provided good encouragement, too. She knew the tightly fitted dress and plunging neckline was a show stopper. She knew she looked good in it. But Zonny made sure to tell her *exactly* how good she looked. 'Murder worthy' was the term he had used. He had also suggested they both go play poker afterward. His idea was that she would be so distracting that everyone else would instantly become shite at playing. She had to laugh. It wasn't a bad idea. However, tonight, she had a greater purpose.

After Knox's latest outburst, she had decided someone on the council of five was still their best bet. But with the uneasy feeling around Commander Pryde, she felt almost paralyzed with fear. If she passed the journal off to the wrong person, all of Jaze's work would be for nothing. It was because of those fears that last night, she had begun copying the first few pages of his journal. They only got one chance to give it to the correct person. If given to the wrong person, they could be killed. But even so, his words would remain.

Tonight, she hoped to get Commander Pryde to slip up. To mention anything about Duran relations. Hopefully, he would drink too much and say things he shouldn't. If that failed, she had stored a set of lock picks under her left breast, close to her heart. Will had shown her the basics of how to use them, and although she wasn't confident in her abilities, she was confident in buying herself enough time to use them. It would be all too easy to convince Atticus to invite her to stay later. And surely his home office had to have more personal documents.

Exiting the carriage, Zonny gave her one last wink as she climbed the stairs of the Commander's residence. The perfectly manicured front gardens were the prime example of Jorjin exuberance, the residency being passed down from one Commander to another. Also serving to impress and woo other officials. The front doors were propped open letting in the cool night air. Stepping inside, she noticed the young girl who stood waiting to direct guests further in. Wes smiled in recognition.

"Amala, what are you doing here?" Wes asked the girl. She knew her from a shoe shop in the square.

"Hi, Wes." The girl beamed and dipped her head quickly in greeting. "The Commander was needing extra help for events, and I'm saving up for a trip to Madjai!"

"Oh wow, that'll be a fun trip. If you're still saving up, I'm having a party in December that Rhina will need tons of help with."

The girl stretched onto her tiptoes in excitement, "Oh, yes! Marley is saving up, too!"

"I'm guessing you two are traveling together?" Amala nodded. "I could use both of you. Stop by the house and talk to Rhina. She'll tell you all the details."

"Thank you, Wes! Oh! And right this way!" she said, remembering her duties and directing Wes towards the dining hall.

Wes entered the well lit room, admiring the delicate chandelier and the array of flowers hanging from the ceilings. The Commander's house was comparable in size to the BlakeMoore, but in comparison the Commander's house felt shiny. It made the BlakeMoore feel well used, or *well loved*. She recalled all the dinners her family had with the Pryde's. That was when everyone still lived under the same roof, it seemed a lifetime ago.

Stepping further inside, she noticed a few familiar faces, including Winnie, Atticus's older sister, who was studying abroad. Ida, Atticus's much younger sister, was Winnie's shadow, jabbering her jaw off. Hugo Hao, the trade councilor, stood with them. They chatted with Winnie, asking about her exploits. Next to them stood Commander Pryde and two strangers. She didn't recognize them, and judging by their clothing, they were most likely from Duran. Perhaps this was her lucky night.

Before she could step forward and introduce herself, Atticus broke off his conversation and surged towards her. He looked polished in his dark formal wear. The cut of his coat emphasized his lean frame.

"Wes." he said her name like a praise as he wrapped her up in a hug. Bent to her level he whispered in her ear, "Save me. They're already talking about trade."

"I'll see what I can do." She whispered back, matching his conspiratory tone.

296

He laughed and pulled away but kept his hands on her elbows, keeping her close. His eyes scanned her body. Wes wanted to lean into it, lean into the seduction, but something in his eyes was different. It wasn't lust, it was... joy.

Her stomach tightened in response. Atticus was less than a year or so younger than her, but yet he still seemed to be a boy. It made sense. He was afforded all the protection and coddling as the Commander's child. Winnie, his eldest sister, was the same way. Well, she was, at least until she went away to study. The reminder made Wes feel hollow at first, but then it enraged her. It made her mad for the life she could've lived. For the innocence that could've still danced in her eyes if not for her sham of a mother.

She quickly shut down the thoughts as Atticus's eyes returned to hers.

"This is the part where you tell me I look beautiful," Wes whispered a loose smile on her lips.

Atticus released her elbows and rocked back onto his heels, smiling out the right side of his mouth.

"I don't think beautiful is the right word. When I find a word adequate to describe you, I'll let you know."

Wes couldn't help the little chuckle that left her. Perhaps she was a fool for letting her mother's wishes keep her away from Atticus for so long. Gods, her mother probably would've encouraged a public relationship between the two. Wes shook her head and brought herself back to the present. She wasn't going to let thoughts of her mother ruin tonight. She had far too much to do and far too much to lose.

Soon they all sat down to dinner as staff began bringing out the courses. She had sat in between Councilor Hugo and Atticus, across from her sat the two merchants from Duran, which she had yet to be introduced to.

"I'm sorry, but what were your names?" Wes asked as she picked up a fork.

"My apologies," Commander Pryde said before either of them could speak. "This is Barren." He gestured to the younger man. He was short and stout with a neatly trimmed dark beard. "He trades in a cacti that has healing properties when used correctly."

"You are too kind, Commander," Barren said, his youthful smile warm, "I am a scholar first, a tradesman to survive."

"And this is Aridia," The Commander continued, gesturing towards the woman. She looked to be only a handful of years older than Wes, but the way her eyes narrowed told a different story entirely. She held herself with as much poise as a princess would. "She trades in rare snakeskins." The iridescent bodice of her dress made sense now. It was made up of multiple snakeskins. All of them were black and shifted to dark blue when she moved. Wes looked up to see Aridia staring back at her.

"Blueback racer of the black sands." her voice was low and strong, drawing all attention to her. "I tracked it for ten days before finally killing it." She drew her gaze from Wes to look around the table. "On the tenth day, I knew. Either it was going to eat me, or I was going to eat it. I came out with a full belly." She swept her hand down the bodice as proof and laughs of approval sounded from the table, Wes's included.

"It is quite extraordinary. I've never seen a snakeskin so dark." Wes said, the smile still on her lips.

"Ah," Aridia clucked, picking up her wine glass with a thin hand, "Your jungle hosts much more colorful snakes but generally less dangerous. Desert snakes are unforgiving and lethal." She paused to take a sip of her wine, and Wes got the sense that this woman was just as unforgiving and lethal as the snakes she hunted. "Forgive *me*, what was your name?"

"I am Wes-"

"Wes Blake, my current apprentice, family friend, and business owner." The Commander said, cutting her off. His eyes flicked back and forth between the women, and abruptly, he turned to his eldest daughter, "Winnie, dearest, tell us how life is in Madjai."

Madjai was the southernmost part of the country. Nestled in the mountains it held a cooler climate, creating a slightly different way of life. It was why Wes's father had moved there, to escape.

"Madjai is as usual. Cold. The snow will begin soon, and I will be trapped indoors for the rest of winter." Winnie said with a bored expression.

The sounds of forks and knives clanking filled the silence after her dismissal. Wes took a delicate bite of her food, and when she looked up to reach for her wine glass, she noticed Aridia staring at her.

"You must tell me more about Duran. I've never been and would love to go." Wes directed her question at Aridia, but Barren was first to speak.

"What do you want to know? There isn't much to tell; it's mostly a dry desert." He said, forking another piece of meat.

"Oh, come now, Barren. There's much more to Duran than just deserts. The city itself is a wonder." Aridia cooed and took another sip of wine.

"And where do you hunt your snakes?" Atticus asked.

"Here, there, everywhere." Aridia's response resulted in a shared laugh around the table. She took another sip of wine with a catlike grin. She hadn't touched her food.

"We certainly have a few pesky ones behind our house, you are more than welcome to hunt them down anytime you are in the area." Councilor Hugo said.

"I'd love to." She tilted her head as if sizing up the councilor. "I could make you a beautiful garment or perhaps a pair of boots."

Aridia spoke of the business deal as if she were trading sex. Her voice remained low and seductive.

Atticus turned to her and leaned in, "We should plan to visit Duran City this summer."

"You'll want to visit before summer. The heat is unbearable." Barren said, not taking the social cue that their conversation was supposed to stay between the two of them.

"*You* shouldn't visit at all. It's dangerous right now." Winnie said, chiding her younger brother.

The table went silent as the siblings turned to each other.

"And how would you know?" Atticus raised an eyebrow in defiance.

"Even Father said so." Winnie retorted with an eye roll, rising to the bait.

"I said it wasn't safe for you and three of your school friends to go gallivanting around." Mr. Pryde said, color tinging his cheeks.

"He's quite right. Tourists are often victims of crimes." Barren chimed in.

Winnie grew further aggravated and turned to Aridia, who had sat back in her chair to watch the exchange.

"What do you think, Aridia?"

She leaned to the side and rested her elbow on the armrest.

"I think," she pursed her lips, "The city can be just as dangerous as any new place. However, if you wish to visit, I will clear my home and welcome you and your friends. I believe that will put your father's worries to peace." She turned and looked at the Commander this time, her eyes sparkling, "No?"

Commander Pryde donned a tightlipped smile and nodded once. His eyes would have burned a hole straight through Winnie, but she didn't notice. Instead, she had turned to Aridia and started discussing the details of her future stay. The Commander stayed tight-lipped at the head of the table, only engaging quietly with Councilor Hugo.

When dessert was halfway over, Wes stood and excused herself to go to the restroom. Tiptoeing through the empty halls, she came to a stop in front of the large double doors that led to the Commander's office. With a gleam of hope, she tried the knob. It was locked. She reached into her dress and pulled out the lock-picking tools she had borrowed from Will. Carefully and quietly, she pushed both pieces into the lock and began attempting to work them.

She had never mastered lock picking. When she was younger, Warden was better at it, and when he left, Cleo always had the nimblest fingers. But now she wished she would have observed them a bit closer.

She had been hunched over focusing, when the distant sound of chairs scraping reached her. Cursing softly, she shoved the tools back into the bodice of her dress and hustled towards the restroom. She closed the door with care and turned the lock slowly so that anyone in the hallway wouldn't hear it click.

After securing the lock, she sat on the toilet and cursed her less-than-proficient skills.

Shit.

Shit Shit Shit.

This had been her opportunity to get an inside look at Pryde's office and see what he was hiding. When Duran was mentioned, he had tensed up tonight, and he certainly wasn't going to let his daughter journey there. He knew more than what he let on. And even though Wes wished he was innocent, she had a sinking feeling he wasn't. Even if he didn't cause Jaze's death, he most likely knew something about it. And that meant she *had* to get into that office. A small plan began to form. If she could unlatch a window, she could sneak in tonight. With more time, she could pick the lock and gain access to the office.

She nodded confidently and stood. Now all she needed to do was unlock a window. Walking to the frosted glass window in the bathroom, she peered out into the darkness. To her surprise, a dark shadow passed by, making her tense. A moment later, the shadow passed again, this time going the opposite way. Holding her breath, she waited. When it passed a third time, it clicked. Of course, the commander would have security on the premises. Gods, how could she be so stupid to forget? He wasn't just the leader of Saint Saveen. He was the leader of the northern third of the country.

Sighing, she turned and opened the door with defeat before pausing.

Atticus leaned up against the opposite wall.

"I wouldn't have fixed my hair if I knew you were waiting." She stepped out of the doorway and motioned for Atticus to go in.

"I was waiting for you." He replied, his voice low.

"Oh?"

"Father insisted on showing our guests the gardens, and I wanted to wait for you."

"Not interested in seeing the gardens?" Wes teased, resting her hip against the frame of the door and crossing her arms.

"After you've spent your entire life in them, it gets a little boring."

"Ah, and what should we do instead?"

Atticus stepped off the wall and got close to her, a smirk appearing. "I have a few ideas."

Two stolen bottles of expensive wine later, Atticus and Wes roamed the house, fits of giggles and whispered words flowing between them.

"And this." Atticus paused in front of a portrait of an elderly man outside of the office. "This is where I learned ink mustaches *do not* come off old paintings."

"You did not!" Wes laughed, clutching her wine bottle to her chest.

"Winnie told me to!" Atticus whisper-shouted in defense, holding his free hand up.

"And you listened to her?" Wes teased, leaning closer and shaking her head.

"If you had a sister like Winnie, you'd do it too."

"Would not," Wes said, pulling away and taking another drink straight from the bottle.

"Would too." He stepped closer

"Nope." She shook her head and took a step back.

"Would too!" He said and stepped forward, wrapping his free arm around her waist and pulling her close. Her sharp laughter echoed down the empty hall, his own following.

Wes watched with curiosity as his eyes roamed over her face and then focused on her lips. Her lower stomach tightened.

"We're not done with the tour, are we?" She asked, breaking the spell and motioning towards the locked office doors with a raise of her brow.

He leaned back and took a drink from his bottle, "Of course not."

In a steady stride he walked to the double doors, his lean body stretched until he touched the top of the frame and came away with a key.

Wes silently cursed herself for not looking for a key. Never mind that she couldn't reach the top of the doorframe.

He unlocked the door and returned the key to its hiding spot.

Stepping in together, she was reminded of just how different their two houses were. The BlakeMoore's office doubled as a library and was filled to the brim with well-worn books. The furniture was well-loved and placed so that friends could gather away from the desk. The Commander's office was the opposite. The sofas and chairs were all facing the large wooden desk. Behind the desk were three bookshelves that had been built into the wall. All the books were color-coordinated and looked as if they'd never been opened. This office made it very clear where the focus should be: on the person at the desk.

Wes strutted to the desk and stood behind it as Atticus shut the door behind him. He turned around, and his eyebrows creased at seeing her standing tall behind the desk.

"Practicing for when I'm Commander," Wes said, tilting her head and tracking his movements in the dimly lit room.

He stalked to her side of the desk, and she turned so that her back was to the door. He gently pushed her shoulders so that her ass sat firmly on the desk. Once she was sitting, he sat in the leather chair and pulled her bare feet into his lap.

"Now you're posted up just like the queen you are."

A throaty laugh escaped her. Oh, this was interesting. But two could play.

"Is that how you like to treat women? Like queens?"

He had his hand resting gently on her ankle and smiled, squeezing her ankle.

"I like to treat women however they like to be treated." He said slyly, rubbing a small circle on her ankle.

Images flashed through her mind. She had heard a rumor of him and a woman barking at each other under the bar. At the time, she had laughed it off as a silly rumor about the commander's son. Now, in front of him, with his expectant eyes trained on her, she wasn't as sure.

"You think I like to be treated like a queen?"

"No," he clicked his tongue, "I know you do."

"I'm intrigued. Explain."

"I've seen the type of men and women you take home." His thumb moved slowly over her skin. "By the time you leave, they're worshiping you."

"I fail to see what's wrong with that." She whispered, leaning closer to him in a challenge.

"Nothing," he whispered back.

"And tell me of yourself, Atticus. What do you like? I once heard a rumor... maybe you could put it to rest for me."

"Do tell, I love hearing about myself," he said between huffs of laughter.

"It involved a golden-haired stranger and *barking*."

Atticus's grin twisted to the side of his mouth as he took a swig of his wine, the first sign of him being uncomfortable. But instead of denying it, he only settled into his skin and replied.

"What can I say, Wes? *I like to please*."

A thrill went down her spine. It was the first time she had thought of Atticus as anything more than his father's spawn. Perhaps the prodigal son was something that needed to be investigated further.

"It's a good thing that I like to be pleased," Wes said, licking her lips.

Slowly, Atticus pulled his chair closer, sitting up taller so they were face to face. His hand reached out and cupped behind her head.

"I'd say it's a perfect match."

Without warning, he pulled her close and kissed her, their hot wine breath mixing as the kiss turned needy rather quickly. It took all of a handful of heartbeats before Wes had put down her wine and scooted off the desk to straddle his lap. One of his hands stayed behind her head, and the other immediately reached down to cup her behind and pull her forward. She obliged until she could feel his hardness pressing against her. Her lower stomach clenched as she rolled her hips against him. A breathless moan escaped him as he pulled away.

"Please me." She whispered melodically in his ear.

He stood, placing her back on the desk. In a quick motion, he dropped to his knees and pushed her dress up.

When he kissed her inner thigh, she threw her head back and allowed him to do what he did best: please others.

Wes had sat up to take a drink of wine, and Atticus was still wiping his face when Winnie burst through the door without knocking.

She didn't even flinch at the sight of Wes with her dress pulled up, or at the sight of her brother on his knees before her. Instead she dead panned at Wes and in a bored tone announced they were requested in the garden. Atticus stood, flustered and rushed towards the bathroom muttering about cleaning up.

Winnie stood taller and crossed her arms at the entranceway, refusing to leave Wes alone.

"Ms. Blake," she said in a faux greeting.

"Winifred," Wes replied with a smiling snarl.

Winnie twitched. "Bitch."

"Attention whore." Wes replied sweetly before adding, "I would ask how you are, but Warden says you've already made a name for yourself."

"That's funny, considering your brother has a nastier reputation than me. Word is if you get him drunk enough, he'll give anyone a ride."

"I heard the same about you. Shame you two haven't crossed paths yet." Wes stood and began walking towards the door, "Or perhaps he knows how desperate you are to cross paths with him." She shrugged and left the room, leaving Winnie to steam by herself.

Winnie and her had never gotten along. As children, Winnie was a year older than Wes and Warden, and Atticus was a year younger. The obvious choice was to choose the older child, and they had. Until Winnie had pulled Warden's hair. Wes had then kicked her in the shin and told her to shove it where the sun didn't shine. From then on, when visiting, they would find Atticus instead.

Wes left the office, pulling her dress down before gathering Atticus and continuing to the gardens. Once out in the glow of lamplight, Wes could make out practice swords sitting on benches outside a traditional swordsman circle. Aridia was holding one and testing the balance. Barren was beside her, looking quizzically at the others. As Wes and Atticus approached Commander Pryde looked up, and something akin to worry crossed his brow before he smoothed it out and smiled at them.

"The Commander tells me you are something of a swordsman, Wes," Aridia said, her long legs moving towards her.

It was while watching her legs move that Wes realized she had had a bit too much to drink.

"I dabble," Wes said, pursing her lips and trying to keep her face straight and keep her body from swaying like a sheet in the wind. She didn't feel too successful when Atticus reached out a hand and placed it on her lower back to steady her.

"Oh, don't be modest, Wes." Aridia turned towards the swords, "I know Jorjin is a modest place, but we Duranians like to brag. And I won't be subtle. I am an excellent swordsman. The best in my class, trained by the best teacher north of the border."

"Who might that be?" Wes asked, avoiding a hiccup.

"Sweeny Reed ." She picked up an additional sword and studied it, "He is, of course, old and dying now, but in his prime, he was something to marvel at. I would say I hate to brag, but I don't, and I was named his successor. If snakes ever get boring, I may settle down and start teaching."

She walked with the additional practice sword over to Wes and held it out. Wes winced. She meant for it to be internal, but her twitching cheek told her it was external. She was far too drunk to be worth a damn in a fight, but saying so would not only raise questions, but it would also be disrespectful to Aridia. She was clearly challenging her, and to turn down a challenge was to automatically forfeit.

With a steady hand, she reached out and grabbed the sword. Atticus backed away from her, and everyone else followed, standing outside the circle.

Wes squared her shoulders and dipped her head in concentration; it would take every ounce of her being not to look a fool. Or to throw up.

Aridia stepped sideways, her long legs stretching in front of her. Wes went to follow her circle, but her body moved before her feet, making her do an awkward little stumble. Hot heat rushed to her cheeks and the back of her neck. She wasn't particularly keen on embarrassing herself.

Aridia waited until she righted herself before making the first blow, a smooth and slow swipe at chest height. Wes blocked it with ease, too much ease. It hadn't occurred to her that Aridia would go easy on her. Warning bells began ringing in the back of her mind. Aridia wasn't the type to go easy on anyone that much Wes knew. The only excuse she could think of was that Aridia was giving Wes a moment to sober up.

Wes shook her head, trying harder to concentrate. Once her eyes focused on Aridia, she lunged forward, striking from above. Aridia was quick to react and thrust her sword upwards to block.

Pushing Wes away, Aridia tilted her head down and smiled. Wes wouldn't have been surprised if a forked tongue had stuck out between her teeth, but with no such luck, Aridia struck again, this time quicker.

She darted out like an arrow and aimed low, too low for the taller woman. Wes dropped into a half crouch, blocked the blow, and pushed back. This time, she didn't let Aridia reset. Immediately, she launched a counterattack. Their swords banged against each other as Aridia blocked each blow. She was losing ground fast, but Wes wasn't done. As quick and lethal as one of the snakes Aridia hunted, Wes shoved her sword to the side of Aridia's head, and in a blink of an eye, she got behind Aridia, her sword now flat against the woman's throat.

Aridia and Wes both stood still, huffing from the effort. Wes released the sword and Aridia stepped out of her immediate grip. Turning to face her opponent Aridia smiled. It took Wes by surprise.

"You have great skills. I have seen others train for twice as long as you've been alive and not come near touching what you have. If you're ever in Duran, it would be an honor to introduce you to my master."

Wes blanched and, untrusting of her mouth, nodded.

ANOUK

My night visits have been paying off, I got an additional 50 silver for this information. In the dead of the night the soldiers drag and carry people into the basement entrance. The people they are bringing inside are not the same height or build as the soldiers, most of them are not the same age either. They are not sick. The only thing in common is that they are generally healthy looking and not gray. I have a feeling they will not see the light of day again.

JG

Anouk Rolle, Councilor of War, sat tall in her chair in the Commander's conference room. She had been on the road visiting various outposts for the past week and would truthfully rather be anywhere but here.

One by one the other councilors filed in, and eventually Pryde followed, shutting the door behind him. He waited until everyone was seated before seating himself at the head of the table and beginning to talk.

"Our friends in Duran City have noticed an increase in disappearances in the last few months. They have asked us to investigate and see if any of the missing people have been brought south through Jorjin."

Anouk sighed. Loudly. The other councilors turned to her.

"Why is the disappearance of Duranian citizens a concern of Jorjin?" She asked the question everyone else would not dare.

"The Duran ambassador has asked for our help." Pryde stated, frowning at her. She had always been a threat to him and he knew it.

"What were the circumstances around the missing?" The historic councilor asked.

Pryde gave him a thankful look before answering.

"They all lived in the southern part of The City, all were between 16 to 30, and none were reported missing until days later."

"The Canyon Dwellers have been known to venture into society when running low on food." Anouk pursed her lips.

"Canyon Dwellers eating people. I'm sure The ambassador would love that solution." The trade councilor said, sarcasm thick. At least she wasn't the sole person bothered by this conversation.

"When did they disappear?" The law councilor asked, only his jaw was set. He would not be taking this manor lightly.

"Three of them went missing last Friday night, the other two the night after," Pryde said.

"About three nights ago I had a report of a couple who had failed to return home. Both were under 30, and it took two days until the sister reported them missing." The law councilor said.

"This was in Jorjin?" The Treasury councilor asked now, her soft eyes hardening.

The law councilor nodded.

"A young couple runs away, and five people -out of the tens of thousands of people in Duran- go missing. This is not Jorjinian business." Anouk stated once and for all.

"And what if more go missing? When does it become Jorjinian business? When your family disappears?" The law councilor had risen to his feet, "Your heartlessness remains on full display, Anouk." He said before striding from the room.

Anouk scoffed at his retreating back. Her heartlessness may be on display but his bleeding heart was ever present on his sleeve. Anouk disliked that amount of soft bellied show. Disappearances in either country were not new. People left, people died. And sometimes people bought themselves a new life. Either way it was not her concern.

The other three councilors left the room shortly after, leaving her alone with Pryde.

Alone, he gazed at her differently. Long gone was the benevolent ruler, but rather the sneaky man who would be bargaining with her to get his way. It was his sacrifice to remain in power. It worked in Anouk's favor.

"Out with it, Pryde. Why do you care so much about what happens to the missing?" She said, cutting away any chance for his preamble.

"Our friends in Duran have asked us for assistance. We would be a bad neighbor if we did not provide it."

"*Our friends* in Duran have double the amount of resources we have. I believe they should take care of things on their own."

"Anouk," he said her name with authority, but Anouk took it as a challenge. "It is not ordinary people going missing, but rather their soldiers."

He was baiting her. Anouk had a singular soft spot, her armies. She had cared for them like they were her own children. It was why Northern Jorjin had the most well trained forces.

"We have far too many problems on our side of the border." She rose to her feet so that she could look at him across the table. "I will not be worrying about random nobodies from Duran. When someone worthy of note goes missing, let me know."

KNOX

K nox was surprisingly not the last person to class. It was Wes. And she rolled in looking like shit. He thumbed the gold ring in his pocket and decided that now was not the time.

"Ooh, you look gods-awful." Cleo chided, wrapping an arm around Wes's shoulders and pulling her close.

Wes winced away from the noise and pulled herself away, mumbling words that resembled 'too much wine.'

"So..." Rhyatt raised his eyebrows in question, clearly knowing more than Knox and Cleo did.

"Uneventful." She said, closing her eyes and pinching the bridge of her nose.

"*What* was uneventful?" Cleo asked, her voice a little too sharp.

"I had dinner at the Pryde's last night," Wes opened her eyes and squinted, "I had hoped to look around his home office, but I was followed around by a *puppy* all night."

"His son doesn't trust you?" Rhyatt asked, fists forming at his sides. And perhaps Knox was intentionally blind to a lot of things, but this, this he had known was coming. He had known the night

Rhyatt was almost killed that something had shifted. Even now, he would bet Rhyatt didn't know he was tensing.

"No, that's not the problem. He wanted to be around me *all the time*. However, I know how to get into the office."

Knox wanted to ask if her lock picking skills had finally come to fruition but the ring weighed heavy in his pocket, and he didn't quite feel right joking with her until she had the ring. Cleo said something about looking at it later, but their conversation didn't continue for very long until Tiunda arrived and class began.

For the next couple of hours, they sweated their asses off in class. The sun heated the room to an unbearable heat. When they finally broke for lunch, Knox wondered if he had lost five pounds in sweat alone. He patted his pocket for the ring, and after making sure it was still there, he went outside to look for Wes.

Wes and Rhyatt sat with their backs pressed against a tree, their shoulders touching. Rhyatt passed water to her. She sipped it before passing it back. Knox walked over, wiping the sweat from his brow. When he stopped in front of Wes, she looked up and squinted. There wasn't anything malicious in her stare.

Wordlessly, Knox pulled the thin gold band from his pocket and pinched it between his thumb and pointer finger, extending it to her. Wes studied it for a moment before taking it and slipping it onto her right middle finger. She nodded to him, and like that, it was over. Knox lowered himself to the ground, opting to lie on his back and close his eyes.

The three of them remained like that until Cleo's hurried steps came too close to Knox's head, and he sat up cursing.

"What the fuck, Cleo?"

She only batted his hand away and crouched down next to Wes.

"You'll never believe what Olivinia just told me." Wes raised an eyebrow but didn't uncross her arms or lean up. "She told me that a boy in Scholar Eliza's class told her that Atticus and Wes slept together last night and that The Commander had organized it and *approved*."

In a rush of motion, Wes shot to her feet, and Knox and Rhyatt scrambled to follow.

"That little *liar*." she spat, beginning to pace with her fist clenched at her sides.

Knox's own anger began to bubble at the false accusations of his friend. He looked at Cleo and she had a similar stony expression. But when he looked at Rhyatt he found something between jealousy and pain written across his features.

"What're you going to do?" Knox asked, but what he meant was what are *we* going to do.

Wes paced quicker, two steps, then a sharp turn on her toes, three steps in the opposite direction before repeating. Her mouth was set into a slight frown, and her eyes were focused on nothing at all. Wes's mother had worked so hard to keep her children's personal lives private, and even in her absence, Wes had continued her affairs quietly, ensuring she was not seen and her lovers were not heard. That was one of the reasons she often chose people from out of town or people who had something to lose. She wasn't particularly vocal about it, but Knox knew she wasn't above an occasional threat or two.

She stopped midpace in front of him, "I can't confront him now, everyone will have something to say about that."

"Later? When he's alone?" Cleo asked, mischief glinting in her eyes.

"He won't be alone until after class. No telling what else he'll say between now and then." Knox crossed his arms, his anger multiplying.

And like a sign from above, Atticus and two other boys walked into their line of vision and then up the stairs to the platform. Atticus let out a loud laugh and looked in their direction.

"I wish someone would knock that smug grin off his face. Maybe remind him what happens to liars." Wes seethed.

And the idea seemed good enough to Knox, he turned and began striding towards the brat and his friends. He was vaguely aware of Rhyatts' footsteps behind him. It was probably a good thing, Rhyatt's tall muscular frame was intimidating.

Atticus and his friends were oblivious to the men coming up the stairs until they were too close. Atticus' eyes shifted to Knox, and he put up one hand as a buffer. He opened his mouth to speak, but Knox knocked his hand away.

Atticus looked shocked,, and Knox hated that he had relished it.

Atticus opened his mouth to say excuses again, but Knox swung his fist, connecting with his cheek. He fell to the ground of the platform.

His friends began to scramble, but Rhyatt seemed perfectly capable of handling them.

Dropping one knee on Atticus's chest, Knox bent and grabbed the boy's shirt in his left hand, landing another punch with the right.

Atticus turned his face to the side, sputtering and coughing. Knox could hear the murmurs of students nearby who had stopped what they were doing to watch. He reached into his boot and pulled out a small blade. Atticus turned his head and caught sight of the knife, fear growing in his eyes. He began to squirm under Knox's weight.

"Hold still," Knox said, his voice surprisingly even.

Atticus just moved more, his eyes wide, and Knox leaned closer to his face with the knife.

"Hold still, and it won't hurt as much." Knox tried gripping his chin, "And I won't mess up." he added as an afterthought.

Knox had had his own fair share of liars cuts. And it was true, the stiller you sat the less it hurt and less chance of it being messed up.

Atticus struggled for a moment longer before seeming to think the same thing and stilling. Knox seized the moment and tightly gripped his chin. He was still breathing hard and grimacing, making it rather hard for Knox to hold him.

Knox moved the knife over the top of Atticus's lips.

"Take it in stride, or I'll cut more than your lip."

Atticus narrowed his eyes and in defeat, pushed out his lower lip. Knox took the knife and quickly cut a line down the middle.

"May your tongue taste the lies of your own lips," Knox announced loud enough for others to hear.

He wiped his knife on his pants while rising. More people had gathered to watch the Commander's son be cut at the top of the platform. He turned, and Rhyatt pushed away the other two boys he had been holding by the shoulders of their shirts. Together, the men walked back inside the university, avoiding Wes and Cleo.

RHYATT

T *here is something deeply wrong with the soldiers at the facility. I have counted enough rooms for a thousand, however the food supply is closer to 300. They are not soldiers for the country, their loyalties lie with those inside the facility. They are unnatural in many ways. Their bodies all seem to be crafted by the gods, tall and muscular. All men and all mean. I am not a superstitious man but I am beginning to believe they are possessed. When given a command they follow through immediately and without thought. They are like rabid dogs. Do not get trapped alone with one, I fear they would cut down anyone who stands in their path.*

J

Rhyatt slid deeper into the leather chair of Wes's library.

"There's no way they are possessed," Knox said, reaching for another cookie.

"I agree. Demons are not real, and they *cannot* possess you." Cleo agreed.

"Then why would he mention it? He clearly thinks something is wrong with them." Wes added.

She was the only one who was convinced the soldiers were possessed. Rhyatt, however, was on the fence but he would not be voicing it. Whenever they began to talk about the journal and its contents the conversation usually became very heated.

"There can be something wrong with them without them being possessed," Cleo responded, biting into her cookie with some force.

Rhyatt turned his attention back to Wes, waiting for a response. She was seated directly in front of him on the couch and had taken her boots off hours ago and sat with her legs crossed. Scholar Tiunda had given them the study guide for the midterm and it had been all they could focus on. It was in rare breaks like this where they would scavenge for food and discuss other things.

"What if they've been brainwashed?" Knox asked.

"I don't think that's a real thing?" Wes responded.

"It's not." Cleo sighed.

"Do you think the men that attacked us in the city were their soldiers? Were they possessed? Or brainwashed or whatever." Rhyatt finally spoke, the sound of his voice making him want to be quiet.

"Jaze describes them as rabid dogs who cut down anyone in their path. We were in their path to the journal, and they didn't cut us down." Wes pointed out.

"He also said that they follow commands. What if they were commanded not to kill anyone?" Cleo asked.

"I think it's unlikely. The men at Rhyatt's house were ready to kill him." Wes leaned forward and added, "One of them was also in the group that attacked us in the city."

"One of the men that attacked me was short, about Wes's height, and according to the journal, the soldiers are all tall and muscular. He doesn't fit the description." Rhyatt said.

"So we likely haven't come across any of their soldiers." Knox said and paused, "Then who attacked us? A third party?"

"I still think it was the facility who attacked both times." Wes said, her eyes flicking to Rhyatt, "When they attacked at Rhyatts, they said something about taking me back for testing. It reminds me of what Jaze said about those being dragged into the facility and about the medical experimentation."

"I think they are soldiers," Cleo stated, her tone indicating she didn't care if she was wrong she was simply stating her thoughts, "There is no way they only hire big burly men. You need variety on a team."

"They could've been hired by the facility, not as soldiers." Rhyatt voiced his own thoughts.

"What about hypnotization?" Knox asked, returning to the earlier question.

"That's real, but not on a large scale like what the soldiers would need," Cleo answered.

"So possession," Wes stated, reinforcing her belief.

Cleo rolled her eyes and Knox smiled. Rhyatt only shook his head. He was slightly superstitious but not enough to believe there were 300 soldiers being possessed.

They started to fall quiet, each of them returning to the research or review they had been working on. Rhyatt felt good about the majority of the midterm but was still worried about his swordsmanship. Tiunda had said if he hadn't improved, he would be kicked out. Well, technically, he would be put into a lower level, but he didn't have the time to go through multiple years.

His training lessons with Wes had increased to daily lessons and been lengthened by an hour. She had already scheduled for them to train over the weekend as well. He was worried, but Scholar Tiunda had seen him improve. He hoped she would show leniency towards him. Cleo seemed to think she would.

The clock chimed ten, and Knox nodded off for the third time. Cleo sighed loudly, making it a point to jostle Knox's outstretched legs as she stood.

"If I read *one more word*, I will combust," Cleo announced loudly, waking Knox and gathering her items.

"Please combust outside the library," Wes said in a monotone, not looking up from the passage she was currently reading. The last few hours of study had made them all tired.

"Very well."

"I'll walk you home," Knox said, clambering out of the chair he had been snoozing in.

He didn't have anything to gather, and Wes bid them goodbye without looking up. Rhyatt glanced around at the semi-destroyed library. On every surface, there seemed to be an open book and a pile of notes. The cookie plate from earlier now sat empty. He stretched his legs from his chair as Wes read across from him. He had been reading all about Saint Saveen's time as the commander of the armies, and Wes had been reading others' accounts of her personal life. She huffed and brought the book down on her lap, drawing Rhyatt's attention.

"Every time I feel confident in my knowledge of Saint Saveen, I find something that makes me question if I know anything at all."

"What did you find this time?" Rhyatt asked, placing his own book down on the table.

"Well..." Wes trailed off, her fingers holding multiple pages, "It tells a slightly different version of the original story of the night her family was slain. The original story goes that Saveen was only a young woman when the first wars began. She was the youngest of five siblings; however, none of them had married, and none were out of the house yet. This made her definitively the baby of the family, and they treated her as such. They guarded her from many things, physical and emotional. During the early times of the war, when raiders came to town, Saveen's family acted quickly and stored Saveen under the floorboards, promising to retrieve her when they were gone. The only problem was that the raiders were on a mission to kill as many people as they could that night. Instead of ransacking the home, they killed everyone within. It was a bloodbath. The blood ran so heavy that it soaked through the floorboards and dripped onto Saveen. For three nights, she stayed hidden under the floor. On the morning of the third night, she crawled out from under the house and headed toward the center of town. As dawn broke and people stirred, they gasped in horror as she walked by. She was covered head to toe in dried blood and dirt. Two townspeople watched her walk to the edge of the spring and step into it. By the time they rushed over to help, the clear water was murky and red, and they couldn't see her at all. She stayed underwater for many minutes; everyone who had gathered assumed she was dead, and they would wait until the water settled to fish her out. As onlookers began to leave, something strange happened. Saveen crawled out of the spring, a sword in her hand, and her once light-colored hair was now blood red. She stood and lifted her sword high, the morning light hitting it and emitting a white light. Right then, she swore vengeance against those who had wrongfully fallen in the war.

Soon, she joined the army and climbed the ranks. By the time she was a commander, she had the reputation of never losing a battle. She was the reason the war was won and the reason our town still stands today." Wes paused, considering her words before adding, "She was a woman transformed by the blood of her own family."

Rhyatt studied her, the way her face was downturned, focusing on the book in her hands. Her brow creased in concentration. He almost thought it weird, he had never seen her focus on something so intently. Everything seemed so effortless for her. Even now, when she told a story, the cadences in her voice ensnared his attention.

"Where does the story differ?" He asked.

"In this account, a man claimed she didn't do anything for her family, but instead did it for her lover."

"Her lover?"

Wes nodded, "The man claims to have seen her on the night of the raids, running to her lover's home, only to find her dead as well. He claims to have never seen her return to her own home. It was, of course, three days before she was seen again, so no one truly knows what she did in those three days- but he claims it was her lover's blood that transformed her."

"If it was true, why would it matter?"

She released the pages she was holding and let the book relax into her lap, her gaze looking up to meet his.

"It would not make her a Saint, according to tradition. Her story is one of redemption for lost family that was unjustly taken from her. If instead, it was from a lost lover- no less, a lover when she was only twenty- her actions would be deemed...*bloodhungry*."

"Why would it matter what reasoning she had? She could've considered her lover just as much family as her real one." Rhyatt responded, he hated the way anger seeped into his voice. This was a long dead history, he had no business being upset over it.

"Yes, she could have. But things were different then. Families were closer, and friends were considered risks." Rhyatt twisted his mouth to the side, unsure of how to respond, but Wes continued before he could, "I don't agree at all; actually, it's the opposite."

She gave him a small grin that almost looked sheepish and returned the book to her lap. Rhyatt returned to his. His book detailed many of the battles she had commanded and a few personal accounts from her comrades. He could almost understand what Wes meant about blood-hungry. Saveen had left a red streak a mile long wherever she went. There was more than one account of altercations outside of battles as well.

"Would you have done the same for your lover?" Rhyatt asked, breaking the silence that had settled.

"I don't have a lover, Rhyatt." She replied without looking up.

"Fine. For someone you've been in love with?" He responded quickly.

This warranted a glance from her, a playful smile rising.

"Can't say I've ever been in love."

"Now you're just being difficult." He responded with a roll of his eyes.

"Difficult is my alias," she responded with a cocked eyebrow.

"What about someone you love like family? Knox?" He asked, suddenly very keen to know her answer.

She narrowed her eyes and glanced around, "I'll take one of your fingers if you ever tell a soul, but I don't think I have the stomach to carve someone's heart out, but for everything else she did, yes. I'd wage war for him. And Cleo. And maybe even you." she added with a wink.

"Maybe me?" Rhyatt feigned concern, bringing his hand to his chest.

"Maybe." she stated and then patted the seat beside her, "Come read with me."

Rhyatt obliged and moved so he could sit next to her. She scooted closer, her thigh pressing against his as she put the book on their laps.

"Here." she pointed to a passage, "This says that the man who saw Saveen in the woods was also one of her previous pursuers. When she turned him down, he began to actively dislike her."

"It is possible it was a rumor, made up by him to hurt her," Rhyatt added.

"Possibly. I just can't imagine how awful it must be. This rumor. Losing her family. Watching both parents die. It must've been horrible."

"It is," Rhyatt muttered before he could think not to. He tensed, realizing what he said.

Wes looked up from the page, and in return, he looked down, avoiding eyes that would see right through him.

"I'm sorry Rhy, I didn't mean to-"

"It's okay, it was a long time ago." He reached for the page and turned it, "What's the next personal account?"

Her hand let go of the book and came to rest over the top of his.

"I'm sorry Rhy, I didn't mean to be insensitive. Time doesn't erase the pain of losing someone."

She gave his hand a gentle squeeze and started to pull away. He flipped his hand over and laced their fingers together, keeping her close.

"I don't think I'll ever think of my father as truly gone. I'm still convinced one day I'll walk into our home and he'll be there, asking me why I forgot to pick up eggs on the way home." Rhyatt huffed a small laugh and looked at Wes. Just as he expected, her eyes looked right through him. It made him want to tell her every dirty little secret he had.

"I- he was an amazing man." Rhyatt nodded, "He raised us by himself ever since I was four. He never spoke out of anger. He thought through every decision. He was too smart for his own good. I think he knew he was dying long before he passed. I like to think he didn't tell us on purpose, like he wanted us to remember him before he got sick."

"Did it work?"

"Mostly. We didn't know until it was too late." Rhyatt glanced down, shame washing through him, "I only wish I wouldn't have acted so recklessly afterward. I wasn't there for Adriel like I should've been."

"Everyone reacts differently to grief." She used her free hand to push back a strand of hair that had broken free, "I mean, look at Saveen. She became a *war queen*."

Rhyatt smiled lightly at her, "She may not be the best, but at least she turned it into something useful."

Wes shook her head, "Grief does not have to be useful. Sometimes it is just... grief."

Rhyatt hadn't heard such soft words from her before, and as he stared into those green eyes, he was reminded of how much grief she carried with her. How she lived in this large home alone with just Will.

"Tell me." He said gently, leaving his meaning open to interpretation.

She swallowed and looked back at the bookshelf, avoiding his eyes. When she turned back to him, her brows were pinched together.

"It's strange." She started and squeezed his hand tighter, "I think some days I grieve for those who are still alive."

Rhyatt instantly knew she meant the Mother, Father, and Brother who had abandoned her here.

"When I lost Jaze, it was a different type of grief. A final one." Her jaw set into a firm line, "The truth is, when I was grieving the loss of my family, I knew it was never permanent. I would see them again soon. I figured I was grieving the loss of the life I had lived *before*. But with Jaze..." She trailed off and offered him a small smile.

"Loss isn't easy. Pretending it is doesn't make it any better." Rhyatt said with sympathy.

"I have Will to take care of, a business to run, classes to attend, and a journal to turn in. Pretending it isn't that bad is the only thing keeping me going." Wes said quickly, a slight edge to her voice as she listed her responsibilities.

"But I'm glad I found you. I forget to pretend with you." She added when he thought she wouldn't speak again.

Rhyatt brought their entwined fingers to his mouth and kissed the back of her hand softly.

"I forget to pretend with you too."

RHYATT

R hyatt was running through the jungle as fast as his legs
could carry him. It didn't help that it was pitch black out
and that it had rained only a few hours before. He slid down the
path before righting himself and continuing as quickly as possible
towards the BlakeMoore. Sweat was running down every square
inch of him. His face was the worst as it ran into his eyes and
made them sting. He blinked rapidly, still moving forward, trying
to clear his eyes enough to navigate. He knew he was short on
time, and if he didn't make it... he didn't want to think about what
would happen.

Rhyatt broke free of the trees and ran towards the backdoor of
the BlakeMoore, he tripped up the stairs and grappled with the
door handle. Locked. He knew the front door would be locked
too. Then it occurred to him what the men had said. Her balcony.

He pushed off the door, bounding down the steps and heading
toward the lattice that grew vines up the back of the house.
He grabbed on, hoisting himself upwards. His fingers slipped on
the night dew that had settled. He didn't dare curse in fear of
someone hearing him. He was too scared to think about the fact

that someone could be watching him scale the house at this very moment.

He moved up the lattice, easing onto the balcony with preternatural grace. With his heart thudding in his ears, he reached for her balcony door. The handle was open.

Stepping inside, he paused and scanned the room.

No one.

No one except Wes in her bed.

He closed the door and stepped up to her bed.

He pressed one finger to his own lips in a shushing motion before reaching out to touch her shoulder. He stopped just shy when cold metal pressed against his throat.

Her eyes were closed, but the knife at his throat gave off a very different impression.

"Wes. It's me." Rhyatt whispered, avoiding any unnecessary moving of his throat.

Her eyes snapped open, and a broad range of emotions flashed within before settling on skepticism.

"I need you to trust me. We don't have much time."

She nodded before lowering her knife and pulling back her covers to stand.

Rhyatt glanced out the window before looking back at her. There were so many things he wished he could stop and take in- the sight of her unruly hair, her shirt hanging off her shoulder, the lack of pants, and even the single sock she wore- but his heart was beating too wildly, and the fear coursing through him wouldn't allow any thoughts but survival.

"What is going on, Rhyatt?" Her voice was deep from sleep, and the knife was still clutched in her hand.

"I don't have much time to explain, but we need to hide, and we need to do it *now*."

"Talk fast then. Who is coming after you, and why do I have to hide as well?" Her voice had evened out, and her eyes opened more.

"Not me." He shook his head, "You. And we have to hide because there are too many."

Wes stared at him for a moment before nodding, "Let's get Will."

She turned on her heel, moving silently through the room and into the hall. Rhyatt spent a moment making the bed look like it was slept in before leaving the balcony door unlocked and exiting the room.

Wes was in Will's room, gently waking him up. He sat up and looked around the room in confusion. Wes steadied a hand on his shoulder, they seemed to communicate wordlessly and without direction, Will stood and placed his hand in Wes's.

Wes looked up to Rhyatt. He nodded in support, his own heart still hammering away in his ears.

She led the way out of the room and back into her room, where she stopped in front of her large ornate mirror. Rhyatt had never given it much attention, but as she began to push it, he realized it was on a swivel. In seconds, the mirror opened up to a hole in the wall, big enough for a handful of people to stand in.

The bottom edge was only up to their shins, Wes picked Will up and placed him inside. She quickly motioned for Rhyatt to follow. He stepped in silently, a moment later she joined them. And in less than thirty seconds she was pulling the mirror closed, hiding them away.

For a moment, the enclosed space darkened, but then Rhyatt swore he could still see out into her room. Perhaps it was just his mind playing tricks on him. He shut his eyes and reopened them, only this time, the room was clearer.

It was a two-way mirror. He had only ever read about them, never saw them in person. Rhyatt thought to ask Wes about its origins later. There were many things he wished to know about it.

He was pulled from his thoughts by a gentle bump from Wes. Her back was now pressed against his side. He looked down at her. Will stood in front of her. She had one arm across his shoulders and chest, and her free arm gripped the knife. Rhyatt eased his arm around to rest on top of hers. In response, she leaned closer. He could hear Will's uneven breath and could feel the slight shake in Wes's knife-hand. And worst of all, he swore he could still hear his own heart pounding.

They stood still, looking like a horrified family painting, when a faint click of a doorknob made them all tense.

The balcony door eased open, and Blondie slinked inside, his tall, slender frame not meant for being sneaky. He scanned the room before motioning to two others. Greasy and Grumpy followed. Rhyatt had nicknamed them such at the bar.

The three of them stepped further into the room, eyes darting to and fro. Blondie and Grumpy held knives, while Greasy held a rope. They began checking under the bed and in the closet, still remaining quiet.

Rhyatt felt Wes tense even further as they watched the scene unfold in front of them. She was as tense as a cobra, ready to strike. Only it would do no good. He didn't doubt her abilities but rather the consequences of such.

He gave her arm a quick squeeze, and in response, she pressed further into him.

"She's supposed to be here," Grumpy grumbled.

"Your informant must be bad." Greasy said, turning to Blondie.

"He ain't bad." Blondie whispered back defensively, "He said she doesn't have a schedule. You're more likely to run into her by accident than on purpose."

"It's no accident she isn't in bed tonight." Greasy responded, stepping closer to Blondie.

"He told us as such, and we took action-" Blondie stepped up, ready to argue, but Grumpy raised his hand, halting the argument in its tracks.

"We haven't yet wasted our time. Search the house. Take no prisoners." Grumpy nodded, a malicious grin on his face before the three men walked out the door into the house together.

After the longest ten minutes of Rhyatt's life, Grumpy was the first to return. He stepped into the room, and alone, he must've felt emboldened. He leaned down to the pillow on the bed and took a deep inhale.

A shiver of unease coasted down Rhyatt's spine.

Grumpy straightened and looked around, his eyes landing on the mirror.

Will, Wes, and Rhyatt simultaneously stopped breathing.

Grumpy walked to the mirror, seeming to stare directly at them. Common sense told Rhyatt that he was only staring at himself, not at the three of them hiding behind the mirror. Nevertheless, his blood ran cold as the intruder stood inches away from them.

He stared at his reflection, seeming to study it.

His lip curled back, revealing neat teeth.

Rhyatt couldn't breathe.

The intruder took the knife he had previously sheathed and held it up to the mirror, tapping the glass twice.

"That's very rude of you." He said, his eyes trained directly ahead.

A cold tendril of dread seeped into Rhyatt's very soul. In that moment, a million scenarios ran through his head. If the man went to break the mirror, he would push Will and Wes to the back and take the brunt of the blow.

"Very rude of you to walk around with seasoning in your teeth," Grumpy said to himself.

He pressed the knife to his teeth to pull free a speck of pepper that was lodged between his lower teeth.

Rhyatt flexed his hand only to realize he had been gripping Wes far too hard. She let out a slow breath. Will didn't move.

Greasy and Blondie reentered the room empty-handed, and Grumpy turned to them, pretending he had never seen his reflection.

"No one seems to be home tonight."

"Four other bedrooms, all empty."

Grumpy nodded and said to Blondie, "Ask your informant where else she goes."

Blondie nodded, and the three of them headed towards the balcony door. They closed it, and the room was quiet again.

Only it was different. The space had been sullied, even though they had not touched anything within their immediate vision.

Wes moved and pushed Will against Rhyatt. He pulled the boy close.

Wes stepped out, creeping to the balcony, looking out before locking it and coming back. She motioned for them to exit the wall.

Rhyatt lifted Will out, then followed and gently pushed the mirror back to its original spot.

Wes gripped Will's shoulders, "They're gone."

He nodded slowly, his eyes wide. Shocked.

Wes pulled him closer in a hug, "They're not coming back." She assured him, although Rhyatt didn't think she believed her own words.

"Why were they here?" Will asked, sounding more curious than scared.

Wes looked up to Rhyatt.

"They were thieves." Rhyatt lied. And the worst part was he looked Will in the eye to do it. He looked up to Wes. She knew better but didn't say a word. "They think that Wes is the only person who knows what your code for the safe is."

"We don't have a safe." Will furrowed his brow.

Rhyatt was at a loss of what to say. He was halfway into a lie and refused to back out now. Luckily Wes interjected.

"We do have a safe."

"Where?"

Wes shook her head, "If I told you where, then it wouldn't be a secret."

Will looked up at her and Rhyatt could tell the next week would be spent turning the house upside down looking for the hidden safe. The thing that almost struck him as funny is that he wouldn't put it past Wes to actually have a hidden safe.

"Let's go downstairs and start making breakfast so Rhina doesn't have to do as much." Wes encouraged.

In the kitchen it became very clear Wes and Will only knew how to cook meat and eggs, which left the biscuit making to Rhyatt. He took Will to the island and together they worked on the biscuits.

Rhina came in before dawn and angrily clucked at Rhyatt for his dirty appearance around the food. Wes pulled her aside rather quickly. Rhyatt presumed she was passing along the events of the night. Rhina reentered the kitchen and proceeded to help. A handful of minutes later, Wes returned, this time fully clothed and with boots on. She gave a quick nod to Rhyatt.

"We're going to run a few errands. Eat without us."

"Where are you going?" Will asked quickly, and Rhyatt saw Wes tense.

"Rhyatt and I have to help the workers this morning." She stepped up to him, rustling his hair, "I'll be back in time for the market. Why don't you take a nap after breakfast."

Will scrunched his nose in defiance. Wes laughed at him as she placed a kiss atop his hair.

Dawn had not yet broken but the moon was too far gone to produce any solid light. Silently, Rhyatt and Wes slipped across the dark land, heading in the direction of the bunks. She waited until they had stepped into the trees before speaking.

"What really happened?" her voice was icy cool. An edge he hadn't seen about her.

"I'm sorry Wes. I didn't mean to lie to you, but I didn't want Will to know, and I know it seems-"

"Rhyatt." She cut his rambling off, the intensity of her focus burning him.

"I was at the bar, and it was getting close to closing time when I heard a group of men say something about 'the Blake house.' I got closer to listen, but they started talking quieter. By the time I realized what they were planning, the barkeep was closing, and there was only a handful of us there. I left to try to find the law councilor's office, but when I stepped outside, I saw six other men waiting. The guys from inside joined them and continued making plans. The councilor's office was in the opposite direction of you. It seemed like an easy choice."

"What were they planning, Rhyatt?" His name almost sounded like a threat on her lips.

"They were going to take you. Their only goal was to capture you alive. And they will be trying again. Whoever hired them has deep pockets."

Wes's pace faltered, unnoticeable to anyone who hadn't spent time with her.

"Is that why you look so awful?" She asked, the slightest tease in her voice.

Rhyatt was shocked. Only moments ago, she had been very worked up over this, to the point of sounding threatening. Or so it had seemed. Now she teased him? It didn't make sense.

"Are you not afraid?"

She shrugged her shoulders, "Fear is useless. What is needed is action."

It was then that they stepped through the trees to the small clearing where the workers were housed. Inside, light flickered as shadows walked to and fro in the windows. Wes walked up the short stairs to the first cabin. With the side of her fist, she banged on the door thrice before throwing it open.

"Meeting in five." She yelled into the house.

She repeated the same to the second house before returning to stand where Rhyatt stood by the message board.

Slowly, men and women trickled out of the cabins, gathering in front of them. Rhyatt felt his cheeks heat in a flush of nerves. He didn't enjoy being in front of so many people. At least it was still dark, and no one could make out the color on his face.

When Wes deemed enough people were in front of her she began to speak, loud and clear.

"Good Morning. My apologies for calling a meeting so early, but it is urgent." She paused and looked around. "Some idiot has spread a rumor that the BlakeMoore is a good place to rob. Anyone with a brain will soon discover that there is no treasure inside the house. Rather, it is invested in livestock and equipment stored away in the barn. However, the rumor mill turns faster than the wind can blow, and a few out-of-towners are already a little too curious. In order to protect our livelihoods, we will be starting a night watch. If everyone commits to a four-hour shift with a partner, then everyone will only be on watch once a week. Payment for being on the watch will be double."

A ripple of murmurs went through the crowd.

"From here on out, if you see anyone strange on the property- or asking about it in town- please let me know. If I am unavailable, let Rhina know." She took a small step back, "Thank you for taking time this morning. For those of you working today, have a good day. For those of you off, I hope to see you in the market later." With a nod of her head, she dismissed them. Turning, she tacked a signup paper on the message board behind them.

It was on their way back that Wes veered from the path, heading away from the house. Rhyatt almost blindly followed, but he was unsettled by her nonchalant attitude. He suspected it was put on, but even after telling himself that, he couldn't help but be bothered by it. He stopped at the edge of the path and called after her.

"Where are you going?"

"We are going to the hot spring." She replied, pausing to turn back to look at him.

"Hot spring?"

"You look like you could use its healing qualities," she turned and began walking again before adding, "And I could use the relaxation."

They walked for a few minutes before they reached a rocky patch of earth where the trees didn't grow. In the dim predawn light, steam wafted upwards from what seemed to be a hole in the ground. Rhyatt crept closer, his boots scuffing on the uneven rock. The hole in the ground was about the size of two bathtubs put together, and inside was murky dark blue water. He scrunched his nose as the steam hit him.

"It smells awful."

"The worse it smells, the better it is for you."

Rhyatt turned around to comment on how he didn't think it was true, but the sight of her half-undressed made him pause. Her shirt was off and she was working on kicking off her boots. She looked up and saw his wide eyed expression.

"No clothes allowed in the spring. Messes with the balance."

She finally succeeded in kicking off her other boot and began shimmying her pants down her legs. She began to pull her undergarments off and Rhyatt looked down, intently studying the rock beneath his feet. Light gray. Small patches of dark green moss. Occasional blots of white rock. Not sharp. Not smooth. A decent rock.

"Are you coming?" Wes asked as she walked by Rhyatt, completely nude.

"Yes," he responded a tad too quickly.

A gentle laugh came from her direction, followed by the sound of sloshing water.

Rhyatt began peeling off his clothes, layer by layer, with his back still turned. As he placed them in a neat pile beside hers, he noticed the mud caked on his shirt and the tiny rips in it. He glanced down; his arms were disgusting and smeared with mud. No wonder Rhina had complained.

Glancing over his shoulder, he saw Wes had her back turned. In a hurried motion, he slipped off his undergarments and hustled to the spring. Wes stood still as he eased into the water. When it covered his chest, and he found a spot to sit, she turned to face him. The tips of her short hair were wet, and her green eyes reflected the faint light of the early morning dawn. He studied the definition of her jaw, the sharp cut of her cheekbones, and the contrasting gentle curve of her nose. Out of all her features, the delicate nose caught his attention more often than not. The rest of her features seemed harsh when compared to her nose, but he rather liked it.

His gaze drifted back up to her eyes and he found that she had been studying him as well. His thoughts turned instantaneously to the too broad width of his shoulders. The size of his chest. The stubble that was growing on his jaw.

"Are you not worried?" He asked, pulling himself away from his insecurities.

Her mouth drew into a tight line, and she moved her arms around in the water.

"I am." She said with a sigh. "But I've learned to control what you can and let the rest go."

"You think the night watches will help?"

"I do. At the least, they will give me a warning. A chance to hide Will."

Rhyatt nodded. He understood the need to protect a younger brother well.

"Do you think they were looking for me because of the journal?" She posed it like a question, but he could tell she already knew the answer.

Rhyatt nodded, wishing he could lie to her, "I think the same people who came after me are coming after you. I think the only reason they want to kidnap you is to use you as leverage to get the journal back."

Wes nodded, the line in her mouth tightening, "They probably connected us through that damn rumor."

Rhyatt grimaced, remembering how his actions had caused a week of whispers and stares.

"I'm sorry-"

"Don't." She cut him off, but the light tone of her words eased him.

He shook his head at her, leaning back further and resting his arms on the outer rim of the spring. He watched as her eyes traced down his chest and across his arms, all the way to his fingertips. She inhaled deeply. And very suddenly, Rhyatt was all too aware that they were both unclothed. He was now very aware of her naked collarbones and the tops of her breasts sitting out of the water.

"I don't think I ever said thank you for the warning this morning." She said parting her lips and licking them.

"You would've done the same for me," Rhyatt said, not liking how quickly his voice grew gruff.

She stood, the water only going to her waist. Rhyatt made it a point to keep eye contact with her as she closed the distance between them. He made it a point to ignore the droplets of water that ran down her body, down her stomach, dripping off her breasts.

Wes leaned over him, resting one arm on the rock behind him. Rhyatt's breath hitched and then got caught in his throat.

"Is there any way I can thank you?" She asked, tilting her head slightly.

Rhyatt swallowed, "You would've done the same."

"This isn't about me."

She was so close that he only had to sit up, and they would be face to face. Her face was tilted down to look at him, and her hair hung loose, creating a curtain-like effect on either side. He wished to run his fingers through her hair. To discover what it felt like. He wanted to know if she liked it as well. Perhaps he would instead settle on tucking it behind her ear. That wasn't too much, was it?

She shifted her weight backward, pulling away slightly.

"Tell me, Rhy, why do you not touch me?"

"Because you haven't given me permission."

She stood up straight, a smirk appearing. "You have permission."

Before he could grab her waist and pull her closer, she moved away and returned to her seat across from him.

"But for the next half hour, I want you to *touch yourself*."

His own sinister smile grew.

"Is this a punishment?"

She shook her head, blinking and looking up at him from dark lashes.

"It's a reward." She sat up so that her breasts were entirely exposed. "A reward for getting to me so quickly." Her hand rose out of the water and gently ran her fingers across her collarbone, then her middle finger led the way down between her breasts. It kept going further down in the milky water. "A reward for how *hard* and *fast* you must've run. " Her arm was straight down the front of her body. Her fingers were presumably between her legs.

Rhyatt could no longer ignore the erection that had grown and was now throbbing. He eased his arms into the water, his right hand knowing what to do. His jaw clenched as he watched her eyes flicker and her tongue lick her lips again.

"Think about how this should have been you between my legs." She rolled her hips, her other hand grabbing her breast. Her perfect nipples already peaked.

Rhyatt's eyes took in every inch of skin she was showing, his thoughts running rampant. He licked his lips, wondering how hers would taste. How good her breast would feel in his mouth. How his teeth would graze her skin as he kissed her all over. His grip tightened on his dick, and an involuntary moan escaped the back of his throat.

"*Rhyatt.*" She said his name in return, and it took every ounce of control he had not to go to her. Not to grab her and show her how much he *did* want to touch her. How many times he had *thought* of touching her. How much he wanted to make her scream his name.

His speed increased as he watched her body move rhythmically. Gods, she was almost too much for him to handle. He didn't think he would last long while watching her.

A little gasp escaped her, and her chest heaved up and down as her mouth parted.

"Gods dammit Wes." Rhyatt shook his head, his voice too deep, his thoughts too clouded. "You make me think *very* dirty things."

Her brows went together as a small laugh collided with her pleasure.

"I'm glad." She whispered as her panting increased.

She bit her lip, and another moan escaped the back of Rhyatt's throat. Her eyes rolled upwards, and her face twisted. Rhyatt increased his speed further, his rhythm getting messy as he intently watched her every move.

"Rhy." She moaned his name before going still, her mouth parted as an orgasm racked through her. Her arms shaking silently. Rhyatt followed her into oblivion, a sharp gasp and stilled arms his only signs of finishing.

The dawn finally broke into sunrise as they both came down.

Rhyatt's mouth turned up into a lopsided grin, "Now I have something to think about when I'm alone." He winked at her and, with renewed confidence, stood and exited the hot spring, his naked body on full display.

WES

Wes's eyes had not stopped moving around the market. Half the time, her attention was on Will. The other half she spent searching the faces of the marketgoers. She was looking for three specific faces.

So far, there hadn't been anything out of the ordinary. She asked around, but the only strange thing from the night before was that the blacksmith's son, a man known for having too much to drink, hadn't come home. Wes assured the blacksmith that he would be back soon. He always returned. Her next objective was to visit the out-of-towners' tents and booths. It was a busy market day, and she had counted twelve booths run by nonlocals. Rhina was almost done shopping, which meant she could keep an eye on Will while Wes looked around.

Wes sat on the edge of a retaining wall watching Will play jacks with another young boy. A tall frame with dark, curly hair caught her attention. Her eyes flicked up to see Rhyatt walking towards her. He was freshly showered, his hair still wet on the ends. His clean shirt was pushed up past his elbows, the small cuts he had gotten this morning still raw and bright red.

Rhyatt waved at her, a smile on his lips, and slipped through the crowd to her. After seeing his naked body this morning, it was going to be hard to imagine much else.

"Adriel says hello," Rhyatt said, taking a seat next to her.

"How many times has he asked you about training with me?"

"Everyday." Wes laughed and Rhyatt shook his head, "No it's serious. Sometimes twice a day."

"Once we get through this midterm, he can come over whenever he wants."

"He'll be thrilled to hear that." Rhyatt rested his hands on his thighs, leaning forward, "Better be careful, or all his friends will start showing up too."

"Maybe that's my new plan: train a bunch of pupils and put it on a resume. It would show my dedication to future careers."

"What *do* you plan to do when we graduate?" Rhyatt asked, his voice laced with caution.

Wes exhaled a little too loudly, a touchy subject she had come to some unpleasant conclusions.

"I had hoped to join the thirteenth legion, a special division of Jorjin's army. Only the elite are selected. They travel around the country, and sometimes others." She explained before glancing out to where Will was, "But I think I will be needed locally for a little longer. Business is good right now. Perhaps I will expand." She paused to bump his shoulder with hers, the touch tingling. "What about you?"

Rhyatt scoffed, "I didn't think I'd make it this far, to be honest. I'm not entirely sure what strings Lita pulled, but I don't deserve to be at university right now."

"I don't believe that's true." She interjected.

"Maybe not, but I had only completed a year of university in Duran before leaving to work at a printing mill. I know there are large gaps in my education."

"What did you study in Duran?"

A sheepish smile spread across Rhyatt's lips, "Culinary arts of the world and communicative journalism."

"Ooh," She made an impressed noise, "Didn't know you were such a scholar."

Rhyatt waved his hand in the air as if to clear it, "It's different in Duran, you start immediately learning your skills. General education is more of a second thought. But now here I am, hoping to receive a general degree from Jorjin."

She patted his knee, "It's never too late to continue."

"I'm not going back. Not if I can help it."

His words were final, and Wes wanted to dive into them, to ask him more about his dislike of his home country. She wanted to know everything about him. In his life. But every time she was around him, time seemed to pass more quickly than normal. Like now, Rhina was approaching them, a bag of goods on one arm and a glass of something in her other hand. She smiled a wide grin at the pair of them before sitting down on Wes's other side.

"Scorching day out today." Rhina laid the bag down beside her, and took a sip of her drink. "Merchants may leave early if the heat persists," she glanced at Wes, "May want to look around while you still can."

Wes nodded, standing. Rhina had a sense for things like that. She knew when Wes was antsy and knew how to soothe her.

"Thanks Rhina. Will has money if he wants anything."

They rose and walked away from the relief of the shade. Wes led him towards the tents and booths of the busy market.

"Feel like doing some investigative journalism?" Wes asked.

Rhyatt cocked an eyebrow at her, "What are we investigating?"

"There are twelve nonlocal merchants here today. I figured we'd give them a visit to see if you recognize any from last night."

"Clever." Rhyatt nodded, and they walked towards the first tent she had marked. Inside were dried herbs, some were crushed in jars, others hung from the wooden ceiling of the tent. The interior was cooler than outside, the sun unable to scorch penetrate the thick canvas ceiling.

Wes walked around looking at the herbs, occasionally bringing one to her nose and sniffing them. Rhyatt followed behind her, pretending to be interested. She settled on a branch of small pale green herbs in a circular leafs. There were more bunches of this herb than any other in the tent.

"What is this one called?" She asked the merchant who had been watching them with a hawk's vision.

"Sage." The merchant replied.

"Where is it from?"

"East of the river." The merchant clipped his words, clearly annoyed.

Rhyatt shook his head. He didn't recognize the merchant.

"Thank you," Wes said before exiting the tent.

They reentered the bustling market, heading towards the next stand. They sidestepped a booth carrying a large basket of bright-colored berries before turning left.

"You never told me what you plan to do when you graduate," Wes stated.

"Like you, I may be needed locally for a bit longer." Rhyatt ducked a low-hanging beam.

"Until then?"

"I thought about talking to Scholar Tiunda and seeing if there were any openings in the primary schools. Will has opened my mind to so many things. I think I would enjoy working with children."

Wes agreed. And then the image of him running with a gaggle of children following behind him flooded her mind. She could see him standing in front of a group, gently talking to them, encouraging them, nurturing them in the way he did. She rather liked the idea.

"Promise you won't let them tie you up to play tag?"

His laugh exploded, and he clutched his stomach. Wes smiled at the sound.

"You haven't forgotten that yet? How will I ever live it down?"

"That's the secret, Rhyatt. As long as I'm living to remind you, you never will."

"I guess I can deal with that." He winked at her before ducking into the tent they had been walking towards. She followed him, their arms brushing as they looked at the jewelry inside.

This merchant was far more welcoming, saying a greeting as they entered. They returned it and stopped in front of a table of rings and pendants. The rings were decorated with jewels of all colors and shapes. Some of the jewels were bigger than the rings they were mounted on. Rhyatt stood thumbing a hanging necklace while Wes bent lower to the table. Among all the bright jewels and silver shiny enough to see your reflection, there was a pendant made of gold, but no jewels. Instead, it was a heart with a miniature sword going through the top. Her fingers brushed the heart.

"The heart and sword. A symbol with many meanings." The merchant spoke, leaning over the opposite side of the table to get a better look.

"It's beautiful." Wes breathed, admiring it.

"What does it mean?" Rhyatt asked.

"Some say it is a sign of betrayal. However, this pendant is very special, it was made from a pair of wedding bands. The heart represents life, while the sword represents strength. It is a subtle accent piece that could be worn every day, showcasing the strength of life within its owner."

The merchant smiled down at them, and Wes returned the pendant to its spot.

"Someone would be lucky to wear it."

CLEO

I have been trying to wrap my mind on how this large facility is able to function. What are they selling to keep it running? I believe one of their exports is the soldiers themselves. The possessed soldiers are easily controlled and the wealthy of this country enjoy people they can pay to be quiet. I believe the other export is a clear fire accelerant. One of the containers caught on fire in the dead of night and the bright green explosion left me blinded for many minutes. Whatever it is, it's rare and likely cost.

Jaze

Cleo tucked her legs underneath herself as she curled closer to Wes, the journal on their laps. They had locked themselves away in Wes's room so that no prying eyes, like Will's, would see.

Cleo didn't miss the clutch Wes kept on the journal at all times. Even Cleo did not know where the journal was kept hidden. She knew where Wes kept the business ledgers, where extra coin was hidden, what bank vault and what combination was used. But Wes had not told her where she was keeping the journal hidden, only that it was safe. Cleo wished she could say Knox was not the cause, but she was too observant to lie to herself in that manner.

Wes did not trust Knox with the journal, whether it was fear of him doing something irrational or fear of him burning the thing in a drunken rage. That much was unclear.

They sat alone in her room, the late morning sun shining through the windows and casting the room in light. Wes flipped another page in the journal, and they continued reading together for the second time. The majority of the journal was full of monotonous daily life. It was curious how often Jaze had made the crossing to Duran, yet none of them had noticed. Or perhaps Wes had noticed his comings and goings, but because of the nature of their relationship she had kept quiet. It made sense if Wes kept tabs on others yet told no one.

"There is something off about their business model," Cleo stated, her fingers running along the page, "If Jaze is right and they rent their soldiers out, how do they pay them? Or are they providing something besides monetary payment?"

"You don't have to pay people who are possessed," Wes stated. She was still holding onto the idea that the soldiers were possessed.

Cleo frowned, "They are not possessed."

"When we meet one, we can ask them how they are paid," Wes responded.

Wes had been on edge ever since the break in, Cleo continued to forgive her for the little snipes, today she was faring decently.

"What about the fire accelerant he mentions? You said he was killed by LiquidFire. Is this the same thing?" Cleo asked, turning back to their most recent journal entry.

"Yeah, about that," Wes said, one side of her mouth drawing into a grimace, "I may have done some research and found out that the Council knows of Liquid Fire's existence and has gone to great lengths to hide it."

"Wes." Cleo warned, "How did you come by this information?"

"That doesn't matter," Wes waved her hand through the air, "No one knows that I know."

"I doubt it." Cleo rolled her eyes and chose to move on, "I wonder what it's made out of? Maybe that grain he mentioned, he mentions it a few times and always says it is unmarked."

Wes winced, and her grimace returned.

"You know what it's made out of, don't you?" Cleo asked, frowning.

"Yes." her grimace turned into an uneasy smile that was almost comical.

"Spill."

"It's made out of green mountain corn."

Cleo frowned even deeper. Green mountain corn was only grown in high elevations, which meant it was extremely prevalent in Northern Jorjin. At her internship, she had been privy to much of the classified history but had never read about the creation of Liquid Fire. Another thought occurred to her.

"Wes. You had some corn stolen from you a few years ago. It was maybe a year or two after you had taken over."

Her friend paused, the gears turning in her mind.

"I did. It wasn't a lot, and when I reported it to the Trade Councilor, he passed me along to his subordinate who was in charge of agriculture. They said they would keep an eye on it in town and at the border, but for only one bin, it was likely being broken up and sold."

"What if they were stealing it before they could buy it?" Cleo asked, her own gears turning.

"We could look into it, but what if it's just a coincidence," Wes said.

"Or we look into it and find a pattern but still don't know who stole it. The Councilors likely didn't care to investigate very far, which means we're back to square one."

"What if we focus on whose growing it?" Wes countered.

"We could, but it's not only Saint Saveen that could be growing it. Anyone in the mountains could be growing and exporting it all the way to Oan in the East."

"Well fuck Cleo." Wes's temper flared, her voice rising, "I want to focus on something. My home is under attack, and I feel no closer to this than before."

Cleo's eyes softened, and she reached a hand out, resting it on top of Wes's.

"We're going to figure it out. Let's focus on the mountain pass. That is the only way things come in and out of the country in the North. If the grain is being passed by without papers, then someone is being paid to let them through. We need to figure out who."

Wes sighed and nodded. They could work with that. It was likely between the two of them in the governance offices that they could even get a list of workers at the pass.

The walk home for Cleo was slow. She had left home early to avoid her parents; now, it was past lunch, and she was as ready as she could be. Walking through the square, she glanced up to the second and third-story windows of her family's flat. It sat over a clothing shop. Her parents had picked the location almost 15 years ago. They liked that the flat was over a clothing shop rather than a bar or eatery. Less noise and less smells, they had explained to a young Cleo. It still held true many years later.

Slipping around the back of the building, she stepped inside the antechamber that opened up to the stairs, after taking off her boots she ascended the steps. Without checking if it was locked she opened the flat door, sunlight almost immediately blinding her.

That was her favorite part about the flat, how many windows sat on both sides of the building, allowing the sun to shine through, illuminating the space so that not even a shadow could hide. Her other favorite parts included the high ceilings, the spacious common rooms, and the redwood that was throughout the flat. It was different from that of the dark woods found in the jungles of Jorjin; it had reminded her parents of their home overseas.

Mother Nafin looked up from the book she had been reading on the couch. She smiled and opened her mouth to summon her Father, but he was exiting the study before Cleo could fully close the door. His eyes shone with happiness at seeing her, and it made her slightly remorseful for the conversation that was to be had.

"We have missed you." Father Nafin said, pivoting to the kitchen to prepare Cleo lunch.

"I was needed," Cleo said, straightening her spine as she stepped further into the room, an equal distance between each parent.

"Needed or wanted?" Her mother marked her page before placing the book down on a coffee table.

"The trunks you bought me for my trip to Genvi are far too large," Cleo stated, not letting her voice lean one way or another.

Father Nafin paused his movement in the kitchen to look at his daughter. He was too smart to risk a glance at Mother Nafin.

"You can take all of your belongings, and if you decide to come back, we will pay for their return." Her father nodded at his own words.

"I *am* coming back." Cleo insisted.

"Dearest, it is becoming less and less safe the longer you stay." Her mother spoke now, rising from her seat.

"I am working on fixing it." She gently pleaded.

A look of shock crossed Mother Nafin's face, and before Father Nafin could chime in, Cleo spoke again, "You all work tirelessly to fix and maintain Genvi, I want to work to better Saint Saveen."

"Saint Saveen is not your home. You were born a daughter of Genvi." Father Nafin had set down the fresh apple he was cutting and stepped out of the kitchen so that he was closer. A twinkle of hurt shone in his eyes.

"Isn't it my home?" Cleo asked them both, "I have lived here over half my life. I have grown in their education, I have learned their traditions, I know their histories, their laws, and their way of life. Even now, I am offered a job with the Historic Council once I graduate. I may have been born a daughter of Genvi, but Saint Saveen raised me."

Cleo did not enjoy the harm she caused her parents as they both took in her words. Neither did she enjoy how she had told them of her job offer. She had been excited to receive the formal offer last week, but she had told no one. A few beats of silence later, her mother spoke.

"And if we do not welcome you back?"

"Then I will still return." She inhaled deeply before continuing, "I am delighted to visit my brothers but make no mistake. My trip will be a visit. Not a move."

Cleo knew her gentle-mannered parents would not argue with her, so she turned back to the door, wishing to walk off her anger and let her parents grieve her words alone.

"This business with 'fixing' Saint Saveen. Will it get you hurt?" Her Father asked.

Cleo looked over her shoulder and lied, "No."

She did not tell them that the still-fresh scar across her stomach was from her attempts at fixing Saint Saveen. Neither did she mention that Wes's home now had a night guard. Nor that in Duran they had been attacked. Cleo cherished her parents, but they were gentle souls. Being raised in Saint Saveen had ensured Cleo would not carry their gentle Genvian ways.

RHYATT

The doctors take smoke breaks and it is one of the only times I am able to hear their conversations. Today they spoke of a young woman in Jorjin who might be able to cure their current dilemma. They say the gems are working but they are no closer to any medical advancements. The woman in Jorjin was once a patient here and now displays extraordinary skills. There is an older doctor who knows the details of how she was cured but will not tell anyone. It will be next year before they take her, they have made a deal with someone. I hope I can find out her identity and warn her before they come for her. I fear once she is hauled through those doors she will never see the light of day again.

JG

Rhyatt and Wes went into town after a quick dinner to look at swords. Knox was working in his father's shop, and they went to visit him. Rhyatt thought Wes looked very serious even as her eyes gleamed at different weapons. Her face stayed neutral while those damning green eyes darted around and widened when picking up a new toy. Even now, as they walked home, she had a smug grin on her face. The growing clouds overhead did nothing to dampen her spirit.

"What has you so excited?" He asked.

"Huh?" Wes blinked and turned her head, coming out of whatever thought she was deep into.

"What's on your mind?" Rhyatt asked again, taking smaller steps so they stayed aligned.

"I think I'll purchase a new dagger for my Ad Aetatem Ceremony. Something nicer that can be passed down to Will and his children."

It was not lost on Rhyatt that she did not mention the blade being passed down to any of her children but rather to be passed down through her youngest brother. He would have asked her about it, but the lack of knowledge on the Ad Aetatem Ceremony was more curious.

"The Ad Aetatem? That is your birthday ceremony, correct?"

"Not just any birthday." Wes tilted her head in emphasis, "Your coming-of-age birthday. Twenty-two. Double numbers for double luck."

"Why wait until you are so old?" Rhyatt asked and a sharp look from Wes had him amending his statement quickly, "Not that you are old. But rather why not when you turn twenty or even younger like sixteen in Duran?"

The crease between her brows eased.

"It is tradition more than anything else." She sidestepped a dip in the road before adding, "You are coming, right?"

"I didn't know I was invited." Rhyatt fought the urge to look away or look down at his boots.

"Yes, everyone that's important to me should be in attendance."

Important. To her. It was strange. Rhyatt knew he was important to two different people, Lita and Adriel. And he was important to them because they shared the same blood. But he and Wes did not share blood. Nor did they share years and years of a friendship like her and Knox or Cleo. Rather they shared a few months. And she still deemed him *important* to her. He smiled at the idea.

"As someone who is important to you," Rhyatt began with a smile, "I want to take you and Will on a picnic soon, there's a cool spot I want to show you."

Wes smiled back at him, "I love picnics."

He opened his mouth to respond, but a loud boom cracked overhead, making Rhyatt jump.

"We need to get home," he said, a sense of urgency entering his voice as all thoughts about birthdays were abandoned.

"It's just thunder." Wes shrugged, glancing up to the sky that was only visible in patches through the thick tree coverage. She glanced upwards as if awaiting an old friend to appear.

"Yes, but I don't want to die from lightning," Rhyatt said, his steps quickening. His long legs were able to quickly outpace Wes.

He looked back from a handful of feet ahead.

Only Wes wasn't hurrying. She wasn't even moving anymore, just staring at the sky.

"Wes." Rhyatt hissed, fear creeping over him as the wind began to pick up and the clouds that had been following him grew darker.

"It's the first thunderstorm of the season." She said with a sigh, her eyes softening.

He strode back to where she had stopped on the road.

"Yes, but it's dangerous, and I don't want to die. I have a birthday ceremony to attend."

Wes's eyes flicked down to him, and her hair began to stir in the wind.

"Who said it was dangerous?"

"Edde, Jalon, Aghan." Rhyatt listed a few of his friends from Duran. Wes only raised her brows. "All of Duran said."

"Duran doesn't have thunderstorms." Wes countered, a playfulness entering her tone as she walked past him. She continued at a leisurely pace. It might have been slower.

"We won't get struck by lightning?" Rhyatt asked, returning to her side.

"No," she said sweetly and without any other explanation.

Rhyatt fought the urge to walk faster and instead kept in step with her.

The first raindrops fell. Big, fat raindrops. Cooler than the air around them.

Wes laughed, turning her palms up to the sky as they grew more and more frequent. In a matter of seconds the rain turned into a downpour, soaking the jungle and the dirt path they walked on. The constant hum of birds and insects was replaced with the steady beat of rain.

"We should hustle." Rhyatt raised his voice to be heard.

Wes stopped again. This time, her hand darted out to grip Rhyatts. As their hands connected, thunder boomed overhead, making Rhyatt jump and Wes smile.

"Rhyatt." Her voice was serious, although the smile on her face told a different story, "I promise you we will not get struck by lightning. Are you worried about the rain? Surely you won't melt."

"I won't melt," Rhyatt said quickly.

"Then please, enjoy the first thunderstorm of the season with me." Her head was tilted slightly, and that little cunning smile was so persuasive that he wouldn't have said no, even if he wanted to.

Rhyatt nodded.

And without warning she pulled on his hand, forcing their walk to continue off the path and instead in the trees. Under the canopy the rain was lighter, the drizzle still plastered Wes's hair to her face and made her eyelashes stick together. Rhyatt could feel droplets of water dripping from his hair, soaking his shirt and making it stick to his skin.

As Wes pulled them further into the foliage, he was reminded of the night they went swimming, and she led him to the cave. How much he had trusted her then. She had not let go of his hand then and wouldn't now.

Ducking under a fallen tree, she motioned for him to watch his head. When they both emerged on the other side, a flash of light touched the tree, which was a handful of feet in front of them.

Deafening thunder sounded, and Rhyatt swore he had jumped a foot into the air.

Wide eyed and slightly terrified he looked at Wes, only to discover she was already looking at him, a brow raised.

"Told you *we* would not get struck by lightning."

"You didn't say anything about the trees that surround us from every angle!" Rhyatt's exasperated yell only fueled her fire.

She gave him a sickly sweet smile before continuing onwards, their hands still connected.

The whole walk to The BlakeMoore they held hands, sometimes it felt like Rhyatt was pushing her forward rather than her leading them. Every step he thought of the lightning strike. How quickly it had come and gone, how bright it had been. But the strangest thing had been the tiny little branch of lightning that had left the tree and reached for Wes, gently tapping her chest before it was gone again.

WES

"**W**hy can't I take my own horse?" Will complained from his spot atop a bucket in the barn.

Wes shot him an annoyed glance before answering the question she had answered twice before.

"Because when we get back, it'll be late. And you'll be tired. If we take two horses, I'll be stuck untacking both of them."

"What if I promise to do it myself?" Will asked, attempting to work yet another angle.

Wes sighed, toeing the line between parent and sibling. It was always the little fights that made her dislike the situation. She was tempted to step into the sibling role and say fuck it. Allow him to take his own horse and then complain when he had to do extra work before bed. The other side of her told her this wasn't a good idea. It was the side that usually won.

"Will," she sighed, her hands resting atop the saddle she had been tightening, "I know you can do it, I believe that. But you would still end up going to bed too late. And then tomorrow, your teacher will be mad at me for letting you stay out so late."

Will paused, considering her words. She continued before he could think too long.

"And if you get in trouble at school, we won't be doing late-night adventures anymore."

Will seemed to have a moment of clarity because his whiney attitude fell away, and his shoulders straightened. The sense of adventure must've been enough. He stepped off the bucket and inched closer to the horse Wes was tacking.

"What if I do better in class and get all good scores?"

"When- not if -your scores improve, you'll have to continue to show up on time and keep the good scores," Wes said with optimism.

"So, in theory," Will began mischievously, "If my scores are bad, I don't need to show up on time?"

Wes sent her brother a glare and a silent curse. 'In theory' had been his favorite new phrase since comprehending what a theory was. His theories had ranged from illogical to impossible. She envisioned he would end up a chemist, testing theories to his heart's content.

"No. *In theory*," She said, copying his tone, "If your scores are bad, you need to show up early."

Will scrunched his nose, "Good thing my scores aren't bad."

"Just because they aren't failing doesn't mean they're good." Wes jerked on the saddle before adding, "Rhyatt says you're improving, though."

Will nodded slowly at the compliment and stepped back, allowing Wes to lead the horse out of its stall.

"What about after my birthday?" Will asked, still persistent.

Wes sighed with a smile, "After your birthday, you can stay up later."

He smiled up at her, content with his small victory.

When they arrived at Rhyatt's, he was waiting for them atop his horse. A saddlebag bulged from the left side, promising a feast when they arrived at their picnic destination. The location of which Rhyatt still had not told Wes. The not knowing bothered her. When they were on their way, headed south and up a crop of rocky terrain, Wes turned and asked him.

"Where are we going?" She asked, Will perking up in front of her.

Rhyatt gave her a sidelong glance, still not telling her.

"Would you *please* tell me where we are going?" she tried again.

"So, Wes Blake does know how to say 'please'. Hmm."

Wes parted her mouth in shock as Will twisted around to see her face.

"She doesn't say it often." Will chided, too happy to take a fun dig at his sister.

"I don't *not* say it often."

"When was the last time you said it?" Rhyatt asked before quickly adding, "Besides 10 seconds ago."

Wes snapped her mouth shut and tried to summon the last time she had said please. When was the last time she had asked someone for something? Someone who wasn't her employee or someone she wasn't giving instructions to.

"Earlier this week, I asked you to please pass the corn."

"That's a lie." Will shook his head, messy brown hair flopping with the action.

"I agree with Will. You actually turned to Knox and said, 'pass the corn.'"

"You two were too busy laughing to hear me." Wes tilted her nose up in a haughty motion, making both boys roll their eyes.

Their conversation was quickly halted when the trees thinned and led into rocks that jutted upwards. Rhyatt led them forward, taking his time as the climb grew steeper. Wes wanted to ask if he was taking her to the top of a hill to finally push her over, but the steep terrain put distance between them, and without yelling, she would not be heard. They climbed slowly and gently, the horses knowing what to do.

When the rocky terrain evened out and the trees thickened again, Wes was thoroughly lost. She could hear water rushing nearby but had no clue where she was.

Rhyatt dismounted in a quick, graceful motion, immediately stepping up to assist Will down. Once his feet were on the ground, Rhyatt beckoned him to assist in tying his horse to a fallen log. To Wes's shock, Will went and did not complain. He even helped carry the picnic supplies without complaint.

"Are you ready to see our final destination?" Rhyatt asked.

"Yes." Wes paused before adding, "Please."

Rhyatt smiled at her, and Will giggled, the blanket he carried swinging from his hands.

He motioned them forward, and together, the three of them wove their way out of the trees and into a meadow of white clover perched on a cliff. The sound of rushing water grew louder. Wes and Will pushed forward, eager to see where the edge of the cliff went.

They reached the edge, and Wes wrapped a hand around Will's shoulder, keeping him close.

The cliff dropped steeply, and below them, to the left, was the beginning of the waterfall. From their vantage point they could see the river that flowed into the waterfall and also see the pool below that turned into a trickling stream. The late afternoon sun cast everything in a golden glow. The light mirrored off the moving water.

Wes looked over to the jagged cliffs that served as a backdrop to the magnificent waterfall. Where the rock was vertical it had been covered by a dark green moss, and anywhere there was a ledge vines and ferns grew in droves, flourishing in the wet spray of the falls. The calls of the jungle birds seemed non-existent here, only the rushing of water.

"Can we go to the bottom?" Will asked, turning to Rhyatt who now stood behind them.

"Another day," Rhyatt promised and nodded to where he had set up the small picnic.

They sat down on the cotton blanket and ate dinner, each of them enamored with their new view. Wes was so taken by it she didn't notice when Will tried to eat dessert first. It was Rhyatt that raised an eyebrow and sent Will's hand in a different direction. A few months ago, no one but Wes alone was able to dissuade Will from his set path, whether it was dessert or potentially criminal activity. Now Rhyatt did it with the mere raise of an eyebrow. It was nice how close they had gotten.

When the sun set, Will went to the edge of the cliff and placed his back against a rock, half leaning back to look up at the stars. Within moments, he was nodding in and out of sleep. He was a safe enough distance from the edge, so they let him be.

"When we first met, you called Will a force of nature." Rhyatt stretched his long legs out.

"I did," Wes replied, remembering one of their first conversations.

"I think I've decided which force of nature he is."

This piqued her curiosity, "Go on." she encouraged.

"A tornado."

Her laugh was light as she threw her head back.

"He came in and spun me around. Changed a lot of things for me."

"He tends to do that." Wes sighed, "I hope I'm doing right by him."

Together, they looked out at Will, his eyes now completely closed, no longer fighting sleep.

Rhyatt rested a reassuring hand on her knee, "You are Wes."

"I hope I'm not messing up my little tornado."

"If he's a tornado, do you know what that makes you?" Rhyatt asked, and Wes appreciated the distraction before she could doubt herself too much.

"What? The cow that gets caught in the tornado and thrown around?"

This earned a sweet laugh from Rhyatt, and she smiled at the sound.

"No," he shook his head, that wide grin still plastered on his face, "The thunderstorm that follows."

She raised her brows, motioning for him to continue.

"Powerful." He nodded, "And mesmerizing to watch, even if I was once afraid. You bring fresh air to things. You certainly light up my sky."

She blinked, not trusting her words at the moment. He said it so casually as if it were a fact everyone knew. To distract herself, she began to think of what natural entity Rhyatt embodied. And that was the problem. She didn't think there was a thing in this world as pure as Rhyatt.

"Then you must be sunset." She settled.

"Do tell." He arched his brow.

"Golden. You are what people wish they were. Good and kind. Your light touches everything around you. People are often sad when you're gone."

What she didn't say was that he was more like a sunrise, bringing golden rays into the world. But Wes hated waking in the morning, and she could never hate Rhyatt. So she settled on sunset, equally as golden.

Rhyatt looked down, the corners of his mouth upturned and color in his face. She loved making him blush. The closer they got, the easier she knew how to.

"That was kind of you." He said, looking back up at her.

"Only for you." She looked over and saw that Will had finally fallen asleep. On silent feet, she rose and draped a blanket over him. A few more minutes wouldn't hurt. She returned to where she and Rhyatt had been seated, he was taking up the majority of the space of the small blanket. She didn't let that deter her and instead sat in between his legs.

"This okay?" She asked before leaning back into his chest.

"Mhm." He hummed his approval and wrapped an arm around her. She snuggled into his chest, unsure what territory this fell under. As long as they didn't have to talk about it then it seemed like it was fine.

"How have the nightmares been?" She asked, turning her head to see him.

"You don't want to hear about it."

"Tell me anyway."

Rhyatt paused, staring at her intently as if to check the sincerity of her offer.

"Some are recurring, and others only happen once. There is one where I'm outside of a bar, and I attack someone. Only once they are on the ground does the person change and become someone I love." He paused as if searching for the strength to continue. "A few nights ago, I woke up from a dream, and I was standing over Adriel. My hands were around his neck. I was... I was choking him."

Wes laid her hand on his arm, gently squeezing. She couldn't begin to imagine the fear that had gone through him upon waking. He had been heavily affected by the attack on his home.

"I fear I am a bad person." He said quietly.

"Most people think they are a better person than they actually are. But you," Wes shook her head with a sympathetic smile. "You think you are worse than you are. And I hope you know you're wrong."

He paused, his eyes staring directly into the core of her being. And she felt it, the tug between them. Their faces were closer than ever, and his lips were parted. In that moment, Wes felt like nothing more than a girl about to jump off a cliff, unsure of what lay at the bottom. It could be water, it could be sand.

Rhyatt leaned forward, their lips mere centimeters apart now.

"May I kiss you?" he whispered.

Wes froze.

Reality crashed around her.

She was not just a girl. She would never be just a girl again. She was William Blake's caregiver. She was the only parental figure he knew. And Rhyatt... Rhyatt was the only mentor he had. Not just a mentor, a friend. If she kissed him now, she would be on edge until it ended. She would live in fear of a snappy comment driving him away and ruining the trust he had built with Will. She could not do that to Will. She would not ruin something that had gone so good for him. Not after she had ruined her family.

Her tense body gave Rhyatt the answer he needed to know, but she still forced the words.

"We shouldn't." she leaned away from him. "It's not fair to Will... he really looks up to you, and I don't want to ruin this for him."

There. She had said it. She had drawn her line in the sand. As long as he was Will's mentor, Wes wouldn't cross the line. No matter how much it hurt her. No matter how much it hurt Rhyatt. Will deserved to have both of them, separately, involved in his life. She had scared him enough with all the heat around the journal. She owed him one good thing, even if it meant sacrificing something close to her.

CLEO

C leo strode into the BlakeMoore library with her head held high and a letter in hand.

Knox and Rhyatt sat on the settee together, Rhyatt was reading aloud and Knox was slowly drifting to sleep. Wes was at her desk, a fountain pen in her hand as she wrote a letter, likely to Warden.

"The Historic Councilor gave me this. He asked me to burn it." Cleo said proudly, lifting the letter in the air.

Knox was the first one to grab it, arousing from his sleep rapidly. Wes was on her feet and by his side, she quickly wrestled it away until they both held an edge.

"It's the Commander's seal," Knox observed.

"I'll save you the time of reading it." Cleo perched on the arm of a winged back chair. "Commander Pryde is taking a trip in three nights. He has asked the Historic Councilor to stay home and say they were in meetings all evening."

"That's not suspicious," Rhyatt muttered.

"Where do you think he's going?" Cleo asked Wes, hoping she would be privy to his goings.

"He hasn't mentioned leaving. He could be going anywhere. To a lover, to a trade deal, to Duran?" She replied, her fingers working to open the seal and read it for herself.

"Should we follow him?" Knox asked.

"No." Cleo and Wes responded in unison. Both women turned to look at each other, mischievous smiles forming.

"Commander Pryde's home will be without the Commander..." Wes trailed off.

"What a perfect time to take a look around." Cleo smiled at her friend.

Cleo gripped Rhyatt's outstretched hand and planted her foot firmly on his knee. Pushing upwards, she folded her limbs to fit easily through the window of Commander Pryde's home.

Her feet hit the marbled bathroom floors without as much as a sound. In the darkness, her eyes could only make out the faint shape of the room.

Wes's hand appeared in the window next. Cleo grabbed it and hauled her friend through it to the other side. Wes was not as quiet.

Cleo pressed her fingers to her lips and hushed her softly.

Knox was next. He was neither quiet nor graceful.

After a harsh shushing from both women, Rhyatt's hands appeared. Knox and Wes stepped forward, each grabbing a forearm as they had to physically pull his broad shoulders through the tiny window.

He was partially dumped on the floor with a thud.

Cleo put a hand on Wes and Rhyatt's shoulders but quickly pulled away as both of them shocked her palms.

"Ow." She whispered loudly.

"What?" Knox whisper-yelled back as they all unscrambled.

"They both shocked me." She rubbed her palms together before flicking her fingers out.

She didn't miss the hard stare Rhyatt gave Wes. That was the look of someone who knew more than her.

"Are you going to share your secret with the class?" Cleo raised an eyebrow.

"Sometimes we shock each other when we touch," Rhyatt said on an unsteady breath. He glanced at Wes before continuing, "Today, we shocked you."

"That's... not normal," Cleo said. Looking between the two of them and trying to fit together a puzzle that was missing a piece or two.

Knox leaned forward, a devilish smile appearing, "Does it shock you everywhere or just the body part that is touched?"

It took approximately two heartbeats for Rhyatt to realize Knox's meaning and for a dark red flush to spread over his cheeks and down his neck. Wes only cocked an eyebrow as if she was considering why she herself had never thought of it.

"Is this why you can't take your hands off each other? Is it constant? Is it pleasurable?" Knox's voice rose above a whisper as he asked question after question.

"We haven't tested the theory." Wes's emotionless response silenced Knox.

He held his hands up in mock surrender, but the grin on his face promised he would question them individually as soon as he had the chance.

"You're sick," Cleo said, passing Knox and heading for the bath-room door.

"And twisted," Knox added with a touch of glee.

They all gathered around the door. Wes was the one to crack it open an inch and peek out before shutting it again and nodding that it was all quiet in the Commander's residence.

They crept down the darkened hallway, four quiet sets of feet avoiding the hardwood and instead aiming for the rugs. They were right about the house being almost empty. Atticus had left before dinner but had still not returned. Ida, the youngest Pryde daughter, had not come home at all. Winnie, the eldest, had gone back south weeks ago. The last of the house staff had left minutes after 2 AM. They moved quickly through the dark and silent house.

They paused in front of a set of double doors, Pryde's home office. Wes stepped forward and reached upwards on her tiptoes. She was nowhere near reaching the top of the door frame. Cleo watched her struggle for a moment before she stepped forward, but Rhyatt was already speaking.

"Let me." he whispered and then waited until she stepped away before he stepped forward and grabbed the key. It had been this little song and dance between the two of them for days. Constantly stepping out of each other's paths, barely touching.

Rhyatt extended the key to her, his fingers placed the furthest away.

She took the key, and seconds later, the large doors were opening.

The four strode into the darkened room, the only light coming from the moon shining outside.

They split among the room quickly, deciding before they had arrived who would search where. Cleo had the desk, Knox the bookshelves behind it, and Wes and Rhyatt were on the room as a whole.

Cleo had her work cut out for her as she sat down at the desk and began meticulously opening files. She was only halfway through the first drawer when Knox joined her and took the left side of the desk.

Soon, Wes and Rhyatt were out of areas to check. They wandered back to the desk and hovered over Cleo and Knox.

Cleo shot them a sharp glance, "You're in my moonlight."

She motioned towards the little streak of light that came from the large windows.

Wes and Rhyatt sidestepped.

"Now you're in *my* light!" Knox whined.

"Maybe you two should check his bedroom." Cleo said, annoyed to have them standing over her.

Wes opened her mouth to argue, but Cleo gave her a steely stare. And for once, the woman did not argue.

Wes and Rhyatt disappeared into the house, leaving Cleo and Knox alone at the desk.

"Do you think they'll be testing their new shock theory out upstairs?" Knox asked when he was sure they were out of earshot.

Cleo raised her brows at him.

"Do you really not know?" She asked conspiratorially.

"Know that they've been avoiding each other like the plague for a week?" Knox pursed his lips in triumph, "Oh, I know that. But why?"

"She told him no." Cleo leaned closer to Knox, smiling.

"Told him no to what?" he asked, his whisper growing excited.

"He finally got the nerve to kiss her, but he asked her first."

"No, he didn't."

"He did. And you know how she is," Cleo waved a hand in the air, "She had a moment too long to think on it and over-thought it. She told him no."

"That bastard."

"I know." Cleo agreed and opened the last drawer, pulling out a ledger.

"They're going to start a fire with all that friction if they don't let it out soon."

"Even worse, she wants me to go out with her. A girls night."

"I'm not invited?" Knox asked, the pitch of his voice rising with hurt.

"You're not a girl, are you?"

"If I'm invited out, I'll be a girl for a night. Wig and everything."

"I'd pay to see that." Cleo stopped her chatter as her fingers ran across the notes of the ledger.

It was not uncommon to grow and sell grains in Northern Jorjin, but The Commander's notes mentioned each grain by its name, except 'grain1' was written multiple times. She ran her fingers along the numbers, flipping the pages and finding the other excerpts. It was mentioned once a week, never in a pattern, but always the same cost. $2948.76.

"Knox," Cleo whispered, pointing to the notes in front of her.

"There are over half a dozen grains grown locally, and all of them are labeled *except* this one."

Knox looked over her shoulder and followed her fingers.

"Do you think it's the green mountain corn?" he asked, but Cleo was already turning backward through the pages.

"It has to be. Why else would it be labeled as grain1?"

Cleo's fingers stopped on the bottom of the page. All five of the councilors' signatures were listed along with the Commander's. She pointed them out to Knox.

"All five of the Councilors signed. This could mean every single one of them knows about the corn being sent to the facility." Cleo felt her shoulders sag with her words.

She thought of how she would tell Wes of the correlation and began to wish Wes had been the one to find it. She wondered if Wes had felt this dread every time she shared something new about Jaze's death or the journal. It was an awful, oily feeling that she wished she could hide from.

WES

Wes sat in a chair at the window of the grave-watcher's home. It was tradition that no one saw you until midnight, so after waking the morning before her birthday, she left the house and spent the day among the tombs. It hadn't been a terrible way to spend a day. She had brought her sword and some paperwork to occupy her time. Either way, it was better than spending the day at home. Her mother would be coming in today, and she wanted to see as little of her as possible.

Wes spent a fair amount of time on her hair and makeup. She had wanted to hire someone to do it for her but Knox had talked her out of it, citing the tradition of being alone all day. After finalizing the look she put on the dress, a gorgeous yet expensive thing. She had it custom made, even helping in the design process. It was the most stunning thing she owned.

Wes watched out the window as the hour got later. Thirty minutes til midnight was when Tiunda, Will, and Rhina arrived together. The three of them entered the tomb, and a faint light was emitted from the door. She wasn't shocked her mother didn't arrive first. She would be surprised if her mother wasn't the last to arrive.

Shortly after came Cleo and Knox, arms looped, with Rhyatt trailing far behind.

She inhaled sharply as he turned, and his face came into view.

He sauntered across the yard, hands in his pockets. He was dressed in the traditional all black clothing, a stark contrast from his usual light and airy choices. His dark curls had been neatly combed away from his face and he wore an expression she didn't understand.

All in all, he was something to look at. Even the shirt he wore had been perfectly tailored to showcase his broad shoulders and tall height. As he stepped into the tomb, Wes found herself wishing she could watch him walk away just a little longer. But she had spoiled that for herself.

RHYATT

Rhyatt descended the stone steps into the tomb, hoping and praying no one could tell how nervous he truly was. He had asked Lita about the rite; she had only preached about what an old aged honor it was to be invited to one. She had spoken about how you only invite people you trust. Then shortly after she had berated him about having one of his own, even though it wasn't his culture.

He stepped into the small moss laden candle lit room and noticed how few people were here. He recognized a handful. He recognized Will, Knox, Cleo, Rhina, some of the farmhands; there were four or five others he had never seen before.

Before he could introduce himself, Will was beside him, wrapping his arms around Rhyatt's waist and pulling him in for a hug. Rhyatt smiled warmly down at the boy, returning his hug and patting him gently on the back.

Will pulled away and looked up, a tinge of color in his cheeks, "Stand beside me."

"I wouldn't want to be anywhere else," Rhyatt responded, letting Will guide him to stand next to Knox.

Knox bumped his shoulder and nodded to him in greeting, his shoulders tight and jaw locked. If Rhyatt wasn't mistaken, Knox was just as anxious as he was. Cleo stood on Knox's other side, her spine straight and eyes focused forward. She didn't share their nerves. He wasn't sure if the cool and capable Cleo had nerves to share.

The sound of shoes scuffing the stone pulled Rhyatts attention back to the entrance where he saw a woman in her forties enter the room. Her long dark hair was pulled away from her face, showcasing emerald eyes that Rhyatt knew all too well. He had never seen a portrait of Mrs. Blake, but as she entered the room he had no doubt this was her. From the way she carried herself to the sureness in her gaze.

As if proving it, Mrs. Blake walked to where Will stood and patted his head in an attempt to smooth down a cowlick. Will leaned away, attempting to hide a grimace. Mrs. Blake straightened herself, her eyes landing on Rhyatt.

"And who are you?" Her voice wasn't what Rhyatt expected. It had none of the appealing gravel of Wes's. Instead, it was hoarse. Like she'd spent all her life screaming.

"This is Rhyatt," Will said rather defensively.

Mrs. Blake visibly bristled before pausing and seeming to contemplate what she would say.

"What a name, *Rhyatt*." She said his name like it was a curse. It made Rhyatt want to curl into himself.

"It is a testament to patience and peace," Rhyatt replied, taking a steadying breath.

"Ah." She made a noise of understanding and opened her mouth to say more but the chiming of the clock interrupted her.

The room went silent, everyone turning to face the low podium and clear tub at the center. Scholar Tiunda stood on one side of the podium, her face angled towards the entrance. Everyone else followed her line of vision.

A light breeze circled through the room and sent the candles flickering. The yellow light danced along the moss-covered stone walls. And then the lights stopped their dancing, instead burning bright.

The bells were still chiming when she stepped into view. Her bare feet and legs peeked out of her dress as she descended the steps into the room. Rhyatt's lips parted at the sight. He had never seen her look so beautiful. Except beautiful wasn't a powerful enough word. She was exquisite, otherworldly, truly an entity.

Her short curls had been smoothed, and her dark hair was a contrast to the white and cream-colored gown she wore. Oh. The dress. The tailor must've spent a lot of time on it. The top was tight fitting, a deep V going down the front of her chest. Rhyatt thought it must've stopped right before her snake tattoo. The sleeves were long and billowed out from her body, resembling a cape. The dress was perfectly fitted until her waist, and from there, it became loose. The fabric moved with her hips and puddled on the floor. As she approached the podium, he noticed two slits in the skirts of the dress that went up to her mid-thigh.

The clock stopped chiming. Wes picked up a match and a long, skinny candle. With a single hand, she lit the candle and passed it to Scholar Tiunda. Scholar Tiunda walked to Mrs. Blake with the candle held gently in hand.

"With this flame, we will light the way for Wes Blake. Please bestow your good wishes on it."

The Scholar closed her eyes for a moment, then reopened them to pass the candle to Mrs. Blake. Mrs. Blake took the candle, closing her eyes for an even briefer amount of time, and then crouched to hand it to Will. Will copied them, his little face scrunching and his lips moving without words. When Rhyatt took the candle from him, he silently wished Wes all the happiness in the world and handed it off. The candle made its way around the room, each person holding it and silently wishing. By the time it reached the last person, the wax had begun to dribble down the sides. The Scholar took the candle and returned to her side of the podium.

"Wes, please present your hands."

Wes placed both of her hands on the podium, the Scholar tipped the candle over and the hot wax dripped onto her palms. Rhyatt looked at her face, but she showed no sign of pain.

"Your wishes have been bestowed on her," Scholar Tiunda said to the crowd, "Now may your flame light her way, not only tonight but also through life. The rite will begin now."

Scholar Tiunda placed the candle off to one side of the podium before straightening and continuing.

"One will make mistakes in life, but it is responsibility that separates the youth from the fully-fledged. The fully-fledged will acknowledge their missteps and strive to do better. Wes will now present her own account of her missteps. In doing so, she will unburden herself and go forward unstained."

Wes reached into a pocket that had been hidden by the fabric of her dress and withdrew folded papers. The small stack of papers had to have been at least four pages with ink on both sides. Her fingers gripped the papers tightly as if afraid of anyone seeing their content. Rhyatt wondered how many 'missteps' she had written down. How long had she poured over the papers in her hand. How many unhappy memories she had dredged up to write them. And most selfishly of all, he wondered how many times he had caused one of the missteps.

Wes held the folded stack of papers up to the flame. They caught quickly, flickering and dancing up the paper towards her fingertips. She held the papers over the podium, watching them. From where he stood, Rhyatt could see the reflection of flames in her eyes. Her eyes stared with intensity as she watched her mistakes burn. When the flames licked too close to her fingers, she placed the burning papers on the podium and watched them burn from there.

When the flame fizzled out, and there was nothing but ash, she placed her hand on the podium, covering her palm in ash and then placing it across her heart. It left a dark handprint in the center of her chest.

"No one may hold my past against me, for I have made peace with it." Her voice wasn't the casual tone she usually had. Nor was it the tone of the leader she had when speaking to her workers. It was something different. Something confident yet monotone. No room for interpretation by anyone.

"Responsibility has been taken." The Scholar announced, "The fully fledged are independent of others. They are capable of caring for themselves without any outside influence. Independence will be shown over the course of Wes's life. However, tonight, she will show us what she has worked towards for months."

Wes stepped away from the podium and walked to the entrance, where a dark cloth had been covering a square object. She pulled it free, revealing a cage with a chicken sleeping soundly inside. Bending low, she reached into the cage and retrieved the chicken. It clucked indignantly at being woken.

Will tensed beside Rhyatt as the chicken was carried back to the podium. His small hand soon gripped Rhyatt's arm, and his body turned towards Rhyatt instead of his sister.

Wes placed the chicken on the podium, both hands holding it. She shook her sleeves back, and with her free hand, she wrapped them around the chicken's neck.

Will turned his face to bury in Rhyatt's side. Instinctively, Rhyatt placed his free hand on the back of Will's head, shielding him from what was about to come. Rhyatt himself looked back up, unable to tear his eyes away for more than a second. The room fell utterly still. The only sound was that of the chicken.

Her hands tightened, and in a quick motion, the chicken ceased to live. The *snap* of its neck was quiet enough that Rhyatt didn't think Will heard it.

With light feet she placed the chicken back in its cage and returned the cover, hiding it from view. Rhyatt loosened his grip on Will and in turn he relaxed as well.

"I do not turn away from the slaughter, for it will keep my belly from weeping," Wes said, her voice still that strange mixture, void of any tale of emotion.

"Independence has been proven." Scholar Tiunda announced, and Will slowly turned back to face his sister. "The fully-fledged are rational. They think through their actions and analyze their options in order to optimize their outcome. Tonight, Wes will be given a test. There are no right or wrong answers. Only rational decisions."

Scholar Tiunda pulled a sealed scroll from her robes and handed it to Wes. Her fingertips worked to open the seal wax and unraveled the paper. The room watched as her eyes darted along the paper, reading the test. Once her eyes reached the bottom, they flashed up to Scholar Tiunda, the briefest of emotions flickering across her face before her eyes returned to the paper.

She read the paper once more, and Rhyatt swore she was struggling to keep her face blank. He had seen her try to stay neutral on subjects before, and this was similar. She tilted her chin up slightly before lowering the paper.

"I would save the second." She stated without blinking.

"And what of the consequences of allowing the first to go?" Scholar Tiunda asked.

"I cannot live without the second. Nothing would change if the first was to go." Wes stated and pressed her hands flat onto the podium.

"Legally?" Scholar Tiunda implored.

"I am confident in my ability to arrange something," Wes responded.

"And the third? The fourth?"

"It would be upsetting, but I still choose the second." Wes reaffirmed her choice.

Rhyatt's interest in the test rose, but as soon as he wondered if he would get to read it later, Wes picked the scroll up and tilted it into the fire.

"Rationality has been shown." The Scholar announced, and her tone shifted, "Wes Blake, you have passed the three tests of the fully-fledged. Congratulations."

Wes closed her eyes and dipped her head, relief flooding through the room. Scholar Tiunda reached into her ceremony robes and pulled out a small dagger, it was gilded in gold and it appeared to have a 'W' on the pommel. She held it over the podium, offering it to Wes.

"Wes will now choose her *confidebat*." Scholar Tiunda said as Wes accepted the dagger and turned towards their part of the circle.

He had only been told briefly about confidebats. It was an honor one of the fully-fledged bestowed on their peers. One's confidebat was to hold them accountable. Wes had a small scar on her right collarbone where Knox had asked her to be his.

Wes glided towards them. She stopped in front of Knox and held the dagger in between them, flat in her palms. They stared into each other's eyes, and the corner of Knox's mouth twitched. Scholar Tiunda had silently followed Wes and now stood behind her.

"Knox, do you accept the position as Wes's confidebat?"

"I do," Knox said, his eyes never leaving Wes.

"Let it be bound in blood." Scholar Tiunda said.

Will's grip on Rhyatt tightened as Knox took the dagger from Wes. He slowly raised the tip to her left collarbone. In a quick motion, he pressed and dragged the dagger toward her shoulder, a horizontal line of blood swelling at the sight. A bead of blood left the cut and flowed down to the center of her chest, in between her breasts, until it stopped at the fabric. The red was stark against the white of her dress.

Knox passed the dagger back to Wes and pulled the collar of his shirt loose, showing his bare skin. She leaned forward, pressing the knife below his right collarbone. With an equally quick motion, she cut him. Only his cut was vertical, resembling a scratch. Blood welled under his cut, but it didn't flow as freely as hers had.

"It has been bound," Wes announced, her chin tilting up.

Knox softly repeated the words after her. Wes and Scholar Tiunda stepped away from Knox but did not return to the podium. Instead they stood in between the podium and the glass tub. There was a stone on the ground that was darker than the rest, this seemed to be their focus.

Wes twisted the dagger so that the tip was pressed against her opposite pointer finger. She poked it, and red blood swelled, threatening to drip onto the darkened stone they had gathered around.

"You have yet a long road to go, but your ancestors will be watching over you. Join your blood with theirs and rise to their expectations."

Wes bent and smeared her bleeding fingers across the stone. The bright red blood turned dark as it seeped into the stone. The stone seemed to like the blood, accepting it all and adding it to its long list of patrons who had given a small sliver of themselves to it.

"Lastly, be cleansed by the water." Scholar Tiunda motioned to the glass tub.

Wes stood, her shoulders pressed back as she strode to the waiting water. Gathering her skirt with her chin held high, she stepped one leg in and then the other. Her dress still hadn't touched the water. With a flourish, she threw the skirts out and sat down. She had a hand on each side of the tub as she slipped in. Once seated, she continued to recline until her head was underwater. Only then did she put her hands in, completely submerging herself.

Although the tub was made of glass, you couldn't see much. Just a blur of flesh and white colored fabric. That was until it started changing.

The water began to darken drastically, and the white of the dress disappeared. Someone on the opposite side of the room gasped. Rhyatt looked down at Will, who still clutched his arm, and he wasn't shocked. He looked over at Knox to find him smiling.

The water was now black, and not a single thing was visible inside. It gently sloshed against the edges.

The top of her dark hair peeked out of the tub, and slowly, so smoothly, did her entire head appear, eyes already open. In a smooth motion she stood.

The room was quiet with awe and shock.

Her white dress was now the deepest shade of black, and the tub's water remained black as well.

Not only was her dress changed, but her demeanor was different. Her hair was slicked back, and her makeup that had once seemed simple now seemed darker, more daring.

She had transformed into a dark goddess. Rhyatt starred in adoration.

"I present the fully-fledged Wes Blake!" Scholar Tiunda announced, and the room broke out in cheers.

Wes smiled without showing her teeth. Rather, she glanced around the room for the first time, surveying the people in front of her.

WES

From the moment she stepped out of the water, Wes was not alone. She was instantly swarmed by her friends and family. Even as she exited the tomb, the grave watcher approached her and congratulated her. The ride to her home had been on a carriage where family surrounded her. At her party, she was surrounded by even more people. She knew her mother had invited additional guests, but she had done so as well. Now the gardens felt too full, people spilling over and outside the warm glow from the thousands of candles. The only upside was that a busy party made it easier to avoid the people she didn't want to see.

She timed her escape perfectly. The plan was to be seen for the first twenty minutes of the party, then she could disappear in ten to fifteen minute increments. As long as she reappeared every so often she could minimize the amount of time she was actually available.

Wes slipped in the back door, closing it quietly behind her. This first break could be the longest, she decided as she bound up the stairs with a plate of food in hand. Entering her room, she forwent the lights, instead strolling to the balcony. She left the door open as she stepped out and sat on the settee closest to the edge. From here, she could hear the party, but no one could see her. She doubted they could hear her.

She popped a grape in her mouth when she heard her bedroom door click open. Turning, she saw Rhyatt, his tall frame turned away from her as he shut the door. A mixture of emotions rose in her throat as he crossed the room and stood in the frame of the balcony.

"I thought I saw you sneak away."

Damn. Had she been that noticeable?

Rhyatt shook his head as if reading her thoughts, "No one else saw."

"I just wanted a moment alone," Wes said as if that would explain it.

Rhyatt nodded, "I understand. I just wanted to give you this."

He stepped closer, his hand going to his neck, pulling a golden chain out. There was a familiar pendant hanging down. She watched as his strong fingers worked to unclasp it. Once it was free he stepped closer to her, holding it out.

"Happy Birthday Wes."

Wes stared down at the gold pendant, the sword bisecting the heart perfectly straight.

"The pendant from the market." She said in awe, "Put it on me?"

Rhyatt nodded, and she turned around. She could feel him radiating heat when he stepped closer.

"You said someone would be lucky to wear it and I thought that lucky person should be you." He said as his fingers closed the clasp and brushed against her skin. "Done."

She turned around and smiled at him. She wanted so badly to hug him. Instead, she settled on grasping his arm.

"Thank you, Rhy." She nodded sincerely. This was probably the most thoughtful gift she had ever been given. Rhyatt looked down at his shoes.

"I'll leave you be. I just wanted to give you that."

"No." She said a little too harshly for her liking. "Sit for a minute." She corrected her tone.

He continued to look down at his shoes, and for a moment she thought he would decline and leave. It is what she deserved. But against all odds, he nodded. They sat down on the settee, just enough space between them so that their legs wouldn't brush. Silence surrounded them and Wes feared this is how it would be from here on out. She hated the thought that they would never joke with each other again.

"I've missed talking to you," Rhyatt said tentatively.

"I do miss your wit." She admitted.

And your smile, your laugh, your jokes...

He smiled softly down at her, and that was all it took.

"All you have to do is ask, and you shall receive."

"I wish everything was that easy." She said with a sigh.

Rhyatt's smile faded, and he furrowed his brow.

"What would you ask for?" He asked earnestly.

"Many things. A way to get rid of this journal. A way to keep my home safe. A way to deliver justice for Jaze." Wes looked up to the stars, unable to look at him as she spoke, "Maybe a way to kiss a man without feeling guilty."

Rhyatt's breath hitched. Wes tensed, knowing saying these things didn't make it any better.

"I wish we could be different people sometimes." He replied, the slightest shake in his voice.

Wes looked back at him, a smile brewing as she thought of the idea.

"And who would you be? Romeo?"

"No," Rhyatt responded matter-of-factly. "Romeo dies. I'd be a man named Clyde. Clyde Edgar. And I'd work on a boat."

Her smile widened. She had forgotten how easy it was to be around him, how relaxed she became. He made her smile with such ease.

"You can't swim Rhy." She stated.

"I said I was working *on* a boat, not *in* the water."

"If it capsizes?"

"Then my crew is fired."

Wes shook her head. He was tireless.

"Okay. I'll be Rose. Rose Numan. A general of a naval army. Maybe I'll sink your ship."

"Hmm." Rhyatt tapped his chin, pretending to think, "It sounds too close to a real career for you. With a name like Rose, you need to be a florist."

Wes rolled her eyes. Her mouth parted in faux shock. Still, her smile remained.

"I promise to come buy flowers from you every time I make port," Rhyatt swore.

"I guess it wouldn't be *that* bad then." Wes leaned forward, "Tell me more about this mysterious Clyde."

"Where to start?" Rhyatt mused, "He was born on the sea and gets sick on land. He's seen three mermaids and lived to tell the tale. He only drinks whiskey."

Wes let out an involuntary laugh.

"And is he a gentleman? Or an old sea dog?"

"He's not old at all." Rhyatt's lips twitched, "And of course, he's a gentleman."

Wes leaned closer, hating that she had missed talking with Rhyatt this much. But he was here now.

"I should've known," she said.

Rhyatt nodded, enjoying his own storytelling as well.

"He does have this *thing* with a girl, though."

"Oh?"

"Well, not a girl really. A mermaid. The first one he ever saw. She instantly captivated him. He was unsure of whether to be amused or to be afraid. She had dark hair," Rhyatt leaned forward reaching out to coil a lock of her hair around his fingers, "And a breathtaking smile. He hoped to one day kiss her."

"Men who kiss mermaids drown," Wes said with a hint of sorrow.

Rhyatt nodded slowly, releasing her strand of hair, "Clyde knows. He would happily drown if that's what it took to kiss his mermaid."

He leaned back, putting space between them. Wes saw the movement and panicked, fearing the distance. She leaned forward, but she was now far too close to his face and he wasn't moving anymore.

He paused, clearly waiting for her to say something.

A million words ran through her mind, but none seemed accurate to describe what he meant to her. Words would not do justice to the emotion he evoked.

Maybe touch would.

Wes reached her hand out, placing it gently on Rhyatt's cheek, pulling him a fraction closer.

He closed the distance, and their lips collided.

Soft and gentle at first. Two friends unsure of what boundaries they were going to cross. But soon, the current passed between them, and the kiss turned urgent, needy. Wes hadn't crossed the line in the sand. She had obliterated the whole beach.

She paused just long enough to bite his bottom lip and tug. A soft moan came from the back of Rhyatts' throat as they broke for air. But Wes wasn't willing to keep her hands to herself for more than a second. She pushed him back and straddled his lap, her hands going to his hair. He gripped her thighs.

Wes kissed down his defined jaw, loving the way his rough stubble felt against her lips. His hands tightened in response. She kissed lower until her lips rested on the side of his throat. A quick nibble had him pulling her further into his lap.

Wes closed her eyes as her lower abdomen tightened. She could feel him through his pants. The slits in her dress had allowed the majority of her legs to be exposed, and his rough hands took pleasure in touching them.

She leaned closer, her breast pressing against his chest, and pressed a kiss to the side of his jaw. He jerked his head towards her, a hungry kiss swallowing her breath.

Instinctively, she began rocking her hips, enjoying the movement.

"Are you sure you won't regret this?" Rhyatt asked, out of breath.

"It's my birthday, let me live a little." She replied, shutting him up with a kiss.

His hands went higher, his thumbs rubbing her inner thigh. He made slow, methodical circles against the soft skin there.

She pulled away, this time dipping her attention lower. She left a trail of kisses along his collarbone before running her tongue up the column of his neck.

"Feel what you do to me." She whispered, canting her hips towards his fingers.

He kissed her again, this time slower, his tongue swiping across her lips. His hand went under the dress. He ignored her panties, tugging them to the side.

His long middle finger pushed between her lips, sliding down to her entrance. Slowly, he pushed his finger inside her.

She tilted her head back, biting on her lip to keep from making an ungodly noise, and gripped his shoulders.

He slowly pulled his finger out before pushing it back in and curling. He pumped his finger again before pulling it completely out.

Wes opened her mouth to protest at the same time Rhyatt added an additional finger, plunging deep inside her. Her back arched, and a gasp escaped.

He pumped his fingers in and out of her, slow and tortuous, making her tense after every thrust.

His pace began to quicken, and she tilted her head upwards. Rhyatt seized the moment, attacking her neck. Kissing and biting every square inch of her. He lowered his mouth until he was kissing the tops of her breasts, only stopping at the start of the fabric. She hummed her approval.

He leaned back and studied her face. There was something so different about him. His eyes had darkened, and his jaw was set. Wes had never truly considered Rhyatt dangerous, but right here, right now, he looked like he could be. It turned her on more than she could manage.

She rocked her hips, effectively riding his fingers. The friction building between her thighs was tortuous.

Rhyatt licked his lips, his mouth slightly parted as he tilted his head. He pulled his fingers out of her and slowly brought them to his lips. Keeping eye contact, he placed them in his mouth, sucking them clean.

His cheeks hollowed, and Wes clenched around nothing, inhaling sharply. When his fingers were free of his mouth, she pounced on him, their lips smashing together desperately. He wrapped his hands around her ass and stood, picking them both up. Without stopping their kiss, he carried them to the bedroom.

Inside, he tossed her onto the bed like she was a sack of flour. A girlish laugh escaped her. Rhyatt looked down at her, that dangerous look dancing in his eyes. Grabbing her behind the knees, he yanked her to the edge of the bed.

In seconds, he was kneeling between her legs. He bent forward and kissed the inside of her knee. Her abs contracted at the touch of his lips, warm and wet. But this was only the beginning. Rhyatt began a trail of soft kisses up her legs, pushing the dress up to her waist when it got in the way. When he reached her panties, he paused. His warm breath sent shivers down her spine. Lightly, he pressed a kiss to the fabric. Wes fought the urge to squirm.

His fingers came up to play with the sides of her panties as his lips kissed the opposite leg. When his lips stopped at her opposite knee, he twisted his fingers in her panties and tugged them down. The force made her gasp.

Rhyatt tossed the panties behind him and repositioned himself. He wrapped his arms under her leg so that his palms were gripping her hips. He positioned his face right in front of her.

Another soft kiss to her inner thigh. His breath grazed her inner-most parts as he turned to kiss the other thigh.

"Tell me how much you want it." His voice was husky and reverberated through her.

"I want it." She whimpered, burning desire growing deep within.

"Tell me." Another kiss.

"I fucking want you Rhy." She said breathlessly.

He smiled up at her, "That's all you had to say."

He leaned forward and licked her from her entrance to her clit. Her hips bucked against him. He only tightened his grip on her. He did it again, stopping at her clit and circling it with slow and deadly precision. Her hands reached down and grabbed his hair again, pulling it as her body began to rock against his tongue.

Rhyatt moaned, the sound reverberating through her and earning a whimper. He stopped the circles to gently suck. Her grip tightened in his hair. He sucked harder before pulling away, a sinister slurping noise filling the air.

"You're fucking divine Wes," he whispered before returning to his work.

Her body responded in kind. She felt like all of the currents were running between them, making each touch that much hotter. Making each kiss, each lick, that much more unbearable. She felt like she was going to burst at the seam.

Rhyatt released one hand from her hip and placed it in front of his face, pushing two fingers inside her. Where they rightfully belong.

Her throat bobbed at the mix of sensations. Her hands released his hair and twisted in the sheets instead.

"Godsfuck," she whispered, her hips moving quicker, encouraging his fingers and tongue to work quicker. He obliged.

The hand on her hip dug deeper, and it registered in her mind that this should hurt, but it didn't. It was far from hurting. It grounded her in this moment.

His fingers pumped in and out of her, and his tongue flicked across her in rhythm. Her back began to arch, and she moaned his name as her walls clenched around him, and she orgasmed.

RHYATT

R hyatt rocked back onto his heels, gently placing soft kisses down Wes's thighs as she came down. His hands came to rest on his thighs as he listened to her shallow pants. Rhyatt exhaled. It felt good to be a pious man worshiping at the altar.

The bedroom door was thrown open, and golden light spilled into the room.

"Wes, I was thinking-" Knox stood in the open doorway, frozen.

Both Rhyatt and Wes scrambled for the edge of the dress, pulling it down over her exposed stomach and thighs.

Knox looked back into the hallway before taking an exaggerated step into the room and shutting the door behind him. An evil grin appeared.

"I didn't know the party was in here."

"What do you want?" Wes said with a ragged breath as she propped herself up on her elbows.

Knox leaned his back against the door, crossing his arms and analyzing the scene before him. Rhyatt gazed downwards, hating that Knox could probably see his arousal all over his face.

"I saw this coming, but not tonight. Certainly not tonight." Knox switched his focus to Wes before continuing, "I'd mistake you for a queen for how many men get on their knees before you."

Wes had no immediate response. The air hung heavy. Knox tensed and waited for his retaliation. But Rhyatt surprised himself when it was *him* who let out a dark chuckle. He looked away, covering his mouth. Wes rolled her eyes and pushed herself up into a sitting position.

"What did you need?" She asked again. Her breathing had returned to normal. There was almost a certain calmness to it.

"Just came to let you know your mother is looking for you. Something important." He huffed a little laugh and added, "I'm glad I was the one who came to look for you."

Wes stood, her dress brushing against Rhyatt as she walked by. He contemplated grabbing her wrists and asking her to stay. But as she crossed the room, he knew he couldn't ask that of her.

"Not a single word to anyone." She glanced back at Rhyatt, "Either of you."

Rhyatt nodded, and she turned back around to Knox.

"As you command, *Queen Wes.*"

She motioned for him to move. He sidestepped and she exited the room, leaving the two men alone.

Rhyatt stood, stooping to dust the dirt off his knees. He rolled his sleeves down and straightened his collar. Knox watched quietly, still standing close to the door. Rhyatt drug his palm down his mouth, wishing he could still be between her legs. He shook his head, hoping the thoughts would stay away for the rest of the night.

He straightened his spine and took a deep breath before walking to the door. When he reached it, Knox clapped him on the back.

"Don't worry. She always keeps the ones she likes hidden."

WES

Wes found her mother in a throng of people, her laugh carrying and making others around her smile up at her in adoration. She was the perfect picture of poise and confidence, no matter the situation. Wes sometimes hated her mother for it, even worse she suspected her mother hated Wes for the lack of the qualities. She was more like her father.

Wes straightened her back, a tightlipped smile appearing on her face as she approached the group. Her mother noticed her immediately but waited until her sentence was done to comment.

"Wes, dearest." Mrs. Blake cooed, separating herself from the group.

"Knox said you were looking for me," Wes said, keeping her voice even. She had learned that unpleasant behavior got her nowhere when it involved Mrs. Blake.

"Yes." her honeyed words stuck to Wes's skin as she motioned them towards the house. "Where did you run off to anyway?"

"Just needed a moment alone," Wes replied, finding her voice smaller than she would like.

"Soak it up while you can." She said with cool indifference as they ascended the stairs, "Girls like you don't get to have 'moments alone.'"

Wes joined her at the top of the stairs, only Mrs.Blake didn't turn to the door, she turned to her daughter. Mrs. Blake reached a finger out, tapping underneath Wes's chin. Wes automatically held her head higher. She had a hatred for her mother's tricks.

Satisfied, Mrs. Blake pulled the door open and strolled in, not waiting to see if Wes would follow.

Wes stood for a moment, trying to contain the mass of emotions that onslaught her every time her mother was in the same vicinity. She took a deep breath and strode through the door and found her mother approaching the library doors.

"What does that mean?" She asked, and this time, her voice did not fail her.

Mrs. Blake stopped in front of the doors, turning to face Wes, a sad smile on her eyes.

"You and I both know you've always had eyes on you. The older you've gotten, the more people have watched."

She reached out and ran her thumb across her daughter's cheek. Wes jerked at the touch before stilling herself. But Mrs. Blake had noticed. She sighed and pulled her hand away.

They entered the library, and Wes was sure to close the doors behind them. Mrs. Blake had taken a seat on the couch and motioned for Wes to join her side. She obliged but left as much space as possible between them. She clasped her hand and noticed the stacks of papers on the table. The only problem was that Wes had spent days cleaning the library and knew for a fact that she had not left anything out.

"What is that?" She asked.

Her mother's face twisted into something that could be construed as a prideful smile. It turned Wes's stomach.

"Like I said, Wes dearest, the older you have gotten, the more people have paid attention. And how magnificent you've done these past few years. You've held the highest retention rate the farm has ever seen. The workers are loyal and refuse to do business with others. The Trade Councilor says you've increased the trade value almost double. You're expanding into winter crops."

She paused and reached a hand out to clasp Wes's. This time, she was prepared and didn't flinch away.

"Wes, you're running everything better than my mother and father did. The business is flourishing." Mrs. Blake paused, smiling in that prideful way. "That's why I've decided it's time for you to take over completely. The house, the farm, the business. As of today, it's all yours."

Mrs. Blake handed Wes the papers that had been lying on the table. And there it was. Right there on top. As of October 24th, Wes Blake was the owner of the BlakeMoore house, its surrounding lands, and any of its businesses.

Wes swallowed. Then flipped through the documents once, twice, thrice for good measure. It was all there.

"What about Warden? Father?" She asked after a moment of silence.

"This was never your father's to give away." She dismissed him before continuing, "As far as Warden, you are welcome to bring him on as a business partner, but you are the firstborn child. This is your right. You *deserve* this."

Wes swallowed again, her throat feeling tighter. She could agree that she deserved the BlakeMoore, all the time and effort she had put into it the past five years. However, she couldn't help but worry about everyone else in her family, even when they didn't seem to worry about her.

"I don't understand." Wes muttered, "How will you all survive?"

Mrs. Blake cocked her head and lowered her voice as if talking to a confused child.

"We have all been surviving just fine. It is time for you to rise to the occasion, Wes. This is yours now, and I have no doubt you will surpass every expectation."

Wes looked back down to the documents, they had been drafted almost a year ago. Not too long after her last birthday. A thought occurred to her and she looked up, her gaze turning stony as she fixed on her mothers eyes.

"What about Will?" her voice shifted on his name. An edge far too sharp.

Mrs. Blake dipped her head, breaking eye contact. The coward.

"That is entirely up to you. If you wish for William to be raised in the BlakeMoore, I can arrange for you to become his guardian. If you no longer welcome him in your home, he will accompany me to Oan."

"He stays," Wes said before her sentence was finished.

"Are you sure? A young boy can be a lot to handle, new estate owners included. I don't mind to-"

"I've been *handling* him just fine. He stays." The edge of her voice clipped, turning into something far more viscous.

Mrs. Blake nodded.

"He stays."

Wes wanted to breathe a sigh of relief, but the relief in her own mother's eyes conjured an entirely different reaction. Rage. The room seemed too small, the air too stale, and her breath too raged. She angled her body away, hiding her face from her mother's vision. Her hands gripped her bare knees, and she focused on taking deep breaths. The boiling thing inside her continued. She began counting backward from one hundred. At 89, her hands began to shake. Strangely enough, the shaking hands distracted her. She silently cursed herself. She had done more than enough to calm them, yet now, gripping her knees, they shook. She released them, ignoring the dark handprints left in their wake. She faintly wondered if they would bruise.

"I need to return to the party," she announced, rising quickly.

She was halfway to the door when her mother whispered *Happy Birthday*. Wes pretended not to hear it, instead continuing outside. She didn't stop moving until she was back among the partygoers. She found Zonny and Leroy chatting with one of her older cousins. She stepped up and smiled at them, effortlessly joining the conversation.

"No, if you do it that way, you'll lose a thumb."

"Yes, but if you do it your way, it'll take twice as long. I'd rather risk my thumb and eat my lunch quicker."

"Well, if you are to be stupid, you might as well be thumbless."

Wes nodded along, occasionally laughing when others laughed. She looked deeply involved in the conversation, and that was all that mattered.

Inside, her mind was tumbling. Falling down and down. Spiraling into a seemingly endless abyss. She hated this feeling. She hated everything about how she currently felt. Hatred was strong, but it was the only thing she could manage right now. The light from the candles blurred, and she found herself struggling to not let her emotions show. Staying collected was something her mother valued, and even now, even hating her mother, she followed her rules.

Small hands wrapped around her, and a warm face buried itself in her back.

Wes hesitated. Then she turned around, wrapping her arms around Will. He squeezed her tighter, burying his face in the folds of her dress. She squeezed him back. He would stay. He wasn't going anywhere. He stays.

They stood like that, uninterrupted, unspeaking, removed from everyone and everything. They embraced and held each other like they were the only two at the party.

After a few moments of stillness Wes hooked her hands under his arms and hauled him up so that he stood on the tops of her feet. Returning her arms to their hugging position she began to walk slowly towards the stairs. They had done this many times, not so much since Will had gotten older. She stopped at the stairs and he looked up at her. His eyes were glassy but his mouth was set in a hard line. Such a hard expression for such a young boy.

He reluctantly let go of Wes and walked up the stairs. She followed him up and all the way inside until they reached his room. Wes shut his door as Will began taking off his shoes.

"You were listening," Wes said softly.

Will dropped the shoe he had pulled off, and it landed with a thud on the floor.

He looked down at the discarded shoe and nodded.

Wes slowly crossed the room and sat down on the bed beside him. Will continued to look down at his shoes.

They sat in silence, a shared emptiness. Two siblings constantly disappointed by the people who claimed to be family. Two siblings who had reverted to a mother/child relationship because of their family's failings. Two siblings who felt utterly alone in the world.

"Thank you for not sending me to Oan." Will's voice broke on the city's name, and Wes wrapped her arms around him, pulling him in close again.

"I would never send you away." She promised, giving the top of his head a kiss.

"Thank you for not letting her take me." Will corrected.

"Nothing has changed. You're not going anywhere. You belong here, with me." Wes clutched him, if he refused to break out in tears then neither would she. She had to be the strong big sister he depended on, no matter what.

"I know," he said weakly.

"Good." she kissed his head again and spoke into his hair, hoping the words would seep directly into his mind. "I love you far too much to let you go. You belong here Will."

They stayed in an embrace until Will drifted off to sleep. Stroking his hair, she tucked him into bed fully clothed. The boy deserved rest.

RHYATT

Rhyatt, Cleo, and Knox were in the kitchen eating leftovers and talking to Rhina when the last guest said goodnight. The majority of the party was cleaned up, but for the last half hour, no one had seen Wes. Rhyatt told himself it was late, and she had many guests to attend to.

The three of them left together, saying goodnight to Rhina and telling her to tell Wes goodbye for them. They walked down the driveway headed for the road when something caught Rhyatt's eye. A light was coming from the storage barn.

"Is someone in the barn?" Rhyatt asked, his nerves immediately going on edge. Last time there was an unexpected visitor to the BlakeMoore, they had tried to kidnap Wes. Cleo and Knox clearly remembered this, too.

"Let's check it out," Cleo whispered, giving each of them a loaded glance before pulling a knife from her boot.

On silent feet, they started towards the barn but stopped in their tracks when the sound of glass shattering broke the silence.

Knox was the first one to take off in a sprint towards the barn.

Soon came the sound of glass shattering, this time louder, more violent. All three of them sprinted towards the barn. Cleo was the first to reach it, with her hand on the door she waited for Rhyatt and Knox before throwing it open and the three of them burst into the room.

They hadn't been prepared for what they saw.

In the middle of the barn, Wes stood, her teeth bared and breathing heavy. Her dark dress was rumpled, and the bottom looked tattered. In one hand, she had a half-drunk bottle of rum, in the other was an empty bottle. Without warning she launched the empty bottle at the opposite wall.

It exploded, sending colored glass raining down in a ten foot radius. She reached down, into a box and pulled another empty bottle, preparing to throw it at the wall.

"What's going on?" Knox asked, stepping further into the room and into the shatter zone.

Wes's eyes cut to him before focusing on Rhyatt and Cleo, who still stood in the doorway. She gave them a lazy smile with far too many teeth, then proceeded to take another drink.

"She gave me the house," Wes announced a tad too loudly. She had clearly had a lot to drink. "And the land. And the business. She gave me *everything*." Her word ended with a snarl, and she cocked back her arm, another bottle exploding against the wood.

Knox moved quickly, coming to stand at her side. A bit too close, Rhyatt thought.

"So we're celebrating?" he asked.

Wes dipped her shoulder and drove it into his chest, sending Knox stumbling backward and her wobbling after him. She quickly righted herself.

"You don't understand." She yelled. "It's a cop-out."

Cleo and Rhyatt had moved further inside, coming to stand on either side of Wes. Cleo held her empty hands up in a show of goodwill.

"What do you mean, Wes?" Cleo asked, her voice calm, controlled.

Wes turned away from them, returning to her box of bottles. She swooped down, picking up another and throwing it with all her might.

"You won't understand." She spat, bending for another bottle. She took another drink before launching the empty one.

"Make us understand. We want to know." Rhyatt spoke, creeping closer. He had never seen her this undone, and it felt like he was intruding.

She turned her attention to him, and suddenly, he wondered if he should have kept his mouth closed. The center of her attention seemed like a terrible place to be right now. She stepped forward, pointing her finger at his face.

"She's spent the last five years in Oan doing gods know what, fucking gods know who. And the first opportunity she sees to give it all up - she takes it. This is the easy way out for her. Out of Saint Saveen. Out of the BlakeMoore. Out of her family." Her voice had steadily risen until she was yelling again. Her eyes were wide, and her nostrils flared as her voice leveled out, and she continued. "That's what my newfound *ownership* is. A way out. And she fucking took it."

Rhyatt felt like he had been punched in the stomach as he looked into her eyes. So much rage. Anger. All hot and burning. He didn't know she handled so much of it. She turned away, picking up another bottle.

"She stopped wanting this family the day a piece of it stopped wanting her. It was always all or nothing."

The bottle burst, punctuating her sentence.

She looked at Rhyatt and laughed, a type of laugh he hoped to never hear again. She seemed to see through him into his soul, the way she always did, only this time with her seething rage it frightened him what she was capable of. She seemed to see the worry and mock it.

"I haven't even told you the worst part." her guttural laugh echoed as she looked back to Knox and Cleo before focusing on Rhyatt again. "She wanted to take Will back to Oan with her. Send him to school there." She shook her head violently as Rhyatt's heart dropped at the thought of losing the boy.

"What did you do?" Knox asked, stepping forward to be in line with Rhyatt.

"I told her I'd take guardianship over him." She looked at Knox with a glare. "You should've seen the look on her face. You would've thought I offered her gold, not to take her youngest child."

Her eyes turned glassy, and she looked down. Realizing the half full bottle was still in her hand she turned and hurled it at the wall. It broke, the remaining liquid painting the wood a darker shade. Her shoulders sagged and she looked back up at her friends, shaking her head. Her mouth twisted, the rage began to melt as something else brewed.

"She planned this. Almost a year ago. And tried to disguise it as a gift. She doesn't want us..." she trailed off, her voice now impossibly small. "And Will doesn't deserve that."

With her head down and her shoulders slumped, she looked nothing like Wes Blake. Long gone was the woman who laughed in the face of danger. What was left was a shell. A shell of someone who had spent so long pretending to be something else. It wasn't pity that went through Rhyatt. It was sorrow and rage. Rage at her mother for failing her so enormously.

"You don't deserve it either, Wes," Cleo said before closing the gap and wrapping her arms around her friend. Without hesitation, Wes returned the hug, sagging against her like it had taken everything out of her. Knox stepped forward, hugging her other side. Rhyatt followed suit, the three of them surrounding her.

A gasp of air escaped Wes, and her body shook as she sobbed.

"Why doesn't she love me anymore?" she asked.

No one had an answer, so they all just held her tighter.

WES

Whomever is sending the grain without paperwork has went silent, no shipments in three weeks. The doctors complain of other departments in the facility, they loosely refer to one person as the snake. The snake does not 'wear a gem' like the others. I have yet to learn what wearing a gem means. I think they are creating something with the fire accelerant. Bombs seem like a likely answer but perhaps it is these 'gems'.

JG

Wes spent the entire day at the child-appropriate Samhain festival. Her, Rhyatt, and Will had walked around, Will tugging on one of their hands and asking for either of them to shell out for something ridiculous. He had first asked Wes for a sausage on a stick, which she had bought. Next, he asked her for an apple slush drink, which she had also bought. After that, he asked for a wooden ax. Wes had promptly told him no and that maybe he should look at something like the spinning tops. Will had instead waited until she was out of earshot and asked Rhyatt for one of the overpriced slingshots. He had bought it. Wes had given him a nasty look when she found out. His other requests were a sharpened dagger, a vile for keeping poison, and a toy that supposedly gave you amazing hearing. After the slingshot, Rhyatt had put his foot down. Will didn't bother to ask Wes. After Will had gotten second place in the costume contest, he was ready to go home, likely realizing no more toys would be bought. None that he wanted anyway. That had been a handful of hours ago. Now he was safely at home with Rhina and Wes had joined Cleo and Knox at the bar for a drink before the night version of the festival began.

"The world just gets dumber and dumber." Cleo mused as the three of them watched two men fight over who spilled whose beer first.

"I've heard that intelligent people have fewer kids," Knox replied as the men resorted to kicks.

Wes flicked a speck of dirt off the shoulder of her costume and turned to Knox, "I've always seen you with a yard full of kids."

He turned to scowl at her but stopped when he saw her smile. She sent him a friendly wink and swayed to the music. He shook his head and sipped his drink in response.

"Maybe that's why I've never seen myself with kids," Cleo said, holding her glass in front of her mouth.

Knox swallowed the rest of his drink and laughed, "What're you talking about? We're all going to have enough kids to make a miniature army!"

Wes laughed, the movement sloshing some of her drink onto the floor, "On holidays we can have mini battles."

"I can't wait for my kids to show your kids whose genetics are better." Knox puffed his chest and nodded confidently.

"Uhm, hello." Cleo cleared her throat and motion to her long outstretched legs, "My children will clearly be running laps around yours."

Wes waved her hand in the air, "You both may have advantages, but it is also about *who else* is in the gene pool." She smiled a crooked smile, her drink kicking in. "I hope you both fall hopelessly in love with short uncoordinated people."

Knox barked a loud laugh that made others look and Cleo shook her head as she stood, gathering their cups to get another round. She stopped in front of Wes, bending to make her point.

"To even the playing grounds, I hope you fall for someone big and tall and strong." Cleo's eyes flickered up, then back to Wes, a mischievous smile growing. "Speaking of, I think I found the perfect *gene pool* for you to pull from."

Cleo darted away before Wes could make sense of her friend's comment. She turned her head to see Rhyatt, dressed as a cowboy, coming her way. Behind him trailed Adriel. She smiled at Rhyatt's costume, loving the bandana wrapped around his neck.

"You're one step ahead," Knox whispered to her before standing and waving them down. Wes got up and joined Cleo at the bar, ordering two more drinks for Rhyatt and Adriel. The wings of Cleo's angel costume brushed Wes's shoulder as she leaned on the bar.

"Did Will have a good time today?" Cleo asked as they waited.

"He did." Wes nodded before glancing back at Rhyatt. It seemed that any time Will spent with Rhyatt was a good time. "We saw your parents a few times," Wes added.

Cleo looked over at her with raised eyebrows, "I'm sure you had lengthy conversations."

"If you consider ten words or less lengthy, then yes."

Cleo laughed her little angelic laugh. The costume really did suit her. She shook her head before staring straight ahead again, something burning her up. Wes knew good and well not to push Cleo, she would speak when she was ready.

"When I visit my brothers after graduation, they really want me to stay there."

Wes didn't miss how Cleo said she was visiting her brothers, not returning home. Her parents still called Genvi home, but Cleo had stopped referring to it as home some time ago.

"Do you want to stay?" Wes asked, her tone cautious.

"No." Cleo shook her head slightly, "I don't know where I want to go yet..." She trailed off before looking back to Wes, "I sometimes fear they will send me over and refuse to buy me a ticket back."

"They wouldn't."

"They might. They've been worried about the safety here for some time." Cleo's eyes darted to the door and back, "The disappearances aren't easing their worries."

The bartender chose that moment to set down their drinks, Wes handed her a few silver pieces, insisting she keep the change. Cleo and Wes loaded the festive drinks in their hands and turned toward where Adriel and Rhyatt had joined Knox.

"Let's not think about it too much tonight. I just want to have fun." Cleo said before they joined the others.

"Nice costumes, boys!" Wes said in greeting. Adriel lit up at the compliment, and Rhyatt blushed.

"Here." Cleo passed the drinks to them and raised her own in a cheers motion.

"To fun." She raised her glass higher.

"And genetics!" Knox added.

RHYATT

I t had taken them an hour to secure a cards table inside the festival. In that time they had had approximately six more drinks. Rhyatt had spilled half of one down his front when someone knocked into him. He had been surprised at how quick to anger Wes had been, but now she sat to his right, her eyes focused on the cards in her hand. Knox sat to his left, with Cleo beside him and Adriel beside her. Adriel had been trying his hardest to make Wes laugh. He had to admit his brother could be funny when he wanted to.

"-And he looked at me and said, 'you wouldn't know your willy from a brown snake on a rock.' But I'm from Duran City and didn't know that a brown snake was actually a snake! So I argued with him." Adriel nodded his head, and Knox burst out laughing. Rhyatt shook his head with a smile.

Olivina and a younger girl he presumed to be her sister had walked by earlier and were walking by again when Olivinia waved to Rhyatt, and he waved back. She and her sister turned towards them.

"Hi," Olivina said with a big smile, "You guys remember my sister, Olea," she motioned to her younger counterpart.

A chorus of hello's came from the table.

"Why don't you sit down and play a game with us?" Wes invited. When Olivina nodded and began to look for a chair, Wes stood.

"Have mine." She shot Olivina a flirtatious smile and motioned to the chair.

"I'm actually going to look for my friends," Adriel stood and motioned for Olea to sit.

Wes took a standing space beside Rhyatt, her hip resting against his chair and using the back of the chair to steady her. He noticed her cheeks were rosy and her movements fluid, but he had been drinking too. He could feel her warmth without touching her. When he focused again she and Olivina were talking.

"And your mother?" Wes asked, taking a sip of her drink.

"She says she is tired of having Tomas home, but I think she is lying." Olivina nodded.

"He was always her favorite child. The firstborn." Olea added with a roll of her eye.

"Did Tomas like Budojin?" Knox asked, not looking up from the tail end of the card game he and Cleo were finishing.

"Oh, he loves it. He talks about it all the time." Olivina said.

Wes shifted her weight from one foot to the other. Then, she shifted again, moving her hand. Rhyatt looked at her face, studying those sharp features, looking for any sign of discomfort.

"Do you want to sit?" He whispered to her.

"Don't mind if I do." She replied, and before he could move, she sat down in his lap. His hands moved automatically to keep her from falling. One on her hip to steady her and the other on her knee under the table. As he touched her skin, the current began pulsing through them, passing back and forth quicker and quicker until he could feel it constantly. He sighed and leaned into the touch. In turn, she leaned back. Her back pressed against his chest. He felt the heat rise to his face. This close, all he could smell was her. The salt of her skin, the citrus in her hair, and the ever-present lingering smell of honeysuckle. If he leaned closer, he could *taste* her.

"After we graduate, we should take a trip to see Tomas in Budojin." Wes was saying to Olivina.

"We could stay at the inn with hot springs in every room," Olivina replied with enthusiasm.

"Only if you promise to be my roommate. I wouldn't want to get lonely." Wes said with a wink.

Olivina blushed, and her sister laughed at the flirting. Knox and Cleo only shook their heads, but Rhyatt felt something different than wry amusement. He felt a kernel of something hot and sticky building in his chest. Perhaps a bout of jealousy. He tightened his hand on her waist and told himself he shouldn't be jealous. Wes could do whatever she liked, even if the idea of her sharing a room did make his chest tight.

Wes moved, scooting her ass further up his lap, sinking further into him. Her movement made every thought of Olivina disappear. As she moved around, his thoughts scrambled. The short skirt of her costume- that damn bat costume that she made look entirely too good- was riding up, exposing more of her thighs.

The sound of cards shuffling refocused him. Cleo and Knox had finished their game, and Cleo shuffled, preparing for the next round.

Cleo dealt, her hands moving quick and efficient until the cards were in six piles and then passed out to each player. Rhyatt chose to use his left hand, wanting to keep the other on her knee. He enjoyed the contact a bit too much. So much that he was willing to let her see his cards as long as he continued to have that hand on her knee. She didn't seem to mind because her cards were also on full display for him.

The conversation around him picked up as the game began, but Rhyatt wouldn't be able to focus. Wes leaned forward to place her card on the table. As she settled back into him, Rhyatt breathed deeply. The warmth of her body was distracting as it was, but the extreme warmth where she sat on his leg preoccupied every other thought. A question began to form.

After Wes and Rhyatt had put down their cards, Rhyatt swallowed, his courage coming in liquid form.

"Are you *aroused*?" he asked, his lips brushing the outer shell of her ear.

She turned her head towards him slowly, like a predator-tracking prey. And that's precisely what danced in her eyes as she looked up at him. He didn't know if bats preyed on cowboys, but he was sure they would tonight.

"You should find out." She whispered back.

Then, as if she hadn't just invited him to do something explicit, she turned back to the table and intently watched the card game unfold. Rhyatt was baffled. And worst of all, he was entirely too tempted. His grip tightened slightly on her knee, and he thought about it. The way she sat, her lower body was under the table, and nothing would be seen. Rhyatt blinked rapidly, attempting to refocus on the game.

She laughed at something someone had said, and it moved her waist. He tensed, the movement causing friction. She leaned back, twisting at the waist to pull his ear closer. Her lips hovered, not touching, as she whispered.

"Find out."

Rhyatt did not resist this time. He slowly moved his hand up her knee onto her soft thighs. Gods. Why was she so soft?

His hand crept higher, going up her inner thigh, under her skirt, until his thumb met the fabric of her underwear. He swallowed at how hot and wet she was. He thought back to her birthday and how good she had felt, how he had pleased her. He wanted to do that again.

He pressed his thumb against her through the fabric and watched her face. She had turned back to the game, and the only inclination she had felt him was the flare in her nostrils. He pulled the fabric away and pushed his pointer finger between her lips. Gods. Oh gods. His finger slid into her wetness, going down to pause at her entrance. But Rhyatt wouldn't give in yet. He moved his fingers to her clit, pressing down and gauging her response. She blinked rapidly. He smiled, a thrill running through him.

He began slow circles against her. She jerked into his hand, and Rhyatt fought not to lay down his cards and use his other hand to control her hips, to move them against him.

Wes leaned forward to lay down another card. She had been careful not to move her hips anymore. But as Rhyatt leaned forward to lay his card down he used the movement to his advantage, sinking his middle two fingers inside of her.

This close, he heard her sharp intake of air. No one else noticed.

He pushed his fingers deeper into her, and in turn, she canted her hips towards his palm.

It took everything in him not to moan aloud. Judging by her widened eyes, she was struggling with a similar battle. He drew his fingers out before pushing them back in.

His thoughts turned. The current between them had been amplified until he felt like they were humming. And oh. The feeling of being inside her. He considered the possibilities. He could untie his pants and pull himself free and fuck her right there in the middle of the card game. Her skirt could cover where they met. No one would have to know. How good she would feel around him.

Her free hand came to rest on his thigh, and his thoughts were broken. His pants were far too tight. He knew he should put a stop to this madness. He thrust his fingers back into her, and her hand moved so that she was stroking his erection through his pants.

It was his turn to twitch.

She stroked him up and down. It was around that time that he finally dropped his hand of cards, and they fluttered to the ground.

Maybe right here wasn't the best place, but there was plenty of space. He needed to be alone with her. On his knees in front of her, making her scream. That's where he needed to be, and he couldn't do it here.

"Let's go get a drink," he said, pausing his movements.

She placed her cards down on the table and nodded.

"Meet me behind the duck."

Wes had left the table first, and Rhyatt had waited a few minutes before getting up to follow. He wound through the festival goers, tipping his hat as people parted to let him pass. He had reached the first row of businesses in the square when he turned his head and saw Adriel rushing towards him, a smile of excitement on his face. He considered dodging his brother but feared he would follow instead.

Adriel reached him, and without stopping, he grabbed Rhyatt's arm and pulled him into the mouth of a small alley. Rhyatt allowed his brother to pull him along.

"I just heard something *very interesting*." Adriel breathed.

Rhyatt arched a brow, he enjoyed his brother's company but right now he had other things on his mind.

"Can this wait? I've got somewhere I need to be." Rhyatt said, taking a step back.

"No." Adriel shook his head quickly. His eyes were lit in excitement.

"So me and Lila were- well, it doesn't matter what we were doing- we overheard two people talking. They were talking about a grain trade that was happening tonight. They were just the guards, but they are getting paid a hundred silver for less than thirty minutes of their time. One of them complained about missing the festival, and the other said that the trade *had* to be done tonight while everyone is at the festival." Adriel took a deep breath before continuing, "I know you said to be careful and let you know if I heard anything weird, so I thought you might want to know."

Rhyatt paused, assessing Adriel. His brother had been easily excitable, but this did seem very intriguing. A trade deal happening not only in the middle of the night but also in the middle of the festival. It was something important.

"What else did you hear? Did they say anything about where or who the trade was for?"

Adriel shook his head, and Rhyatt sighed.

"I'm going to meet Wes behind the lucky duck, go find Cleo and Knox, and bring them back. Only Cleo and Knox."

Rhyatt found Wes leaning up against the back side of the lucky duck. Her dark hair and costume blended into the shadows. When she saw him she stepped forward, a smile appearing. Rhyatt stopped an arm's length away, fearing what would happen if he touched her.

"I know we agreed not to talk about the journal, but Adriel may have something." He said and her smile fell flat. Tipping her chin up she spoke.

"I'm guessing it's good?"

He nodded, "Cleo and Knox are on their way."

"Good." She turned her face away as if hiding something.

Adriel returned with Cleo and Knox in tow and he recounted his tale again. They had asked the same questions that Rhyatt had asked. Adriel still didn't have the answers, however with each one he had gotten giddier. Rhyatt didn't like it. He was far too excited about the thing that had been plaguing them for months. That had threatened their life multiple times. That had put Will's safety at risk.

"We need to see who is involved," Wes announced, although Adriel remained.

"If we can find out what is being traded, it will narrow it down," Cleo added with a nod.

"The council members won't leave the festival early. It would draw too much attention." Knox said, and Rhyatt gently placed his hand under his brother's elbow, attempting to tug him away from the conversation.

"Then we see who leaves. Make a note and compare it to staff lists of the council members." Wes planned aloud.

Rhyatt gave Adriel's arm a harder tug, but Adriel planted his feet. Rhyatt leaned closer, knowing the others could hear but not caring.

"I don't want you involved with this." His voice was low, a caution rather than a threat.

"What is 'this'?" Adriel asked the group, ignoring his brother.

Wes and Cleo glanced at Rhyatt apologetically, realizing their mistake. However Knox did no such thing. A gleam shown in his eyes and Rhyatt was reminded of how much the lot of them had had to drink.

"This," Knox said loudly, spreading his hands, "is potential treason- for both us and others- that we have no clue who is doing and have been chasing our tail for months. That little conversation you overheard will either help us or send us on another wild goose chase." Knox finished with a smile.

Rhyatt seethed, taking the two steps and closing the distance between him and the blonde-headed boy.

"What part of 'I don't want him involved' did you not understand?"

Rhyatt knew Knox could be an ass, he believed that was behind them, but now he had involved his little brother. It crossed a line Rhyatt didn't like. His nostrils flared, and his hands curled into fists.

A hand touched his arm and he turned, expecting to see Adriel, instead Wes stood at his side. As soon as he saw those green eyes the fight died from him. He couldn't do that, not when she would be the one to break it up.

"What's done is done," Wes said, her voice soothing. She looked to Knox and added, "The less he knows, the better."

"But I can help." Adriel quipped.

Wes released his arm and stepped away, Rhyatt followed her lead and stepping away from Knox and turned to Adriel.

"No, you can't. Go find Lila and keep quiet." Rhyatt's tone shifted, and the statement became more of a command. He turned so his back was to the group, and only Adriel could see his face.

"I want to help." He started again.

"What you want and need are two different things." His body tensed as he grew more aggravated.

"It sounds like you guys need all the help you can get." Adriel countered, crossing his arms. Rhyatt inched closer, gritting his teeth.

"I said no. I don't care if I have to drag you away, kicking and screaming. Go find your friends."

Adriel's eyes widened, "I was just fine while you were gone. Just because you have your shit together doesn't mean you can act like dad."

Rhyatt froze, realizing what he had said.

Their father had always joked about dragging them away, kicking and screaming. But he was a gentle man and never once followed through. It was his term of endearment. Now Rhyatt had weaponized it. His chest caught as he wondered what his father would think of him now.

"Perhaps he could cover Knox," Wes said, her voice breaking the fragile silence, "Knox can stay inside the festival. It would look less suspicious if he was with someone."

Rhyatt paused. He knew his brother had as much spine as a fighting cobra. Trying to argue this one out would only waste time and hurt feelings, which he had already done enough of.

"Not a word. To anyone. And afterward, you leave it alone."

"Of course," Adriel replied, trying to curb his enthusiasm.

They refocused on their tasks. Knox and Adriel would circle the festival, focusing on the farmers. Cleo would take the second floor of the lucky duck; from there, she would be able to see the festival from one window and see the entire dark second ring of the square. From there, she could easily see who came and went and watch them if they went north, making it easy to follow as well. Rhyatt was on the south side and, unfortunately, on the ground level. He would only be able to see and follow people who came through the south exit. Cleo suggested that Wes be a distraction instead of helping with surveillance. She had wanted to argue, but she had quickly seen the usefulness of it. Rhyatt didn't agree at first. Wes was the best fighter, but they wouldn't be fighting tonight. The bigger the distraction she caused, the less likely they would be going on wild goose chases of random festival goers choosing to leave early.

Knox smiled mischievously, "This is going to be fun to watch."

"Fuck you," Wes muttered, her heart not in it.

"Adriel. Shall we go get a drink? Get away from this lot." Knox asked and motioned away. Adriel nodded and followed him as they broke away from the group. Cleo was next. She pretended to wave at someone before walking in their direction. That left Wes and Rhyatt alone.

"I'm sorry about including Adriel," Wes said as soon as Cleo was out of earshot.

"He would have argued until he was blue in the face."

"Nevertheless, I am sorry." She repeated, sincerity in her voice. She began to walk away but Rhyatt called out for her.

"Wes." she stopped and turned back, her brows lifted in question, waiting on his words. And there were so many things he could tell her, that he already forgave her, that he wished this was over. "Make it worthwhile."

She dipped her head, a tight-lipped smile, "I will."

And she walked away, heading for the center of the festival.

ATTICUS

Atticus had been hovering near the drink table when she approached him. That was the curious thing about Wes Blake. She wasn't the prettiest girl, but the way she carried herself, like she was worth double her weight in gold, it made her *intriguing*. After the ordeal with the liars cut, he had sworn that he would stay as far away from her as possible, but as she had wove her way through the crowd to him, he hadn't budged an inch. He blamed it on her intrigue. Or perhaps it was the thrill that followed her.

"Dance with me?" playful arrogance coated her tongue.

He found himself powerless to do anything but nod, extending his hand to her. Together, they cut towards the dance floor, partners spinning and laughing in the glow of the gas lamps. The song was fast and upbeat, instantaneously drawing them in.

Wes tugged his hand, and they were dancing, spinning rapidly around each other. A stringed instrument picked up pace, causing the others to follow. The dancing area turned heated as drunken fools laughed and ran out of breath, trying to keep up with each other.

Atticus's anger at the liars cut faded and he became embold-ened by the other dancers floundering, he hadn't had nearly as much to drink as he wished, and broke his stride to grab Wes's waist, hauling her body flat to his and continuing the dance in close quarters. Atticus wondered where his father was. And even worse, he wondered if his father was watching them at this very moment.

Her laugh ricocheted off the cobblestones as she looked up at him and smiled. The dark wisps of her hair became wild and messy as the dance moved them faster. Atticus continued to hold her close.

Her laugh had gained them a few glances but his dancing had gained them even more, he noticed attention from other dancers and bystanders alike. If he was a wiser man he would be embarrassed by all the attention they were drawing. But he was Atticus Pryde. He had grown accustomed to it at a young age. He smiled down at the woman in front of him. The woman that was as much mystery as myth.

They continued the speed and close dance until Wes pushed free and pulled herself away just to bring them together again. She made the motion over and over in a showman-type way until even Atticus was laughing along with her.

"Excellent dancing, Miss Blake." He cooed in her ear when they were close again.

"Only the best for you, Mr. Pryde."

Atticus wrinkled his nose at the nickname, "Call me what you will, but *not* Mr. Pryde."

"Very well, Atti." She hummed, pulling away for a twirl. He tugged her closer until she was once again pressed against him.

"I *love* that nickname." His voice was low in her ear and he felt the goosebumps go down her arm. Being this close reminded him of the night of the dinner. How warm she was, how her breath had smelt of wine, only tonight she smelt of rum and something earthy.

"Good." She said, untangling them and sending them back into the previous rhythm.

He felt the distance immediately. They were too far apart. He knew he wouldn't kiss her in the middle of the circle, but this far away, it made that very obvious. Atticus knew Wes had a set of rules she followed about public relations; he knew the whole Blake family did, but that didn't stop him from wanting to break them. If he kissed Wes in the middle of the town square, perhaps everyone would forget about the rumor of her and Rhyatt. That was the thing he really wished to erase.

The song eased to a close, and a slow romantic melody replaced it. The drums lessened, and the strings picked up instead. The soft music made people talk quieter and sway together.

Wes turned a slow spin, her short skirt flaring out, before hauling herself against his chest. Her exuberant green eyes looked up at him through thick, dark lashes. Atticus used the song to his advantage and wrapped his hands around her lower back, pressing their bodies closer together. She raised an eyebrow.

"How risque of us." She whispered.

"There's nothing risque about this, Wes," he replied, his voice soft.

"You're right. Nothing special about two friends dancing very close." She raised her brows as if tempting him to say otherwise. Did she know how those rumors bothered him?

"Two friends?" He asked.

"Mhm." She nodded before looking down and smiling.

"We could always be more than friends," Atticus said, his hand leaving her back and coming up to cup her face.

She leaned into his palm. Her face was warm, although her skin was not flushed.

"I'm sure we'll be married in a few years." she laughed softly.

Atticus stroked her cheek and moved closer, so they were only a breath away.

"We could." He nodded slightly, "We would be the most powerful couple in Saint Saveen."

The shine left her eyes, and Atticus immediately sensed he had messed up. Perhaps it had been a bad idea.

"We would." Wes agreed, and she stilled their dance, leaning forward on her tiptoes to place a kiss on his cheek.

It felt like a flame had taken to his cheek when she leaned away. He was tempted to touch the spot and make sure she hadn't cut him.

The song came to a close, the artist stepping away from their instruments for drinks.

Wes leaned away from him but managed to grip one of his hands.

"Drinks?" she asked.

"Lead the way." Atticus motioned to one of the bars stationed nearby.

She wove through the crowd ahead of him, and he watched the way she moved and how others parted to let her through. He envied it. He found himself straightening his spine and imitating her. There was an extra factor he could never get right.

She had handed the bartender two coins before Atticus could even stop walking.

"You should have let me." He eyed her with disappointment.

"I owe you a drink or two." She said, looking at his bottom lip. "I'm glad it's healed."

Atticus looked down, fighting the embarrassment.

"I didn't tell them we slept together." He said.

Wes tilted her head and waited.

"I may have mentioned that we had fun, but it was only to two people. I have no idea how it got twisted and spread."

Wes considered before nodding.

"We both know the university has nothing better to do than gossip." She said.

Atticus smiled back at her, "I can agree with that."

"How fast do you think the rumors of our betrothal will spread?"

"Huh?"

"Our dance. It might as well have been our official statement saying we are to be married in the spring." She took a sip of her drink and dared him to play along.

"Oh." Atticus paused, pretending to think, "I think by the morning we will both have bakeries offering to make our cake."

"Is your favorite still chocolate?" Wes asked, taking a step away from the bar and forcing them to walk in front of the tables of seated party go-ers.

"Yes. Yours was orange!" He responded, remembering the details from their childhood, "And Warden liked lemon better."

"He did." She smiled softly, her eyes focused forward. Not looking at anyone in particular but rather seeing through them.

"Wes, I-" Atticus was cut off by a man bumping his shoulder.

He turned to see the Trade Councilor.

"Hey, oh. It's you two." The councilor paused his speech when he realized who he had bumped into.

"How are you tonight, Councilor?" Wes asked, her voice lilting.

"Doing quite well, it's an excellent night for a festival." The Trade Councilor spoke quickly. His dark beard wasn't as trim as usual Atticus noted.

"It is," Atticus said a tad too curtly. He didn't wish to talk politics or talk about anything related to his father, but staying near the Councilor would ensure exactly that.

"The weather cooperated thankfully. I couldn't imagine how many plans would've been ruined if it had rained." Wes said, continuing the conversation against Atticus's will.

"Would have had to reschedule a lot of things." The councilor replied and turned to say something to Atticus, but Wes interrupted.

"A lot of businesses would've been very upset. Lots of trade going on tonight."

That was odd, there were no trades going on during the festival, it was a time for rest. A glint of anger appeared in the councilor's eye as he refocused on Wes, the wheels in his head turning.

"It would have been a shame. Tell me, Miss Blake, where is young mister Will tonight?" There was no mistaking the edge to the councilor's voice. He felt Wes's hand tense on his arm at the words.

"I believe he is too young to be out so late," Wes said, her tone poisonous.

Atticus wasn't sure what Wes and the Councilor had against each other, but it was glaringly obvious they were both teetering on the edge of a knife, waiting to see who would fall off first.

"Ah," the Councilor smiled not so kindly, "Let us hope he is asleep in his bed."

Her hand tightened beyond comfort on his arm. He shifted his weight to bump her hip. Her grip released, and she blinked at the councilor.

"He is. I always keep track of my wards."

WES

Wes threw open the doors of the BlakeMoore, not caring how loudly they banged against the wall. The stolen horse still sat outside as she ran up the stairs, heading towards Will.

As soon as the thinly veiled threat left the councilor's mouth, her heart began to beat rapidly. A small drum banging against her ribs.

The entire ride home, horrible thoughts entertained her. She had seen every possibility, and every single one made her gut turn. She had told herself not to worry. Will would be exactly where she left him. She refused to think that he wouldn't. She had come to depend on him just as much as he depended on her.

Not stopping, she pushed open Will's door and huffed a sigh of relief when a Will-shaped lump rustled under the covers.

"Wes?" his voice groggy from sleep.

"Yes," she whispered. Crossing the room, she sat on the edge of his bed, gently rubbing his head and flattening his hair. He curled towards her, leaning into her touch. In seconds, he was asleep again.

He had fallen asleep, yet Wes's heart still thundered in her chest, refusing to be silent. He was safe. Safe. For now. She couldn't help but wonder how long it would be until his safety was called into question again? How long until she was rid of this journal?

WES

"**W**hat the hell happened to you?" Wes asked Cleo as she entered the barn. Cleo was covered head to toe in a black ash. Both Rhyatt and Knox turned to examine her.

"While *you two* flirted with the entire town, I crept down alleys and got stuck in a coal container." Cleo lifted a pointed finger to Knox and Wes.

Wes grimaced and wanted to apologize to her friend, but Knox spoke first.

"We thank you for your great sacrifice." His voice was haughty as he bowed at the waist.

Cleo narrowed her eyes at him and stepped forward, intent on getting to him, but Wes's nerves were too high. She needed to know everything, now.

"What did you find out?"

Cleo huffed and motioned for them to sit on the bails of hay. Once they were all seated she began.

"Colin Frevey was the first I noticed to look nervous. He was looking around and constantly checking his watch. When he left the square, I set about following him. This is what is odd: he went in a circle, crossing his own path before stopping behind a shop. I saw a young woman with a hood walk up to him. I decided to get closer -and this is where it was my poor decision to choose the coal container- but from there, I could hear the conversation perfectly. Colin is selling something to the woman's employer, and whatever it is, Colin wants a pretty penny for it. He promised to produce double if given an advance. The only other thing is that Colin asked if the new shipment should be delivered to the new site or to the old one. The woman said to use only the new site from now on. They would 'prepare' it from there."

"What is Colin selling?" Knox mused.

"That's the question that keeps him in business. For now." Wes responded, crossing her arms. "Any other news?"

"None of Colin's staff were at the festival." Knox said before adding, "Many councilors seemed to be on edge. I wasn't the only one who noticed."

"The Trade Councilor seems to know more than we think. He made a thinly veiled comment that some may construe as a threat." Wes added.

She told them about the threat and why the stolen horse was now sitting outside. It was agreed that he was more than likely guilty in the endeavors. It made sense that the trade councilor would be in on a deal allowing the grain to pass through the city untaxed and unaccounted for.

Shortly after they began to leave, the hour was late. It was Wes who asked Rhyatt to stay behind.

As Knox closed the door behind him quietly, Wes turned to face Rhyatt. She felt her features shift into something unknown, something vaguely discomforting.

"I need a favor from you." Her voice was strong, stronger than she was feeling at the moment.

"Anything." He responded, stepping closer so that she had to crane her neck. And she believed it. He was the type to do anything for her.

"Can you start walking Will home from school on the days of your mentorship? Will you also add some self-defense lessons to your mentoring time? Things that would work against adults. Teach him without his weapons first, then add them in. He has two knives he keeps under his pillow." She paused, hating the words she was about to say. "He needs to know how to kill someone twice his size."

Rhyatt's breath seemed to be suspended in the air as he looked over her carefully like a scared animal. And she hated even more that that was how she felt. She had worked so hard for so long to see that her brother would be given a life without the sorrows she had known. He wouldn't have to learn business at a young age because she had. He wouldn't have to work hard in the fields because she had. He wouldn't have to be the best swordsman around because she had. She had hoped he would never have to endure the hardships she had. But now she asked Rhyatt to teach him how to kill.

"Are you sure this is a good idea?" He asked.

"No." She released a long sigh, her eyes briefly closing before opening again and reinforcing her ferocity, "But it is necessary."

"I understand." Rhyatt nodded. Perhaps he did understand. Wes still did not know the full story, but she knew Rhyatt had left Adriel when he was needed the most. In a sense, he understood doing the things that are necessary.

"May I ask you something?" He asked as the silence became too much to bear. She was thankful for him breaking it.

"Yes. I'll even answer you honestly." She replied with a slow smile. If she didn't return to her usual self she was afraid she'd get bogged down in all her thoughts.

"Why do you flirt with him like that?"

"Who?"

"The Commander's son."

She cocked her head, pretending to consider his question.

"Sometimes flirtation gets better results than threats. It takes a connoisseur to know when to use what." She shrugged before adding, "Flirting gets secrets out of people without them even knowing."

"Is that why you flirt with me? To get my secrets?"

"No." Wes mused. "You'll tell me your secrets when you're ready. I wouldn't want to hear them before that anyway."

Rhyatt chuckled and seemed to think for a moment. "Either way, you should be careful flirting with him like that. He looks at you like you hung the moon."

"I hung the moon *and stars*. Thank you for noticing."

"I agree." Rhyatt frowned, "But you know what I mean."

Leftover rage boiled to the top and Wes found herself turning on Rhyatt quicker than he could keep up with.

"The way you speak suggests I am not actually interested in him."

"Are you?" he replied just as quickly.

"Maybe." She retorted instantly. And instantly regretted it. To her, a 'maybe' meant no, but she wasn't able to admit it. She could tell from the way Rhyatt's jaw ticked that he did not understand that. She could tell he was hurt by the answer. It wasn't her place to be hurt by her own words, but she was. If her pride wasn't such a terrible beast, she would take it back. But pride cometh before the fall.

An air of awkwardness hung between them, and she was the first to look away.

"Thank you for helping him. He really looks up to you."

Perhaps flattery would help.

"He's like the little brother I never had." Rhyatt paused before explaining, expecting the question, "Adriel is younger, but when you're only 18 months apart, you stop feeling like a big brother and more like twins."

Wes swallowed, the admission catching her off guard. "You're the big brother he never got to have. I will never be able to thank you enough."

Rhyatt paused, his eyes focusing on hers. He squinted marginally. So small of a squint she wouldn't have recognized it any other time, but just as he was learning her she was learning him.

"Why does your brother live with your father?"

She had been expecting this question, this topic, for some time. She had even thought about ways to explain it to him while leaving out all the gritty details. But now that it was asked, she only took a calming breath, blinked, and began the story of how her family fell apart.

"About five years ago, Warden and I found out Will was not our father's son. Somehow, this information leaked, and soon, my father knew. That summer, he asked to be repositioned in the south providence. He was moved swiftly and asked Warden and I to join him for a summer holiday. Will was still too young to travel, and we saw it as a break from our normal lives. We spent the summer having the time of our lives. Before returning for school,

Father asked us to move in with him permanently. We both said yes. We headed back to Saint Saveen one last time to pack our belongings and tell Mother of our decision. When we arrived, the house was in disarray. All of the staff but Rhina had left, and the farm had only been half-ass tended to. And Will-" her voice broke softly on his name, "He was tiny. He looked like he'd lost half his weight, his hair was falling out, and he refused to talk to anyone. We spoke to Rhina and found out that Mother had only been home for a handful of days in the past three months. She had taken a new job in the East and bought an apartment there. She knew what was happening to Will and didn't care. Warden wished to go back to Father and convince him to take in Will as well." She paused and shook her head, recalling fond memories of her brother, "I love Warden, I really do. But he is a wishful thinker. He thinks everything can be solved so easily. I knew differently. Will is the reason Father ran away. He wouldn't send for him. So I stayed behind, and Warden went back to try to convince Father to allow all of us to stay together."

"He never sent for you," Rhyatt whispered.

"No," Wes stated, glancing at her shoes. "He was a good man, but sometimes even good men can't rise to be the better man."

"I'm sorry."

Wes shook her head, "Nothing to be sorry about. I've lived the past five years without any consequences. I even inherited a home, farm, and business from it."

"But you had to sacrifice so much." He said, an inkling of pity in his eyes. She loathed it. She was not to be pitied.

"And I would do it all again." Her voice raised, and she wondered if she was telling Rhyatt or herself. "However many hardships I have endured, I have come out on top. I have earned everything I have, and I have fought tooth and nail to get it. When I fall asleep at night, I don't wonder what's going to happen to me. When I spend money, I don't feel guilty."

Rhyatt studied her, the inkling of pity gone instead, curiosity replaced it.

"You are lying about the last one." He said almost playfully.

She paused, her fervor cooling. How did he always know her lies? How did he pick them out so easily?

"You have a tell." He said, answering her unspoken question.

"And what is it?" She asked with an exhale.

He cracked a smile. "If I told you, you'd learn not to do it. Then I would never know if you're lying."

She cocked an eyebrow, "What if someone robs me, and I have to lie to them?"

"Only a fool would try and rob you." He replied, and she agreed.

"You never know." She said, crossing her arms, "The world is full of fools like you."

"Like me?" He put his hand to his chest, mouth wide, feigning hurt.

"Exactly like you," Wes replied with a small smile, knowing the world was that much better with people like Rhyatt in it.

KNOX

K nox got home late again. Which meant his Father was angry. Again.

It was unfortunate because Knox had enjoyed his night. He hadn't known Rhyatt's brother would be much the opposite of him. Rhyatt was calm, endearing, and mostly polite. Adriel, on the other hand, felt like a summer night when you had no responsibilities the next morning. Compared to the absolute shitstorm they had been suffering with the journal, it had been nice.

Now, walking through the front door, all the sweet dreams faded as Knox saw his father. He was seated in his usual chair, the usual anger written across the lines in his face. Knox wasn't sure the last time he had seen another expression.

He shut the door, not attempting to be quiet.

His father did not raise his head as he spoke, "Who was Jaze hanging around before he died?"

The question hit Knox like a punch to the gut.

"What?" Knox whispered. His right hand instinctively going to the ring on his left hand. The twisted metal reassured him.

"Don't play dumb with me. You're dumb enough as is." He looked up, taking in Knox's messy hair and costume. Knox felt small as his father analyzed him and came away disappointed.

"He was around us." Knox lied, refusing to take a step further into the room.

"What about the Blake girl?"

Dread crept up behind him, prickling the hairs on the back of his neck.

"She and her brother were with us." He said, deflecting the question he had a sinking suspicion his father was leading up to.

"Did she spend a lot of time with him?" he leaned forward.

Knox swallowed, attempting to straighten his spine.

"They were close." He said with a casualty, he did not feel.

His Father rose from the chair but did not come closer.

"Tell me the truth boy, were they together?"

"I don't know what they did when they were alone," Knox replied, a kernel of anger digging into his hollow chest. Because he had not known what they did alone. He hadn't even noticed them being alone. His closest friend and cousin had been sneaking around for months, but he had not noticed. How good of a friend did that make him?

Knox shook his head, growing tired of the well of emotions the topic had brought up. He huffed and turned to walk towards his bedroom.

Rough hands gripped his collar and shoved him against the wall.

Knox's father looked at him through hate-filled eyes, his liquored breath making Knox's stomach turn.

"Your aunt has been told some confusing things and asked me to straighten them out. So tell me the damned truth. Was Jaze fucking the Blake girl?"

Knox blanched at the blunt disrespectful words. He pushed his father's arms off of him, disgusted at the touch. He meant to defend her. To defend him, them both. But he understood that would likely lead to blows, he was too much of a coward at the moment.

"Yes." He hated the word as soon as it left his mouth. "They had a secret romance. Is that all you wish to know?"

His father took a small step back, motioning for Knox to walk away.

"That is all I wanted to know." A small smile slipped appeared on the older man's face. Something bad would come of this, Knox could tell.

"What do you plan to do?" he dared to ask.

"The town should know that Jaze spent his last months tangling with a Blake. Even in death, it will be an honor to have been the one she loved and lost."

"Wes is not an object to be won or a prize to bestow on someone." Knox's voice rose, that anger bubbling to the surface again. "It does no good to air his personal life now."

"He is a dead man. It will not hurt either."

Knox cringed away at the harsh reminder.

"There are things you do not understand. Talking about her- about what happened between them- will do nothing but bring sorrow."

"I understand everything, boy. He was preparing to marry a Blake before his untimely death. What else is there to know?"

"Don't lie." Knox snarled, stepping closer.

"Who says I'm lying?" His father sneered.

"Jaze wasn't going to marry her. He was leaving for the army."

"Was he? Or was he preparing to better himself to be a good husband?"

"Stop fucking lying!" Knox yelled, his breath ragged.

But his father did not stop.

"He was going to marry her before he died in a fire. Such an *unfortunate* accident."

"It wasn't an accident." Knox corrected.

Something in the back of his mind told him he should shut up. But he could still feel it, the heat from the blazing barn. He could still feel Wes's sweat-slicked skin as she fought against him. He could still hear the crackling and groaning of the old wood as the barn collapsed and the fire soared higher.

"What did you say?" his father's voice was a quiet rumble.

"It wasn't a gods damned accident." Knox stepped closer, so now it was him towering over his father, "And you need to keep quiet, otherwise the same fate will fall upon our house."

His Father didn't waste time before his open-handed palm reached across the space and smacked the side of Knox's head.

Knox stumbled sideways in disbelief. And for the first time in his life, he did not stand idle and allow the next blow to hit. He moved to the left, sending his drunken Father crashing into the wall. A painting of his mother fell to the ground in the commotion.

"Come here boy."

Knox froze at the words. He knew what would come next if he stayed still. He knew his next conscious thought would be awakening in his mother's arms. A damp cloth wiping any blood from his face. But Knox could not take that tonight. He could not go another round with his Father and explain away the bruises.

So when his Father swung again, Knox swung back.

Knox's legs were burning as he ran along the dirt road leading to the BlakeMoore. He did not like running, but with the adrenaline pumping through him, it was a good outlet.

As he approached the house, he slowed his steps to a walk, careful not to disturb anything hiding alongside the moonlit pathway. From the road, he could see a gas lamp burning in the library. He crept up to the window, trying to see if Wes was in it or if the light had been left on.

She sat alone at the desk, her hair was a mess, as if she'd been running her hands through it constantly. She was no longer in her costume, but the oversized shirt she wore was buttoned incorrectly and sat strange on her shoulders. She had asked Rhyatt to stay behind a few hours prior, but the tiredness on her face did not seem related. She looked... wary.

Knox paused. He had never seen his friend like this. Even in their casualness, she sat tall and proud. Alone, she did none of that. Did she always look like this when she was alone?

Suddenly, his problems with his Father seemed trivial in relation to the attack her home was under. He remembered the guards she had posted in the attic watchtower. Stepping back he looked up, and could see their shifting forms. He waved, and one of them waved back, the metal from their crossbow reflecting in the moonlight.

Knox turned away, it was close to 3 in the morning and the fact that Wes was still up meant he probably shouldn't bother her.

He reached the end of the drive and knew he didn't want to go home, and he didn't want to be alone. The bars seemed too busy, and Cleo would already be asleep. But he knew someone else who was nearby.

Knox walked with light feet through the newly worn-down path. The trees were too thick for much moonlight to get in, so he was forced to stumble every few steps. His face burned from the single blow his Father had managed to land.

He cleared the jungle and crept towards the house, being careful not to step on the neatly planted garden. The small cottage was pale in the moonlight, and he could easily see which window he needed to go to. It was the only one without curtains.

Knox stepped up to it, attempting to peer inside, only darkness.

He took a deep breath before rapping his knuckles against the window. Loud enough to disturb whoever was inside but not loud enough to wake everyone in the house.

He waited, listening as someone stirred inside. A figure stepped up to the window and worked to undo the latch before pushing it open.

Rhyatt leaned out the window, his sleep-ridden face shifting to anger as he saw Knox. Perhaps this *was* a bad idea. He was likely expecting Wes, not Knox.

"Who did this to you?" Rhyatt asked.

Knox sighed, feeling his shoulders sag as he nodded. It was safe.

"My Father." His voice cracked as Rhyatt crawled out of the window and wrapped his arms around him.

"Tell me what happened," Rhyatt said, his voice rough.

Knox leaned into him and told him every horrible thing his Father had done and said to him.

RHYATT

R hyatt slowed his stride, attempting to keep pace with his friends. Wes, Cleo, and Knox had opted to eat lunch at one of the small parks in the garden district. He smiled as a semi-cool breeze blew through the buildings. The beginning of winter was only weeks away, and although the trees would not shed their leaves like they did further south, the temperature would cool enough for him not to sweat every step he took.

"No, she said it *wouldn't* be on the final exam," Knox argued next to Wes. They had been fighting over the review for half a day, and it had become tireless.

"Then why would she put it on the review?" Wes replied.

"Because she listed everything on the review."

"No." Wes shook her head, "She only put the important things."

"If it's only important things, then why is the review half a mile long?"

Wes turned her head to look at Knox. "It's going to be on the exam."

Rhyatt rolled his eyes. He had committed almost every question and answer on the review to memory.

"Why can't you both just study the entire review and aim for 100%?" Cleo asked, she was also tired of this ongoing argument.

Knox mumbled something that sounded similar to *fuck you* as they entered the square and began walking across it.

"What about some good news? When does Warden come home?" Cleo said, ignoring Knox's muttering.

"The 20th. He wanted to come home early to prepare for our joint Ad Aetam celebration." Wes said, the argument leaving her.

"Is your Mother still insisting on hosting that?" Cleo asked.

"Yeah, it's been like two months since your birthday," Knox added.

"Yes." Wes side stepped a loose paver, "Father is coming into town for it. But at least Nan will be there."

Wes's voice softened on her Nan's name. Rhyatt had learned that her Nan lived somewhere in the swampy lands of Central Jorjin and that Wes had a fondness for her. Rhyatt was nervous to meet her. He was nervous to meet most of Wes's family after meeting her mother. His biggest concern was Warden, the twin brother who had abandoned her.

"Tell Nan to bring some Pralines. She does an ama-" Knox cut himself off mid-sentence and stopped in his tracks.

Rhyatt turned his head, quickly trying to figure out what was wrong. He followed Knox's line of sight and found him at a man across the way.

The man was double their age and resembled Knox in the face. Upon closer inspection, the man was a smidge taller than Knox, and his short hair was a light brown. It dawned upon Rhyatt that this man was likely Knox's Father. Hot and sticky anger flooded his system. His fists balled at his sides.

"Go through the shops," Wes said gently to Knox.

"We'll meet you at the park." Cleo's gentle voice added.

Knox began moving, cutting behind them and working his way towards the nearest break in the buildings. How did the women know that Knox did not want to see his Father? Had they done this same song and dance with him before?

They continued walking, and as they got closer, he noticed.

The older man's eyes widened before narrowing at them. He marched up to them, his steps a bit unsure.

"Where is he?" The man asked, anger and annoyance lacing his voice.

"Why do you want to know?" Rhyatt asked before either Cleo or Wes could respond.

He turned to face Rhyatt, assessing him like he hadn't noticed he was there before. He took in Rhyatt's size before turning back to Wes and Cleo.

"Can anyone tell me where my *son* is?" he asked again.

"Up your ass and to the-" Wes was cut off by Cleo.

"We don't know."

The man looked between both women. He treated Rhyatt as if he didn't exist.

"I know," he said simply.

Rhyatt tensed, but Cleo and Wes did not.

"Know what?" Wes asked.

"I know it wasn't an accident. I know Jaze was murdered." He paused, watching them, "And I think it's high time someone else in this town knows too. You kids aren't telling the proper authorities."

He laughed and shook his head, his feet already turned away, "I think I'll go have a chat with the Law Councilor now." He took a step before focusing on Wes, "You won't be exempt from punishment because you were his bride-to-be."

The color drained from Wes's face as he walked away.

"He won't believe a drunk like you!" Cleo yelled, her voice catching the attention of a few nearby pedestrians.

"Should we go after him?" Rhyatt asked, unsure what to do.

"No." Cleo responded, "There are too many people. We need to go to Knox."

Cleo and Rhyatt started walking, but Wes stood still. He turned around, calling her name. She blinked rapidly before taking a step forward, falling into step with Rhyatt as Cleo went ahead.

"Why did he say that? About the bride-to-be?"

Wes shrugged, "Everyone wants me to be something I am not."

WES

Wes stepped into the park with Rhyatt at her side. Cleo and Knox were perched on a picnic table. Cleo's bag was half open, and various papers were spilling out of it. She had two papers in her hand and appeared to be cross-referencing them.

"What in the fuck are we going to do?" Knox asked as they approached.

"I have *no idea*." Wes sighed, returning her focus to the various papers in Cleo's lap, "What are you working on Cleo?"

Cleo snapped her head up at the sound of her name. Her big brown eyes were wide, and a small smile was forming. She was onto something. Stretching forward, she handed Wes the document she had been looking at.

"Collin has three properties, two of which are declared as farmland. The third is residential. None of them are declared as growing corn of any type." Cleo said before turning around to grab another document.

"So he is growing undeclared?" Wes asked.

"No." Cleo shook her head and began unfolding a map with a stamp in the bottom right corner. It said 'Saint Saveen History Department.'

"The residential property is listed North of town." She laid the map down, pointing to the rough area in which the property was in. "It is surrounded by other properties and has no direct roads."

"Wait..." Wes paused, a memory surfacing, "Collin lives in town. He lives in that small cottage behind the governance building. His wife owns it."

Cleo nodded. "Exactly. Why would he need a residential property a mile away from town and miles away from any of his farmland."

"We need to go. Now." Knox said, springing off the table and into action. He began to gently place the documents back into Cleo's pack.

"What happens if we find something?" Rhyatt asked unease in his voice.

"Then we can go to the Council or tell the town. Someone somewhere has to care."

RHYATT

They left the small park and began heading north towards the property. Cleo and Wes navigated, keeping them out of the square and off of the busier streets. The buildings began to be sparse as trees rose and towered around them, and the road narrowed. They kept a brisk pace, but chatter still happened around Rhyatt. He didn't speak often.

Perhaps it was the slight terror that Knox's Father would land all of them in jail for keeping quiet about a murder, or maybe it was the looming final exam that would determine if he graduated from University. A degree he likely didn't deserve but wouldn't turn down, for Lita's sake. In a week, they would be given the written test, and a week later, they would be given the physical portion. He had somehow gained confidence in the written portion, and he was even more confident in saying he would likely do better than Wes and Knox. Both of them were smart, but Knox didn't listen in class, and Wes slept through the majority of it. Running the business took a toll on her. He and Cleo seemed to be the only ones in the group who paid any attention. It was the physical aspect he was concerned about; his lessons had been going smoothly, but he had only been learning for a handful of months. He would be up against those who had had their whole lives to learn.

Someone bumped his shoulder, and he was pulled from his thoughts. Wes stared up at him with an eyebrow cocked. He gave her a tight smile, and she understood he didn't want to talk about it.

Unfortunately, Knox didn't understand as well.

"What's got you in a knot over there, Rhy-Tie?" Knox's voice sped over the nickname as if it was common. It was not.

"Just worried about the physical portion of the exam," Rhyatt responded, not in the mood to come up with a lie.

"You'll pass," Knox said, a knowing nod.

Rhyatt thought about the words of assurance he had heard repeatedly from his friends the past few days. They did nothing to ease his anxiety.

"What happens if I do fail?" He asked, curious if retaking it was an option. He didn't have another semester to waste.

"You're not going to fail." Wes said with a sigh before adding, "You learned from the best."

His thoughts were wound so tight he couldn't manage to crack a smile at her jest, "What happens if I do?"

"Rhyatt. You've bested me twice this week. It's unnatural, really. I wouldn't worry about it." Knox reassured him. But he still wasn't convinced.

"What if I go against Wes?" He countered.

"Then I'll let you win." She said with a flirtatious smile.

"No, you wouldn't," Cleo said.

"And you would fail?" Rhyatt asked.

"They're not going to fail their star student, are they?" Wes countered.

"The test isn't like that." Knox began as Cleo led them off the road and into the trees, "It isn't passing if you win and failing if you lose. They watch for skills, how well your foot placement is, your balance, your attacks and defenses."

They crept deeper into the forest, their feet crunching on dry debris as they went.

"How many people usually fail?" Rhyatt asked.

"None," Knox answered.

"Two or three," Wes said at the same time.

Rhyatt didn't miss the glare Knox sent to Wes.

"What Wes *means* is that two or three people usually fail the written exam. If anyone fails the physical portion, it usually means they put in no effort." Knox said.

And Rhyatt was slowly starting to believe that he might make it by. He had certainly put in the effort. He was also noticing a pattern. How both women stayed mostly quiet. How neither of them were good at easing Rhyatt's doubts and how, on the other hand, Knox was soothing him. It was odd, but the more he thought about it, the clearer it was. Both Cleo and Wes had the confidence of a tiger who knew it was the best thing in the jungle. They both had lived a life where confidence was their only defense. Second-guessing themselves wasn't an option. Knox however, had not. Knox had been good at encouraging Rhyatt because he too needed encouragement at times. For the briefest second, Rhyatt pitied Knox. How many years had he spent with Cleo and Wes, who were terrible at boosting confidence?

"This is where the original property ends." Cleo announced before pointing up a steep hill, "On the other side of this hill is the valley in which the new property begins."

The group looked up the hill in union. It wasn't so steep they would have to crawl, but it was steep enough one misplaced step and they'd likely tumble downwards. At least it wouldn't be a far fall.

"Up-up and away," Knox said with faux cheer before beginning the steep trek.

The others followed in silence, the only sound their feet hitting the ground. It had been a few days since it had rained and the ground was solid, unfortunately that also meant that dried leaves crunched loudly as their feet struck them.

They made quick work of the climb and, in a few short minutes, stood atop the hill looking down on the small valley. Sure enough, there were three buildings below. One was a massive barn, newer by the looks of it. It had a metal roof reflecting sunlight and a thin silo shooting off the side. To the right was a house, smaller and sagging, reflecting its old age. In between the two was a barn, but it looked more like a shed with the larger barn looming nearby. It had to be even older than the home. Sun streamed through the holes in the wooden planks that made up its sides.

"Well, shit. What do we have here." Knox drawled, folding his arms across his chest in triumph.

"I knew there was something odd," Cleo said, a smug grin of her own appearing.

Wes was the only one who didn't smile. A small victory was just that, small. He watched as she surveyed the area, her keen eyes squinting against the sunlight.

"We need to take a closer look. We need something to prove the journal's claims." She said, her voice and posture slipping into a cool calm. The others responded equally, taking on a business demeanor as she began to speak.

"We split up. Get in and out as quickly as possible. We are looking for information, records, notes, labels, anything of the sort. Do not get sidetracked. Move quickly and quietly. If you find anyone, you come back here immediately." She paused, looking at Knox. "Do not engage. I don't want to see a single scratch on any of you." Her eyes drifted to Cleo and paused, "Not a single scratch."

Cleo nodded. And Rhyatt remembered the day at his house when the men had attacked, how guilty Wes had looked when Cleo had gotten hurt. If one hadn't known how the events happened, they would have thought Wes was the one to injure her.

"Knox, take the small barn. Cleo, go to the far side of the house and wait for me. Once Knox has entered the barn, Rhyatt will go to the big barn, and I will join Cleo in the home." She nodded her head, "We're in and out, twenty minutes top. We meet back here. No one, and I mean *no one* sees us."

A small smile played on Cleo's lips, "Like ghosts?"

Wes paused, a crack in her all-business attitude. She gave the smallest smile and nodded.

"Why would you want to join the legion of ghosts when you have your own right here?" Knox asked, his arms spread, motioning to their group.

Her smile finally cracked open, "When I join, I'll hire the whole lot of you."

"As you should," Cleo said, walking towards where she was to wait.

"I agree," Knox added as he took a step downwards. "See you in twenty."

Silently, they both disappeared into the greenery, leaving him alone with Wes. She stayed focused on the smaller barn, watching it as if she were an eagle and it was prey.

"You know you're going to pass, right?" She asked, eyes still forward.

"No. I don't know that." Rhyatt admitted.

"I wouldn't lie to you, Rhy. I have no doubt you are going to pass." She turned her head to him, a nod in place. "Now go in and be swift." She said with a nod of her head.

He obeyed, heading down the back side of the hill, his large stride moving him faster than had been allowed earlier with the group. In seconds, he was on the edge of the treeline. He paused, taking a deep breath before darting towards the barn. It almost felt strange to run this quickly with this much grace. It was nice to have a purpose, even if the purpose was to just look around a barn.

He came to a halt outside the large doors, both of them stretched up twenty feet in the air and were at least 10 feet wide. He gave the right handle a slight tug and the door opened with ease. The bright sun outside did not enter barn, instead only cool darkness awaited him. He took a steadying breath before stepping inside.

The cool air surrounded him, and so did the darkness. A moment later he was falling to his knees, his body shutting down. He was barely conscious as his face hit the dirt.

WES

Wes reached Cleo on swift feet. She was crouched down behind a tree, her long legs folded underneath her effortlessly. Wes raised her eyebrows in silent question, Cleo nodded, signaling it was safe. She rose and together they crept towards the house.

The house was old, partly covered in vines and growth from the untamed forest around it. That didn't take away from how clean the porch was of debris. Wes didn't see a single leaf, much less a speck of dirt. As they crept closer to the door, it was obviously maintained, the glass clean and free of mold. It was a contrast from the various green growths all over the building.

Wes stepped forward and turned the door knob gently. The door opened without a creak. Pushing the door open, she stepped into a small but clean kitchen. Cleo stepped in behind her and shut the door.

Together, they crept towards the hallway. There were three different rooms, all of their doors wide open.

"Empty," Cleo whispered.

"And very clean," Wes said, wiping her finger along the wall as they entered the first room.

It was clearly a woman's room, in the right corner sat a four poster bed with pale gauze curtains hanging down. To the left of it was a tall dark wooden chest of drawers, cosmetics and jewelry sat atop. In the left corner a rack of clothes and two thin chairs, not made for comfort.

"Someone lives here," Cleo said aloud, echoing Wes's thoughts.

"Let's start looking," Wes said, unease coiling around her spine.

Cleo took the chest of drawers, and Wes took the rack of clothing. She pulled the garments towards the front and began emptying out pockets. Nothing. NothingNothingNothing. Sighing, she flipped through a few more pairs of pants, taking note of how they had been folded. She pulled forward more tops, which were far lighter in color and the palest tan possible. More of a dirty white, in her opinion. But she paused, her fingers rubbing the fabric. The lighter clothes were woven tighter. The threads of the fabric did not shift as she rubbed them. Odd. This was not Jorjinian clothing. The tight weave would never allow for breathing. It had to be Duranian. Tight enough to not let sand in, lightweight to be breathable, and light in color to keep cool in the neverending sun. The realization did not go without weighing on Wes. She dug through the Duranian garb's pockets and came up with nothing. Not a single pocket had anything. Not even a piece of lint. It was meticulous. Sanitary.

"Anything?" She asked Cleo as she emptied another pocket.

"Just undergarments and jewelry. The jewelry is odd. Some are antiques. Others are cheap costume jewelry. But all of them are well taken care of." Cleo responded, her voice muffled as she kept her head down to dig around.

"The clothing is weird too. Looks like this woman spent enough time in Jorjin and Duran to need wardrobes for each." Wes pushed all the light-colored clothing forward and revealed nice evening dresses. She paused as her fingers went out to the first one. A red one with hand-dyed lace and silk. A rather costly dress. A rather memorable dress. If she had worn this dress in Jorjin recently, someone would know. Wes pulled the dress off the hanger and held it up. But the garment behind it caught her eye.

A dress with a snakeskin bodice. A snakeskin so dark that even when the light hit it, it was only the darkest blue. It belonged to Aridia, the snakeskin traitor from Commander Pryde's dinner party.

"Cleo." Wes whispered, the unease had traveled up to rest at the base of her neck.

Before she could speak, a door slammed, and the slight rattle of glass sounded down the hallway.

Panic rose in the back of her throat.

The only way in *and out* was the kitchen door.

The windows were too small, and there was no other way out.

Wes reached for her sword, only to find an empty holster and only her small dagger beside it.

The panic welled until there was a thumping in the back of her skull.

Fight. Fight. Fight.

But that was an impulse. And last time, the impulse had gotten Cleo hurt.

"Hide." She whispered at Cleo, already grabbing her elbow too tightly. "Under the bed. Now."

"What?" Cleo asked, the faint sound of voices coming from the kitchen.

"Now." Wes snapped, her whispered voice too sharp. Too panicked.

Cleo listened the second time and folded her limbs up as she began to scoot under the bed. She was still scooting in when the heavy thud of boots began making their way down the hallway.

"Come on," Cleo whispered, her hand held out. But the footsteps were getting closer.

"Stay hidden until you can run," Wes said, an apology already forming for later.

"Wes-"

"I meant it Cleo, not a single scratch on that pretty face."

Without another word, Wes stood straight up and took a step away from the bed, instead facing the chest of drawers. The footsteps came to a halt outside the door.

"You are not Aridia." A man's voice said. His words were clipped and official.

Wes turned around to face him, a lazy smile on her face. He was tall and broad. Just as big as Rhyatt was. If she had her sword, it would've been quick, but fortune did not favor her. He wore a uniform the color of sand. In his belt sat different pouches and weapon holsters, most notably the wicked long dagger.

"Are you disappointed in who I am not?" Wes asked, slinking one hip to the side and resting her hand on it.

"No. You are not allowed in here." He said, his voice a strange mixture of business. His eyes stared straight through her.

"Aridia told me to wait for her," Wes said with a sigh, as if inconvenienced.

"No." The man said, his nostrils flaring.

"Who are you talking to?" another man's voice said from down the hallway as he approached.

"Wes Blake." The first man responded as the second one, dressed exactly the same but a bit shorter and thinner, appeared beside him in the doorway.

The second one smiled, his eyes strangely not as cool as the first.

"We've been waiting for you, Miss Blake."

Wes fought the urge to snap at them and correct them on her name. But now wasn't the time nor place.

"Why have you been waiting for me?" Wes asked, her hand sliding off her hip and instead gripping the hilt of the dagger.

"To capture you." Said a third man, standing behind the first two.

A 3 to 1 odds wasn't spectacular, not without her sword. But it was doable. All she needed to do was draw them out of the house so that Cleo could make a break for it.

She pulled the dagger from its sheath, "I'm afraid I don't want to be captured today."

Without waiting for them to respond, she darted forward at the first man. He reached his arms out-no weapon in sight- and tried to... tried to grab her. Wes went low to avoid his meaty hands and managed to slash his thigh. It was a shallow cut, but still, blood poured from it.

He didn't flinch. Nor look down at his leg, instead he charged forward, aiming for her again. The other two stepped into the room with him. The first man attempted to grab her arms, but she was quicker and much lighter on her feet. She twisted out of his reach and when his back was turned she kicked him.

Now, she faced the second and third men. The third had the same cloudy look as the first. But the second... It was odd how clear his features were in comparison. She stopped looking at their faces and looked down to see what weapons they had.

Only they had none.

Their weapons remained strapped to their belts. Only their bare hands were raised.

The second one motioned the third forward. The second man was in charge here.

The third man charged at her, but Wes was armed, and he only had his hands. When he was close enough, she sidestepped him and kicked the back of his knees, sending him downwards. Wes took advantage and got behind him, placing her dagger to his throat.

"Don't move unless you want to die." She said between gritted teeth.

But he moved. He moved even after she told him what would happen. And the blade was sharp and his movement was quick.

In a second, his throat was slit, and bright red blood began to pour out.

The man did not reach for his throat. No. He had no regard for his lifeblood that was leaking to the floor. He reached for Wes.

His blood sprayed onto her face and chest as his meaty hands clasped her shoulders.

She cringed away. The only thing stopping her from screaming was the fact that Cleo was under the bed and would come scrambling out if she cried out. So Wes stayed quiet.

The man's hands went to her throat and began to choke her. She gasped and clawed at his hands. He was choking too. Guttural sounds coming from him as he choked on his own blood. That did nothing to deter him. He continued to press on her throat.

Her nails dug into his arms as she clawed at him. In disgust, she watched as fresh cuts welled where her nails had been. The man was not affected.

But his blood flow slowed. And his grip loosened.

He was dying.

He was dying and refused to hold his own throat, to hold his own blood in. He would rather strangle her. It was dedication. She'd give him that.

As his grip loosened, he fell to the floor, the light fading out of his eyes. Wes didn't have long to process before the first man was behind her, continuing the failed strangulation attempt.

She resumed clawing at him. She couldn't find her balance on the blood-slicked floor to kick him, but she managed to stomp his toes. He was the same as the first: no reaction.

She reached her hand up to find his face and felt around until she found his eyelashes. She dug her two fingers inwards. People are rather sensitive about their eyeballs. He was no exception.

He stepped away, howling and clutching at his now bleeding eye.

The only problem was Wes didn't realize how much strength she'd lost while being strangled, twice, that is. Once he let her go, she slumped to the floor, her face towards the bed. From there, she could see a wide-eyed Cleo. Gently, Wes shook her head and willed her friend to stay in place. 'No,' Wes mouthed.

A sharp pain shot up Wes's spine as the second man landed a kick to her back. She gave Cleo a smile, her eyes bloodshot and face covered in another man's blood.

Another kick landed on the back of her head, and darkness surrounded her.

WES

Wes hated the taste of blood. From the first time she had busted her mouth open at seven years old, she knew that she would gladly avoid bleeding from her mouth. It was the sharp, salty tang that bothered her. As her senses returned to her, that was the first one to register the blood in her mouth. She couldn't be sure if it was her own or the man whose throat she'd slit. She didn't care to think about it too much.

She tried to open her eyes but struggled; her eyelashes stuck together, dried blood, and gods know what else coating them. Once they were free, harsh light assaulted her. Squinting, she blinked in rapid succession and attempted to make sense of her surroundings.

She was in an office of sorts, with one window and one door, on opposite sides of the room. In front of the window was a large desk, heavy by the looks of the solid wood. She was slumped in the corner of a settee, two cushioned chairs faced her and a simple rug was beneath it all.

Blinking again, she looked down to her lap. Her wrists were bound tightly in rope. Kicking her feet out, she found the same.

She wouldn't have been surprised if she was gagged as well. She twisted her ankles, testing how tight the ropes were. Very tight, apparently.

"Don't panic." said a man's voice from the now-open doorway.

She hadn't been panicking, but it was odd that the man had opened the door without her knowing. She blinked and forced her eyes to focus on the outline of a person. She should've felt angry that her sight was betraying her, but all she felt was calm.

The man closed the door and stepped further into the room, taking a seat across from her.

The Commander.

Wes's eyes narrowed on him as he crossed his ankle over his knee and leaned forward.

"Sorry about those." He motioned to the restraints, "They didn't think the legs were necessary, but I did."

She felt her face warming as the dots connected.

"Why?" She asked, her voice much rougher than she remembered.

"Because you are oddly talented, and escaping seems highly possible with you." He said simply, leaning back into the chair. He pressed his shoulders back, and Wes thought he looked like an overstuffed bird.

"Not the restraints." She said between gritted teeth. Her face was rather swollen, and she felt it with every word she spoke. "Why are you betraying your own people?"

Pryde blinked, turning his head slowly so that his full focus was on her. Wes stilled and forced herself to remain as tall as she could in the sinking cushions. She would not give him the satisfaction of lording over her.

"*Betraying?*" He pursed his lips, "I am *saving* our people. They are paying us so well that citizens will be paying half the taxes for the next 10 years. I am not foolish enough to broker a deal that did not benefit us."

Wes wanted to recoil at his words. *Our people.* As if they were friends working together, not enemies on different sides.

"It's always been about the money." Wes nodded, the disdain evident on her face.

Pryde sighed slowly, uncrossing his ankle and leaning forward again. This time his forearms rested on his legs. For a moment he studied Wes. Not in the way a father would a child, but rather in the way a doctor would a patient.

"You are too young to heed my message and will forget everything about today, but I hope you hear this and hear it clear, for one day, you will be commanding my armies." He paused, leaning closer. "Sometimes you must do what is best for others because not everyone is privileged enough to see the whole picture."

He leaned back a fraction and waited. Wes would have made him wait all damn day, but even her curiosity got the best of her.

"What don't I see?"

Pryde let a sliver of a smile take hold, proud of himself.

"What everyone fails to see is that I made a proactive move to protect our people. Duran would have taken what they wanted by force. I made a deal to protect us and allowed us to profit."

She could feel the blood beginning to boil inside of her. The Commander's sole purpose was to make decisions that were best for the town, to protect its people, and to protect the northern borders. Yet Pryde had done the opposite. He had only protected the ones he deemed worthy. He had blown open the Northern borders.

"Do *you* see the whole picture, *Pryde*?" She said his name like a curse. "Do you know what they do in those facilities? Do you know whose people they use in there? You are aiding murderers and kidnappers." She huffed, her voice raised as she continued, "Do you know who hired Jaze? Who had him killed?"

Pryde paused, his chin lifting. "I do not." He stood swiftly. "Wes, you do not understand now, but I hope you will one day soon. Atticus will need you."

He turned and began walking to the door. Wes wanted to rage. How dare he speak of her and Atticus as if it was a predetermined destiny. How fucking dare he.

"What did you mean I will forget everything?" Wes calmed herself enough to ask.

Pryde paused, his back to her. Ever so marginally, his shoulders seemed to deflate. As if of all the questions, this was the one that sucked energy from him.

He turned towards her, his feet staying rooted in front of the door. His smug grin had been replaced by one of sorrow. Wes's stomach tightened.

Pryde glanced at his watch, then to the door, then back to her. "I'm telling you this as a friend."

We are not friends.

"You were a patient at their facility ."

Wes froze.

"When you and Warden were young, you fell. Got hurt. You couldn't move your legs. Your parents found no cure here, so they looked in Duran. You came back cured, completely normal." He shook his head. "That should've been the end of it. But they saw you. Practicing with a group of soldiers this summer. And someone remembered your name. They are interested in how you healed, how their methods have progressed. And, of course, how talented you are."

"I'm talented because I work hard." Her voice was a whisper, whether from the hoarseness of her throat or the information she had received, she did not know.

"I have no doubt that is a factor." Pryde said with a kind smile, "They will keep you for a month and see what effect they had. Afterward, you will be returned without your memories. I will make sure you can go through with graduation."

Wes's eyes widened. This couldn't be real. "Graduation?"

"I am sorry." He shook his head. "After the first attempt to take you, I made a deal for them to wait until after graduation. But now that they have you, they won't wait. You shouldn't have come here today."

He turned his body back to the door. Whatever he was about to say, he was too much of a coward to say it to her face.

"Please tell them where the journal is. It will make things go quicker, and your time with them will be easier."

He pulled open the door and stepped into the hallway, leaving Wes reeling.

Wes was on her feet, hobbling to the desk before the sound of silence could surround her. Before the gravity of the words would come crashing down. Pryde didn't know what he was talking about.

Leaning against the desk she used her bound hands to pull on the drawers. Every one of them was locked.

She dropped to the ground, looking underneath the desk for a key, for a pen, for anything. But nothing was out of place. Everything had a spot, and it was all under lock and key. She pushed herself back, contemplating the best escape. The window was three floors up, and without her bonds broken, she wouldn't make it anywhere. But if Rhyatt, Knox, and Cleo were watching from outside, they could cut her free. They could only cut her free if they saw her on the way down.

Wes inched towards the window and looked out. The building's new metal would make it impossible to climb down. It was a very tall three stories up, and the fall alone would break a few bones. There was a rolled wheat crop below, but even if she hit it she would risk a broken bone, if not a broken neck.

The door creaked open and Wes froze, her shoulders going rigid. A soft click signaled someone entering the room. This time she was able to hear it.

Slowly, she turned around.

Aridia stood in front of the open door frame.

Wes had met the woman when she wore snakeskins, now Aridia wore commoners' clothes. Clothes so close to what Wes wore daily. Jorjinian clothes to be exact. It made her look... strange. It should have taken away from the princess persona, yet somehow it did not. Aridia seemed to be a chameleon, able to blend in with her surroundings while still maintaining her attitude.

Aridia's eyes scanned over Wes, a frown appearing after studying her face. A genuine glimpse of sadness flitted across those beautiful features.

"They shouldn't have hurt you so." She said with a shake of her head.

"Yes. I've heard slaughterhouses don't like bruised livestock. I'm sure I won't fetch as much now." Wes replied, the venom lacing her voice. She had beaten Aridia in a fight, but Aridia was smarter than that. She was much smarter than Wes had credited her for.

Aridia's frown deepened as she pushed the door closed behind her. It was then that Wes noticed she held a small bucket with a cloth draped over the side. Did they plan to waterboard her?

She noticed Wes's gaze and spoke, "Come sit."

Aridia sat on the edge of the settee, the bucket on the floor in front of her. Wes considered not moving, instead making Aridia drag her to the couch. But stubbornness wasn't going to get her anything right now.

Slowly, very slowly, Wes moved her tied feet forward. Aridia glanced down at the ties, amusement plaguing her features.

She stood, the embodiment of grace, the fluidity reminding her of Cleo, and strode to where Wes was behind the desk. A quick flash of metal and the ropes at Wes's feet were uncoiling and slumping against the ground. Wes studied her now free ankles, she wondered if underneath her boots were red marks. It certainly felt like there was.

Aridia returned to her seat, and Wes followed, still cautious.

When she sat, she perched herself on the edge. In case Aridia decided to stab her mid-sentence, she could at least attempt to roll away.

Aridia picked up the cloth and dipped it into the bucket of clear water. She slowly rang it out, the sound of each droplet of water echoing in the silent room.

"Hold still." She said softly before lifting the cloth to Wes's face and cleaning it.

Wes tried not to pull away from the cloth, from the sting that radiated down her face and down her throat, as Aridia gently rubbed away the dirt and blood. She was very curious to see what type of nightmare she looked like after the man's blood had spilled down her.

"I heard you put up quite a fight," Aridia said, attempting to start a conversation.

"Yes," Wes said between gritted teeth.

"I wish they would've taken better care with you."

"You and me both," she hissed as Aridia touched a tender spot.

"We will get you taken care of," Aridia said, her voice cool, an attempt at calming.

"Why are you putting on this big sister act?" Wes asked, jerking away from the now bloodied cloth.

Aridia placed the cloth in the bucket, and the water swirled red, deepening with each passing moment. She looked back up at Wes and smiled, a smile that hinted she knew more than her.

"I am not *your* big sister, Wes." She picked up the rag and squeezed. The water dripped a muddy red into the bucket.

"Would you like to know whose sister I am?" Aridia continued, unbothered.

"Ask me anything else," Wes responded, and although the sarcasm in her voice was clear, Aridia raised her eyebrows and asked her a genuine question.

"Why do you protect the journal?" Her voice was serious, kind even. Because of the genuine question, Wes decided to give a genuine answer.

"He asked me to."

"Your dead lover?"

Wes nodded. No one had ever called him her dead lover. He had been called many things by strangers and friends alike. But not *her dead lover*. The sadness of his absence threatened to intrude on her churning thoughts.

"What is the corn used for?" Wes asked. Aridia blinked at her, "I know you use it with the soldiers. But I mean - how?"

Aridia nodded and placed the cloth back in the bucket.

"Green Mountain Corn is the hottest burning grain on the market. It is very easily turned into LiquidFire."

"You use LiquidFire to control the soldiers?" Wes asked.

"No." Aridia sighed, "We use LiquidFire to make rubies to control the soldiers. And because of your capture, I will have to take my first ruby."

Wes did not speak because she did not understand. The soldiers did not care if they lost life or limb. No pretty jewel could make them behave like that.

"The Ruby–Queens Blood Ruby to be exact–are made about the size of your head. They are split into tiny pieces. Whoever has the largest piece controls the rest. Our Captains have the large pieces inserted under their skin close to their hearts. And our soldiers have the tiny rubies inserted on their neck." Aridia leaned forward and touched a spot on Wes's neck, a few fingers directly beneath her ear. "They are placed under the skin right here."

Wes froze at the contact but did not shy away. Aridia did not wish to harm her.

"How does a ruby make hundreds of soldiers bend to your will?" Wes asked, wondering if this was a joke.

"Ah," Aridia pulled her hand away and returned it to her lap. "My Father says, 'Science is magic that we comprehend, and magic is science we do not yet understand.' He considers the rubies to be a science now. But I still think they are magic. Until I understand how the queen's blood alters the ruby, they will remain magic to me."

"Which queen is supplying you with blood?" Wes asked and began to mentally tally the countries that still held monarchies.

On this continent it was less than 5. None of their Queens were remarkable. But perception is not always reality.

"She has long been dead," Aridia smiled and the edges of her mouth twisted, "Your Saint Saveen was blessed by the lands. That blessing ran through her blood until the day she died. Luckily her body was well preserved in a tomb under your city. Almost twenty years ago my Father exhumed it." Aridia leaned forward, sharing a secret, "It is rumored her blood was used on you the night you came back from the dead."

"Why are you telling me all this?" Wes asked, leaning away.

"Because soon you and I will be bound together. Rubies plunged under our skin. When that time comes, I am going to tell you to forget every bad thing that has ever happened to you. I am going to tell you to forget that you and I were ever on the opposite side of this. I am going to tell you that we are friends. That we share our secrets, that we work together, that we are doing the best we can for medical advancements. Because Wes, they are going to try and turn you into a mindless being," She leaned forward and whispered, "but I will keep you close. I will be the protector you never had."

Aridia stood, and Wes was shocked by the seriousness of her words. Aridia would not free Wes, but she promised not to let her suffer. And Wes wondered for a moment how her new life tied to Aridia would be. How the ruby would work when she was forced to forget. Would she forget Jaze first? Or rather, would she forget Will and her friends first? If Aridia did not force her to forget, would she always remember while doing others' bidding? A life of mindlessness seemed so simple yet so complex.

Aridia was halfway to the door when Wes called her name.

"Aridia." the woman paused and looked back, awaiting the question. "Tell me one last thing before I am ushered into this new life. Do you know who had Jaze killed?"

"No." Aridia blinked before adding, "I do know who hired him."

WES

A soldier in a sand-colored uniform came to collect her. He was tall and broad like the others.

"Stand." He ordered, his voice was flat. Devoid of any emotion. Wes wondered if he had been experimented on like her. Or was he just a product of the *blood rubies*? As she stood, she looked at his neck and noticed the smallest pink scar against his brown skin. A mindless soldier, then.

He grabbed her arm above the elbow and steered her towards the door. She considered tugging away from him, but she was attempting to be less impulsive. She wanted to at least understand where she was going. Likely to tell *the others* where the journal was. She was, at minimum, curious to see who the others were. However, she wouldn't be speaking about where the journal was. They likely didn't suspect it to be at her home; otherwise, The Commander would not waste time questioning her. Which means they either believe she hid it or had it on her person. The thought that someone had likely searched her unconscious body made her skin crawl.

The soldier shoved her when she didn't move as quickly as he would like. Wes stumbled out of the office door and onto a platform.

Her eyes adjusted as he led her forward. They were inside the large barn. The office had been on the third floor. The second floor was a square with a hole in the middle, showcasing the bottom level. The second floor looked to be a maze of barrels. There were two or three sizes, and she could see the ramps that would allow them to go to the bottom. As they descended the stairs, Wes could make out the first floor. It was set up the same with an empty space in the middle and various wooden storage containers throughout. There were one or two grain wagons parked near the doors. From here, she could see the soldiers. 17 visible ones. She assumed it had originally been 20, the one walking with her now, the one she had injured, and the one she had killed.

They stepped onto the bottom level and turned, giving Wes a direct line of vision to two kneeling men.

She felt her heart drop into her stomach.

Knox and Rhyatt both had their hands tied in front of them and looked up at her as she walked forward.

Wes concentrated on not tripping as she walked by Knox. His lip was busted, and blood had run from his lip down his throat and dried. Unlike her, the blood had not been cleaned. He had some bruising around his jaw beginning to appear, but besides that, he looked *okay*.

Rhyatt, on the other hand, looked unharmed but was pale, and his brown eyes were wide and restless.

There was more at risk besides her own skin now. She had to be smart, she had to be calculated, otherwise two of her closest friends would meet the end of their fate.

Once on the other side of Rhyatt, the soldier kicked the back of her knees. She kneeled and was held upright by his hand on her shoulder. He released her a second later and stepped backward, joining the other soldiers.

Wes huffed a stray hair out of her face and looked up to see the line of people in front of her.

As expected, The Commander stood tall with a frown. Unexpectedly, the Trade, History, and Treasury Councilors.

"Fucking traitors," Wes said, spitting at the ground in front of her.

"Hello, Wes." The Trade Councilor cooed, smiling at her.

Wes tilted her chin up, refusing to let her terror show.

Aridia stepped forward, her gaze going behind Wes to the soldiers a few feet behind her.

"Thank you all for your hard work in capturing them. We recovered our lost experiment," she looked at Wes before moving to Rhyatt, "A traitor, and the kin of our dearly departed Jaze." She said as she looked at Knox.

Wes could feel her heart beating in her ears. She knew who had hired him, and she was going to rile Knox up.

"We only need one last thing before we can return to Duran." Aridia returned her focus to Wes, "Tell us where his journal is."

"Bend over, and I'll fucking show you," Wes said, the smallest of smiles forming. Gods, she might be about to face down death, but she refused to cower before it.

"I told you she'd be like this." The Trade Councilor said, smirking, "She's got too much of that cunt of a mother in her."

Wes ground her teeth together and curled her lip, squashing down the instinct to deny she was anything like her mother.

Aridia held up a hand, silencing the Councilor as she strode to the spot in front of Wes. She bent down, her body gracefully folding in on itself, and took Wes's chin in between her thumb and pointer finger. Long gone was the sisterly act, and instead, a determined grin had replaced it.

"I do not wish to resort to violence." She said.

"Do what you must," Wes responded, unblinking.

Aridia stared at her for a moment, her stunning eyes moving slowly over her face. She pursed her lips and stood.

"Very well. I will leave it to your peers to get the location of the journal. I am ready to have this mess behind me." Aridia turned towards the waiting Councilors and Commander. "You have an hour to retrieve the information from her. If you fail, you will die."

Aridia walked around Wes and stopped next to the soldier who had brought her down.

"See it through. And remember my command."

Without another word, Aridia headed towards the large doors and slipped between them, fading into the bright afternoon sun.

The air in the barn shifted. It had never been *light*, but now there was an uneasy heaviness. Aridia had promised death to the Councilors and Commander if they were unable to make Wes talk within the hour. With 17 soldiers and only 4 of them, the Jorjinians were outnumbered and outmatched. She knew some of them stayed active in their swordplay, but they were all older. The soldiers were youthful and strong. They did not fear death. Wes, Knox, and Rhyatt likely couldn't take all 17 at once. If they spread the soldiers out, they would be able to make it. However, if they were free, their objective would be to run, not fight. She wouldn't risk her friends' lives.

The Councilors looked at each other with unease before looking at the Commander, waiting for instructions. Ever the faithful servants. Wes however was not going to wait for them to talk first.

"What is it like being on a Council of Traitors? Do your families know?" She asked her voice loud in the otherwise quiet space.

The Trade Councilor stepped forward, the first one to stop reeling from Aridia's threat, and stopped in front of Wes.

"You know nothing, little girl." He said, his hands moving in a vague gesture.

"So your families don't know?" Wes asked.

Her head and body were whipped to the side as the Councilor backhanded her.

She had hit a nerve. Good.

Blood welled in her mouth and covered her teeth before dripping out of her mouth with slobber. She smiled at him, letting it run down her chin.

His eyes widened, and his jaw set in response, "Save us the time and tell us where the journal is."

His voice had an odd edge. The Trade Councilor had always been quick to anger, but this was different. It resembled *desperation*.

"Do you think your families will cry at your deaths? Or will they bury you in an unmarked grave once they learn the truth?" She asked, the blood smeared on her lips.

She was prepared this time when his hand struck her. She stayed upright, and only her head followed the flow of the slap.

"You've got too much of that bitch-of-a-Mother in you." He snarled, his face inching closer to hers.

Wes swallowed and straightened her shoulders. She would not rise to the bait. She would not refute him.

The Commander stepped forward, standing a few feet back from the Trade Councilor. His arms were crossed, and he was frowning. Clearly, he believed the threat was real too. They now had less than an hour to find out where the journal was.

"Wes, save us the time and tell us where the journal is. We will let you rest before you are transported tonight. There is no reason for excessive violence." The Commander said.

The Commander did not mention Knox or Rhyatt's fate, and that terrified Wes more than she would admit. She watched him talk and turned back to Trade. She had started something and planned to finish it.

"The night of the festival, I had the journal with me. You were so close." Wes pouted, "Isn't that sad? Now, when I don't check in on Monday, the journal will be given to the Central Commander."

The lie came off her tongue easily enough and judging by the Councilor's sharp breath, he believed it. The Treasury and History Councilor glanced at each other. The Commander stayed still. But the Trade Councilor's face was mottled, and his teeth were clenched. Wes had him worked up.

"I want to say this so you'll understand my intentions. I plan to tell you *nothing* for the next hour. Not a word about where the journal is located. And when they kill you, I plan to watch with a smile."

Wes smiled at the eloquence of her words. Cleo would be proud.

Trade launched forward, closing the gap between them, and wrapped his hands around her throat.

Her eyes bulged as she tried to inhale and was unable to.

Noise exploded around her, and the other two Councilors yelled at the Commander to stop this madness. Knox and Rhyatt had both tried to get up and were being held down by the soldiers standing behind them.

"You fucking bitch." Trade said, spittle leaving his mouth.

Wes blinked, trying to force air down her crushed windpipe. She opened her eyes in time to see a soldier shove Trade off of her. It was the soldier Aridia had spoken to, the same one that had brought her downstairs.

Trade pulled a dagger from his belt and pointed it at the soldier. The soldier was unfazed.

"You cannot kill her," he said, his voice even despite the chaos that had erupted.

"What if I do?" Trade asked, stepping closer to the soldier. To the soldier's credit, he was unblinking. Those blood rubies were good.

The sound of a dozen different boots stepping closer made the Trade Councilor pause. He instead turned towards Rhyatt.

"Not him either." The soldier stated.

Trade's temper flared, and he sent his dagger flying at Knox. It landed in the outside of his thigh.

"I can't kill anyone, but I will die in an hour," Trade yelled, his voice echoing in the space.

Wes spared a glance at Knox. He was looking down at the knife and frowning. He wasn't freaking out, and blood wasn't pouring out, only little drips. She didn't have half the medical knowledge as Knox, but if he was calm, then she suspected he would likely be okay.

"Ouch," Knox yelled.

The Trade Councilor began to pace in front of them, the others stepped back and were watching him with worry. He was not good under pressure. Even the Commander stayed silent. Whatever was coming next would not be good, but Wes would face it head on. If they found out the location of the journal was in her home Will was at risk, and that was something she couldn't handle.

Trade stopped in front of Wes and turned his head in a serpentine fashion. He stared at her with a wicked smile.

"I cannot kill you, but I can cut into you." he unsheathed a dagger from the opposite side of his waist.

Wes looked at him, her throat too raw to speak.

Trade used the knife to split open the sleeve of her shirt, going all the way to the shoulder. His movements were jagged and made the fabric tear. Wes held her breath as he looked over his shoulder to the councilors, "Join me and cut the boys. Let's see who speaks first."

Now Wes's heart was truly pounding. She just hoped both of them could stand it. The Councilors knew they couldn't kill without the soldiers striking them down. That didn't mean as time went on they wouldn't become more desperate.

Treasury left her spot and stood in front of Knox. She jerked his blonde curls, forcing him to look up at her.

History did not move. He stood still beside The Commander. Neither of them had the stomach for blood. Trade stared at them, waiting for one to step forward.

"Join me." Trade demanded, his voice loud through his clenched teeth.

"I don't take commands from you." The Commander responded, crossing his arms and standing his ground by the History Councilor.

"So you'd rather us die?"

"Finally drawing the line at harming your own citizens?" Wes croaked, her voice too ragged to speak louder than a whisper.

"I'll do it." The soldier behind Wes stepped forward, grabbing a knife from his belt. When Trade turned to question him, the soldier spoke again, "Burying four bodies is time-consuming when it hasn't rained in days."

The soldier grinned and shrugged at Wes, the first sliver of a personality showing. He had the ruby, she had seen the scar. And until now he seemed emotionless, functioning solely on the commands he had been given. Wes watched the soldier as he turned to Rhyatt, cutting open his sleeve the same way. Rhyatts hands curled into fists at the closeness of the soldier.

"Would anyone like to tell us where the journal is?" Trade asked loudly.

No one spoke.

"Make a cut," he announced and used one of his hands to grip Wes's arm while the point of the blade pressed into the top of her shoulder, and he drug it down.

Wes clamped her mouth shut as white-hot pain erupted down her arm. He was going deep. She wouldn't yell out. She would take the pain with the knowledge that Will was safe.

A yelp from Knox made her head snap in his distraction. Red blood raced down his pale skin. His face was scrunched in pain. Wes's chest felt like it was caving in as she watched him suffer.

She had thought it would be Rhyatt to call out. When she looked at him, he was stony-faced, staring a hole through the soldier who was making the same long vertical cut on him. The blood didn't flow as quickly from him.

Wes fought back the urge to wince as the blade stopped on her wrist bone. She looked down at the long vertical line. It ran from her shoulder down to the ropes binding her wrists. It was unbroken. She, Knox, and Rhyatt all shared the same long wound. Blood coated their arms and spilled onto the floor.

"What about now? Does anyone remember the location of the journal?" Trade asked.

The Commander shook his head, but he wouldn't interfere.

Trade turned to the soldier standing in front of Rhyatt, "Can I take a finger? Is that *acceptable*?"

The soldier stared down at Rhyatt, thinking about something. When he looked back up, he nodded.

"Aridia should have just told *you* to get the information if there were going to be so many rules." Trade muttered, bending to grab Wes's hands.

She began to panic. Fingers were kind of important body parts for sword wielders.

She jerked her tied hands backward, curling them into fists. The Councilor grabbed at her, yanking her arms forward. She brought them up to her chest and used the bottom of her curled hands to strike the Councilor in the nose. He staggered backward, blood beginning to drip downwards.

He used the back of his hand to wipe it away before raising his knife to point at her.

"You're dead."

He stepped forward, the knife arching into the air.

A deafening explosion shook the ground.

The Councilor fell backward, and there was smoke in the air, clouding everyone's vision.

Wes scrambled towards the door, she struggled to push herself to her feet and decided to stay on the ground. She glanced around, the smoke was filling the room quickly and the sound of coughing was becoming louder and more frequent.

Before she could begin to crawl, someone was gripping her bound wrists and yanking her towards them.

Instinctively, she pulled away.

"Let me cut your ropes," Knox said.

She blinked rapidly, her eyes watering. Knox's blonde curls shook wildly as he wrestled her wrists away from her and began to cut the ropes.

The ropes fell to the ground, and Wes felt a sense of relief. She was no longer helpless.

"We need to get out," Rhyatt said from beside her.

She snapped her head in the direction of his voice. How had he gotten free?

"Yes." She croaked and accepted their help.

Together, the three of them ran towards the door, the light making beams through the thick smoke billowing out of it. In the bright afternoon they ran towards the ridge they had come from, the adrenaline making quick work of climbing the hill. At the top they sagged against the tree.

Wes leaned against her knees, trying to catch her breath and not cry at the pain that tore down her raw throat. She needed water.

"That was Cleo." Wes croaked and gestured towards the barn that now had a pillar of smoke flowing upwards.

"Where is she?" Knox asked, his voice panicked.

"She'll come here to meet us." Wes assured him, looking at him and nodding.

She turned her attention to Rhyatt, who was staring at Knox's leg which still had the knife in it. No wonder he had run slower than normal.

"Knox, you have a knife in your leg," Rhyatt said, bending to get a closer look.

"Yes, I was there when it happened." Knox sniped as he straightened and began to unbuckle his belt. With swift efficiency, he jerked it from the belt loops, wrapped it around his leg above the wound, and began tightening it. He jerked it tighter and tighter until it was pressing into his pants, and the skin around it was spilling out. Knox looked up, glancing from Rhyatt to Wes.

"I need you to pull the knife out as slow and straight as possible." He said to her, his voice calm as he turned to Rhyatt, "As soon as it's out, I need you to press *firmly*."

Wes took a deep breath and stepped forward with Rhyatt. She positioned her hand around the hilt but didn't touch it. Rhyatt looked at her and nodded, his hands ready to cover the wound.

"Are you ready?" She asked, Knox nodded and she grasped the handle and began to pull.

"Fucking bitch." Knox spat between clenched teeth.

Wes continued to pull, the blade resisting. She gave it one last tug, and it was free. Rhyatts hand instantly covered the wound, applying pressure.

Ten minutes later Rhyatt let go of Knox's leg and Knox used his torn shirtsleeve to bandage the wound. It was not perfect but the blood flow had slowed to a trickle and Knox had said he could make it back to town like this. However Cleo still hadn't left the barn. The smoke had dwindled to a small plume but *no one* had left the barn. None of the soldiers nor the councilors.

"Where is Cleo?" Wes asked no one in particular. When Rhyatt shrugged, and Knox shook his head, the hair on the back of her neck began to rise. It had been too long since the explosion had happened, and yet she was not back. Wes knew what she had to do. She wouldn't leave her friend behind.

"I'm going back in for her." She stated, picking up the knife that had been in Knox's leg only a few moments ago.

"I'm going with you," Rhyatt said, standing to his full height.

"Me too," Knox said. He, however, did not stand. Wes frowned at him.

"I don't think you are going to do us much good." She motioned to his injured leg. "Stay here in case she gets out before us."

Knox's face hardened, and Wes could tell that whatever he was going to say would piss her off.

"Is that a command?"

She bit the inside of her cheek and stared him down. Her adrenaline was still pumping, and she couldn't tell if it was a mockery or a genuine question. Even worse, she knew that he would follow her answer.

"No." She said in an attempt to be casual, "But once we're in, you need to be able to hold your own."

He smiled a wide-toothed grin at her, "I can do that."

Rhyatt shook his head and opened his mouth before closing it again and pressing his lips together. There was no argument left. There was only Cleo.

Wes ran ahead to the small shed. She was inside and pilfering for tools before Knox and Rhyatt had made it halfway down the hill. Rhyatt had looped an arm around Knox, and together, they walked quicker.

There wasn't much inside. A few old gardening tools with wood handles and rusted metal ends. A rotten shovel that crumbled in her hand made her question if they would make it out alive. But then she spotted it. A scythe with a sharp blade that only had sparse signs of rust. She picked it up and discovered it was lighter than expected. Good. This would be her weapon of choice. Gathering a hoe and a decent shovel, she crept back into the bright daylight.

Knox and Rhyatt had made it to the side of the shed. She handed them each a farm tool turned weapon. Anything was a weapon if you tried hard enough, and in their hands, they would make sure death followed.

"Killing blows for the soldiers." She said, glancing back at them and memorizing their features. There was no way all of them were coming out of this without scratches to their pretty little faces.

WES

The three of them ran towards the barn. The heat of late afternoon made sweat roll down their foreheads and spines.

Rhyatt was the first to reach the barn door. He braced his hands on the handle and pulled it open with great effort. Running inside with their makeshift weapons raised, they paused, understanding why the soldiers had not come for them.

On the ground floor lay a handful of bodies on fire, all of them still. Crates and barrels had been pushed off the second floor and had busted on the first, scattering grain and a powdery substance. On the second floor, a small fire started from the explosion and took over one large container of unknown flammable objects. The soldiers were scattered. The ones in sight were desperately looking for someone. No one seemed to care about the bodies that lay on the floor burning to crisp.

Their pause was short lived as the soldiers nearest the door noticed the trio and turned, coming towards them with weapons raised.

The first one to reach them aimed for Wes, his arms outstretched with a knife in his right hand. But he was slow and untrained.

Wes stepped forward just to sidestep his grip as he got close. Before he could step out of range, she took the scythe and swung it, connecting it with flesh.

A meaty plop signified she had taken his head. She didn't need to look to see. She didn't want to look.

Instead, she ran towards the stairs. Cleo was most likely still on the second floor. Knox and Rhyatt could handle the first floor while she got Cleo, and they escaped.

She was halfway up when another soldier came down the stairs. He had the upper hand, but he was coming towards her far too quickly. And he only carried a small dagger with him.

Why did they all keep their swords sheathed? Was it the 'no kill' order on her?

Wes raised the scythe, poised to strike, but the soldier skipped a few steps and was too close for the blade. Instead, the wooden handle smacked into his neck, and a sickening crack sounded.

His body was still in movement far after he was dead, and she watched in horror as he tumbled down the remaining stairs, limbs flailing.

This was quickly becoming nasty business.

Wes continued up the stairs. It was strange how her legs did not scream at her. Instead, it was her left arm that jolted in pain with every step she took. The only consolation she had was that it had stopped bleeding, and the blood on her hands was now dried.

Wes reached the second floor and glanced down. Rhyatt and Knox were holding their own in separate corners, a trail of bodies behind them. But her attention snagged. Each man now had a sword, and the enemies they fought also had swords. It was puzzling. The soldiers attacking her had not drawn swords.

Focusing back on the second floor she stepped forward to view in between the rows of crates and two soldiers immediately saw her. These two already had swords drawn.

They approached her like they would a hurt animal. Slow and cautious, one hand outstretched.

"Come now, Miss Blake, we don't want to hurt you." One cooed.

"That's unfortunate." Wes rolled her neck, "Because I want to hurt you."

She sprung forward, the scythe arching through the air towards the first soldier.

But he was quick. Quicker than the others, and stepped back out of her range. The second soldier had been waiting, and as soon as Wes's defenses were down, he lunged, aiming low.

And his blade struck.

She had moved, but not enough.

The fabric of her pants hung open right above her knee, and a line of bright red blood dripped down.

With an open-mouth look of shock, she glanced down at the wound dripping red on her pants. Somehow, her pants hadn't been cut during the entire ordeal. Until now, at least. She huffed a sigh and watched as a drop of her blood dripped from her leg down, past the grated floor, and onto a curly blonde-headed boy below. She wanted to laugh but instead promised to laugh with Knox later.

She looked back up to her attackers. They were looking at her knee and back up to her. Something like fear on their faces.

Gripping the scythe with both hands, she stepped forward and swung at them. The first man moved in time, but the second did not. The scythe sliced across his bicep, cutting open his shirt. It seemed fair. He ruined her pants, and she ruined his top.

The first man stepped behind Wes, and panic swelled at her disadvantage.

She pivoted, the scythe swinging wildly, and maneuvered behind the man.

Her chest bumped his back as she used her hurt leg to kick the back of his knees and knock him to the ground. She placed the wooden handle of the scythe against his throat and tightened her grip.

She looked up and was met with a sword gently pressed a few inches beneath the hollow of her throat.

Impulsive.

She clamped her jaw in defeat. How could she be so stupid? So impulsive to not think through the consequences. What about Cleo? Maybe if they took her, Cleo could go free and take Knox and Rhyatt with her.

"Let them go and I'll come willingly." Wes stated, her voice didn't shake although her hands had started to.

"You'd come willingly?" the man pressing the sword against her skin asked.

She swallowed, unable to think of another option. She would go willingly if they would be safe. She hated herself for it. That she would leave Will, but he would still have Rhina and Rhyatt. That would have to be enough.

"My life is not worth-"

Thwack.

Wes recognized the sound. Although the last time she had heard it, the knife had gone through an eye socket.

The soldier fell in slow motion.

The sword clattered to the ground first. Then he fell to his knees. And finally landed face-first on the metal grated floor.

The knife was embedded deep in the base of his skull.

The man under Wes's scythe made a sound similar to a cry.

Wes pulled the scythe tight against his neck and pressed deep, attempting to make it quick.

He clutched at his throat as he fell forward, lying beside his fallen friend.

"The second floor is now clear," Cleo announced, coming out of the shadows.

"Are you okay?" Wes asked, her eyes scanning Cleo, searching for any wounds. There were none.

"Not a scratch on this pretty face." Cleo chirped, stepping forward to retrieve her knife, "Seems you can't say the same."

Wes smiled crookedly at her friend. "I did not promise the same thing."

Cleo only rolled her eyes and motioned down the steps where Knox and Rhyatt still fought. Both now wielded swords. "Shall we?"

"Someone has got to save them." She replied, taking the first step downwards.

"Oh, Wes," Cleo said from the landing, her height magnified.

"Yeah?" Wes looked up at her, that concern creeping back in.

"Do not ever sideline me again." Her voice was serious, and even as she looked down at Wes.

Wes nodded. "I promise." She whispered, and they both bound down the stairs.

Cleo veered left to help Knox and Wes right for Rhyatt. As she jogged forward, she couldn't help but watch Rhyatt and his form. How far he had come. His offensive moves still needed work, but defensively, he was doing amazing. It didn't look like anyone had landed a blow to him at all.

Rhyatt blocked an attack that could have easily taken off his head. His attacker stumbled back, but Rhyatt was slower with the counter attack. He struck and his attacker blocked it, stumbling back from the force.

That was alright. His attacker had just stumbled into Wes's reach.

She swung the scythe, and it sliced through the air, leaving the attacker dead and Rhyatt pouting.

"You're welcome," Wes said with a cocky grin.

"I had it under control until I saw you," Rhaytt grumbled, using the back of his hand to wipe sweat from his forehead.

"Am I that good-looking?" Wes arched an eyebrow at him, and he only rolled his eyes.

"Something like that." He said with a faint smile. And for a moment the pain and exhaustion of her body went away and she was in the garden, under the tree practicing with Rhyatt. Even as chaos sounded around them, she felt a glimmer of calm with him.

"Let's clear the floor." She nodded to where Cleo and Knox had gone, and together, they followed their trail.

When the first floor was clear, they gathered in the center where they had been tortured less than an hour ago. They quickly realized a few important people were missing from the dead, and presumably, no one had left. The Councilors and Commander were unaccounted for.

Cleo pointed upwards to the third floor, the only place they hadn't been.

Silently, they ascended the stairs, Wes leading, Rhyatt behind her, Cleo in the middle, and Knox following up the back.

RHYATT

R hyatt hadn't been awake to see Wes brought in, but he had seen her come down from the third floor. Her cheek was slightly swollen, and her face set into determined lines. It had stirred unbearable emotions from him.

They reached the top of the stairs and crept closer to the door. Wes looked at Rhyatt and made a kicking motion to the door.

He stepped forward and obliged, kicking the door. It flung open and banged against the wall.

Rhyatt rushed in, and seated closest to him was the Trade Councilor.

His body reacted before he could think.

He blinked. One moment, he was standing in the entryway; the next, he was standing above Trade, the blade of his sword protruding through the councilor's throat and out the back of the chair, the hilt pressed flush against his skin. Beady eyes stared back at him.

"Stop."

He looked over his shoulder to where Wes stood, her eyes wide and mouth slightly parted. The gash on her arm had stopped bleeding, but his white-hot anger remained.

Perhaps he had been too hasty in killing the councilor. It would have been better if he had suffered. Maybe if he had more time, Rhyatt could have delivered the exact same cut and blows the councilor had delivered to Wes.

Wes exhaled and turned to the desk in front of the window. Rhyatt looked over and saw the commander sitting calmly and the two other councilors standing behind him at the open window as if they had been waiting for someone.

"We just want to talk," Wes said, her chin tilting downwards.

He turned back to the dead councilor and pulled the sword out. The action must have seemed more threatening than he realized because the next few moments were a blur.

The Historic Councilor pushed open the window and wrapped his hand around the Treasury Councilor's waist before shoving her out the window. He turned to follow her, but a throwing knife now protruded from his chest. He fell to the floor like a dead weight.

Cleo's hand was still in the air. Knox had his hands on his hips, and Wes had crossed her arms, frustration evident on her face.

Rhyatt was the first one to move, rushing to the window and looking down.

"She landed in hay and is running for the tree line. Shall we follow?" Rhyatt asked, his tone surprisingly formal, even to him. He sounded like he had given similar reports before.

"No," Wes said, shaking her head and stepping forward to the desk. In a quick motion, she rose and sat on the lip of the desk, one leg hanging off and the other stretched before her. Her bloodied scythe rested in her lap.

She glanced at Rhyatt, then back at Cleo and Knox before inclining her head towards the couches. Cleo and Knox sat together on one couch, leaving Rhyatt to sit in the chair next to the deadman.

The Commander looked at them under heavy lids. What reason did he have to be tired?

"I have a few questions for you." Wes's words were clipped.

"I am at your mercy." The Commander replied, a slight arch in his eyebrow.

Rhyatt did not know the Commander well enough to know if the tilt in his voice was a jab or the way he spoke. Rhyatt had only seen the Commander in passing. And here. He hadn't made a good impression.

"Tell them what you told me. About the facility. And me."

The Commander scrutinized her but did as she said. "When Wes was a child, she got hurt and could not walk. The facility was the only place that healed her. They would have forgotten, but her swordsman skills are remarkable. So remarkable that they remembered her name and that she had once been a patient. They came to me where I bargained for them to wait until after her graduation, where they would then take her for a month to do some testing. She would be returned without her memories."

Despite the sweat slicking his body, a cold chill ran down Rhyatt's back. Testing. They would have done testing on her, like a sick animal.

"Where was she hurt?" Cleo asked.

"Her back." The Commander turned his gaze to Cleo, assessing her.

"Her spine?" Cleo responded, crossing the hand that gripped a knife over her arm.

The Commander nodded and looked back to Wes, waiting.

"You left out the first attempt to take me." irritation coated her voice, "Was that the night before a market?"

"When they linked you to the journal, they became..."

"Fearful." Wes supplemented. "It appears even The facility could see what a traitor you were and that giving you unlimited intel would be a mistake."

"Perhaps."

"I digress. What test would they have run on me?"

"I do not know."

"Pryde." She warned, her voice that of a mother warning a child what is to come if they don't obey.

"I would tell you if I knew." he lied.

Rhyatt stood, his sword no longer hanging loosely in his hand but at the ready. The Commander's eyes widened at him, and true fear absorbed his features. The Commander was *afraid* of Rhyatt. And Rhyatt liked it. He liked the kernel of fear that was showcased on The Commander's face. If for no other reason than that, The Commander had harmed them all.

"Your blood." The Commander said, looking back to Wes, his words rushed. "They would have taken your blood, asked you to do exercises, to examine the original wound. They would have tried to replicate the process."

Something told Rhyatt that was the least of what they would do.

"When will they come for me again?"

"I do not know." Rhyatt lifted his chin like he had seen Wes do so many times before, and The Commander continued quickly,

"But if I had to guess-I would say they will take today's loss poorly and come again within the month, with more reinforcements."

"Are the people within my home safe?" She asked, and he could almost hear her say Will's name. Rhyatt tensed.

"Yes. Part of our bargain is that they would not harm nor take the innocents."

"Was Jaze not innocent?" Knox asked, rising from the couch.

"That journal damned him. You all know it did." The Commander said, an edge to his voice.

"No. *You* damned him by bringing that mess here." Knox stepped closer, his cheeks gaining color again.

Rage was a complex emotion, and Knox did it well.

"I did what I had to." The Commander yelled, his face shaking. There was more than what was being said.

Knox stepped forward again, but Cleo rose to block him. He didn't dare push her aside. Rhyatt took a step closer to Wes, prepared to do whatever she asked.

But she only raised her right hand, pausing the commotion. Rhyatt studied that hand. The knuckles that were shiny from scars, a few new cuts speckled across them. He saw the way her nail on her middle finger was cracked all the way down. How splatters of blood and dirt covered her hand making it an entirely different shade.

Turning her focus back to the Commander, she took a deep breath. "I will ask you only this once. *Eligere?*"

The *choice*. Scholar Tiunda had called it the choice in class. It was a long dead tradition of giving the captive a choice. A choice between fighting or surrendering. The choice was only given between two equals. If The Commander chose to fight he would fight Wes to the death. If she perished he would be allowed to go free.

"Wes." Cleo hissed, disapproval radiating from her. Rhyatt's worry built on hers. Wes was in no condition to fight. Her injured arm had been clutched close to her since they had left the shed.

"Do you not think it is fair?" Wes snapped back.

Cleo pursed her lips and replied, "No. I do not think he deserves your respect."

"It is alright, Cleopatra. I choose to be your prisoner." The Commander answered.

Cleo stood taller, "I do not think you deserve that either."

Silence hung heavy at Cleo's statement. Rhyatt agreed. He presumed Knox did too. Wes was the only one who he was not sure which side of the line she fell on.

"We will tie him up and return to town," Wes stated.

Cleo and Knox glanced at each other, the former said, "There are horses tied in the woods, I will ready them for our return."

She strode out the door, and Knox followed, saying he would help. Wes planted her feet on the ground and stood from her resting spot on the desk before speaking to Rhyatt.

"Go help. I have something else I must do." She said, but it was not a command. He knew her well enough to know that it was a suggestion.

"I will stay." Rhyatt shook his head, and he swore a glimmer of relief showed in her eyes.

"You are not going to like what comes next." Her words were hollow.

"I will stay with you." He repeated and meant it.

She walked to where the dead councilor lay and knelt down.

"Atticus will be saddened to hear about this romance." The Commander gestured between the two of them, but his hand fell to his side as he saw what Wes was doing.

She had picked up a dagger and was now slicing into the fallen councilor's chest. Each cut going deeper and deeper. She paused and put her hand inside his chest cavity. A moment later, she retracted her hand.

Covered in bright red blood up to her elbow, her fist clutched the man's heart. Exactly how her necklace had shown.

Rhyatt watched as Wes touched the necklace, leaving a bloodied print on her disheveled top. He saw the ideal form in her eyes as she remembered the double meaning behind the symbol. Strength. Or Betrayal.

Carelessly, she tossed the heart onto the desk. The Commander sat and stared, horrified. His horror increased when she grabbed a discarded ax. Using her good arm, she swung it at the councilor's neck. It did not separate fully. She raised her hand and tried again. This time, the head separated from its body.

She gripped the hair, picked up the severed head, and placed it on the desk next to the fallen man's heart.

Picking up the dagger, she strode to the other fallen councilor. Neither man had the strength to watch as she repeated the process a second time.

THE VIEW FROM TOWN

The four university students had rode into town with Commander Pryde in tow right before sunset. Three of them had looked very battered, while the fourth, the ambassador's daughter, sat clean and pristine in her saddle.

When they reached the square, whispers and waves of shock circled the citizens.

Wes Blake, the eldest Blake child, led the horse The Commander was riding to the center. Clasped in his hands was a sword, two hearts piercing it. The murmurs grew as Blake dismounted and reached into The Commander's saddle bags.

Gasps and cries of shock echoed as she pulled two severed heads out. When she mounted them on the gate surrounding the well, a few people fainted. Two sets of dead eyes stared back at them. Two heads previously belonging to two beloved councilors.

They betrayed us. She yelled. *But their traitorous hearts bleed no more.*

Soon, the remaining two councilors came forth and questioned the four students, the story quickly unfolding as medics tended to their wounds.

As they told their story of the evil facility in Duran, The Commander sat quietly. He did not deny a thing.

When they left, the townspeople knew their names and knew the strength within all of them. They knew Knox Greene, the metal worker's son turned medic prodigy who had slayed his enemies with a garden tool. They knew Cleo Nafin, the ambassador's daughter, who had evaded capture and assisted her friends without a scratch on her. They knew Rhyatt Valvidez, the newcomer to town who had picked up excellent swordsman skills in a matter of months and defended his new friends. They knew Wes Blake, the young businesswoman who had taken the pain and led her friends into battle. They looked upon the group and knew many things: how fierce they had been, how loyal they had been, how fearless they had been. But the citizens knew one thing above the rest. They had bled for their town, bled so the citizens wouldn't have to. Neither of the two remaining councilors could say the same.

WES

Wes stepped into her darkened room and heard Rhyatt shut the door behind her. She had a faint memory of them walking home together after being seen by the doctor. They held hands at one point.

Stepping further into the room, she paused, staring at nothing in particular.

The events of the day seemed to be written in reminders across her room. The antique sword strewn across her vanity made her think of the councilors' hearts and how she had skewered them. The single piece of sugar cane sitting on her table reminded her of the scythe and how easy it had been to decapitate her enemies. The flower crown sitting on her bedside table reminded her of her Will and how her family would now be at risk. And lastly, the mirror reminded her of the journal. And Jaze. And his death. And how she and her friends had almost met the same fate as him. How she was going to be taken captive. She shouldn't be in her room right now. She should be halfway to Duran, where she would be locked up and examined like an animal. But here she was, alive and well, while 20-something soldiers and councilors lay dead.

A cracking noise gained her attention.

She looked down at where she kneeled on the hardwood floors. The cracking noise had been her knees hitting the ground.

She leaned forward, palms jerking out to catch her, but before she could, a pair of strong hands gripped her arms. Rhyatt wrapped himself around her, holding her tight against his chest. She leaned into him, the smell of dirt, blood, and antiseptic strong on him. Her breath became ragged and unmeasured. Squeezing her eyes shut, she willed herself to pull it together, to get up, and to continue as she always had.

She was Wes Blake. She couldn't falter now.

But her body didn't understand who she was, what she had to be. Her body faltered. She felt the fight leave her and she held tight to Rhyatt. It was always him.

Long minutes passed before she could breathe normally again. Rhyatt's hands released her and instead, roamed down to her boots and began unlacing them. She watched as his perfect hands worked on the blood and dirt covered laces. There were large splotches of filth that had dried and made the laces hard and stuck together. He worked them free with care. Once done he pushed himself to his feet and extended a hand.

"Let's get you into bed." His voice was soft in the quiet room.

She shook her head. The last time she had gone to bed this disgusting, she had hated herself the next day and had spent too many hours scrubbing sheets.

"I need a shower." She replied, taking his outstretched hand and letting herself be pulled upwards. Once they were toe to toe she added, "You need one too."

Rhyatt didn't complain as she led them to the darkened bathroom, they didn't bother lighting a lamp as Wes turned the water on and took off what remained of her torn shirt. He followed suit and they stepped in together, the water was still warm from the sun.

It was seconds before red began swirling into the drain. Wes watched as the rivulets ran down her legs. A touch on her arm brought her attention back to the present. Rhyatt's fingers rested gently on her elbow by the long cut. In the dark, the stitches looked more severe.

Wes looked at Rhyatt's matching cut and the droplets of water that clung to his arm. His hadn't been as deep like the soldier was against hurting them.

"Wes," he said, his voice low.

"I'm sorry." She cut him off before he could say anything else, "I am so sorry for what I've gotten you into and I am so sorry for what you've had to do all because you were friends *with me*." her voice wavered and her eyes began to water.

Rhyatt cupped her chin, tilting her face upwards to look at him, "Everything I have done has been of my own free will, and I regret *none* of it. I would repeat tonight's events ten times over if that meant you got to come home. You," he trailed off, struggling to find the words. Wes picked up where he left off.

"I'm glad I met you. I'm glad we're *friends*." Wes said the word but knew it wasn't accurate as they had their naked bodies pressed against each other.

Rhyatt leaned forward and pressed his forehead to hers; one hand remained on her cheek while the other found her free hand, and they intertwined their fingers. She leaned into it, the water rolling off of their faces, and she gripped his hand and felt the tangle of emotions settle into her chest.

"When we first met, what were you thinking?" Rhyatt asked.

"I was thinking you would be a challenge and I would finally have a worthy opponent." She smiled lightly, remembering how he had been tucked into the shadows when she first arrived but as soon as he had moved she had spotted him.

"Maybe one day I'll prove to be worthy of facing you," Rhyatt replied, his mouth curving into something like a smile.

"You already are worthy. More than you know."

He clutched her close as the water washed away their troubles, and once they were as clean as they could manage they crawled into bed and tangled their limbs. It was hard to tell who was holding who as they drifted into sleep.

WES

It had been two weeks exactly since Wes had revealed the secrets of Pryde. And it had been a whirlwind two weeks. Uncoincidentally, the barn, house, and shed on Collin's property had burned down the same night. It would've caused suspicion, but Aridia was seen leaving town less than an hour before. Wes, Cleo, Knox, and Rhyatt had been well enough to take the written portion of their final exam a week after, but they had been given a month extension to heal for the physical part. They had passed the first portion, Cleo scoring the highest -closest to perfect in the whole class- and Knox, the lowest, tying with five others and still *very* good scores.

Wes's mother had arrived days afterward, the news traveling fast. She had spent the past two weeks preparing for the Yule party, which was to simultaneously be Wes and Warden's delayed birthday celebration. It was odd. It was the first time she had visited since turning the title over to Wes. It was Wes's house now, technically, but while her mother visited, it felt... off. It was a similar experience with explaining things to Will. Wes had been honest, leaving out the gory details and going straight to the point. Her mother, on the other end, had tried to paint Wes as a hero, encouraging whimsical tales of her. Wes tried to remain calm and answer the majority of Will's never-ending questions.

"What will happen to him?" His face scrunched in curiosity. It had been the most recent talk everywhere. Who would be the next Commander?

"He will remain imprisoned until he has his trial and faces his punishment." Wes struggled to keep a neutral tone in her voice.

"And who will become the new Commander?"

"The townspeople will vote on a new one. That person will either accept or decline."

"Will you vote for yourself?" Will asked with childlike wonder.

"No." Wes laughed softly, "People don't vote for themselves on things like this. Besides, I wouldn't make a very good commander."

Will shook his head, his hair was overdue for a haircut and it flopped into his eyes, "I think you'd make the best Commander."

"Well, good," she reached out and ruffled his hair out of his eyes, "because I'm the Commander of this household, and you're stuck with me!" She bent lower and led a tickle attack; one her brother had quickly returned.

Hours later, Wes sat alone at her vanity, attempting to smooth the bandage around her hurt arm. The Yule party would be the busiest time of the year for the Blakemoore, and she didn't want the gnarly-looking wound to be a topic for discussion. The excitement would hopefully be centered around her father and Warden's late arrival. She had gotten word that snow had delayed travelers. It seemed very in style for the Blake men to arrive late to their own party.

She patted the skin-colored bandage and left her room, already vowing to return later when the party was in full swing. Maybe she would get lucky, and Rhyatt would appear again. Maybe, if she was even luckier, Knox would *not* appear afterward.

She floated down the stairs into the busy household, temporary workers running to and fro, placing last-minute decorations in the foyer, or moving food dishes from the kitchen to various places in and outside the home. Avoiding any interaction, she ducked into the kitchen to find Will, except he was not there. She had expected him to be at Rhina's side taste-testing a custard pie. Instead, Wes found Rhina alone, her hands kneading dough as she barked orders at one of the workers.

"Have you seen Will?" She asked, smiling kindly at the woman.

Rhina's face was flushed with heat but returned the smile after doing a once over of Wes's attire.

"My gods! Look at how good you look!" She waved her floury hands at Wes's black dress, the same she had worn for her birthday. Rhina knew as much but still gushed at her.

"Will?" Wes asked again, trying to hide her smile at Rhina's motherly gushing.

"Down by the creek. Rhyatt went down after he arrived, and when Will's school report came, he went to find him. I think it's good news." She added with a conspiratorial raise of her eyebrows.

"Or it's bad news, and he's asking Rhyatt to run away with him," Wes said.

She stepped out the back door, clutching a handful of her dress to keep it from dragging the ground. Outside, the air had only a faint chill even though the sun had set an hour ago. Goosebumps rose along her exposed back in the night air. She cherished the warmth she got from each lantern placed in the garden.

As she reached the edge of the garden the sloping hill came into view, a low fog rising from the creek down below. Gingerly stepping in the wet grass she continued downwards, carefully studying the ground where she stepped and avoiding particularly muddy areas.

It was her keen focus on the green ground beneath her that made the sharp contrast of white paper stick out that much more. She bent to pick it up, the corner slightly wet.

Unfolding the paper, she noticed Will's name at the top and below his scores for this semester. All of them were satisfactory or above! There were even a few *excels*! In the comments, one of his teachers had written a quick note:

Will has improved drastically throughout the semester. He is a bright boy and will do even better next semester if the progress continues. Although his behavior needs some help, he is a fine young man!

Wes practically gushed at the raving review. Will had only ever barely skated by. Now, his teachers had written about how bright he was. Of course, the behavior was still a work in progress. But the rest was there.

She knew the reason this was the first semester he had scored so well. Rhyatt. Rhyatt was all to blame, or thank. He had unnerving patience with Will, explaining math equations two or three times. Spelling words forwards, backwards, upside down, and inside out. Him and Will had created a bond and in turn Will had listened to Rhyatt, learning from him instead of giving up and quitting. Rhyatt really did belong in a school house teaching.

A feeling of comfort surrounded her like a warm blanket on a cold night. Look at her boys, working together so well. She beamed, folding the report up and continuing forward.

The fog parted around the folds of her dress, stirring it into the air and making it difficult to see. When she reached the creek, her right foot squished into ground that was too soft. Pulling back, she looked down the length of the water for any sign of Rhyatt or Will.

At first the fog didn't let her see anything, but after stilling herself she was able to see the shape of a mop of brown hair further down.

"Will!" she called to him.

Stepping towards the solid ground, she started to make a loop towards him, avoiding the creek bank.

"When were you going to tell me about these amazing scores?" She said, her head down and focusing on the ground again.

He did not answer. She stepped onto the soft ground again and paused, using her hand to fan away the fog. A small section cleared, and she could see that Will was lying down, his head facing the water. His clothes would be covered in mud and he would be lucky to only have to change and not take another shower.

"Hey. I saw your scores," She lifted the paper and stepped closer, but her mouth froze, and every muscle in her body stopped short.

His arm was twisted behind him, and his head lay at an odd angle.

She stepped closer until his small face was in view.

His face was pale, and his lips blue. He wasn't breathing.

No.

NoNoNoNoNo.

A gargled scream tore from her throat as she stepped forward and dropped to her knees beside him.

"No." She said again.

Grabbing his shoulders, she pulled him up towards her. He was soaking wet. His white dress shirt was plastered to his skin.

He was not breathing, and he was cold. So cold.

She laid him down and began the compressions she had been taught. One hand clasped over the other, she pressed on his chest in a rhythm.

"Help!" She managed to scream, pressing on his tiny chest. "Help! Someone Help!" She screamed again, her voice more frantic with every passing second.

"Will. Come back to me Will." She commanded, her voice a harsh whisper.

But the dead do not listen. They do not take commands nor give them.

"Someone help!" She screamed again and faintly could hear the sound of people coming from the house.

She pressed on her brother's chest again and again.

She would've continued all night.

A horrible crack reverberated through her hands, up her elbows, and to her chest.

She paused.

She had broken his ribs.

She had broken his ribs, and he was not back. He was not alive. And he never would be again.

William Blake was dead.

Her hands clenched into fists as she doubled over, her forehead resting on his cold, wet body. Hot tears streamed down her face, leaving streaks of makeup in their wake.

She sobbed into the boy as her chest cracked open, all the love pouring out onto the ground beside him. Her brother was dead. She was sure she should lie down beside him and wait to die. After all, she had failed him. It was her responsibility to keep him safe, and she fucked up that.

She let her hands grip his tiny body, and with it, all the possibilities faded away. He would never ride a horse by himself. He would never learn sword fighting with her. He would never introduce his lovers. He would never get a coming-of-age ceremony. He would never get to grow up.

Grief surrounded her. Overwhelmed her until it swallowed her whole.

Rocking back onto her heels, she turned her face to the sky and raised her arms, her fingertips reaching for the gods. And she screamed for them. Begged them to help.

As she screamed, the air became charged, and loose pieces of her hair stood on end.

White lightning cracked from her fingertips and shot into the sky.

The lightning touched the sky before returning to her outstretched fingertips.

Immediately, she slumped to her side in silence. She landed alongside her fallen brother. Her eyesight went blurry, but she still heard the roar of thunder directly above her. She was dying. And that was okay. It was what she deserved.

Her hearing went in and out, she could make out the sounds of people behind her. Maneuvering her head, she saw the small crowd that stood stock still. They looked at her but did not approach. Rhina was at the front, and her face was frozen as silent tears streaked downwards. She parted her mouth and whispered Wes's name.

Wes was too much of a coward to look at them. She had failed, and Will had paid the price. Turning her head the opposite way, she stared across the creek, the dark cover of trees making it impossible for her to see anything with her fading vision.

She waited to die.

But death was not so easy for her.

Across the creek she saw movement and struggled to focus on it. Two figures were emerging. Both men.

They got closer, and she recognized the first one as Rhyatt. Behind him was another man wearing the facility's soldier uniform. It was the same soldier who had escorted her in the barn and had cut Rhyatts arm.

Wes opened her mouth to yell a warning to him, but she only gasped for air.

She watched in silent horror as the soldier got closer to Rhyatt.

Rhyattt stopped at the edge of the creek. The soldier stopped beside him but did not attack.

She blinked and focused harder, their outlines still blurry. But Rhyatt was wet. His knees were dark and stained. The forearms of his shirt were soaked through.

Her vision swam again. She blinked, and they were above her. The soldier picked up Will, and Rhyatt picked her up.

Against his still-beating heart, her head fell to the side, and she slipped into a comfortable darkness.

Wes and Rhyatt will return in *Nevertheless We Persist.*

GLOSSARY

Chief Commander of Northern Jorjin and Commander of Saint Saveen

Bence Pryde

Intern - Wes Blake

Trade Councilor

Hugo Hao

Law Councilor

Irem Momani

History Councilor

Martin Knoe

Intern - Cleo Nafin

War Councilor

Anouk Rolle

Treasury Councilor

Viraan Hansen

Terms

Eligere- The *choice.* Usually given from the winning leader to the losing leader that they respected. Traditionally, the choice referred to the losing party being the winners willing prisoner, or the two would engage in battle til the death.

Confidebat- An honor a person bestows on their trusted comrade, most commonly during their coming of age celebration. The Confidebat is tasked to hold the bestower accountable to the vows they have made.

Acknowledgements

Writing a book is a massive feat and wouldn't be possible without the amazing people who supported me along the way. They are listed in alphabetical order.

Austin, my oldest friend. Our friendship is old enough to drink, 21 years! Thank you for always encouraging me to be my authentic self. You are a light in a dark room and everyone who knows you gets to be touched by something amazing. I hope you enjoy this cinematic masterpiece.

Dalton, my dear husband. Our love is something straight out of a book, that's what makes writing love scenes so easy. I am forever grateful to have you in my life. You are the ultimate hype person. I wouldn't be surprised if most of my sales come from people you convince to read it. Thanks for being my #1 fan.

Loretta, my most talented friend. I can't remember why I hated you, but I'm sure as hell glad I got over it. Watching you grow as an artist has been amazing, having your art on the cover of my book is literally a dream come true. Thank you for reading the roughest draft and seeing potential in me.

Mom, my beloved mother. When I was a little girl you told me 'you can do anything you set your mind to.' 27 years later I decided I could write a book! You have never once doubted me (even when you should have) and for that I am forever thankful. Thanks for pretending the sexy scenes didn't exist.

There are many other friends and family that have supported me along the way, but these four read the book at its worst. If someone loves you at your worst then they deserve you at your best.

Augusta Ren writes fantasy that makes readers constantly question "When do they kiss?" and "How did we get here?"

Originally from Western Kentucky, she now resides in Louisville with her husband and two cats. When she's not writing, you can find her looking for treasure at thrift stores, crafting something odd, or pretending to be a Victorian ghost. She's a certified foodie who loves traveling and hopes to live a thousand different lives before she dies. In the meantime, she'll settle for living through the characters in books.

Find her on TikTok @AugustaRen and Instagram @AuthorAugustaRen